Dear Reader:

I'm delighted to present to you the first books in the HarperMonogram imprint. This is a new imprint dedicated to publishing quality women's fiction and we believe it has all the makings of a surefire hit. From contemporary fiction to historical tales, to page-turning suspense thrillers, our goal at HarperMonogram is to publish romantic stories that will have you coming back for more.

Each month HarperMonogram will feature some of your favorite bestselling authors and introduce you to the most talented new writers around. We hope you enjoy this Monogram and all the HarperMonograms to come.

We'd love to know what you think. If you have any comments or suggestions please write to me at the address below:

HarperMonogram
10 East 53rd Street
New York, NY 10022

Karen Solem
Editor-in-chief

THE FIRST TIME

His hands moved to her neck, tangling in the hair at her nape. She ran her hand across his chest, feeling the hard muscles through his shirt, and touched the soft chest hair where the top buttons were undone. His special fragrance mingled with the odor of burning wood from the stove.

"Martha," he murmured, "why did we wait so long?"

"I don't know." In a recess of her mind she did know, but at this moment she didn't want to remember why.

Harper Monogram

Heartbreak Trail

BARBARA KELLER

HarperPaperbacks
A Division of HarperCollinsPublishers

If you purchased this book without a cover, you should be aware that this book is stolen property. It was reported as "unsold and destroyed" to the publisher and neither the author nor the publisher has received any payment for this "stripped book."

This is a work of fiction. The characters, incidents, and dialogues are products of the author's imagination and are not to be construed as real. Any resemblance to actual events or persons, living or dead, is entirely coincidental.

HarperPaperbacks *A Division of* HarperCollins*Publishers*
10 East 53rd Street, New York, N.Y. 10022

Copyright © 1992 by Barbara Keller
All rights reserved. No part of this book may be used or reproduced in any manner whatsoever without written permission of the publisher, except in the case of brief quotations embodied in critical articles and reviews. For information address HarperCollins*Publishers,*
10 East 53rd Street, New York, N.Y. 10022.

Cover illustration by Diane Sivavec

First printing: September 1992

Printed in the United States of America

HarperPaperbacks, HarperMonogram, and colophon are trademarks of HarperCollins*Publishers*

❖ 10 9 8 7 6 5 4 3 2 1

To Connie,
for all the reasons that she knows,
and to Charlotte,
because she inspired one of my
favorite characters.

1

Arizona Territory, March 18, 1877

The silence jolted Cole Wingate out of his half sleep. Before he caught himself, he strained against the irons and felt their edges cut into his wrists and left ankle. He ignored the pain, listening for sounds from outside the wooden shack.

In the noontime warmth the cicadas should have been ticking their irregular rhythm. But the only sound was the soft swish of a creosote bush moving in a breeze, brushing the sandy soil. Earlier the animal noises had paused when light footsteps and a skirt rustling told him a woman was going along the path to a privy. This was different. Even the croaks of the ravens had died away. His senses, sharpened during months of depending only on his wit and intelligence, told him something was wrong.

Where mud for chinking had fallen out between the upright logs of the shed wall, sunlight filtered through in thin, irregular lines. He stretched as far as the chain between his left ankle and a corner post allowed and peered through the nearest gap. It gave him a distant view of the corral but not of the stage station. The other passengers and the deputy marshal who'd chained him here should be finished with the noon meal, but no one was in sight. In the distance, a horse whinnied. Though everything looked all right, Cole's uneasiness persisted.

A single gunshot cracked through the silence. The air exploded with gunfire, then screams and shouts. Cole lunged upward, his heart racing, before the ankle chain caught and dragged him back. Somewhere a horse gave a high-pitched cry. An Indian ran into Cole's narrow field of vision. He crouched beside the corral, rested a rifle on the railing, and shot in the direction of the station. The screaming grew louder, more frantic. Cole heard the crackle of fire and smelled smoke. It was wood smoke, not the acrid smell of blazing chaparral. All the wooden parts of the adobe station building were old and dry. They'd catch fire and burn easily, especially the brush roof.

Savagely Cole jerked at the ankle chain encircling the corner post. The wood splintered a little more at its edges but held. Rage erupted in him until it seemed almost strong enough to burst the iron bonds.

Through the gaping logs he saw smoke billow past the corral. The crackle of flames increased. Cries rose to a desperate pitch. He heard a crashing sound. The roof must have burned through and fallen in. The gunfire slacked off, then started again in bursts. Cole guessed that people were running out of the station. The waiting attackers were shooting them down one by one, like rabbits from a burrow. His stomach clenched in revulsion.

A spark fell on a nearby creosote bush and flared into a blaze. Again he jerked futilely at his chains, cursing. He could only watch grimly as the bush burned and hope it didn't set off the rest of the brush near the shack. Finally the flames died without spreading.

Sporadic gunfire continued for what seemed long enough for the army to come from Yuma. When the last screams died out, Cole realized the attack couldn't have lasted over fifteen minutes. The fire was burning with a whooshing sound as it devoured the last of its meal. Men called to each other, but they were too far away for him to hear what they were saying. Through the crack Cole watched two men pull agitated horses from the corral. The amount of gunfire meant that there were more than those two attackers. When the Indians returned for the last horse, one of them started in Cole's direction. Though the shack was a good hundred yards from the corral, the Indian walked toward it as if he intended to look inside. If he did, he'd find Cole trussed like a wild turkey ready for the spit.

The only thing in the shed that might be used as a weapon was a rusty shovel in the corner, and it was too far away for Cole to reach. His heart beat at a punishing pace. Sweat poured down his face, trickling into his eyes. He didn't move to wipe it away. The chain between his wrists might jangle.

Someone out of sight shouted. The Indian coming toward the shack turned and hurried back out of Cole's line of vision. The crackle of flames subsided and the voices diminished. He heard the sound of hoofbeats, at first loud, then fainter. Finally they died out. The desert noises began again.

Cole wiped the sweat off his face. His muscles ached from draining tension. He leaned back, trying to find the least uncomfortable position. The next stage ought to come through in a day or two. A matter of enduring thirst and waiting until—

He sat upright, rigid with memory of a conversation on the stagecoach. Today had been the last time the stop on this route would be used. The spring had gone dry, and a new station had been constructed south of here. Supplies and horses were to be moved tonight. When this stagecoach didn't arrive in Yuma, eventually someone would come here to see what had happened. But would anyone come close enough for him to be heard?

His life couldn't end this way! He'd been in a bitter rage about going to prison—the unfairness of it, the prospect of being shut up. But he might escape from prison.

Harvey Lippincott's face rose up in Cole's memory, the eyes hard and mocking, the white-mustached mouth curved in a sneer. Cole let out a roar of rage and pain and smashed his fist on the ground. "You son of a bitch," he shouted. "You won't get away from me. I'll send you to hell yet!"

Again nearby cicadas retreated into silence, disturbed by his bellows. He leaned back against the wall and took a deep breath, forcing control to return. All he could do was wait and endure.

The creak of a hinge snapped him erect. The low door was opening. Cole braced himself, silently cursing that the shovel was out of reach, gripping the wrist chain taut. It was no match for a gun but it was all he had. The door opened farther. A shaft of sunlight widened and sliced across his legs.

Someone called, "Who's in there?" A woman's voice!

He wet his lips before he could answer. "A passenger. From the stage."

"Come outside," she ordered.

"I will, if you'll help me," he said, in what he hoped was a reassuring tone.

A woman's figure appeared in the doorway, silhouetted against the glare from outside. She held a piece of wood that looked like a discarded fence post. As she hesitated in the doorway, he realized she was probably near hysteria.

He tried again for a soothing voice. "I thought I was the only one the Indians didn't find."

"I hid behind the privy." Her voice was low and even, without the agitation he expected. Slowly his muscles unclenched again. "They weren't Indians," she continued. "Indians wouldn't have missed either you or me."

He almost asked why she was sure but checked himself. He didn't want to sound as if he were disagreeing with her. "If you can help me unlock these cuffs, I'll see what I can do to get us away from here."

She moved closer and pushed back her bonnet. He remembered her. She and the middle-aged man with her were already on the stage when Cole and the deputy marshal guarding him got on in Tucson. A young woman, thin and quiet. He'd been too absorbed in his bitter thoughts to pay much attention to any of the passengers. About all he'd noticed was that she could have been pretty if she weren't so unhappy looking. Now she was staring at his manacled hands. For a minute he feared she might bolt.

But she didn't. Instead she said in an oddly controlled voice, "Oh, yes. You're the murderer."

Anger that still lay close to the surface threatened

him, but he forced it back. "Have you seen what it's like out there?"

She gave a shudder, quickly suppressed. "I haven't gone close. I can see bodies on the ground."

"Can you find the deputy? The keys to these irons were on his belt."

When she didn't move toward the door, he said bitterly, "If you get me loose, lady, don't worry. I won't do anything to you."

She laughed.

Astounded by her laugh, he watched her turn and go out the door.

Smoke drifted upward from the shell of the stagecoach stop. The remnants of door and window frames smoldered in the blackened adobe walls. Martha Turner walked slowly toward it, dreading what she would find. Instead she chose to think about the man in the shack.

Her first impression when he and the deputy had boarded the stage in Tucson was of a dangerous man. His face looked sinister with its dark brown beard and angry, dark brown eyes. An army lieutenant already on the stage had eyed the chained man nervously, perhaps because his young wife was with him. Even so, Martha had felt a stir of sympathy for the prisoner. She and he both had jailers with them—the difference was that he was in chains. In the two days' travel from Tucson, she hadn't paid much attention to him. From what the marshal had said during one of the meal stops, the murderer had killed a man he was traveling with. He'd denied it but a witness had testified to the murder. Because he came from a prominent family and had never been in trouble before, he'd been sentenced to prison instead of hanging. Just now he spoke as if he'd been educated, but that didn't tell much about a man's character out here.

Near the entrance of the burned building, eight bodies sprawled, some in contorted positions. Martha knew that if she hadn't been in the outhouse, she'd be lying here too. She moved hesitantly among the bodies, forcing herself to check that no one lived. Joseph Adams lay on his face, and she was grateful she couldn't see his wounds. Tears rose painfully in her throat. She'd hated his control over her, but he'd served her grandmother well in other ways. He shouldn't have died because of a duty as the family's lawyer. The middle-aged wife of the station owner still wore the apron she'd never need again. An old grief threatened Martha's control. Her mother had worn just such a blood-stained apron.

Shakily Martha went on with her grim hunt. The army officer's young wife lay in a crumpled heap. Her husband's body was in front of her. At the sight of him, Martha's stomach revolted and almost destroyed her thin shell of composure. The upper half of his face was gone. She backed up, whirled, and started away. After a few steps, she halted.

She gripped her trembling hands together. "No, you can do it," she admonished herself. "You've seen worse than this."

Keeping her gaze away from the lieutenant, she continued searching until she found the deputy. Martha knelt beside him. His guns were gone, but attached to his tooled leather belt she found a ring of keys. Her sweaty fingers fumbled with the metal, but it remained stubbornly attached to the belt. Flies buzzed loudly nearby, hovering over wounds on which blood was congealing into sticky masses. Nausea threatened her again. In desperation, she unbuckled the belt, held onto the buckle and pulled hard. Finally the body rolled sideways, as if in a last moment of life.

She staggered backward, gripping the belt. The keys jangled against each other like a harsh warning, and the sound brought up the fear and horror that lay waiting in her stomach. She doubled over and retched onto the ground.

When she could stand, she stumbled across to the corral. She dipped the edge of her skirt in the horse trough and wiped her mouth and face. Nearby an old bottle lay in the dirt. She held the hem of her skirt over the bottle, submerged it in the trough, and let the water filter through. Soon she had enough to drink and to take to the man in the shed.

It was time she must decide whether to free the murderer or leave him in chains. She clutched the bulky keys as if they could give her the answer. Did she want to become his jailer and wait for someone to rescue them? Or strike out on her own? There were no guns left on any of the bodies, and the stick she'd abandoned was no defense. The prisoner was a large, muscular man. He could easily overpower her.

During the years that her life and sanity had depended on her perception of the people around her, she'd learned to read clues of voice and body. Somehow she thought he wouldn't harm her. And maybe he could help her with the only thing that still mattered to her. If she were wrong, he might kill her. In spite of the warm March sun, she felt a chill. There had been times in the past ten years when she'd almost wished for death. Not now. Fear clutched at her chest. In spite of it, she started for the shed.

* * *

Cole heard the returning steps. When his heartbeat slowed, he recognized how uncertain he'd been that she would come back. He'd grown up around women who looked and sounded like this one—well-dressed, educated, proper. Like his mother. He knew what to expect from women like that, but not this one. She'd seemed unnaturally calm. That made her unpredictable.

The door swung wide, letting in a rectangle of desert glare along with the young woman. "Did you find the keys?" he asked.

She looked at him, not answering right away. Finally she said, "Yes. But if I release you, I want your promise to help me."

"I said I'd try to get you someplace safe so you can go where you were headed."

"That's not what I want."

The trapped feeling was stifling him. "Then what the hell do you want?"

"There's someone I must look for in eastern Arizona. But I may need help. Do you promise to help me?"

"Look, lady, the law wants me. I'll see that you get to safety. But I can't promise anything else. Once we're out of here, you can find someone else to help you."

"No, that won't do." She took a step forward, the keys in her hand just out of reach. "Unless you swear you'll do what I ask, I won't give you the keys."

At that moment he felt like strangling her with the chains. "And you expect a murderer to keep his word?" he snarled.

"I don't know if you're a murderer. But I think that

if you promise, you'll do it." Her voice still sounded confident, but the keys jangled slightly as her hands trembled.

So she wasn't so sure as she tried to appear. She might be crazy—very likely was. But she had figured him right. Once he made a promise, he'd keep it. At least, he always had. Whatever she wanted must be damned important, or she wouldn't take a chance on him. Eastern Arizona was the general direction he wanted to go. And he had no choice. Later maybe he'd ignore his conscience and get rid of her. Once he was free, her bargain wasn't worth much. "All right, I'll help you."

"You swear?"

"I swear!"

She held out the keys. "Do you want me to try them?"

"No. I'll do it." It was bad enough to be shackled; he didn't want her taking the irons off. He hated the humiliation of being in someone else's power.

He forced the heavy key until it grated and the band around his left wrist opened. His left hand worked more awkwardly, but finally he freed his right wrist. When he unfastened the fetter around his ankle, relief made him almost dizzy. His left boot lay to one side, and he pulled it on. His whole body ached as he rose. He stamped his foot into the boot, restoring some of the sluggish circulation.

"Your wrists," she said. "They need tending to. I could—"

"They'll do." There wasn't time, and he didn't like the idea of being obliged to her for anything more.

She handed him the bottle of water. He drank eagerly before stepping around her to the door. Outside he stopped, blinking in the afternoon sunlight. She followed him, and he had a good look at her. She was about midtwenties, he guessed. She was tall for a woman, thin without being angular. Planes dominated her face—straight eyebrows and nose, squarish jaw. Strands of light brown hair had come loose from the coil at the back of her head. Nothing striking about her appearance—except for the intense blue of her eyes, regarding him with a wary but determined expression. Her expensive-looking gray traveling dress and educated way of talking suggested money. This was no rough frontier woman.

He gestured toward the burned station. "I have to see for myself. You can stay here."

"No, I'll go with you."

"All right," he said and wondered as he started toward the ruins whether she wanted to make sure he didn't desert her.

Before he reached the bodies, he steeled himself not to let them bother him. He'd never been able to look on death without being upset by the tragedy of it. Quickly he moved from one to the other of the men. He stopped and studied the man who'd been traveling with the woman, then crouched and measured his arm length against the arm on the corpse.

"What are you doing?" she asked.

"I need different clothes. This man looks about my size." Cole rose and looked at her. This might be her husband's body. "I'm sorry if it bothers you. Was he related to you?"

"No. But please, could we move away from here? I want to ask you something." She turned and hurried over to the unburned corral.

He followed, glad enough himself to leave the carnage. When he reached her, her face was pale but composed. "Why do you want someone else's clothes?" she asked.

"The marshals will be looking for me. It's not healthy to be myself just now."

She studied him a moment and said, "Are you planning to have it appear you died here?"

"Yes."

"What is your name?"

He hesitated, but she already knew enough about him that his name didn't matter. "Cole Wingate."

"I'm Martha Turner." Still watching him intently, she said, "If you want to go on as someone else, you could be the lieutenant. He was about your size and coloring. Your hair and beard are darker than his, but you and he look quite a bit alike. I noticed the resemblance when we were on the stage."

Cole frowned. "I couldn't claim to be an army officer."

"Why not?"

"He'd have too many friends who'd know him."

"No, he wouldn't. While we were on the way to Tucson, he was telling my . . . the man with me about himself. He tried law but didn't like it. A friend helped him get a commission in the army. This was his first posting. He and his wife were on their way to join a regiment in Yuma that's to be stationed somewhere in Arizona Territory."

Cole thought about her information. If she was right, taking on the lieutenant's identity was a possibility.

"The stage company knows who was on the stage," she continued fiercely. "If you want them to think you're dead, it has to appear that someone else survived. The last place anyone would think to look for you would be in the army."

Without answering, he turned and skirted around the bodies toward the stagecoach. Trunks and leather bags had been broken open and rifled in an apparent search for jewelry and money. And guns—there were none left. Cole hunted until he came to a metal trunk stamped in gold letters, Stephen Baldwin, with a newly stenciled U. S. Army below the name. Still inside was a flat leather case that held Lieutenant Baldwin's enlistment papers and orders: to report to Fort Yuma to join the Twenty-fifth Infantry Regiment. It was coming from San Francisco, for assignment in the Arizona Territory.

Cole sat on his haunches, considering. During his wandering he'd known and worked with a lot of people, including a lawyer. He could fake that background, provided no one on the army post knew much law. Medical records might be a problem, and there was the age difference. But the army had a reputation for sloppy records. It would be easy to lay differences to some mix-up. With his beard, he looked as close to twenty-four as twenty-eight.

He stood up and read through Baldwin's papers again. Impersonating an officer of the United States Army was a serious charge. But he wasn't risking much—with a murder conviction already hung on him. Martha Turner's idea just might work, long enough to do what he had to do. But what about his promise to her?

She was still standing by the corral when he returned carrying the leather case. "You were right about Stephen Baldwin," he said. "New to the army. Going to be stationed in Arizona."

"So you intend to be Stephen Baldwin?"

"Yes. For now."

"Then you need a wife. I need to be someone else too. I'll be Elizabeth Baldwin."

Startled, he began, "But that wouldn't—"

Her head went up and her back stiffened, like a female bear about to defend her cub. "You promised to help, and this is what I want to do."

Her tone of authority raised his hackles. "Look, lady, I didn't agree to go along with any crazy plan you thought up. Don't you have family who'll look out for you? I can take you to them or wherever you were going."

Her lips tightened. "No! That isn't what I want."

"Impersonating Baldwin might not work," he protested. "Then I'll be on the run again—if I get away."

"I'll take that chance. Are you a man of your word or not?"

They glared at each other while calculations raced through his head. If he went along with her plan, she'd have something at stake too. Things might not turn out the way she wanted, but she wouldn't betray him. Finally he said, "All right. But I don't see how this helps you."

Her rigid stance relaxed a fraction, and he realized that she wasn't as confident as she sounded. She declared, "Never mind that. A wife will give you an explanation for being alive."

"What do you mean?"

She gestured toward the still smoldering building. "How can you explain why you weren't burned or shot? If you and I had been outside, away from the building at the time, that would be your excuse."

"You mean—tell them we went out for a walk?"

Color crept up her throat into her face, but she didn't hesitate. "No one would believe we'd go for a walk far enough away from the station that we didn't get back until it was hopeless to help the others. You'll give it as the polite explanation, but everyone will know what we were doing."

"In the sagebrush?" he protested.

Though the flush hadn't receded, her voice was composed. "You don't think that happens?"

She was right, and it irritated him. He gave her a deliberately slow look and let his mouth curve into a grin. "You want to show me?"

Anger flared in her face—anger with a touch of what could be fear. "No! That's not part of our bargain. We have a . . . business arrangement until I accomplish my purpose."

"And what is that?"

She turned so that he couldn't see the expression on her face. "I'm looking for a child. A part-Indian child."

He waited for her to explain, but instead she turned back and said, "I think you have a purpose too. Something you were shouting about in the shed. And you need to stay in Arizona to do it. Otherwise it makes sense for you to leave the area."

"You got that right. So maybe I'll help you as long as you want. Or maybe I won't." It satisfied him to shake her assurance a little. "Don't bank too much on believing that I keep promises." He glanced up at the sun lowering toward the horizon. "It's time to get started. We have a long walk ahead of us."

She looked thoughtful. "Yes, I suppose Lieutenant Baldwin and his wife wouldn't stay here. The Yumas don't come this far east, and the Pimas and Maricopas are peaceful. The raiders got the horses, so they won't be back. But the Baldwins didn't know that much about the country."

He didn't ask about her knowledge of Indians—he wasn't anxious to answer any questions himself. "We'll need what supplies we can salvage. Go through the Baldwins' belongings. Choose what will help us and destroy the rest. And I have to do something with the bodies."

"You mean bury them?" she asked.

"No. It would take a couple of days to dig the graves. When this stage doesn't get to Yuma, someone will come to find out why. They can do the burying. For now, I'll find a place to put the bodies so animals can't get to them." He thought a moment, then asked, "Did you notice if there's a root cellar?"

"The station-owner's wife went outside and brought back a jar of preserves. She went around to the back, I think."

He circled around the adobe and found traces of a path. It led to a low rise with a slanting door set into it. When he pulled it up, he found steps dug out of the earth leading down into a crude cellar. He backed out and found Martha waiting. "This will do," he said.

She took a breath as if steeling herself and said, "Shall we start now?"

That was too much. Even if she was a little mad, hauling bodies was no job for a woman. "I'll do it."

"No." She stood, her chin at a determined slant, her gaze holding his steadily. "It will be faster if we work together."

He held in his protest. She was right. Uncomfortably he said, "Then you'd better put on gloves. And cover up your dress. It's going to be a bloody job."

Her face paled, but without replying, she whirled and started toward the scattered luggage. He watched her as she walked away, her back still defiantly straight, her skirt swaying with her motions. He admired her guts, but he couldn't figure her out. She hadn't told him anything about herself. He hadn't told her about himself either. They were going to be in a tricky situation together. For the scheme to work they needed to cooperate, not antagonize each other. He had the feeling that he'd walked into more than a scheme to fool the army.

2

Martha stripped off her bloody gloves and pinafore. Her impulse was to throw them as far away as possible. Instead she took them to the watering trough and sponged off as much blood as she could. She would need them again—not, she prayed, for a task like the one just finished.

Together she and Cole Wingate had carried all the bodies except Stephen Baldwin's to the cellar, but Cole had insisted on dragging them inside by himself. He'd spared her that part. With a rock and nails he'd salvaged from the shed, he pounded pieces of charred board across the door. She was glad that he also took care of searching pockets for anything overlooked by the raiders.

During it all, his expression of cold purpose hadn't changed. She decided he was a hard man—or he had enormous control over his feelings.

The breeze that whipped spirals of dust across the corral felt chilly, reminding Martha that March nights could be cold in the desert. She still had to look through Elizabeth Baldwin's belongings for anything that would aid the impersonation. When she reached the coach, Cole was crouched beside a metal traveling trunk.

He motioned toward a small pile of papers beside him. "I found Baldwin's medical records and their marriage certificate. I'll burn the medical records in the shed. The certificate might be useful if we need their signatures. Put anything of his wife's belongings there to be destroyed."

Martha knelt on the ground beside a small leather trunk with the initials *E. P. B.* on it and hesitated, her hands on the lid. It seemed wrong to pry into someone else's life, Martha thought—and realized how foolish her reluctance was. She was planning to appropriate Elizabeth's life, not just pry into it.

A packet of letters would be valuable clues to the woman she would pretend to be. She put those aside to save. Toward the bottom she found a slender package wrapped in a scrap of blue satin. Inside was a cardboard folder embossed with roses that opened to show a sepia-toned photograph. Stephen Baldwin, rigid in a dark formal suit, sat and stared into the camera. An unsmiling Elizabeth Baldwin stood beside him, one gloved hand on his shoulder. In her other hand she held a bouquet. Someone, perhaps the photographer, had arranged the train of her dress so that it fanned out in front of her. The Baldwins' wedding picture. What hopes for a life together had ended so brutally?

"Did you find anything to burn?" Cole was standing over her.

She rose slowly and held out the picture. "I suppose this has to be destroyed." To her dismay, she felt her throat tighten and moisture form in her eyes. She thrust the photograph at him and knelt again, keeping her face turned away.

Cole looked at the picture, but he was thinking about Martha and not the photograph. The emotion in her face made him uncomfortable. He'd about decided she didn't have any womanly feelings. In that case, it wouldn't bother him so much to cut out and leave her in Yuma, if that's what he decided to do. Still, no need to consider that now. They were a long way from Yuma, and there was one more job to do here.

"I put your trunk and Mrs. Baldwin's on the other side of the coach," he said. "Pick out a few things you'll need to carry between here and the next stage station."

She rose and faced him, a frown on her face. He could see she didn't like orders from him, but until they reached safety, he wanted it settled who was in charge. "And take your time about it," he added.

"Why?" she said, a trace of challenge in her voice.

"Because I plan to burn the shed with what looks like my body chained inside. Right now I'm going to swap my clothes with the lieutenant's. Unless you want to watch, don't hurry back."

She stood her ground a moment longer, and then retreated.

As soon as she was out of sight, he forced himself to undress the young officer's body, then stripped. Though the air was cold, by the time he finished putting his grimy clothes onto the corpse, sweat ran in trickles down his torso. He could smell death on himself along with the stink of the Tucson jail. No matter how important time was, he had to wash. Naked, he went to the horse trough and sponged off until he felt cleaner. He went back to the lieutenant's trunk and found clean underwear, then put on the blood-spattered uniform. It was a little tight across the shoulders and chest but otherwise wasn't a bad fit. He tried on the boots and discarded them as too tight. Fortunately his own boots were new enough to pass.

Martha was still behind the coach. She was just closing Elizabeth Baldwin's trunk as he walked around. A small bundle with a belt strapped around it lay beside her. At his step, she looked up, and her eyes widened.

"Do I look enough like the lieutenant?" he asked.

Martha found herself so disconcerted that momentarily she could only stare. He did look quite a bit like Stephen Baldwin, but it wasn't the resemblance that startled her. In the uniform Cole Wingate appeared different—competent, but not so wild and dangerous. He was handsome, something she hadn't noticed about the man in chains.

His face creased in an impatient frown. "Well?"

"You look like him, except that your hair and beard are ragged."

He smiled with irony. "We didn't have mirrors in the Tucson jail, and the barber wasn't eager to come around. Are you finished here?"

"I've moved my belongings into her trunk," she said. "I found these keys." She held up several trunk keys. "They don't fit any of these trunks."

"We'll take them along anyway. Anything else to destroy?" She shook her head. "Then I'll get on with burning the shed. After that we'll leave."

Martha followed Cole, wondering how to respond to his assumption that he would make all the decisions. She was sure she knew more about traveling on foot in the desert than he did. Silence was best for now.

When they reached the body, he hoisted it up on his shoulders. "Bring the papers," he said, and started for the shed. She picked up the small stack with the blue-wrapped photograph on top and followed.

When they reached the shed, he disappeared inside with his burden. After a thud came the muffled rattle of the chains. Cole reappeared and took the papers from her, then went back inside. Martha started away, not intending to watch, but the odor of burning paper drew her back. Cole came out the door holding a piece of burning cloth that he laid next to the outer wall. The first wisps of smoke curled around the cracks in the boards. As the dry wood began to smolder, the smoke thickened and finally burst into flames.

One part of her wanted to leave; another couldn't. It was as if the flames were destroying her. Someday she would be Martha Turner again. But for now Elizabeth Baldwin was taking her place. It was a bizarre feeling. She glanced at Cole to see his reaction, but he had already started back toward the ravaged coach. She followed, wondering what he was thinking. On the one hand, it might be prudent to ask him about his murder conviction. But at this point it was probably better not to know. It might be crazy to trust him, but the help he could give her was worth the risk.

When they reached the stagecoach, he took out a leather bottle. "Get water in this. I'll take another look for a gun, but I think the Indians, or whatever they were, got them all."

While he searched through the scattered objects, she went to the watering trough and filtered water through a clean handkerchief into the bottle. When it was full, Cole had collected an assortment of objects: a small hatchet, a knife, matches, some twine, two extra jackets, and a tin of crackers that had been in the marshal's bag. He put them, along with Lieutenant Baldwin's papers, into a large pack. By the time he was finished, the sun had set. Cole went back to check the shed. "It's burned down enough," he reported when he returned. "Let's get started."

"We need to decide what route to take," she pointed out. "According to a sign that was inside the station, we're ninety-six miles from Yuma. The next stop is about twenty miles."

"We'll generally follow the Gila River. We have to stay off the stage road. I don't have a gun. So we can't risk running into anyone."

"But the lieutenant and his wife wouldn't know the country. Even if they were cautious about Indians, they'd have to keep on the regular route to find the way."

For the first time Cole smiled with something like amusement. "Along with my clothes, I guess I have to change my thinking." The edge returned to his voice as he added, "From murderer to honest soldier."

She wished he hadn't reminded her of his conviction. He waited a moment, as if challenging her to comment, then picked up his large bundle and the water bag and struck off along the ruts used by the stage line. Envying the freedom of his stride, Martha took her package and followed.

Ahead of them to the west the sky still glowed behind the far hills. Before long Cole was several yards ahead of her. She quickened her pace as much as her hampering clothing allowed. As the distance between them increased, her muscles tightened with the effort to catch up.

Despite her belief that the area was mostly safe from

Indian attack, she was afraid. The ground was dry, and each footstep stirred up a cloud of fine dust that could give their presence away to any observer. It had been ten years, but memory could still resurrect the terror of being the last one alive, facing the Apache warriors. The men in her family couldn't protect her then, but Cole seemed harder, stronger. He should be more considerate than to get so far ahead, she thought angrily, and knew that her anger was at herself too. She was finally free, and she didn't want to have to depend on him or any other man. But fear made her hurry after him.

His figure was becoming indistinct in the growing darkness before he finally stopped and waited for her. "Are you going to have trouble keeping up?" he asked.

"I'd be ahead of you now," she retorted, "if I didn't have to dress like a white woman. You try wearing a long skirt and petticoat and see how fast you walk."

"Yes, I see." He started again at a slower pace.

As Cole walked, he wondered why she'd said *white* woman. She looked white, with her light brown hair, blue eyes, and pale skin.

Martha's complaint about his pace led him to look for a stopping place earlier than he would have by himself. There was no kind of cover up on the mesas, so he veered off through the chaparral to a shadowed defile where the bases of two bluffs met. He stopped and started to ease his pack off his shoulders.

"No, not here," Martha said. "The moonlight will shine in here in an hour or so." She marched past him up the slope where the bluffs intersected, and stopped. Looking back at the sky as if measuring the angles, she put her bundle down.

After his surprise abated, Cole examined the position of the moon in the sky. She was right. He should have noticed that. Though the air was cold, his neck felt hot under the high blue uniform collar. Slowly he followed her and set down his pack and the water bottle.

She was already seated on the ground. He stood, flexing his shoulder muscles and examining the landscape for movement. He pulled out the extra jackets and handed her one, then found a spot, smoothed away rocks and gravel, and stretched out. It was too bad they couldn't have a fire, but the light would give away their location.

As his fatigue lessened, he realized how hungry he was. He sat up and took the tin of crackers out of the pack. "This is all we have," he said. "Without a gun there's not much chance of getting game, but in the morning I'll make a sling shot."

She held up something long and thin and said, "I saw rabbit droppings down below. I've made a snare from the twine. I'll put it out, and we'll probably have a rabbit to cook when it's light enough for a fire to be safe."

Too surprised to respond, he watched as she picked her way back down the slope. He could see only the moving dark outline as she walked a short distance, crouched down briefly, then started back. More than ever she was a puzzle to him.

When she returned, he passed her the tin of crackers. She devoured one, then took another and ate it slowly. "I was very hungry. Are there enough for one more?"

"Go ahead. You seem pretty confident we'll have meat." She took two before passing the tin back to him.

His stomach was clamoring for food, but he limited

himself to four crackers. At times he'd gotten along on less than that. The crackers had about as much taste as paper. He opened the leather water bag and offered it to Martha. She drank from the narrow opening and returned it. As Cole put it to his mouth, he thought that he'd drunk from the same bottle as another man countless times without paying attention to it. Sharing with Martha seemed . . . intimate.

Curious, he studied her dark figure. She sat huddled in the extra jacket, her knees against her chest and her arms wrapped around them. "Where did you learn to make a snare?" he asked.

"Someone I once knew taught me."

He waited, but she didn't say more.

From the position of the moon, he guessed it must be about midnight. "I'll watch while you sleep," he offered.

"Why don't you go first? I'm too keyed up for sleep just yet."

He wasn't sure he wanted to depend on her, but they were fairly secluded and she seemed to know about wilderness travel. An hour's sleep right now would be enough. He lay back on the slope, looking up into the sky.

If Martha hadn't survived the attack, his last view might have been the underside of the shed roof. Or suppose a detail from Fort Yuma had found him—he wouldn't be looking up at stars at night. She'd spotted a concealed place to stop. And they might have rabbit for breakfast. He was grateful for her skills, but if he could make out what kind of woman she was, the gratitude might come easier.

* * *

The early morning colors of the mesas were changing from purple to rose when Martha found a rabbit in her snare. By the time she returned to the camp with the skinned and eviscerated rabbit, Cole had started a fire with dry mesquite sticks. He'd stuck two forked branches in the ground, one on each side of the fire. Though he'd slept little, he looked rested.

"Good thing you got the rabbit," he said and handed her a long straight stick. "I'm starving."

"Yes," she said, "so am I."

When the spitted rabbit was over the fire, she debated whether to use their water to clean the blood from her hands. "There isn't any grass to clean my hands," she said. "Do you think we have enough water that I could use a little?"

"We can't be sure how far to more water. Here." He held out his arm. "Use my sleeve. It's already bloody."

She moved hesitantly toward him. When she rubbed her hands on the rough cloth, she could feel the firm curve of his muscles resisting the pressure of her hands. It reminded her of his strength—of his masculine power. Quickly she wiped off most of the grime. "Thank you."

She turned to her own small bundle and hunted until she found the paper she wanted. It was yellowed and dingy along the creases. Carefully she unfolded it and spread it out on her lap. After a moment's study she said, "I think we're about ten miles from the Gila River and the same distance from the next stage stop."

Cole looked astonished. "You have a map?"

"Yes." She hesitated, then held it out. "Do you want to look at it?"

After a long scrutiny, he said, "Where did you get a map with this much detail?"

"What does it matter?"

He folded the map and turned it in his hands, frowning. "This would be a curious thing for someone new to the Territory to have. Maybe I should put it in the fire."

"No!" She reached for the map, but he held it back. "It's mine. You don't have the right to decide."

His eyes glinted dark and angry. "I agreed to go along with your idea. That doesn't mean we do everything your way. If anyone gets suspicious of you, they'll suspect me too."

She glared as fiercely back at him. "I'll say it was given to me."

He gave her the map, but the taut muscles around his eyes told her he was still angry.

When the rabbit was brown, Martha removed it from the spit. Silently Cole divided it. The meat was tough and stringy, but they gnawed every fragment from the bones and followed with two crackers each and sips of water. Martha was still hungry and guessed that Cole must be even less satisfied. He didn't complain, and when he broke the silence with, "Thanks for snaring the meal," her continued anger toward him felt uncharitable.

She accompanied her "You're welcome" with a tentative smile and was answered by a brief softening of his guarded expression. For that moment he again looked handsome, which reminded her of something his appearance needed.

While he tossed out the bones and smothered the fire, Martha took a small pair of scissors from her bundle. When he started to pick up his pack, she said, "Wait. Stephen Baldwin wouldn't have such ragged hair and beard."

He looked at the scissors. "You think you're going to do something about it?"

"Yes."

"What do you know about cutting hair?" It was more a challenge than a question.

"Do you see anyone else around to do it?" she said, her kindly feelings fading. "Lieutenant Baldwin had neat hair and a well-trimmed beard. You look like someone from the Tucson jail."

His frown settled in again, but he took off his jacket. After he tied a handkerchief around his neck, he sat down on the ground, facing out toward the stage road. "All right," he snapped. "Get on with it."

Martha went up the slope until she was behind Cole. His dark brown hair covered his ears and neck in shaggy points. It felt soft to her hesitant fingers as she lifted strands and slipped the scissors underneath. As she continued to trim, more of his neck was revealed. Instead of the bared skin looking vulnerable, the heavily corded muscles gave an impression of power.

She also discovered what a difficult job she'd undertaken. When she'd cut her own hair in mourning, she'd used a knife and hadn't cared how it looked. Now it mattered. By following a line an inch above the handkerchief and being careful around his ears, she managed to make the back look reasonably neat. When she moved around to the front, Cole gave her one wary glance, then returned his gaze to the horizon. She took a closer look at the thick mass waving around his forehead and retreated a step.

"I think the top will be all right," she said.

She suspected that her voice had given away her discomfort because he looked directly at her, and crinkles of amusement appeared around his eyes. "The beard," he said, getting up. "You need to trim that too."

Though she concentrated on her task, standing close to him made her more aware of him than she'd been before. She could feel the heat from his body, see the texture of his skin, detect an individual yet clearly masculine odor. Within herself she detected a faint stirring of feelings that shocked her. Perhaps because it had been such a long and painful time since it had been important to her, she'd ignored an elemental fact. He was male, and she was his complement and opposite.

His mustache at the left corner of his mouth was slightly longer than on the right. Nervously she positioned the scissors to trim it. An insect whirred past her head and in her state of tension, it startled her. She jumped and banged against Cole. He caught her with his hand. "You all right?" he asked in a voice that wasn't completely steady.

She looked into his eyes and saw a mirror of her own feelings. Heat rushed up into her face. "Yes." Quickly she stepped back, and didn't dare glance down toward the lower part of his body.

His hair looked as if an apprentice barber had practiced on him, and his mustache wasn't even. At least the beard was respectable. "I think that's the best I can do," she said.

He removed the handkerchief and said, "Then let's leave," but he didn't move until she had turned her back to him.

Cole set a slower pace than the previous evening, and gradually she calmed down. The coach road continued through a level plain, ringed with mesas. Halfway through the morning a spring green line of cottonwood trees appeared to the north. Martha stopped and took out her map. Cole waited while she studied it, then handed it to him. "That must be the Gila River," she said.

He compared the terrain and the map. "Yes. That should make the next stage stop three or four miles from here."

Martha's mouth felt dry with more than thirst. "That won't take very long—and then we'll have to be Stephen and Elizabeth Baldwin."

"Do you want to change your mind?" His face had its usual closed expression that didn't let her know what he was thinking. "When you get closer, I can just disappear. You can say you were the only survivor."

She didn't like that prospect at all. "You wouldn't be able to explain the uniform," she pointed out.

"I can get rid of it. I brought along some other clothes I found."

His caution reminded her how little she knew him. Once the masquerade started, she risked prison too, as an accomplice. "So you were expecting me to give up this idea?"

He shrugged. "I thought you might. It won't be easy. And you looked anxious when you found out how close we are."

"That's not it." She must conceal her feelings better. "I just realized," she said, "that before we get there, we'd better practice our names. And what we're going to say about ourselves."

His eyebrows lifted momentarily in what might have been resignation. "All right. Let's get away from the road a while. Someone may be starting out to look for the missing stage." A brief, surprising grin softened his face. "That'll give us time to get our lies straight."

Cole found a dry streambed. Seated on the bottom, he and Martha were concealed from the surrounding area. She took out the packet of letters. Cole produced Stephen Baldwin's papers, and they exchanged information.

Cole said, "They were married September 5, 1875, in St. Louis. Almost two years ago. He would have been twenty-two. She was probably younger, but maybe not much."

"She had several sisters, but apparently no brothers."

"His medical records didn't show much—that he was healthy enough to enlist. And he was shorter than I am."

"Will that be a problem?"

"Maybe. I'll say that paper was lost in the station fire. There must be a longer record somewhere, but someone would have to send for it. No point in worrying now."

Martha didn't feel reassured, but she went on with her information. "Elizabeth must have been very anxious about living in Arizona. Letters from her mother and sisters are filled with reassurance that it will be all right." Martha thought sadly of Elizabeth—left in that dark cellar. Her mother's and sisters' wishes hadn't protected her.

Another subject cropped up repeatedly in the letters. Apparently Elizabeth and Stephen had wanted a child badly, and Elizabeth worried because she hadn't become pregnant. That was too painful a topic for Martha to discuss with Cole. She tied up the packet and returned it to her bundle.

He stirred restlessly. "Is there more we have to talk about now? When we get to the next station, all they'll want to know is what happened. They won't care what we call each other. We'll have time to work out details before we meet up with the army."

He stood up and took his pack. "You'll have to act less sure you can get along in the desert. Don't make any more snares, and don't tell people what to do, or no one will believe you're new out here." He started back up the side of the streambed.

Martha stared after him, but all she could see was his straight back and purposeful stride. So her desert skills hadn't pleased him. Stephen Baldwin's wife would have suited Cole Wingate very well.

As she followed him, she practiced the name Stephen to herself. It ought to be easy, but she already thought of him as Cole. The shorter, more abrupt-sounding name fit him better.

Closer to the Gila River the taller mesquite provided good cover. Cole and Martha had covered a mile or more parallel to the road when a dust cloud appeared, moving toward them along the stage route. Martha's muscles tensed and her heartbeat speeded up. "That won't be Indians," she said, "because they wouldn't follow the road."

"Yes, I expect it's someone from the next stop."

When the cloud came closer, they could see several mounted men. As the figures emerged more distinctly, Cole exclaimed, "They're soldiers. Must be a detail from Yuma."

Martha restrained herself from reaching out and grabbing Cole's arm. Whether they were ready or not, the first test of their impersonation was upon them.

3

The approaching figures looked like ghosts; dust had turned men and horses into yellow-gray centaurs from a mythic army. Cole counted sixteen soldiers with an officer. When they were within hailing distance, he left the concealing brush and stepped to the edge of the rutted road. He waved his arm and called, "Hello." The man in the lead, a first lieutenant, checked his mount, then advanced slowly. The soldiers spread out and followed, their rifles at the ready as Cole motioned to Martha to come forward also.

When Martha reached Cole's side, she took his arm. As the lieutenant reined in beside them, his dust cloud added its powdery coating to their own. Martha, her throat already dry with apprehension, felt as if she were choking.

The lieutenant, a young fair-skinned man, dismounted. He stared at Cole's blood-stained uniform and his eyes widened. "Are you all right?" he asked.

"Yes," Cole said, "but we're glad to see you." He

sounded relieved and eager, the right emotion for Stephen Baldwin.

The lieutenant's cap had a brass *D* and a smaller number 12 over crossed rifles. "Harold Nelson," he introduced himself, "D Company, Twelfth Infantry."

"Stephen Baldwin," Cole responded smoothly. "This is my wife, Mrs. Baldwin."

Lieutenant Nelson took off his cap and gave a half-bow in Martha's direction. "It's a pleasure to meet you, ma'am."

Martha managed her response in a voice that didn't shake. When her heartbeat slowed, she looked at Cole. He appeared relaxed, even close to smiling.

The lieutenant turned back to Cole. "What happened?"

"My wife and I were on the stage—on the way to meet the Twenty-Fifth at Yuma," Cole said. "When the stage stopped at Stanley's yesterday, it was attacked. Everyone else was killed and the horses taken."

"My detail is on patrol from Fort Yuma." Nelson sounded very young and excited. "We just came through Riley's Springs. Indians tried to raid that station too. They got some horses but no one was killed. Must have been the same Indians who attacked you."

Martha's impulse was to correct him, to tell him the raiders weren't Indians, but Elizabeth Baldwin wouldn't know that.

"It's amazing you got away," Nelson said. "How did you manage that?"

"Yes, well . . . " Cole seemed to be fumbling for words.

Martha's anxiety blazed up again. "Lieutenant Nelson," she interrupted, "are we far from the next station?"

"About four miles."

"If it's possible to go there and rest a little, I would be so grateful."

"Why, certainly, Mrs. Baldwin." The young officer was instantly solicitous. "I apologize for asking questions now. Your husband can tell me later." He spoke to a corporal who ordered two soldiers to dismount and bring their horses forward. "But what will your men ride?" Martha asked.

"Don't worry about them," Lieutenant Nelson said. "Our pack mules are extra mounts." From his slight tone of disapproval Martha wondered apprehensively whether she'd violated a taboo. Maybe officers' wives weren't supposed to concern themselves with the comfort of ordinary soldiers. But, she reassured herself, Elizabeth Baldwin was new to the army and couldn't be expected to know army ways. The soldier who helped her onto the sorrel mare didn't appear unhappy that he had to give up his horse.

Lieutenant Nelson took his place in front. Martha and Cole rode behind him. The sixteen soldiers formed two lines behind them. She felt sorry for the men at the rear, breathing the others' dust. But when the column started off, she forgot about everything but her balance. Her clothing made riding astride on an army saddle very different from gripping an Apache pony with her knees under a loose skirt and no petticoats.

By the time they reached the cottonwood trees that surrounded Riley's Springs station, the strain of the ride had added to her fatigue from the past day. When the lieutenant stopped next to a corral, she wasn't sure she could dismount. She attempted to extricate her right leg from the stirrup and preserve a modesty that rapidly became less important than managing not to fall. Cole swung down from his horse and tossed the reins to a soldier. Quickly he moved to her side and reached up to grasp her waist. As he lifted her, she put her hands on his shoulders and half slid, half tumbled against him.

"Are you all right?" He was still holding her; she seemed to feel the vibrations from his voice as much as hear them. The shelter of his arms and the hard muscles of his body gave her a disconcerting sensation of comfort.

"Yes. I'll be fine after I walk a little."

He released her. She started to step back and found a button of her dress had caught on his belt buckle. "Just a minute," she said, and fumbled to free it. She hadn't blushed in years, had thought she'd never feel that innocent again. By the time she finally worked the button loose and moved away from Cole, heat had crept up into her face. Cole was looking a little unsettled too.

Lieutenant Nelson said, "Please come inside the station, Mrs. Baldwin. After we eat, your husband will be going back to Stanley's with me and some of my men, but you can wait and rest here. Mrs. Riley is the station owner's wife. She was pretty shaken up by the attack here, and she'll be glad to see another woman."

The low station building resembled the burned one; dirty gray adobe walls repeated the color of the desert. Only a row of sunflowers near the building redeemed its drabness.

Mrs. Riley, a thin woman who looked more like the gray walls than the brilliant flowers, greeted Martha with tired sympathy. She soon had coffee, mutton stew, and beans set out on one end of a long plank table. Martha thought she had never smelled or eaten anything better. Cole also attacked his food with relish.

While they were drinking a last cup of coffee, Cole briefly described events at Stanley's.

Soon Lieutenant Nelson got around to the postponed question: "How did you and Mrs. Baldwin manage to escape the attack?"

Cole glanced at the women then put down his cup and got up. "It's about the time you said we should leave for Stanley's. I can explain on the way."

Lieutenant Nelson furnished Cole with a pistol and carbine. Twelve of the soldiers were detailed to go with them. The other four and the corporal stayed at Riley's Springs.

Martha's apprehension rose again as she watched the men depart. She wasn't sure Cole would tell their story so that it was believable. He'd looked shocked when she proposed their alibi.

Mrs. Riley apparently misinterpreted Martha's concern. She said sympathetically, "No use worrying about Lieutenant Baldwin. In this country you have to trust in God and depend on your man's good sense." She filled her cup and Martha's and sat down on the bench. "Still, it's good for a woman to know how to shoot a Winchester for herself. Yesterday me and Mr. Riley was out in the corral. We had our rifles settin' at hand, like we always do. When them Indians come along, we got down behind the bottom rail and blasted away. Them savages got a few of our animals, but they didn't stay around very long."

"Weren't you terrified?"

"Some. But I give a quick thanks to the Lord that I had my rifle and knew how to shoot."

"You are very brave," Martha said.

"Well," Mrs. Riley offered comfortingly, "I don't suppose you know much about rifles. That husband of yours looks like a good man. He'll take care of you. But you get him to teach you how to shoot."

How different her life might be, Martha thought, if she'd known how to use a rifle years ago.

By nighttime, Cole and the others hadn't returned. Mr. Riley insisted that Martha and his wife share the bedroom and only real bed. Martha was too tired to care about arrangements and was asleep before Mrs. Riley could put out the candle. Sometime later she half wakened to the sound of male voices. She recognized one of them as Cole's and was surprised at the relief she felt. That was because, she thought sleepily, she depended on him now. If this Stephen Baldwin died, what would the army do with her? Maybe send her to an astonished and outraged Baldwin family.

By early morning the soldiers were up and preparing to leave. The bodies at Stanley's station had been buried and the Baldwins' small trunks brought on the pack mules. The stagecoach was left behind.

The column left before sunrise with Martha and Cole in their position behind Lieutenant Nelson. At midmorning they reached Antelope Peak, close to the Gila River. The station took its name from a nearby outcropping of dark gray volcanic rock that descended from a jagged top in a series of bluffs, like gigantic steps. Lieutenant Nelson was anxious to push on, so as soon as they had fresh horses, they were off without any chance for Martha to ask Cole how he'd explained their survival.

Another three hours of riding took them to Mission Camp. As they approached the station, Lieutenant Nelson, in spite of his expressed desire to hurry, fell back beside Martha. "We'll stop for the noon meal here. There's a landmark here you mustn't miss, Mrs. Baldwin," he said. "When we get to Mission Camp, I'll let Corporal Green take the men on in. We'll ride out just a short distance so you can see it. Your husband too, of course."

Martha hesitated, then smiled. "That's very kind of you, Lieutenant Nelson."

Lieutenant Nelson sent the men on ahead. He motioned to Martha and Cole, then started off toward the river.

The Gila River wandered back and forth in swoops among a few small cottonwoods and brushy willows. Beyond the river the hills rose to low peaks, except for a single high one. It stood out from the others, as if a giant hand had added it after the others were finished. Its steep sides rose to a jagged top with evenly spaced points.

"That peak across the river looks like a crown," Martha exclaimed. "Is that the landmark?"

"Yes," Lieutenant Nelson said. "The Spanish explorers named it Coronation Peak."

Martha noticed that Lieutenant Nelson's professed interest in the peak seemed considerably less than his attention to her. Uneasily she looked around for Cole. He had ridden close to the bluff at the river's edge and seemed to be staring down into the water.

Lieutenant Nelson glanced at Cole, then edged his horse closer to hers. "While you're in Yuma, your husband may be busy." His voice deepened. "I know the area well and I'll be happy to show you the points of interest."

Martha bristled. She was sure that there must be an accepted standard of conduct for the behavior of one officer to the wife of another. She felt equally sure that Lieutenant Nelson's voice and smile didn't fit that standard. "Thank you," she said, making sure her voice and manner did fit. "I'm afraid I'll be busy too, learning what an army wife needs to know."

He blinked and pulled his mount back a step. "Yes, I see." He looked around for Cole. "Well, we must be getting on to the station."

The hurried meal at Mission Camp left Martha no chance for conversation with Cole. As they were starting out again, Lieutenant Nelson announced, "We ought to make Gila City in three hours' time. It's twelve miles of good road from there into Yuma, so I'd like to go on and report in to the fort tonight."

Dismayed, Martha realized that the lieutenant's plan would give no time for her and Cole to get their story firm before they reached the army post. She was trying to think how to object when Cole asked, "How secure is the road between here and Yuma?"

"Hasn't been any trouble on it for a long time. The Indians who attacked you must have been Apaches raiding out of their territory. They wouldn't come this close to the fort."

"My wife is very tired. If it's safe for us to go on tomorrow without you, I'd like to stay overnight at Gila City."

"Yes, certainly," Lieutenant Nelson agreed. "I can leave two of my men to accompany you in the morning."

Relieved, Martha rode on, grateful for Cole's quick thinking.

Gila City overlooked a bend of the river with flats of sandy beach and clusters of cottonwood trees. Mostly wood-frame buildings lined the main street, with a few adobes. It looked immensely inviting to Martha, with its promise of a place to spend a night, and perhaps have a bath.

They passed a dry goods store and a church, but most of the buildings were saloons or billiard halls. At the station for the Southern Pacific Mail Stage Line, Mr. Berg, the station keeper, welcomed them with a thick German accent and an amiable expression. "Yes, certainly," he responded to Cole's inquiry about accommodations, "I haf a nice room."

Immediately after the horses were watered, Lieutenant Nelson returned and said, "I'll be leaving now with my patrol, all except the men who'll go with you tomorrow."

"My wife and I are very grateful for all your help."

"I'm glad I was of service, Mr. Baldwin."

Martha stood still, her attention riveted on Lieutenant Nelson's departing back. He had called Cole Mr. Baldwin, not lieutenant. She looked at Cole to see whether he was alarmed, but he was smiling and talking with the station owner.

Mr. Berg apparently liked to visit and was in no hurry to see to a room for Martha and Cole. While she schooled herself to contain her anxiety, they sat on the veranda and he talked. She finally decided she'd been polite long enough and rose. The men got to their feet also. "Mr. Berg, I'm very tired. Do you think the room is ready now?"

Reluctantly he said, "I'll ask my wife."

"And would it be possible to have a bath?"

"Yes, certainly." He disappeared into the station.

Urgently she whispered to Cole, "Lieutenant Nelson called you Mr. Baldwin. Not lieutenant. Does he suspect?"

"No. In the army a second lieutenant is called mister, not lieutenant. I called him Lieutenant Nelson because he's a first lieutenant."

"How do you know?"

"I was in a kind of army once."

She wanted to ask more, but Mr. Berg returned. "The room is ready. One of the helpers will get bath water. Lieutenant Baldwin, do you also wish a bath?" he asked.

A grin of anticipation flashed over Cole's face. "Yes."

The station keeper's face brightened. "Then you will wait here with me until Mrs. Baldwin is finished and we can visit some more."

Cole didn't look pleased, but he sat down again.

The extra bedroom was a lean-to added at the back of the station. Their bags were in a corner. The room held a bed that was slightly wider than a cot, and a cane-bottomed chair. An oval tin tub just large enough to sit in had been filled and was next to a braided rug. Martha almost tore her dress in her hurry to strip off her clothes and settle in the water. Though the tub wasn't large enough to stretch out her legs and the water just warm, the bath felt more luxurious to Martha than anything she could remember.

A shiver that was part cold but mostly excitement persuaded her out of the tub. Once she'd despaired of her unknown future so much she'd hoped to die. Now she didn't know what was coming, and she wanted very much to live.

She was almost dry when a knock sounded. Cole said through the door, "Are you finished?"

"Just a moment." Hurriedly she pulled on a clean shift and a dress over that, then called, "Come in."

Cole came in, followed by a Mexican boy. Together they carried out the tub of water. Martha sat on the side of the bed. She hoped Cole wouldn't be too long having his bath and returning. It was becoming hard to stay awake, and they hadn't talked.

The door opened. Cole and the boy entered, carrying the tub, and set it down. After the boy left, Cole took off his jacket and started unbuttoning his shirt.

"You're going to bathe in here?" Martha asked, suddenly wide awake.

"Why wouldn't I?" He pulled off the shirt and undershirt. "We're supposed to be married."

"But—" She stopped. Custom assumed that a husband let his wife have a room to herself for bathing; she was supposed to be a delicate creature. But men didn't need privacy. How many aspects of pretending to be Stephen Baldwin's wife had she failed to anticipate?

She turned around on the bed and faced the wall, curling her knees under her. She couldn't see, but the sounds created a distinct picture. A careful splash, the water sloshing slightly against the tin, a soft bump—maybe a knee hitting the side. Then a long sigh of pleasure. Resolutely she closed her ears and chided herself for a desire to look at him that would have shocked her grandmother. It shocked her a little—the image of him naked that wouldn't go away because it was incomplete.

The water sloshed again; the linen towel squeaked against skin. She heard him rummaging in the luggage, and then the sound of clothing being put on.

"You can turn around now."

She unfolded her cramped knees and turned. His hair and beard were wet. He had on fresh blue uniform pants with a light blue stripe along the side, a sparkling white shirt, and an amused expression. It didn't help that when she was a young girl, giggling with her friends, all of them had longed for a man who looked as handsome as Cole did now.

Silly, childish feelings. It irritated her to recall them. Her mind should be on crucial issues. "We must talk," she said, "and make sure we have our story right."

His face sobered. As he sat down in the chair, his movements looked weary. "Are you married?" she asked, surprising herself.

"No. Are you?"

How should she answer? It didn't matter; he wouldn't consider her married if she told him everything. "No."

He leaned forward, as if to be certain she was listening. "Are you sure you want to go through with this? There's still time to change your mind."

"We told Lieutenant Nelson. And Mr. Berg. It's too late now."

"I could disappear. You could claim I threatened you. Forced you to say you're my wife."

She didn't like his raising the question again. "I want to go ahead."

"You'd be free to go wherever you want," he said. "Look for the child you want to find."

"The prison in Yuma isn't the only kind," she said angrily. "I was a prisoner too. Mr. Adams, the man with me on the stage, was taking me to California. To my brother."

"But Adams is dead."

"Yes, but if my brother learns I'm alive, he'll make me go to California. I must stay in Arizona."

Cole could see how upset Martha was becoming. But what she said didn't make sense. "How old are you?"

"Twenty-five."

"Then how can your brother make you go with him?"

Martha stood up as if her agitation were too great to contain sitting down. "Several years ago I was very ill. My brother was made my legal guardian."

"Won't he help you find the child you're looking for?"

"No, he wouldn't. And he can force me to do what he decides. Because I'm a woman."

She said the last words so bitterly that Cole felt indicted, along with her brother. "For a woman, you're doing pretty well at getting me to do what you want."

A smile momentarily relaxed the tense lines of her face. "But you were in chains when I made you promise."

"You don't need me," he persisted. "Anyone can help you look for a child. Or you could do it yourself. Why get in trouble impersonating an army wife?"

"Because the Apaches are on reservations now. The army doesn't let people just come and go on a reservation. I need a reason for being there."

That made sense. Why would she tie up with a murderer otherwise? Reluctantly he acknowledged to himself that she'd won. Though he'd like to be able to renege, he couldn't. "So, we'll go ahead. But I'd like to know how long we'll have to keep up this masquerade. Do you have a good idea where to find this child?"

She hesitated as if she were choosing each word. "Probably eastern Arizona. I don't know more than that."

"I guess we'll have to wait and see. Before we decide on a story, I want to know something about you."

Her face had a guarded look. "All right." She sat back down on the bed.

A little stiffly they exchanged information. He began. "I'm twenty-eight. I grew up near Tucson. When my father died, I left home and wandered around, doing different things."

"What things?"

"Cowboy, miner, clerk for a lawyer. I did a stint in the militia. Lots of war veterans there. They talked all the time about the regular army."

"It's why you knew about second lieutenants being addressed as mister?"

"Yes. That's about all there is to tell." It wasn't, but it was enough. "What about you?"

"I was born in Texas. I was living there until my grandmother died recently."

He thought of asking who the child was she was looking for, but he decided to let it alone for now. He needed sleep.

She had another question. "What explanation did you give Lieutenant Nelson for why we survived the attack?"

"What you suggested. That we were out in the bushes."

He hoped she would leave it there, but she asked, "That was all?"

"I had to say a little more to account for turning up without a gun." She waited, and his fatigue and irritation dissipated any reluctance about speaking bluntly. "I hinted that you were so hot to get me outside that you couldn't wait and dragged me off when I didn't have my pistol. By the time you had my pants open, I wasn't thinking about anything else."

Her quick intake of air made a soft hiss, and she flushed.

If he'd embarrassed her, it was her own fault. "It still

makes me out a fool," he said, "but it was that or sound like a liar."

"But I don't look like . . . a woman who's . . . I mean, did he believe you?"

"Men know you can't tell much from looks."

"At least only Lieutenant Nelson knows," she said. "Surely he won't say anything."

If he hadn't been so tired, he'd have had a good laugh. "You have a lot to learn about the army. By now all the men with him have heard about us. They probably have a nickname for me already."

"Nickname?"

"Something choice—like Lucky Dick."

Her face flushed again, but this time with anger. "If you're trying to intimidate me into releasing you from your promise, I won't."

"I wasn't going to tell you this," he retorted, "but you insisted."

The belligerent lines of her mouth softened. "Yes, you're right. And the important thing is that Lieutenant Nelson believed you."

"I hope he did." Cole stirred restlessly. The night was getting on, and he needed enough sleep to be alert in the morning.

"When we went down to the river just outside town," Martha said thoughtfully, "he suggested that he'd show me around Yuma. From his manner, I'm sure he did believe you."

Cole felt his anger rising. It was bad enough to be saddled with this woman. Would he have to defend her from other men? Dammit, he didn't need that. And he hadn't been honest with her. Men did judge women by their looks. At first she'd looked plain to him. But the soft clothing she was wearing now showed that she had a body and movements to distract any man. Yes, Nelson probably did believe his story. "What did you say to Nelson?"

"I let him know I didn't approve."

Cole got up from his chair and found the heavy wool military cape and wrapped it around him. "You can have the bed. I'll sleep on the floor." When she looked uncertain, he added, "I've done it plenty of times."

"All right. Thank you. There are two blankets. You take one of them. My jacket will be warm enough." She put on her jacket and blew out the candle.

Cole shifted, trying to get comfortable, and resigned himself to the bare floor. He'd been too long in the Tucson jail. When she'd cut his hair, he'd gotten hard enough to pound spikes in the ground. He'd never be able to share a bed with Martha and sleep.

His last thought before falling asleep was that their arrival in Yuma the following morning would be a hell of a lot different from the one he'd expected. If he and Martha could pull off this deception, he'd never see the inside of the prison. If they couldn't, maybe he wouldn't see it then either. He didn't know what she risked, but he probably wouldn't get a prison sentence. It would be a rope for hanging.

4

Early the next morning Mr. Berg produced a sidesaddle for Martha to borrow, and she and Cole, with their two escorts, left Gila City. In the fresh, chilly air the fragrance of the sage was still delicate. The austere beauty and distant vistas of the desert gave Martha a feeling of freedom. Anything seemed possible.

The road veered south of the Gila River across a smooth plain, letting the riders set a quick pace. At midmorning Martha saw what she thought were low buildings in the distance. She waited for the soldier riding behind her, Private Greaves, to catch up and asked, "Is that Fort Yuma?".

"No, ma'am. That's the town. The fort's north of there, on the California side of the Colorado River."

"What is it like?"

"Like most army posts, ma'am. Not a bad place to be this time of year. In summer, that's different." He grinned. "Folks here tell a story about a soldier who died and went to hell. Next day he came back for his blankets. Said it was too cold down there for anyone used to Yuma."

"I suppose you get to know the habits of the Indians," she commented.

"Have to, ma'am, if you're going to keep them peaceable."

His answer encouraged her. She'd been hoping that it was common practice for soldiers to learn about the Indians in their area.

As they approached Yuma they rode past scattered adobe buildings, most of them one-room houses. A little farther on, regular streets constituted what could more properly be called a town.

Martha noticed men who looked like Americans, along with Mexicans and Yuma Indians. Several men lounged under the veranda of a large whitewashed adobe store. A blond woman, wearing a two-piece dress much like Martha's, came out. Behind her walked a young Chinese boy carrying several parcels. A soldier who had been standing in the shade in front joined her. They walked on in the direction of the river.

The combination of Chinese boy, American woman, and soldier intrigued Martha. "Do you know those people?" she asked Private Greaves.

"No, ma'am. They're not from my outfit. Maybe from your husband's."

Quivers started circling in Martha's stomach. *Her husband's outfit.* What had been an idea was becoming real.

At the far end of the street a large sign over a corral and building announced *Southern Pacific Overland Mail Stage Line*. Cole reined in beside the corral and dismounted. "I'll let the man in charge here know we'll be at the fort. He'll probably want to ask me about the raid at Stanley's."

"Yes," Martha said. According to their story they hadn't seen the actual raid, but Cole would describe the aftermath. She hoped he wouldn't take long. Their next big hurdle was at the fort. She wanted to get that test over with.

After Cole helped her down from her horse, he went inside. The two soldiers dismounted also and lounged at one side, talking to each other. To keep from dwelling on Fort Yuma, she watched the crowd of men around the station. Two Yuma Indian men, one wearing only a breechcloth, and the other in ragged pants, looked on from one side. Near them a Yuma woman in a short bark skirt watched a small boy. Martha wondered that no one appeared to pay attention to the woman's naked breasts. A white woman in public naked to the waist would cause an uproar. Yet there was no difference in the women's bodies, except in the attitude of the men. How well she knew what difference attitudes made!

Finally Cole came out of the building in the company of a large man with whiskers to match his size. He shook Cole's hand and said, "I'll be in touch with Mr. Griffith, the general superintendent. He'll want to talk to you himself."

"I don't know how long I'll be at Fort Yuma," Cole responded. "My regiment will likely be leaving soon."

Cole spoke so smoothly of his regiment that if Martha hadn't known the truth, she would have believed absolutely that he was Lieutenant Baldwin. If he played this part that easily, how would she ever know whether he was being honest with her? Uneasily she told herself it wouldn't matter, as long as she accomplished her purpose.

Mounted again, they headed for Yuma Crossing, where they would take a ferry across the Colorado River. At the north end of the main street they passed a stockade on a rocky bluff to their right, with a square two-story tower on one corner. The bluff rose steeply; its surface resembled a rough sculpture, as if it had been hewn to make it almost a sheer drop.

"That's the new Territorial Prison," Private Greaves said.

Martha glanced at Cole. He appeared to be looking at the prison with only mild curiosity. Surely he was feeling more than that. His ability to conceal his emotions continued to surprise her.

Even before she could see the broad expanse of the Colorado River, she could hear its murmur. When she reached the low, willow-covered banks, she understood how the river got its name; the ripples and swirls of water were a definite red color. On the shore next to the ferry dock two mules plodded in a circle around a capstan, hauling in the rope that was towing the ferry. The ferry, more like a flat platform than a boat, was in midstream, being pulled toward the dock.

A short distance downriver from the ferry metal frames formed a line across the water, as if some iron giant had forded the river and left a portion of its skeleton behind at each step. Again she turned to her escort. "What is that?"

"That's where the Southern Pacific railroad will cross the river. Then folks can come all the way from San Diego right into Yuma."

Would her brother ever cross on that bridge to visit the grave at Stanley's he thought was hers? Probably not for the sister who had disgraced him.

On the far riverbank at the top of the tallest of three mesas, Martha saw a group of low buildings that must be the fort. Shivers of apprehension prickled her skin, but there was nothing alarming about the fort's appearance. A breeze whipped the flag above it. In the sky beyond, a line of dark gray smoke floated above the horizon, marking the labored progress of the locomotive coming from San Diego.

If the stage station at Stanley hadn't been attacked, she would already have crossed the river and boarded the train for the trip to California—and the prison of her brother's authority. Whatever waited for her at Fort Yuma was better than that.

Cole also was watching the far bank, but his emotions were more complicated. If Martha was crazy, he asked himself, was he any more sane? A convicted man, coming to the place where he was supposed to be locked up. Now, that was crazy! When he had promised to help her, he'd figured she would see the idea was a mistake. Well, maybe she hadn't. All he'd thought about then was getting rid of the shackles.

He looked at Martha, noticing tiny lines at the corner of her mouth. She looked determined, but nervous. He had to admit, going into the fort like this was a gamble with the highest stakes he'd ever played for. It excited him. If she changed her mind now, he could just disappear. He'd be better off, but he'd be disappointed.

The mules brought the ferry to the dock, then stopped, and two men got off the boat. As they passed by, one grumbled to the other, "Charging fifteen dollars! Thievery, I call it."

Martha said to Cole in a soft voice, "I have money, but it would be difficult to take it out here."

"No need. They probably don't charge the army."

As Martha walked ahead of him, he speculated enjoyably about where she might have money hidden on her person. Reluctantly curbing his thoughts, he helped Martha onto the ferry, leaving the horses to the soldiers. The operator didn't ask Cole for money. On the far shore another set of mules began their laborious circle around a capstan and as the ferry lurched out into the current, Martha swayed and tumbled against Cole. He grabbed her arm, holding her steady. She grasped a stanchion and straightened up, pulling away from him.

"Thank you," she said, with an almost shy smile.

The smile and the curves of her body resting against him for that moment felt good. Too good. He released her arm. He'd have to watch himself. It wouldn't do to get notions about her. She was already enough of an interference.

When they reached the dock at the other side, they mounted and rode up a steep, winding road to the gates of the fort. Cole identified himself to the sentry, who asked them to wait and sent another soldier off at a run.

Except that the buildings were adobe rather than wood, Fort Yuma was laid out much the same as other army posts Cole had seen when he was with the militia in Missouri: parade ground in the center, flagpole at one end, officers' quarters along one side. Around the rest of the perimeter were company barracks, corrals, and the other buildings needed for an army post.

Lieutenant Nelson arrived. "I'm glad you got here safely. Mr. Baldwin, General Porter's in Major Dunn's office. He wants to see you." He looked at Martha and explained in a polite but formal voice, "General Porter commands your husband's regiment. Major Dunn is the post commander."

"I'll report to the general right away," Cole said. "Is there someplace my wife can rest for now?"

"I've arranged for you to put up in my quarters. I'll bunk in with one of the other officers. Private Greaves will show Mrs. Baldwin there."

Martha said in an equally polite and cool tone, "Thank you. That's very kind."

He gave her a somewhat stiff smile. "You're very welcome."

Cole remembered what Martha had said about Nelson's reaction to her and was glad the other man was being formal. He didn't want to have to take offense. Too many other tricky things to manage.

"I'll join you after a while," Cole said to Martha.

She said only, "Yes," but he could see a faint quiver of her mouth. He'd bet she wished she were the one going to talk to the regimental commander. Judging by the way she acted, she had confidence in herself, but not much trust in anyone else. He gave her a husbandly smile and got a little perverse pleasure from seeing her lips tighten.

After she left, Nelson led the way to one of the larger buildings. Inside the thick walls, the air was cool. A bulky man with a large mustache and a fringe of white hair around a shiny bald crown sat at a desk. At one side a young first lieutenant stood attentively. Nelson saluted, then said, "Sir, this is Mr. Baldwin."

General Porter acknowledged the introduction with a nod, then said, "A miracle that you survived the attack on the stage station, Mr. Baldwin. I want to hear about it, but first, my adjutant will take your papers." He motioned to the first lieutenant, who came forward.

Cole handed over Stephen Baldwin's enlistment papers and orders. He could feel his heart racing the way it did in a poker game when his opponent might be a dangerous loser.

The adjutant took the papers to a desk and began examining them. The general spoke again. "I understand you have a direct appointment from civilian life."

"Yes, that's correct."

"I don't know the senator who arranged it." General Porter's tone suggested that he didn't want to. "We don't have many officers who come to us that way."

So, Cole thought, using political pull to get a commission in the army wasn't popular.

"You've been assigned to C Company," the general continued, "Captain Fisher commanding. Report to him after you tell me about the stage station."

Cole recited his account, telling of seeing the raiders from a distance and being unable to prevent the attack.

"You and Mrs. Baldwin were both away from the station?" General Porter's expression reminded Cole of a schoolmaster who had caught a boy red-handed but was making the culprit go over the story anyway.

The gossip was too good not to have circulated through the fort. Cole fixed his gaze at a point just above the general's head. "Yes, we were getting some air, sir."

The silence reverberated with the general's expectation of a further, humiliating explanation. Cole said nothing.

"Very well, Mr. Baldwin. You were not actually on duty at the time. However, the army expects its officers to be armed and ready for emergencies at all times. This is Indian country."

"Yes, sir. I understand." Cole smoldered inside.

He'd never responded well to a dressing down. Right now he could do with something in his favor. Looking directly at the general, he said, "If I may comment, sir, I believe the raiders were not Indians. Only gotten up that way so the law would be looking for Indians."

The general's expression lost a little of its disapproval. "Major Dunn will be interested in your observations. He's invited you and Mrs. Baldwin to dine at his quarters this evening. We'll discuss this more over dinner."

As Cole left, he reflected that Stephen Baldwin already had two demerits. He wasn't a West Pointer and he'd been caught without his gun. What kind of treatment would C Company give an opportunist and a fool?

From the window of Lieutenant Nelson's room, Martha studied any blue-uniformed figure that seemed to be heading in her direction. It was terrible to have her life in someone else's hands again, even briefly. That she'd chosen—insisted on—joining her fate to Cole's didn't help at this moment.

Afternoon shadows softened the outlines of buildings and mesquite trees. For the first time Martha noticed that a cactus across the way sported brilliant orange blossoms. Closer at hand sprawling plants sent out runners bearing tiny yellow flowers. They reminded her of a springtime with the Apache band. By then the tragedy of losing her family had lessened, and hope, natural to a sixteen-year-old girl, was reviving. She had begun to accept and admire—if not yet love—her Apache husband. A too brief time of growing happiness followed that spring. The bitter years since mustn't make her lose hope for a different happiness again.

More calmly she sat in a wooden rocker beside the window where the sunlight warmed her, closed her eyes, and set herself to wait. Finally she heard the scrape of a bootheel on the hard earth just outside. She was on her feet and partway to the door when it opened and Cole stepped inside, looking weary.

"What happened?"

He said sharply, "It's too late to change your mind. I can't disappear now."

"I just want to know whether the commanding officer believed you."

"General Porter did. I'm not so sure about Captain Fisher, the C Company commander. He didn't have much to say except that he'll talk to me later. You'll see him this evening. We've been invited to dinner at Major Dunn's quarters. Now, excuse me, I'm going to sleep for a while." He shrugged out of his jacket and boots and lay down on the cot.

Martha felt disconcerted. "But don't we need to talk more? What shall I say tonight?"

"As little as possible."

Before she could protest, he added, "I do need to know what made you decide the raiders weren't Indians."

"Why?"

"Because that's what I told the general. The post commander will want to hear my reasons." He gave her a wry look as if he knew she wasn't happy with having to let him take the lead. "I'm depending on you to tell me what to say."

A little mollified, she said, "None of them had tattooed faces. Both the Mojaves and the Yumas regularly tattoo themselves. The Pima and Cocopahs have been peaceable for so long that they wouldn't have been raiding. And the feathers and paint weren't Apache. The fire was started with kerosene. Some Indians might use it, but more likely outlaw Americans. And when they left, they all rode the saddled horses. One of them took time to saddle a particular horse so he could ride it. Indians prefer a blanket and certainly wouldn't bother to find a saddle."

His eyebrows went up a fraction. "How do you know all that?"

She wavered. But one answer would lead to another question. He might react with the same contempt as the people in the town where her grandmother lived. If he did, he might be less inclined to keep his promise to her. "I just know."

He stared at her a moment longer, then closed his eyes. In a few minutes his breathing became even.

Taking advantage of the privacy of Cole's sleeping, Martha looked through her small trunk. She found a golden-brown dress of Irish poplin and changed into it.

Soon after she was dressed, Cole roused. He yawned and glanced at her sleepily, then came awake. "You're ready," he commented, as if he couldn't think what else to say. "You look . . . fine."

He started to unbutton his shirt, and she retreated outside. Before long he joined her, dressed in a uniform she hadn't seen before. Gilt epaulets and braid decorated the long, double-breasted tunic. Over it he wore a scarlet silk sash; a sword hung at his side. Though the regular uniform enhanced Cole's handsome appearance, the dress uniform had a different effect. In it he seemed out of character—his face too angular and his body too strong for this kind of formal display. With his dark eyes and beard, he looked like a highwayman masquerading as a lord. Though the air wasn't cold, her skin tingled and her pulse speeded up—from renewed anxiety, she decided.

"Stephen Baldwin's full-dress uniform fits me well enough," Cole said, "and I borrowed the sword. So far we've had luck nobody would believe."

"Will Lieutenant Nelson be at the dinner?" she asked. She'd welcome even the too forward lieutenant to have someone there who already believed their story.

"Probably not." Cole frowned. "Remember, you call a second lieutenant mister, not lieutenant. We have to be careful not to make mistakes."

She didn't like being scolded. "Elizabeth Baldwin wouldn't know army customs."

"Maybe so, but we don't want any extra attention," Cole said, his tone equally irritated. "Do you know the insignia for the other ranks?" Without waiting for her to answer, he listed them.

As he finished, Private Greaves arrived. He saluted and said, "I'm to show you to Major Dunn's quarters, sir."

Instantly amiable, Cole said, "Thank you, private," and offered Martha his arm. As they followed Greaves along the sandy walk in front of the officers' quarters, she thought that she and Cole were foolish to be at odds so easily. So far she'd had her way; they were here. But Cole, she judged, didn't bend easily to another person's will. Neither did she.

Major Dunn had thick gray hair and a jovial smile. Each of the rooms in his quarters was twice the size of Lieutenant Nelson's single room. Captain Fisher and his wife Harriet arrived shortly after Martha and Cole. They looked a little like sister and brother, both tall and sandy haired with pale blue eyes and narrow faces. He seemed reserved, as if he were waiting to decide what he thought of the new officer and his wife.

Mrs. Fisher greeted them warmly. "Aren't you pleased," she said, "that C Company is going to Fort Apache?"

Martha wanted to laugh with elation. Of all the army posts, it was in the best location for her search. Cole was right: No one would believe such good luck. With great effort she managed to restrict herself to a demure, "I didn't know about the assignment. What is Fort Apache like?"

Before Harriet Fisher could answer, an arriving man, whose red sash encompassed a large middle, took everyone's attention. Martha decided that he must be the regimental commander. She thought Cole had called him General Porter, but the insignia on his shoulder straps was a silver eagle. She hadn't been listening carefully enough. When Major Dunn presented her, the commanding officer smiled graciously and said, "I'm pleased you and Mr. Baldwin are safely here."

She curtsied. "Thank you, Colonel Porter."

His smile stiffened. He nodded curtly, then turned to speak to Major Dunn. Bewildered, she looked at Cole and caught a fleeting moment of exasperation in his eyes.

Two other officers, one with his wife, came in. When they greeted the commanding officer, they called him general. One of them wore a first lieutenant's silver bar but was addressed as captain. Completely perplexed, Martha avoided addressing anyone by name.

At dinner she was seated at the far end of the table away from Porter. While they were eating, Major Dunn turned to Cole. "Mr. Baldwin, I understand you think the raiders at the stage station weren't Indians."

"That's right." Cole went on to give the explanations Martha had provided for him.

"How did you learn about the tribes here, Mr. Baldwin?" Captain Fisher asked.

"When I knew I'd be joining a regiment in the Arizona Territory," Cole said easily, "I started reading everything I could find about the Indians here. Lots of it is nonsense. But there are some good accounts."

The conversation turned to examples of fanciful descriptions of Indian life. But Martha noticed that Captain Fisher was studying Cole with what looked like a distrustful gaze. She stared at the roast mutton and potatoes on her plate, but her appetite was gone.

When she and the other women left the men after dinner, Mrs. Fisher offered to take her to Yuma City the next day for household furnishings.

"Thank you, Mrs. Fisher. I appreciate the offer," Martha said, but she wondered whether she and Cole would be exposed as frauds by them.

Finally the men reappeared, and nothing seemed amiss. Martha would have breathed easier except for Captain Fisher's continued scrutiny of Cole. The evening finally ended with the departure of the Porters, and Martha happily thanked Major Dunn. When she and Cole were outside, she could finally ask him, "What did I do to offend Colonel Porter?"

"Not calling him General Porter."

"But the silver eagle—"

"He's really a colonel. During the War Between the States he must have been brevetted a general. That was temporary. Now he's reverted to his permanent rank, but he still wants to be called general."

Captain Fisher called to them from the veranda. "Mrs. Fisher and I will walk you to Lieutenant Nelson's quarters." There was nothing to do but smile and stroll beside Mrs. Fisher along the moonlit path.

Cole, walking behind Martha, judged from her rigid back that she was upset. He'd been a little on edge earlier, but he felt relaxed now. Everything had gone well. Captain Fisher was talking about Fort Apache, and Cole only needed to listen. It was a small disappointment that he wouldn't be at one of the forts closer to Tucson, but maybe the distance would be safer. He'd find some reason to get to Tucson. Martha had seemed particularly pleased—another piece of evidence about her.

They reached Lieutenant Nelson's quarters and stopped under a kerosene lamp hanging from the veranda roof. Captain Fisher stared at Cole as if he were speculating about something. "Who else was on the stage at Stanley's?" he asked.

Instantly alert, Cole said carefully, "The driver and one guard. And a marshal with a prisoner. The only other passengers still on at Stanley's were a man and woman. From Texas, they said."

The captain remarked, still with the speculative look in his eyes, "It's very lucky you and your wife weren't killed. Most of our officers seem to get in the thick of a fight."

Cole tensed. *What the hell kind of response can I give to that?*

"Captain," Martha said, "I really deserve the credit for our escape." Her voice had a faint tremble but also a touch of defiance—as if she knew she should admit blame but deliberately chose to claim credit. "I asked for my husband's . . . help and urged him to accompany me away from the station. He was looking out for me." As she finished, a genuine blush, deep enough to be noticed in the soft light, stained her face.

In the silence the hum of insects around the lamp suddenly sounded loud and intrusive.

Captain Fisher looked embarrassed. His wife looked bewildered. After a moment, the captain made a stiff good night, offered his wife his arm, and departed.

Martha gave Cole a look that dared him to comment and went inside. As he prepared to follow, Cole decided that she'd settled the captain's suspicions. What he couldn't decide was how a real husband would feel about a wife like her. He'd either admire her or want to strangle her. Cole wasn't sure which.

5

A bugle call wakened Martha the next morning. Someone ran past outside. She peered out from the blankets. Cole, dressed in his field uniform, was sitting on the edge of the extra cot pulling on his boots.

"What was the bugle for?" she asked.

"Morning roll call." He stood up and stamped his foot into the second boot. Picking up his billed forage cap, he went to the door.

She sat up, about to ask where he was going, and changed it to, "What should I be doing?"

He paused, his hand on the latch. "I don't know. In the militia, there weren't any wives along."

"Can you find out? Stephen Baldwin wouldn't know. He'd have to ask."

"No," he said, more forcefully than she thought her request warranted. "I'm already tagged as a man who pays too much attention to his wife. I'm going to find the post barber and then see Captain Fisher. Mrs. Fisher will probably tell you what you're supposed to do."

As the door closed behind him, Martha lay back down and pulled the blanket around her. The prospect of seeing Harriet Fisher that morning wasn't appealing. What would her expression be when she saw Martha again?

Impatient with herself, Martha got up and put on the dark blue traveling dress. Disapproval was nothing new. The story about why they survived at the stage station had been her idea. She had to put up with the consequences. But the way Cole explained it—with her practically pulling his trousers off—was more outrageous than she'd intended. She had a moment of imagining her doing that to Cole—then hastily thrust the image out of her mind.

Martha found a basin and water and washed quickly. Cole might be returning, and she didn't want him to find her partly dressed. She sighed as she fastened the mother-of-pearl buttons on the front of her dress. Though she appreciated that he'd dressed before she was awake, he probably couldn't do that every day. They'd have to work out some arrangement for bathing and dressing. Avoiding Cole would be an awkward and uncomfortable way to spend the next—how long? weeks? months?

She heard a knock. "Mrs. Baldwin?" a man's voice called.

When she opened the door to the veranda, she found a short, stocky man with a black mustache and a cheerful expression. Since arriving at Yuma, she'd learned that the C below the crossed rifles on his cap and the 25 above meant C Company of the Twenty-Fifth Infantry Regiment. So this man was from the company Cole was assigned to.

He pulled off his cap and said, "Private Lane,

ma'am. The lieutenant asked me to tell you Mrs. Fisher has invited you to breakfast. If you're ready, I'll take you along to where she and the captain are quartered."

"I'm ready, thank you," she said and followed the private along the line of houses.

Harriet Fisher welcomed Martha formally but graciously, with no trace of self-consciousness or curiosity. Martha felt relieved. It appeared that the captain hadn't repeated the details about Cole and her.

A little later a blond young woman arrived, the one Martha had seen leaving the mercantile establishment in Yuma City the previous day. "Alice," Harriet Fisher said, "this is Elizabeth Baldwin. Mr. Collins is the other second lieutenant in C Company," Harriet explained to Martha. "He was with us in Wyoming, before he and Alice were married."

After Alice and Martha expressed polite pleasure in meeting, Harriet said to Alice, "Elizabeth and Mr. Baldwin are the ones who escaped an Indian attack at a stage station. No," she said, turning back to Martha, "that's wrong. Your husband said the men were only pretending to be Indians, didn't he?"

"Yes, that's what he thinks."

"My, what a clever man he must be," Alice said in a soft Southern accent. Martha smiled and wished she could say that Cole's cleverness came from what she told him.

Alice went on admiringly. "And you-all walked for miles across the desert! I just know Fred would have to carry me."

Captain Fisher came in with Cole and a short, red-headed second lieutenant, Fred Collins. Apparently Cole had found the barber; his hair and beard were neatly trimmed. The effect was a handsome, well-groomed man—the image of a dashing officer young girls swooned over and boys wanted to be. Martha noticed, with a degree of attention that surprised her, that Alice responded to the introduction with marked animation.

Captain Fisher greeted Martha with polite reserve but none of the distrust of the previous evening. She had allayed his suspicions!. She glanced at Cole and found him looking at her. His eyes expressed a combination of satisfaction and admiration. If he'd had a champagne glass, she would have been sure he was about to offer a toast to her. She smiled happily at him, returning his silent message—they had passed the first test.

As he continued to look at her, his eyes wandered down her figure, and then met hers with a glint of desire, as if he were picturing the imaginary episode and relishing the details. Her cheeks burned so hot she was sure the others must notice. It certainly must convey the impression of a passionate couple. Maybe that was what he intended.

Mrs. Fisher led the way to a dining table where they sat down to breakfast. Afterward, when the men had left, Alice said, "Heavens to Betsy, if I have this much breakfast every day, I won't fit any of my frocks."

"Enjoy it now," Mrs. Fisher assured her. "We won't eat like this on the march."

Martha said, "I don't know much about the army, and I hate to bother my husband with questions. What do we do about food then?"

"We'll go this morning over to Yuma City and I'll help you choose equipment you'll need. On the steamer we'll take up the Colorado River, each officer pays a dollar a day for food. Officers' wives pay the same.

When we start overland from Camp Mojave, rations will be issued to you, and soldiers help out with fires and tents. At Fort Apache you'll have a striker."

"A striker?"

"That's a soldier who works for you. Some of them are quite good cooks."

Martha didn't like the idea of someone in the household who could observe Cole and her. "Isn't it difficult to find a soldier who's willing to be a sort of servant?"

Mrs. Fisher smiled. "Oh, no. It's easier work than constructing buildings or chopping firewood. And the customary wage is six dollars a month. That's almost half a private's regular pay extra. You won't have any trouble getting someone."

"I see," Martha said, planning to have trouble.

Alice sighed. "Fred says we'll camp on the march. I've never done anythin' like that. My daddy didn't want me to marry a soldier. But I thought it would be like West Point—all those boys in their pretty uniforms marchin' around in the daytime and dancin' all night."

"I'm sure you'll adjust to army life and be a great help to your husband," Mrs. Fisher said with a tinge of disapproval in her tone. "I'll go and see about the arrangements for going into Yuma City."

After the captain's wife left, Alice sighed again. "I guess I shouldn't have said that. Half the time I say the wrong thing. Did you know that some lieutenants you have to call captains and majors?"

Martha thought of the abrupt cooling of General Porter's cordiality when she called him colonel. "Yes, I've discovered that."

"Well," Alice said crossly, "I told Fred I'm goin' to

call all of them general. Then nobody will get angry."

Mrs. Fisher returned with Cole. "Mr. Baldwin has business in Yuma City and will escort us."

"A message came from the stage company," he explained to Martha. "They want to talk to me about the attack on the stage. Captain Fisher has given me permission to go."

Even from the short time she'd known Cole, Martha decided he wasn't a man who welcomed having to ask permission from anyone. She hoped he remembered how restrictive prison would be.

With Cole as escort, Mrs. Fisher, Alice, and Martha took an army wagon down to the crossing. The young Chinese boy Martha had seen with Alice the previous day accompanied them. When they reached Yuma City, Cole stopped at the stage office. The rest of them continued on toward the mercantile establishment.

The Chinese boy looked young and frightened. Whenever they passed an Indian, he almost stepped on Alice's skirts trying to stay close to her. "How old is your serving boy?" Martha asked Alice.

"He's twelve years old. Fred hired him in San Francisco. He doesn't speak much English," she confided, "but he's the only servant Fred could find. We call him Willie. In San Diego some other Chinese scared him with stories about how terrible Arizona would be. We had to keep him from running away back to San Francisco. He doesn't even have any parents there."

A boy without his parents. A familiar constriction began in Martha's chest, but she refused to allow the tormenting thoughts that could follow. She'd started on her search.

The dry goods store was like an enormous cave, bright in front with the light from two windows and door, becoming a cavern of dimly lit counters and shelves at the back. It smelled of sawdust, coffee beans, and newly printed calico. Mrs. Fisher said, "I suggest you buy tinware. And some cotton yardage for curtains. There's no telling when your boxes from home will arrive. And often the crystal and china are broken."

Boxes from home? Martha had been so caught up in the urgency of making the masquerade work that since she went through the belongings, she hadn't stopped to think of Elizabeth Baldwin's previous life. Now an image formed in her mind of the shy young woman in a pleasant room, lovingly wrapping china. Maybe a mother or sister was helping Elizabeth pack. They were laughing. Or perhaps Elizabeth was fearful of her new life, and her mother was comforting her.

A lump formed in Martha's throat and spread painfully into her chest. By taking Elizabeth Baldwin's name, she'd appropriated her past too. She felt like a thief.

Martha chose a set of tinware, a cooking pot, and some Turkey red cotton for curtains. And for dividing a room. Knowing how hot Arizona summers could be, she also picked out dress materials. Prices were high, and when she paid with two of the gold coins she'd earlier taken from her money belt, she wondered how long her money would last.

After Alice accumulated several purchases, she said to the clerk, "I'd like to charge these."

The middle-aged clerk's expression set into practiced sympathy. "I'm so sorry, Mrs. Collins. I'm happy to extend that courtesy for families stationed at Yuma. However, my employer won't allow me to give credit to families who are moving on. I'm sure you'd send the money, but the mails are uncertain."

"Yes, I see." Alice reluctantly set aside some of her packages and paid for the rest. "Everything is so dear," she confided to Martha. "Fred says that we must be very careful."

"Yes," Martha agreed, and realized she had no idea how much a second lieutenant was paid. Would she and Cole have money that belonged to Stephen and Elizabeth?

Alice insisted that Willie could carry Martha's bundles as well as hers, but Martha refused. The slight boy already had more of a load than she thought he could handle. To her relief, the clerk settled the argument by offering to have the purchases delivered to the fort.

At the other end of the street Cole left the stage company office and started for the store. He was almost there when the three women came out.

"Mr. Baldwin," Harriet Fisher said, "if you're free now, you can escort us on a tour of the prison." She turned to Alice and Martha. "You mustn't leave Yuma without seeing it. Each time I go there I feel relieved that thieves and murderers are getting their just punishment."

Cole's immediate reaction was to laugh, but only Martha would understand why Mrs. Fisher's request was funny. He restrained himself, saying, "It would be my pleasure. However, I need to make a purchase. If you ladies want to walk in the direction of the prison, I'll catch up in a few minutes."

Martha said, "I'll wait and come along with . . . Stephen." Cole felt his neck muscles tighten, but no one else seemed to notice that Martha stumbled over his name. Mrs. Fisher, Alice, and Willie started off.

"I thought you'd finished your purchases, *Elizabeth*," he said, and felt like saying a good deal more.

"I have, *Stephen*," she responded in a too-sweet voice that didn't sound contrite. "But I'm interested in what you're buying." More quietly she added, "And how you're going to pay for it."

Apparently she knew something he didn't. He swallowed his irritation and escorted her inside. She went with him to the case that held revolvers. "I have several fine products," the clerk assured Cole, "all new. Center-fire cartridges, of course. You might like this Smith & Wesson. The cylinder breaks forward to extract all the spent cases at once. It takes less time to reload."

"Yes, I know. But it doesn't let you decide which cases to eject. Where I'm going, ammunition is more important than speed. What do you have in a Colt or a Remington?"

"This Colt .45 Single Action Army revolver is priced at just seventeen dollars." He pointed to a familiar-looking gun with an unadorned barrel and plain wooden handle.

"Good. I'll take the Peacemaker." Cole looked through the assortment in the counter and didn't see what he wanted. "Do you have a Remington double-barrel derringer?"

"Yes. And we also have a used derringer .36 caliber. I can get them from another case in the back."

Cole didn't know whether Martha could shoot. She seemed to be able to do just about everything else to survive. If she didn't, he could teach her. "I'd like to see them." As the clerk went toward the back, it struck Cole uneasily that he was taking on more responsibility for Martha than their bargain required.

She said softly, "You'll need this," and held out two twenty-dollar gold pieces.

"No, I'll—"

"They won't give you credit," she interrupted, "because you're not stationed here."

The clerk was returning. Cole took the money unwillingly but he had to replace Stephen Baldwin's gun. Otherwise he'd almost rather go without than be rescued by her again. Dammit! A man shouldn't be dependent on a woman.

The clerk held out a stubby, curved pistol. "Even though this is twenty years old, it's a very good weapon. Abraham Lincoln was shot with a derringer like this."

Cole thought that was a strange recommendation. Also two shots instead of one could mean living instead of dying. "No, let me see the double-barrel one. Where can I try it out?" he asked.

"We have a target behind the store. Come this way, please."

After satisfying himself that the derringer wasn't faulty, Cole told the clerk he would take it. Back inside he chose a belt, holster, and ammunition, then paid for the purchases and put on the holstered Colt. The derringer went in his pocket.

Martha said, "You know quite a bit about guns."

"Anybody who lives in the Territory does." He could have added a lot more reasons, but she didn't need to know more than that.

Outside, Cole said stiffly, "Thanks for the money. I'll give you your change later," and started toward the prison at a fast walk.

Martha hurried and caught up with him. "If I apologize for stumbling over your name, will you walk a little slower?"

He stopped and faced her. "If I accidentally called you Martha, I could explain it away. Say it was an extra name. It's common enough. But if you called me Cole, that could put my neck in a noose."

"Yes. I'm sorry."

When they reached the others, Mrs. Fisher led the way up to an arched entrance, the only opening in the high prison wall. A guard stood in front of large iron gates. He doffed his cap and said, "Good afternoon, Mrs. Fisher."

"Good afternoon. I've brought some more visitors. Can someone show us around?"

In answer he pulled out a jangling bundle of keys. A small gate that was part of the larger ones creaked open. A few feet farther in was another wall and another small door set into a large one. The guard rang a bell beside the door and after a moment's wait communicated with someone inside through an adjacent window. The inner door opened, and another guard greeted Mrs. Fisher and then motioned to the visitors to enter. With this much trouble getting inside, Cole thought, it was probably hell for a prisoner to get out. The thought sent a shiver along his spine.

Their guide said, "The prison's not finished yet. So far it has two cell blocks for prisoners." He chuckled. "First ones here had to build their own cells. Dug them out of solid rock. We opened July first last year. Now, if you'll follow me, I'll show you one of the cells."

As he led the way across the yard to another gate, Alice Collins asked, "What kinds of crimes are men sent here for?"

"All kinds. Robbery, cattle rustling, horse stealing, and some crimes you ladies wouldn't want to hear—we have them all. Women too. We'd have a new man right now if the Indians hadn't gotten him."

"You mean the man on the stagecoach that was attacked at Stanley's?" asked Mrs. Fisher.

"Yes, ma'am. That's the one. Name of Cole Wingate."

The muscles across Cole's midriff tightened enough so his jacket felt loose. He saw that Martha's face had lost color.

Mrs. Fisher said, as if she were showing off a prize, "Mrs. and Mr. Baldwin here were on that stage. They were the only ones who survived."

"That a fact?" The guard stopped. "So you saw the prisoner?" he said to Cole.

"Yes." Some spirit of devilry prompted Cole to add, "A dangerous-looking man. Not sure your prison could hold him."

"Oh, dear," Mrs. Fisher interrupted, "I think this is distressing Mrs. Baldwin. I shouldn't have brought it up. Let's go on, please."

The guard showed them through another yard and down steps carved out of the stone bluff. At the bottom they stopped at an iron gate set into the wall. Pick marks told of the work fashioning the walls. Enough light filtered into the dark cell behind the gate to emphasize its desolate appearance. Though the sunlight from above the steps was almost hot, Cole felt the cold of the cell reach into his bones. He could hardly wait to be back up in the yard.

As they walked back the way they'd come, Martha asked the guard, "Are any of the men ever imprisoned unjustly?"

"Well, ma'am, there are always some who claim they're innocent. But juries don't convict a man without good, solid evidence. You can pretty well bet they're all guilty."

Martha said, so softly that Cole doubted the guard heard her, "I'm not sure I could send even a guilty man here."

The guard had heard. He frowned. "We treat our prisoners well. We'll have a bakery and a bathing room before long. Even a library. In the summer this is the coolest spot in Yuma. And you certainly wouldn't want murderers running around loose, now, would you?"

When Martha didn't reply, Mrs. Fisher spoke for her. "We certainly wouldn't."

As the outer gate clanged shut behind them, Martha looked back at it and then at Cole. In her eyes he saw distress. Whether or not she believed he was a murderer, she didn't want to be the one to shut him up in one of those cells.

That evening Martha and Cole were invited to dine in Fort Yuma's bachelor officers' mess. Alice and her husband and two other officers from C Company also shared the meal. Vernon Brown, a middle-aged first lieutenant, had a warm laugh and a graying mustache that was the thickest Martha had ever seen. The other first lieutenant, Peter Dunham, was younger, in his thirties. He wore a uniform that fit so precisely it looked as if a tailor had sewn it onto him. Every light brown hair on his head was carefully combed and his mustache clipped to an exact line. Lieutenant Brown was a bachelor. Lieutenant Dunham explained that his wife was with her parents in New York. Martha was amused to notice that though Alice didn't address every officer as a general, she did call them all captains. None of them appeared to mind, and Peter Dunham seemed captivated by Alice during most of the meal.

Afterward when she and Cole reached their room, he said, "I'm going to walk a while and smoke my pipe."

"I didn't know you smoked a pipe."

"I didn't until today." In the light of the veranda lamp his grin looked relaxed. It was the first time she'd seen him so peaceful. "The post trader does give credit, and I thought a bedtime pipe might be a good habit to take up."

As she went inside to undress, she realized gratefully that he, too, must have been thinking about the awkwardness of their personal arrangements. Even so, she got into bed in her shift and robe and pulled up the blanket. Later on she supposed she and Cole would have a routine worked out so she could change. And she'd be asleep before he came in so that she wouldn't even hear him.

By the time he returned, she hadn't managed sleep, but she buried her head under the blanket and pretended. It helped, but she didn't quite escape picturing his progress as she heard boots tugged off and then clothing rustling. Her heart seemed to pump so loudly she heard it in her ears. Hastily she stifled her images.

The cot creaked as he lay down, then again as he settled into his blanket. Not until everything was silent could she finally fall asleep.

The paddle-wheeled steamer *Gila* arrived the next morning with officers and wives from the regiment which the Twenty-Fifth was replacing. After meeting three weary but happy departing wives at morning tea, Alice Collins walked with Martha back to their temporary quarters. "Those women's dresses are years out of fashion," Alice said. "Do you think we're going to look like that before we leave Arizona?"

Clothes didn't matter to Martha. All the fashionable dresses her grandmother had bought for her hadn't made her happy. But the dismayed Alice needed comfort, not philosophy. "I think you'll always look stylish."

Alice sighed. "I hope so. I just hate it that the Army Regulations lists wives as camp followers. The same as the laundresses."

"Laundresses? Who are they?"

"They're supposed to take in the laundry on army posts. You can surely guess what else they do. Fred says that some of them are respectable—the wives of sergeants and corporals, but I don't know."

Martha said, more mildly than she felt, "I'm sorry for women who have to work so hard to be with their husbands. It's a shame they have to share a poor reputation."

Alice sent Martha an uncertain glance, as if she weren't sure whether she'd been scolded. "Anyway, we're all camp followers. I think that's disgraceful. Fred just laughs about it."

"They've treated us well here," Martha said.

"Oh, you act so cheerful," Alice pouted. "I think you're happy about going to Fort Apache. But then, you're lucky. The army is more important to Fred than I am. Stephen puts you first."

"Oh?" was Martha's startled response.

"I can tell by the way he watches you. And he pays attention when you talk."

Yes, Martha thought, he listens to find out whether I've made a mistake. In spite of that, she felt complimented, as if she had a real husband who cared about her.

When they reached Lieutenant Nelson's room, she said, "I'll see you on the steamer," and went inside. As Martha gathered her possessions, she thought that in one way Alice was correct. The new Stephen and Elizabeth Baldwin had a more compelling interest in each other than most husbands and wives.

When wagons from the fort deposited the C Company officers' wives at the steamer dock, the *Gila* sat waiting. Her rear paddle wheel was motionless, but black smoke drifted from the tall forward stack. Soldiers and a few women were already boarding the barge that would be towed behind the steamer. Martha thought the women must be the laundresses Alice had been disdainful of. They looked quite respectable—and cheerful, too, a trait she admired.

Cole came out to meet Martha. He reached for her as she stepped onto the narrow sideboards and held her arm firmly until she was safely onto the inner deck. "The ladder down to the cabins is steep," he said. "I'll go ahead. Wait until I'm at the bottom and I'll give you a hand."

He descended and reached back for Martha's hand. His grip felt warm and secure. Alice Collins's earlier comment about Cole's interest in her intruded into Martha's mind, and to her chagrin her boot slipped on the last step. Cole caught her and set her back on her feet. Her thank-you felt constrained.

Cole noticed Martha's unusual awkwardness and ascribed it to apprehension about their close quarters on board. He opened the door of the tiny stateroom. "I've been talking to the steamer captain. He says these rooms get too hot for sleeping, even now in the spring.

So everybody takes mattresses and sleeps out on deck."

Her expression relaxed. "So we can go to sleep watching the stars."

"We've done all right so far," he said softly.

"Yes, we have."

They smiled together, in a moment that felt as if they'd known each other for a long time, instead of less than a week. The realization startled him.

He looked at their two pieces of luggage sitting on the narrow lower bunk. It would be polite to help her settle in, but the space was feeling smaller by the moment. Her scent was a combination of perfumed soap and something personal to her. It suggested an image of her bathing, and that led to an unwise tension in his midsection. "I'll be up on deck," he said and escaped.

A door farther along the passageway stood ajar. As Cole passed it to reach the ladder, he heard a light-hearted voice he recognized as Peter Dunham. "You take up too much space, Brown. And you're ugly. If you were a woman who looked like Baldwin's wife, I'd happily spend my time here the whole two hundred miles to Camp Mojave."

"Too bad your wife's not along," Vernon Brown's lower voice answered.

"Yes. Men like Baldwin have all the luck."

Luck, yes, Cole thought as he emerged up on deck. But not the kind Dunham meant. Not with the "business arrangement" Martha had insisted on. He could already tell sticking to it wouldn't be easy.

Loading of the *Gila* appeared to be finished. The high-pressure engines began to clatter and whine. Cole took a last look at the flag and buildings of Fort Yuma on top of the hills. Then, as if pulled by an invisible hand, he swiveled and looked at the prison. If Harvey Lippincott had his way, Cole thought, he'd be there now.

Word of the stage station attack and his supposed death must have reached Tucson. In the concerns of the last five days, Cole had spent little time thinking of his stepfather. Now he pictured Harvey Lippincott's plump face and false smile. The hatred that never completely faded burned in his gut.

Cole knew his mother would mourn his reported death. Would Harvey exult? Cole hoped so. It would make the eventual confrontation between them that much sweeter.

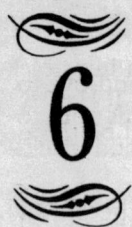

6

Tucson, Arizona, March 28, 1877

In the cemetery at Alameda and Stone streets in Tucson, Emma Lippincott felt a sudden movement from her husband beside her. It broke her absorption in the funeral service for her son. "What is it?" she whispered.

"Nothing."

Harvey was probably feeling impatient, she thought uneasily. During the terrible time of Cole's trial and conviction, Harvey's understanding had been such a comfort to her. But he'd argued against this service. It was the only time she'd insisted on something he disapproved of, and she knew he was unhappy about it. Guiltily she concentrated on the minister's words.

". . . and so we remember the bright lad who passed his happy youth among us. Cole Wingate has gone to that place where God alone will judge him. As Christ forgave our sins, God will surely forgive the weaknesses that led this man astray. Today we say good-bye to his mortal . . . uh . . . spirit, and dedicate his soul to the Lord. Let us pray." Black hats came off and black-veiled heads bowed.

Harvey Lippincott removed his hat. As the prayer began, Emma started to tremble. Soon, he knew, she would be sobbing aloud. He put an arm around his wife's back and felt her lean into him. The support worked; through her veil he could see tears falling, but she cried quietly.

What a farce this was—a service to add Cole's name to his father's tombstone, without a body to bury. Emma was being ridiculous, but it came down to letting her do it or putting up with her hysterics. There'd already been too much of that. Hell, she wouldn't even lie with him these days. If he hadn't needed to convince the whole town he was a model husband, he'd go to one of the houses on Maiden Lane.

The minister's fervent ". . . and let us be thankful that the Lord has taken Cole Wingate to his bosom," penetrated Harvey's thoughts. He joined the others with a loud "Amen." Personally, he'd have liked for Cole to spend hard labor time at Yuma Prison. With some stints in solitary. Still, a few men escaped from every prison, and if anyone could, it would be Cole. His death in a fire was a useful ending. Yes, Harvey concluded, things had turned out to his liking.

The small ring of people around the tombstone began to stir. Harvey released Emma and put his hat back on, being careful not to disarrange his silvery white hair. It was one of his assets. Who could distrust a handsome man who looked like a fatherly judge?

The minister approached and took one of Emma's black-gloved hands between both of his. "You must remember your many blessings, Mrs. Lippincott. Cole has gone to a better life. Someday you will meet your cleansed son and his father again. Until then, you have a husband in this life to sustain you. And for you to serve. In your grief, you must not neglect him."

Emma managed a tearful "Yes, I'll remember."

Good, Harvey thought. He could do with some service from Emma. The minister had something useful to say after all.

Others were waiting to offer condolences. The minister said softly to Harvey, "I admire you, Mr. Lippincott. Few men would be as forgiving as you have been. After all those accusations Cole made against you, to honor him this way shows real generosity of spirit."

Harvey smiled modestly. "Well, Cole was her son. It's natural for a mother to think the best of her child. Even with all the evidence. I understand that."

The minister shook his head. "Not all would. You are a true Christian." With a last admiring look, he walked on.

Harvey smiled his doleful smile and murmured polite responses to the black-clad line of mourners. Soon he and Emma could go home. He'd insist that she have a glass or two of wine to soothe her. Then, since he was certified a true Christian, he intended for her to be a Christian wife and submit to her husband. It would be his private celebration of Cole Wingate's death.

On the Colorado River the *Gila* steamed its way northward, the barges of soldiers and the few laundresses trailing behind like a litter of clumsy pups. Thick growths of willow and arrowweed covered the low banks; beyond them the sage green desert stretched to the horizon on both sides. Gradually the river narrowed and cleared somewhat.

Martha and Cole had developed a routine for the appearance of marriage. He was solicitous of her at mealtimes and made sure she had a place to sit in the shade of the awnings put up on deck. Then he joined the other officers to talk, leaving wives to read and visit and watch the landscape. At night couples went to their staterooms at about the same time. There Martha sat on her bunk, facing the wall, while Cole changed his outer clothing for Stephen Baldwin's loose nightshirt. Cole did the same while she discarded her dress and covered her shift with a robe. They emerged on deck to join the other passengers, all modestly protected by darkness, to sleep on deck. The sleeping arrangements had relieved her of her worries about too much intimacy—as long as they didn't linger in the stateroom.

On the fourth morning Alice Collins, standing beside Martha by the railing, stared glumly at the desert and said, "I hope Fort Apache isn't like this."

"It's more mountainous, and there are pine forests all around," Martha responded. In the next moment she realized Elizabeth Baldwin couldn't describe that part of Arizona. "At least, that's what I've heard," she added.

Along the east bank, the bushy willows swayed and parted. Two young Yuma women appeared and stood looking at the steamer. Both wore short skirts made of reeds. In the sunlight their hair gleamed blue-black, and their bare shoulders and breasts were the color of polished copper.

"Oh!" Alice turned her back to the bank and whispered, "How embarrassin' this is. I'm just glad the men are in the dinin' room now."

Martha had been about to say how pretty the two Indian women were, but she kept silent.

The two Yuma women vanished back into the willows. "They're gone now," Martha said.

Alice turned around. "Do you suppose where we're goin' the Indian women walk around naked like that?"

"We'll find out when we get there." Martha could have assured Alice that Apaches were very modest. The women were always completely clothed, and men and women seldom saw each other naked. But she'd claimed enough knowledge already.

Alice didn't reply, but flounced over to a chair under one of the awnings. Martha didn't mind. She looked down at the water coiling back on itself along the *Gila*'s side and warily considered her changing feelings about Cole. They were conspirators who must look out for each other whether they wanted to or not. That didn't mean they had a special loyalty to each other. She didn't know what Cole's loyalties were, but she didn't intend to develop any allegiance that might interfere with her search.

The Chinese cook rang a bell for the evening meal. Cole appeared and offered Martha his arm, and they joined the others descending to the room which was always much too warm by late afternoon. The menu was the same most days: biscuits, salty boiled beef, and canned peas. Martha ate with little notice of the food and minimal attention to the conversation. Instead she watched Cole and speculated about him. At some time he'd gone to school; she could tell that from his speech. His table manners were good, and he could be polite; those habits were generally learned at home. He'd been in the Missouri militia, which had a reputation for attracting rough and dangerous men. That fit with a murder conviction. Maybe she should risk exchanging information with him. If—

"Elizabeth," Alice said, "if you aren't goin' to have any peach pie, will you please pass it on?"

Martha looked at the faces watching her and then down at the pie beside her place. "I think I will have some," she said calmly, and took a piece.

"I think I'll ask the cook to teach Willie how to make the crust," Alice said. Under her breath she added, "You better stop starin' at your husband. Everybody's noticin' you."

Martha ate her pie as if it were the only thing in all the world that interested her. Maybe, she thought wickedly, when the *Gila* tied up for the night, she should ask Cole to come to their stateroom a little early. They could sit on the bunks long enough to satisfy the expectations of all the men who'd heard the story of Cole's missing pistols.

An inner voice reminded her of her resolution of just an hour or so before. She knew what physical attraction to a man felt like. Cole had too much of that effect on her. To be alone with him too long in the tiny stateroom could be folly. She'd do as usual and watch the soldiers get off the barges and make camp on shore.

After they left the dining room and went up on deck, Vernon Brown joined Cole and Martha. "Only a few days until we reach Camp Mojave," he said. "No more leisure then."

"What happens then?" Martha asked.

"Your husband will be with his men all day. You'll see him only at night."

"I see." Vernon's words brought back the feelings

Martha had been warding off. Knowing it was unwise, she looked at Cole. His gaze was on her, and the thought of what nights alone together could lead to was in his eyes.

"Hello, there." It was Peter Dunham. "How about a hand of three-card monte?" The three men departed for the dining room and a game that would last into the evening.

Martha stayed at the rail, wondering, with a strange little catch in her stomach, about the sleeping arrangements for nights on the march.

7

April 7, 1877

Fifteen days after leaving Yuma, the *Gila* arrived at Camp Mojave. The fort lay on the flat east bank of the Colorado, close to the river. Sunshine reflected off the white sand, outlining the fort with pencil-black shadows. It wakened the aromatic oils of sagebrush and mesquite to compete with the odors of willow and musty river mud.

On the deck Martha waited to disembark. The march would present new challenges. She felt like a child at a party where she wasn't sure how to play the games. But there was a prize at the end she must win.

"Good morning, Elizabeth." It was Harriet Fisher.

Martha said warmly, "Good morning, Mrs. Fisher." The commanding officer of C Company had remained stiff and reserved with her. She liked his wife better.

"You must be sure to check the supplies in your camp mess kit here," Mrs. Fisher said. "It's a hundred sixty-five miles to Fort Whipple. So plan for two weeks. If you don't have a Dutch oven, get one at the commissary. Make sure it has a flat lid for baking biscuits over the camp fire."

"Thank you. I'll do that."

With a smile, Mrs. Fisher moved on. Martha thought she would like Harriet Fisher even more if she didn't give advice so freely, even though it was helpful.

On the dock below the confusion of equipment in haphazard piles was turning into something like order under the shouted commands of corporals and sergeants. Boxes and trunks became orderly piles, and wheels and pieces of wood were assembled into wagons. Two carriages even appeared, as if Cinderella's fairy godmother had set them down in the sagebrush. The soldiers formed double lines, and after a brief conference between a sergeant and one of the officers, the men marched off along two ruts through the sand and disappeared around the corner of the wall.

So far none had reported to Cole. He stood at one side, looking very military in his field uniform, talking to Fred Collins. If an observer had to decide which of the two men was truly an officer of the United States Army, would he choose Cole? Fred was shorter, more slight and boyish looking. Cole's obvious strength gave an impression of force, a man who could command other men. On the *Gila*, he hadn't needed to supervise any activity. The actual tests would come now. Someone reported to Fred and was sent off. Finally a sergeant from the remaining group of soldiers approached Cole. After a brief conference, the sergeant marched his men off after the others and Cole and Fred started back to the boat. Martha was surprised at how relieved she felt.

She turned with a smile to Alice, who was just coming up on deck, and said, "I think we'll be next to go ashore."

Alice's blond hair lay limp and dull around her pale face. "I never want to see any of these places again," she complained.

Fred's tenor voice sounded at their backs. "Never mind. We're off for Fort Apache tomorrow."

Martha could see that Alice wasn't cheered by her husband's words. It was hard not to become impatient with Alice, until she remembered how she would once have felt. "I think we'll like Fort Apache," she said. Alice didn't respond.

Cole came up, and Martha was happy to leave with him. "Where are we going now?" she asked as they walked toward the fort.

"We're staying overnight with the post surgeon." He studied her a moment, then said, "You look . . . excited. And maybe anxious. I'd guess you want to get underway, but you're not sure how it's going to go."

"You're right." Martha was uncomfortable that he could interpret her moods so accurately. "Will you know what to do on the march?"

"As much as any new officer. Better than most." He added with a grin, "I already know to listen to the ones who do know—the noncoms."

She thought about his service in the militia. "I'd guess you were a noncom yourself, in Missouri."

He said, "Yes," but he didn't look pleased at her guess. She decided he too wasn't sure he liked their growing familiarity. Like an alliance of thieves, their partnership made them wary of each other.

Still, they had to reach agreements about some things. Money for one. "Mrs. Fisher says I must make sure we have enough supplies for the march. What about money?"

"Draw against Baldwin's pay. When we get to Fort Apache, I'll look into whether he has money deposited with the post trader. He might have arranged something ahead of time."

"The pay—I guess you'll earn that."

"Is that a compliment?"

She glanced at him, and decided from the smile lines around his eyes that he was teasing her. But she didn't want to be diverted now. "Taking the Baldwins' money—it seems dishonest."

He looked at her, his eyes hard. "Just what do you think we're doing? Not exactly sticking to the law. Stephen Baldwin is dead. I'm not. And I intend to stay alive. If it takes his money to do it, that's what we'll do."

Cole was right. She'd stolen a dead woman's identity, and was quibbling about money. "I have some money of my own, but I don't know how long it will last."

"Don't spend yours," he said shortly.

She wondered whether he was warning her that she shouldn't count on him. That she might be on her own and need her money. Nothing stopped him from deserting her. She was aware of that possibility, but maybe she should keep it more firmly in mind.

Following the directions of the guard at the entrance to Camp Mojave, they found the home of the post surgeon, a large, animated man of middle age. While Cole went off to see to his duties, the surgeon took Martha to the commissary to buy provisions for the Baldwins' mess chest. "Let's see," he said, "you'll need flour, sugar, condensed milk, tea, rice. And soap." Before she could agree, he had collected those and several other items. She accepted the dried apples and peaches, but she refused to buy canned oysters. After she found a Dutch oven left behind by some other camp cook, she charged her purchases against Cole's pay. The doctor helped her arrange for them to be delivered to the company quartermaster, and they went back to his house.

That night Martha retired early and the surgeon kept Cole up late talking.

The next morning Cole was gone before she wakened. She dressed quickly, wondering whether that would be their arrangement on the march. The surgeon provided breakfast before he escorted her outside the fort to the area where the march was to begin.

There the disorder seemed even greater than on the dock the previous day. Dogs from the fort ran around the fringe of the staging area, adding their barks to the braying of the mules and shouting of commands. Gray-white dust swirled up around the soldiers, who were loading boxes and gear into wagons with canvas covers and lashing smaller boxes on the outside. Elizabeth Baldwin's trunk and the box of Martha's purchases were tied on the back of one. The scene reminded Martha of the breakup of an Apache ranchería. When the camp was to be moved, getting under way was as confused as this.

Eventually order came out of the apparent chaos. Most of the soldiers fell in to a double column and took positions at the front of the line. The two Cinderella carriages, pulled by four small mules each, took their place in line behind the foot soldiers. Soldier teamsters cursed teams of six mules into place, attached chains from the remaining wagons to harnesses, and pulled the wagons into the procession. A small group of soldiers lined up behind the vehicles. The laundresses and a few children Martha hadn't seen before climbed aboard a baggage wagon. Martha saw Alice's Chinese boy Willie with the children.

Except that the wagons were all blue, it was like a gigantic circus parade, of the sort that had come to town when Martha was a child. Now she was part of the parade, but she didn't know where she fit.

She looked around for Cole. He appeared, dodging past the wagons, his blue uniform already whitish gray from dust. "You're to ride in the second ambulance," he said.

"Where?" She didn't see anything that looked like an ambulance.

"Over there," he said, and pointed toward two blue wagons that looked like enormous boxes on wheels. "The Dougherty wagons. They're called ambulances in the army." Three women were climbing into the first one. Cole offered her his arm, and they started toward the second vehicle.

The boxlike Dougherty wagon resembled a hearse. Unexpectedly, she wished Cole were going to be nearby. "Where will you be?" she asked him.

"I'll be marching with my troops. They rest every hour. The officers go back and check on their wives then."

That seemed an obscure detail for him to have picked up. "How do you know that?"

He gave her a sardonic glance. "I'm the officer who can't stay away from his wife. Remember? Someone always tells me about the opportunities."

"On this trip when we can all watch each other," she said softly, "everyone can see they're mistaken about your interest in your wife."

"We can't change the story now."

When they reached the ambulance, he returned the driver's salute, helped her onto the box provided as a step, and up into the high vehicle. He was out and away before she could say good-bye.

Inside were two seats, one along each side. Rolled canvas curtains were at the top of all the windows, leaving the carriage open halfway down the sides. The driver leaned down from his seat and called through the front opening, "Private Sperry here, ma'am. I can put the curtains down if you wish."

"No, thank you." The midday sun was hot, and she appreciated the breeze that came through the open windows.

"Elizabeth, it's you!" Alice was scrambling up into the ambulance, assisted by Fred, who nodded at Martha before hastily departing. "I was afraid I'd have to ride with one of those snippy wives from E Company."

"I'm glad you're here," Martha said, not altogether truthfully. Alice happy was a pleasure to be with; Alice unhappy was a chore.

"Mrs. Fisher could have asked me to ride with her," Alice went on mournfully. "The Fishers and General Porter bought their carriages in San Francisco. I wanted to buy one, but Fred said they cost too much."

A bugle call floated across the air. "Listen, Alice," Martha interrupted, glad to have a reason to cut off the complaint. "The column's starting up. We're on our way to Fort Apache." She laughed, sudden good spirits sparkling through her like effervescent wine. There was a place for her in the parade after all. She leaned out the side window to watch.

The double blue column was moving out into the desert like an awakening animal, stretching its joints to propel itself forward in some ancient form of locomotion. Dust boiled up around it. Private Sperry cracked his whip and yelled "Molly!" More cracks accompanied other names, followed by a forceful "Git up!" Harnesses creaked, and wheels groaned. The ambulance started with a jolt.

"Elizabeth, your hair will be a mass of dirt," Alice scolded.

Martha drew back inside, reluctantly recognizing the sound of common sense. "You're right," she said, and stopped, surprised to see tears making slow paths down Alice's face. She reached across and took the other woman's hands. They were cold in spite of the heat. "Alice, what's wrong?"

Alice clutched Martha's hands. Tears came faster. "I'm goin' to have . . ." She trailed off, looking at Private Sperry's back.

Martha didn't need the sentence finished. Envy swept over her, quickly followed by sympathy. No wonder Alice had become cranky and complaining. To face a first pregnancy in strange and unfriendly surroundings—yes, Martha knew very well how frightening that could be. "Hush," she said gently. "It's hard, but it happens all the time. Things will work out."

"How can you say that?" Alice sobbed. "You don't know."

How could she answer? Not truthfully. "I have sisters," she said. Elizabeth did have. "I've helped them. It's frightening—having a first baby—but wonderful."

Alice quieted, and they rode, bracing themselves against the jolt and sway of the ambulance. Martha thought with subdued spirits of Alice's announcement and her first response to it. Envy was a useless emotion, and she couldn't afford useless emotions.

At dusk, the march stopped for the first camp. Private Sperry helped Martha and Alice get down. While they were still stretching cramped muscles, soldiers began putting up tents. Fred arrived. "Come along, Alice," he said. "Our place is over this way. We need to get along so you can see about cooking dinner. Lieutenant Dunham will mess with us."

Alice had started off with him, but she jerked to a stop. "What are you talkin' about?"

"The officers without wives take their meals with the married couples."

"Fred," she wailed, "I can't cook. I don't even do it at home."

"Now, Alice, you make a fine peach cobbler. Willie can help you. And I've arranged for a striker for the trip. You can show him what to do." Alice left, surreptitiously wiping away a tear.

Martha restrained an impulse to offer help. As Elizabeth Baldwin, she would know about cooking in a kitchen, but not over a campfire.

"Mrs. Baldwin, your place is ready." It was one of the soldiers who had been putting up tents. She followed him to a spot at the end of a long row. Alice and Fred, along with a drooping Willie, were standing in front of a tent farther down, and she saw Harriet Fisher at another. Children played near a few smaller tents that were grouped separately. Beyond them soldiers were still setting up a bivouac in their area. The army kept its strict division of officers, laundresses and families, and soldiers, even on the march. Such exclusions seemed wrong to Martha.

She saw Cole striding toward her. With him, half trotting to keep up, was a short, stocky soldier with black, curly hair. Dismayed, Martha knew this must be a striker to work for them. Hadn't Cole stopped to consider what the constant presence of another person with them meant? But perhaps it was just for the march.

Cole arrived. "Elizabeth, this is Private Lane. He's agreed to be our striker, for the trip and at Fort Apache. Mrs. Fisher recommended him to me."

Martha understood the unspoken message. Junior officers and their wives did what the company commander's wife suggested. Maybe a striker's presence wouldn't matter until they reached Fort Apache; things might change by then. Elizabeth would have been grateful. She smiled. "Private Lane, I'm very pleased. It will be such help to have someone who knows how to cook over a campfire."

Lane soon had a fire going with mesquite branches, the mess chest open with the lid propped up for a table, and biscuit dough mixed in a tin basin. While the biscuits were baking in the Dutch oven, he attended to the tent, turning back the flaps and setting up two camp chairs beside the door. He left briefly and returned with buffalo robes, which he spread before laying two mattresses on the ground inside the tent. Around them he circled a horsehair lariat. "That's to keep rattlers away," he announced. "They won't crawl over that."

Martha shuddered appropriately. "Thank you, Private Lane. I'm astonished at how pleasant your arrangements have made our camp," she said with unfeigned appreciation. He smiled happily.

She and Cole took turns in the tent washing away some of the day's accumulation of dust. By the time Lieutenant Brown joined them for supper, they both looked more human. Gratefully she accepted and enjoyed the bacon, coffee, and biscuits that Lane served.

"Good dinner, Mrs. Baldwin," Vernon Brown said. "I'm glad I beat out Dunham for the chance to eat at your mess." He stopped, and his face around his bushy gray mustache glowed pink in the firelight.

Martha could feel her own skin start to heat up. There was only one reason she could think of why the two officers without wives in C Company would vie over eating with Cole and her. If she had to invent a story again, she hoped she could think of one that wouldn't make her so interesting. "You must have heard that Lane would be our cook," she said, and smiled sweetly at Vernon.

"Ah, yes," he said quickly, "I think I did."

Conversation turned to the next day's march, and soon Martha slipped away to the tent. Lane had spread the blankets over their mattresses as if it were one bed. The tent didn't have enough room to move the mattresses apart, which would also disturb the lariat. The best Martha could do was to separate the blankets and put them back folded double. After that she removed her outer clothing and slipped under her blanket.

Determination to be asleep before Cole came in didn't produce that result. Her closed eyes couldn't shut out sounds—of the two men saying good night, the hissing of water putting out the campfire, Cole's footsteps approaching and then entering the tent. She'd listened before to his undressing, but the sounds seemed to fill this small space. When he lay down, she felt as well as heard his movements—the shift of arm or leg to a different position. She started to turn over, and discovered that the ground wasn't completely level. Her motion took her closer to Cole. She put out her hand, and touched his bare shoulder.

She gave a startled, "Oh!"

His mattress rustled, and he said, "Anything wrong?"

"No. I didn't mean to bump you. Sorry."

"No harm done."

His voice resonated in the darkness with a sensual quality. Her hand seemed to have trapped that brief touch of firm skin. The heat from it swirled inside her to an inner core where it joined the echoes from his voice.

She lay motionless for a long time until gradually her arousal dissipated. Not until his breathing finally became steady and rhythmical did she finally fall asleep.

A bugle call wakened Martha at four o'clock the next morning. Mules brayed, summoning their drivers to bring the morning feed. She kept her head buried in her blanket while Cole dressed. When he left, she pushed herself through her dressing. Lane had breakfast bacon, coffee, and bread waiting. While she and Cole ate, Lane struck their tent. They had barely finished before he began packing the mess chest and camp chairs for the day's march.

"Private Lane," Martha said, "you are certainly efficient."

He responded with a gap-toothed smile and a "Thank you, ma'am."

As Cole walked Martha to the ambulance, he said, "You should address the striker as Lane, not Private Lane."

"Why? That makes him sound like a servant."

"It's the army way," he said in an impatient tone. "We don't want to do anything that gets us special attention."

"But—"

"You wanted this. Now we're in it."

There was no answer to that. The man of firm skin and sensual voice had been replaced by an army officer. She didn't like him—and was glad she didn't. It seemed safer this morning.

Subsequent days went along much like the first one. At first the marches were short, but as the men became hardened, they covered more miles. Each day Martha watched the soldiers swinging along with blanket rolls, knapsacks, and rifles, often singing. Occasionally an older soldier became exhausted and rode in one of the wagons until he could march again. None of them complained, at least not in Martha's hearing. As she observed them longer, the demands on them began to bother her. Enlisted men were the backbone of the march, walking their miles each day and having to see to the needs of the officers and their families every evening before they could put up their own tents. It reminded her that once she had been the lowliest of creatures, given no consideration for exhaustion or illness.

"Why don't the soldiers get more chance to rest?" she asked Cole at one stop. "They march and we ride, but they have to wait on us. It seems unfair."

"I think, *Elizabeth*," Cole said, "that you'll get used to it."

Something in his tone cut off her protest. She turned and saw Captain Fisher looking at her with a puzzled frown. It struck her that she'd been expressing an opinion someone like Elizabeth probably wouldn't think, much less say. And it had been overheard by the one officer already suspicious of her and Cole. He nodded at her and walked on, but it wasn't a friendly nod.

The bugle call sounded for the march to continue. Cole left, and Martha vowed she'd avoid Captain Fisher and keep her thoughts to herself. Neither would be easy.

Thirteen days after leaving Camp Mojave, the march reached Fort Whipple, which was regimental headquarters as well as headquarters for the general who commanded the Military Department of Arizona. A mile outside the fort several cavalry officers from Whipple met the march with invitations to the officers and their wives for places to stay. "My wife will be happy to have you and your wife stay with us," Lieutenant Wayne, one of the cavalry officers, told Cole.

"Thanks. We accept gladly."

When Cole and Fred went back to the ambulance to tell their wives, Martha laughed with pleasure. "Wonderful! I'm longing for a bath, and some clothes that aren't covered with dust."

Cole rode alongside the ambulance, thinking about Martha. When she laughed or gave that sparkling smile, she wasn't just pretty. She looked vivid—more alive than most women. More ready for almost anything. For making love. She was damned arousing. God, he'd like to bed her. But the situation between them wasn't that simple.

When the ambulance rumbled past the stockade and into Fort Whipple, it was almost dusk. The fort had the usual central parade ground ringed by offices and barracks on three sides and the line of officers' quarters on the fourth. "It's so pretty," Alice exclaimed, "with all those trees. And the mountains just over there. Oh, Fred, I wish we were goin' to be stationed here."

"Fort Apache may be even prettier," Martha said.

How tiresome a complaining wife was, Cole thought impatiently. He was lucky Martha didn't fuss like that. Suddenly his own thinking caught him up short. My God! He was turning into a husband!

Lieutenant Wayne met the ambulance at the stables. He and Martha and Cole went to the officers' line. As they walked past one of the houses, an Indian came out. He was unusually tall, with long black hair hanging down beside his face. Beads decorated the sides of his buckskin trousers. A large necklace of elks' teeth and a silver medallion hung around his neck and over his vest.

Cole heard a hiss of breath from Martha. When he looked at her, her face was almost white. She was staring at the Indian. Cole put his arm around her, and she shrank back against him.

Lieutenant Wayne nodded to the Indian, who looked at them curiously. As he walked past, Martha pressed closer against Cole, who held her securely. She seemed afraid and vulnerable, a woman in need of protection.

"Now, Mrs. Baldwin," Lieutenant Wayne said, "you

mustn't be alarmed. Black Rope won't hurt you. He came here four years ago with General Crook. When the general left, Black Rope stayed. Someone said he'd quarreled with his people and didn't want to go back."

"He's Apache," Martha said in a faint voice.

Lieutenant Wayne didn't seem to notice that her statement wasn't a question. "Yes. The Apache have a reputation for being cruel and ferocious people. They mostly deserve it. But not all of them are that way. General Crook had a lot of loyal Apache scouts." He turned in at one of the two-story frame houses. "Here's my place. You just come along, and Marian will fix you up with some hot tea."

"Thank you." Martha sounded steady again. She moved away from Cole and followed Lieutenant Wayne.

Cole was puzzled by her reaction. Since they'd joined forces, she'd seen Indians many times. All Yumas or Cocopahs or Mojaves. She'd been delighted that they were going to Fort Apache, in the territory of the White Mountain Apaches. Why did this man upset her?

Marian Wayne was a pleasant woman and the Waynes' quarters were large. Cole and Martha were given a bedroom to themselves, with two iron army cots but with curtains at the window and a rug on the wooden floor. There was even a small room that they used for bathing. Cole waited impatiently while Martha bathed, and he hurried through his own bath. By the time he was finally able to say good night to the Waynes and close the door to the guest bedroom, his determination was fixed.

Martha was already in bed, but he sat on the side of his cot and said, "We must talk."

Slowly she sat up. In the light of the kerosene lamp her eyes looked large and soft and wary, almost frightened. Shadows from the lantern emphasized the bones of her face, but her long braid of brown hair reminded him of a young girl. She held the blanket around her as if shielding herself. Only her shoulders were above it, the white shift faintly colored pink from the skin showing through. He felt the same rush of protectiveness he'd felt earlier, but he suppressed it. He needed to protect himself too. Whether she were reluctant or not, he had to know about her.

"What do you want to talk about?"

"Everything."

She stared at him for a long moment. Finally she said, so softly he barely heard, "All right."

8

The bedroom lamp highlighted Martha's fingers gripping the edge of the blanket. Cole suspected she didn't know where to begin. "Exactly what do you want me to help you do?" he asked.

"Find a boy who's part Apache."

"Who is he? Why do you want to find him?"

She shivered. "I need to put my robe on. Please, turn around."

He went to the window and looked out. Across the parade ground the barracks showed up as dark outlines, each with a row of lighted rectangles along its side. Behind him he heard the rustle of the straw-filled mattress then the click of a trunk lid. An image of Martha intruded, her braid, the color of maple sugar, lying across one shift-clad shoulder. Without the shift the braid would rest on her bare skin, maybe brush her breast. High, full breasts, and—

He caught himself. It was no time to feel like a stud sniffing around a mare in season.

Finally he heard her footsteps and the creak of the camp chair as she sat down. A soft "Thank you" released him to turn around. The braid was hanging down her back, and fortunately her yellow kimono-style robe covered her. She looked up at him, her eyes deep blue like the last sun-tinged edge of night sky. "You're right," she said softly. "There's no turning back. I'll tell you what you want to know. But, please, tell me about yourself first."

He hadn't counted on having to lay out his past so soon. But it was his idea they talk. "Fair enough." He sat down on the other camp chair. "I was born near Tucson. My father had a ranch and some other property, including a copper mine. When I was growing up, all I wanted to do was to run the ranch or the mine. But my mother wanted me to go to school in Boston, where her sister lives. She got her way." His throat tightened with a bitterness he still felt. "I was in Boston four years. Until my father was murdered, ambushed on a trip to the mine."

"The man who killed my father had worked at the mine. The sheriff caught him. By the time I got home, he'd already been convicted and hanged. I was seventeen then. I planned to take care of my mother. Look after the ranch and the mine."

The bitterness colored his voice. "It didn't work out that way. Someone already had his eyes on my mother. Harvey Lippincott. She married him six months after my father's death."

"And you were angry?" Martha asked.

He'd been much more than angry. Memories rushed back, as vivid as if it had just happened instead of eleven years before.

For a while his mother tried to pretend that Harvey

was just a friend, someone she could depend on for advice. That's the way she had put it when she finally told Cole. They were in the sunny dining room, on the east side of the house. A room where his father had sat at the round table and talked about what they would do when Cole was old enough.

"Harvey Lippincott is a widower," his mother had said. "He understands what I'm going through. And he's so sensible, such a help to me about business."

Cole knew how upset she'd been. Keeping his emotions in check, he tried to reason with her. "You don't need to marry again. I'll manage the ranch and the mine."

"Now, Cole. You just started studying law. The best thing is for you to go back and finish. Of course the land will be yours someday. Harvey will take good care of it for you." She took a breath, then added, "The wedding will be Saturday."

The tightly wound spring of grief inside his chest snapped. "No! You can't! I won't let you!"

"Please, Cole." His mother put her hand on his arm. Tears magnified her dark brown eyes. "Don't make difficulties." Her favorite phrase throughout his childhood.

In a rage he ran out of the house, saddled his roan gelding, and left the ranch. In Tucson he went to Ira Gurnett, his father's oldest friend, to say good-bye. For Ira's sake, he agreed to stay overnight. Because he respected Ira almost as much as his father, the next morning he listened when the tall, balding man talked.

"You got to see Emma's point of view, Cole." They were sitting on the fence of the corral behind Ira's house. "It's a hard thing for a woman, living in the West. She wants a man to look out for her."

"I can do that. She thinks I should go back to school. Like a child."

"Well, remember she lost four babies before you, Cole. It's hard for her to realize you're about grown up. Emma's probably thinking she's doing the best thing for you, more than for herself."

"She can't marry Harvey Lippincott. He acts nice, but he's not. Father never liked him."

"Harvey's a respectable man. Most people around here regard him well enough." Ira took a pipe out of his pocket and lit it. After a few puffs he said quietly, "Probably you wouldn't like anybody your mother decided to marry. That's natural enough. And it's hard when your father was murdered that way. But that's behind you now. It's your mother's right to make her mind up about what she does."

Ira's quiet persuasion had worked. Cole didn't go back home, but he did go to the wedding. His mother had worn a ruffled blue lace dress and a big lace hat with blue silk roses on the brim. He'd never forgotten how beautiful she looked. Or Harvey Lippincott's silver hair and black suit. And his smile to match—silver on the outside, black underneath.

Now, so many years later, Cole could say to Martha with outward calm, "Yes, I was angry. Right after the wedding I left Tucson. I went to Missouri and joined the militia. I didn't like that much, so I only stayed a year. Afterwards I did a lot of things in a lot of places. You've already heard most of it. Gambler, bartender, cowboy. For a while I was a lawyer of sorts."

He leaned forward, resting his elbows on his thighs, staring down at his clasped hands between his knees. Martha leaned a little forward too. "You must have gone back to Tucson," she said.

"Yes." He straightened and looked at her. She returned his gaze steadily. Would she believe the rest? "Two years ago. I wanted to see my mother again. I still couldn't stand Harvey, but I avoided him. Then one day I ran into a man who'd been deputy sheriff. He was dying of tuberculosis. He told me that he'd overheard a conversation between someone and a local judge. My father had been murdered by three men, not just the one who was hanged."

"You didn't have any idea there was more than one?"

He gripped his hands together until they hurt. The remembered shock of that discovery still affected him. "No. The deputy didn't know who the third man was, but the second man was Sam Weaver, a friend of his. Weaver had left town years before, and the deputy had kept his mouth shut."

She frowned. "Why?"

"Out of friendship, I guess. He'd just heard that Weaver had come back to Arizona from Mexico. Now that I was back, his conscience was bothering him. He didn't want to die without telling me."

Cole got up and paced the room. Martha watched a few moments, then said, "And you hunted for Sam Weaver?"

"Yes, and I found him. It took a year."

"Did he tell you who the third man was?"

"Yes. It was Harvey Lippincott."

She didn't look surprised. Probably she'd guessed from the bitter way he said Harvey's name. "Do you think," she asked, "that Sam Weaver was telling you the truth?"

"I'm certain." When you threaten a man with carving him up, Cole thought grimly, he usually tells the truth. "I didn't kill him. I wanted to do the right thing. Let justice do its job." He laughed, a twisted, ironic laugh. "On the way back to Tucson, I got careless. Thinking too much about what would happen to Harvey. When we were almost to Tucson, someone jumped me. Hit me from behind. When I came to, Weaver was dead, shot with my gun. The sheriff was conveniently at hand. I had liquor all over me, a lot more than inside, but it smelled pretty much the same. The sheriff figured we'd been drinking, got in a fight, and I'd killed him. That was supposed to account for the knot on my head."

"And you were convicted of Sam Weaver's murder?"

"Yes."

She was frowning again, arguing, as if there were still something to be settled. "But what about the deputy who told you about your father's three murderers?"

"He'd died by then."

"Did you try to talk to the judge he mentioned?"

"That was the judge who sentenced me."

That silenced her, as effectively as he'd been silenced in court. His accusations against Harvey had only convinced the jury that he was hot-tempered, capable of murder. Then he'd compounded it when the verdict was read. He'd tried to choke Harvey. He could still hear chairs going over backward as he lunged. Feel his hands around the soft neck and see the fear in the pale gray eyes before three men dragged him off.

"Maybe I deserve to be called a murderer," he said somberly. "I didn't kill Weaver. But I'll probably kill Harvey if I get a chance."

"What about your mother?" Martha asked.

He didn't like to remember his mother in court. The

way she had cried and pleaded with the judge. But she had saved his life. "She convinced the judge not to sentence me to hanging. Harvey had to pretend to agree with her. That was the only pleasure—if you can call it that—I had from the trial. Watching Harvey try to act like a forgiving stepfather."

He stopped, sick of recalling the past. Did Martha believe him? While he was talking, she'd looked convinced. Now her face was troubled. If she still thought he was a murderer, what the hell did it matter anyway? She hesitated a moment before she asked, "What do you plan to do about it?"

Her question waited, like the interval after lighting a long fuse. They hadn't come to the explosion, but they both knew it was there. "Find a way to prove I didn't kill Weaver. Make Harvey Lippincott pay for killing my father. As soon as I can, I'll get in touch with Ira Gurnett, my father's friend. He'll help me. That's the first step. Then I'll just have to see."

She said softly, "I can understand how you feel. It must be terrible to be convicted of a crime you didn't commit. Who do you think did kill Sam Weaver?"

She believed him! "I don't know who murdered Weaver, but I suspect my stepfather had a hand in it." He sat down opposite her again. "So, that's my story. Now it's your turn."

Cole waited, but she looked down at her hands, clasped nervously in her lap. "Today," he prodded, "when we saw the Apache, you were frightened. You've seen other Indians before and haven't seemed upset. Why this one?"

Martha realized that Cole was giving her a way to begin. "He looked like someone I knew once—a Chiricahua Apache. It was a different man."

That wasn't enough. Cole was looking at her, waiting. She must go on, but she dreaded seeing his expression change. Watching the concern in his dark eyes become distaste or contempt—expressions she'd seen so many times. It would be even more painful because, in spite of trying to convince herself to the contrary, she wanted his approval. More than approval, she realized. When he looked at her the way a man does when he desires a woman, it stirred a response in her she'd thought must be dead. That heat she felt inside of her was dangerous. So if he shrank from her, that would be for the best.

Quickly, before she could lose resolve, she said, "He reminded me of one of the Apache warriors who killed my family and took me captive."

Cole looked startled, then nodded. "I should have guessed. You know too much about Indians. And desert travel. Do you want to tell me how it happened?"

She was grateful for his understanding. "It happened ten years ago. I was fifteen then. My father and mother and younger brother and I were on the way from Texas to California. Benjamin, my older brother, was already there. He wrote to Papa and said how much money he was making and how exciting the country was. So of course Papa wanted to go."

"Apaches attacked you?" Cole said.

"Yes. We were in southern Arizona. We had our own wagon and carriage. Papa had traveled a lot and got along well with Indians. He thought it was safe to travel by ourselves. Later I found out there'd been lots of trouble in that area—Mexicans and Americans raiding Apache camps. Apaches attacking whites. When we first saw the Indians, they seemed friendly. Asking for bread, which Mama gave them. But then . . ."

Noises and images came back, still too clear and

immediate. Shouts, screams, a high wailing sound suddenly cut off. Her mother's apron, splashed with blood. Her younger brother, running in a futile effort to escape. Papa struggling, then on the ground. Brown earth turned dark red. "I don't remember everything. I suppose I must have fainted. When I came to, I could see everyone else was dead."

"Your whole family?"

"All except Benjamin, my brother in California, and my grandmother in Texas."

Cole's face didn't give away what he was thinking. But she knew what most people would suppose happened to her. "They took me with them. None of the men . . . they didn't touch me that way. It wasn't like stories in journals. Apaches don't approve of rape. Those Apaches were Chiricahuas. They traded me to some White Mountain Apaches, who took me to their camp. It was farther north, up in the mountains. After a while, one of the warriors married me."

She stopped, searching Cole's face for a reaction. "Most white people wouldn't say it was a marriage, but it was," she said, challenging him to deny it.

"You must have been very frightened." His voice was quiet, with none of the disgust she feared.

"At first I was. But Deniibesh, my husband, was a good man." The Apache name felt strange on her tongue after so long not saying it aloud. "His name means Sharp-Knife. It fit him. He was always using his knife to do things that made our life easier." She dared Cole to say what her brother had said to her—that her husband was a savage who was no better than the men who had killed her family.

Cole, his expression still unreadable, said, "The boy you're looking for. Who is he?"

Her right leg began to tremble. She put her hand on her knee to stop it. "Nilchi Bidahsaa is my son."

Saying his name aloud brought back a surge of memories. Of lying in the wickiup, with the sun streaming in the east opening, when Sharp-Knife first saw their baby. The pleasure she felt in his pride. It was then she realized that her early fear at the touch of this alien man had become affection and respect. A kind of love. Not the intense love she soon felt for the baby her husband was holding so gently, but for Sharp-Knife's value as a man.

"How did you get away from the Apaches?" Cole asked.

Black memories crowded out good ones. She swallowed, trying to make her voice work. It came out as a whisper. "My husband was killed on a raid against Navahos. His brother's wife hated me and wanted her husband to kill me, but he wouldn't do it. So she persuaded him to send me to another Apache band. My brother Benjamin had come from California and been searching for me. He was offering a big ransom. I was very sick, and the Apaches I was with decided to take the ransom right away, before I died." In the silence she could hear Cole's breathing, but she couldn't look at him.

"Is that why you asked why the regular soldiers aren't treated better, because you think they're treated the way you were?"

He looked questioning, maybe kind. Nothing more. "Yes. I was a slave. After Sharp-Knife died, I had to do exactly what I was told. Like the soldiers."

"What happened to your son?"

Her throat constricted, and tears filled her eyes. She struggled to hold them back, but one spilled over and ran down her cheek. "My husband's brother and his wife kept my baby with them. I haven't seen him for seven years."

Cole heard the quaver in her voice and saw the tears. His impulse was to put his arms around her and comfort her. But she was holding herself stiffly erect, not acknowledging or wiping away the tears. Clearly she didn't want comforting from him.

He got up and stood by the window so that he didn't have to look directly at her. "Did your brother help you try to find your child?"

She gave a laugh that wasn't a laugh. "Help me hunt for a half-breed child? No. Besides, at first I was too sick to do anything. Benjamin took me back to my grandmother. By the time I was well, he'd returned to California."

"What about your grandmother?"

Martha's words tumbled out, as if they tasted too bitter to stay more than a second in her mouth. "My grandmother agreed with everyone else in the town—that a woman who'd lived with an Indian was disgraced. A normal woman would never want to think about it again. Since I kept insisting I must go back for my child, they concluded I was crazy. My grandmother arranged to be made my guardian. When she died, the court made my brother my guardian. The man with me on the stagecoach was Grandmother's lawyer. He was proxy for my brother until he could deliver me to California."

Cole didn't know just how he felt about her story, but she was looking at him and he had to say something. "So you found me, and we made a deal. Do you have any idea how to go about finding—what did you say the boy's name is?"

"Nilchi Bidahsaa. It means Pinecone." Her face softened as she said the name. "He loved the taste of pinecones, the tiny ones. He'd put them in his mouth and suck on them. The sharp points didn't stop him."

"So exactly what do you expect me to do to help you find Pinecone?"

"I'm not sure. See that we get to Fort Apache. Then I'll decide how to search."

Her phrasing set off a warning in his head. "Hold on. *We'll* decide how to search. And we'll make sure we don't do anything to make the army suspect we aren't Stephen and Elizabeth Baldwin."

"Yes, of course. And I know you have your own problems to solve."

Her tears were gone. Her face was flushed, her eyes determined. She didn't convince him that caution would be the first thing on her mind. Not by the way she talked about her child. He'd have to wait and see, and keep a close eye on her.

Later when he lay on the iron cot, discreetly separated from Martha's, he stared up into the night-dark ceiling and mulled over his reactions to her story. A white woman, really just a girl, captured by Indians and forced to take an Indian husband. None of it was her fault. But the image of Martha, lying with an Apache man, pulled at him. Dammit, he didn't want to think of her that way. But it was hard not to.

Cole detested people who could only react according to their prejudices. He'd seen too much of that in Missouri after the war—Yankees and Confederates still hating each other. The trouble was, he'd already been aroused by her, and now he couldn't separate that feeling from this new image. Damn! He was no better than the people in her grandmother's town.

* * *

Over the next three days, with minimal duty for the officers of C Company, Cole spent most of his time escorting Martha to social events arranged by the families of the officers stationed at Fort Whipple. In spite of his resolve to suppress his feelings of attraction to Martha, Cole found himself observing her closely.

He was already thoroughly aware of her body—the sway of her walk, the way the tiny row of buttons down the front of her dress emphasized her breasts. Her light brown braid, coiled at the back of her head, lost just enough tendrils of hair to make the curve of her neck inviting. Now he watched for other signs—how often she looked at men. Whether her laughter had a special, free quality. He thought it had. On the other hand, she generally acted modest and proper. Even his mother would approve of Martha.

Ironically, in the bedroom privacy that Cole's fellow officers probably envied him, he and Martha had established an impersonal routine. In the mornings he dressed while she still slept, or pretended to. At night he lingered over his pipe and then went to the room and undressed in the dark. He couldn't tell whether she was already asleep. Sleep didn't come too easily for him those nights.

On the last evening before C Company left for Fort Apache, the regimental staff officers were hosting a dance.

All the officers were to wear full dress uniforms. Cole preferred the field uniform because its looser fit allowed more room for the difference between his frame and Stephen Baldwin's. In the Waynes' guest bedroom he muttered a few curses as he pulled on the tailored light blue pants and tight double-breasted tunic.

He could hear Martha and their hostess talking somewhere in the house. He'd come in without seeing either of them. When he emerged into the outer room, he forgot about his appearance in his surprise at Martha's. She was wearing a silky dress with a billowing skirt that floated around her, emphasizing her movements. The color fell somewhere between blue and green; he'd seen mountain lakes that looked that way from a distance. The neckline was modestly high, but the bodice fit snugly over her breasts. It was the kind of dress that was sure to attract male attention.

His high collar, stiff with gilt embroidery, rubbed against his neck, which was suddenly very warm. It helped some when Mrs. Wayne said to Martha, "You'll have the handsomest husband at the ball."

Martha smiled at him. "Yes, I agree."

Lieutenant Wayne appeared, looking as stiff in his uniform as Cole felt, and they left for the dance.

The ball was held in the commanding general's house, which had several large rooms. Furniture had been removed from the one that served as a ballroom; strips of bright red cloth covered the windows and hung over the doorway. Two trumpets and a horn from the fort band made up the orchestra.

Cole and Martha danced the opening waltz. She felt light and supple, following his movements easily. He noticed her perfume, a scent that reminded him of roses. Once as they swung around, the edge of his right epaulet brushed her cheek, leaving a faint red streak. As if he'd put his brand on her. "Sorry," he said when they finished. "Does that hurt?"

"No." She ran a finger across the mark. "Not at all."

Later he thought that claiming ownership of her in some way wasn't a bad idea if he wanted to dance any more. Like any army post, Fort Whipple had far more men than women. Martha was beleaguered by requests for dances. She seemed to enjoy the attention. Maybe too much, he thought. He noticed that Peter Dunham danced closer than he would have with another man's wife. And caught himself feeling like a jealous husband.

When Martha returned to him after a series of dances, she said, "Have you seen Alice and Fred Collins? I'd like to speak to Alice."

He'd had plenty of time to look around. "They're in the next room."

They found Alice sitting on a cane-backed chair, looking pale and somewhat gloomy, with Fred beside her. She brightened when she saw them. "Elizabeth, you must make Fred dance with you. He loves to dance, but I'm simply too fatigued this evenin'. Mr. Baldwin, you'll stay here and keep me company, won't you?"

With Cole's assurance he'd be delighted and only a slight demur from Fred, Martha and Fred went back to the dancing room.

Alice sighed and lost her bright look. "Everyone wants to dance with Elizabeth."

"When we reach Fort Apache and you're feeling better," Cole said, "every man there will ask to be your dance partner. I'll be among the first." He was being polite rather than honest, but Alice looked in need of gallantry.

To his surprise, tears appeared in her eyes. It had been a lot of years since his mother drilled him on polite small talk. He must be very rusty.

"I'll never feel like dancin' again," she said.

There wasn't a polite comment for that. If he were honest, he'd tell her to quit whining. Act more like Martha. It startled him to realize that he was thinking like a husband again. The second time in one night.

Fortunately before Cole had to say anything more, Fred returned. "Mrs. Baldwin is dancing with Lieutenant Dunham," he explained.

Cole excused himself and went into the dancing room. Martha wasn't there, nor was Peter Dunham. The questions about her that had plagued him since hearing her story echoed in his mind like hounds in full cry. He looked into the room for serving cakes and punch. Neither Martha nor Dunham was around the lace-covered table.

Outside on the veranda the smokers stood under the blue clouds that were forming around the overhead lanterns. There, at the far end, Peter Dunham leaned against a post, talking to a captain from E Company.

Where the hell was Martha?

Cole stepped casually off the veranda, then picked up his stride going toward the Waynes' quarters. Lanterns from other verandas made circles of light that reached out onto the path. He passed three buildings when he caught a flash of color off to one side. Quickly he turned in that direction and saw Martha. With her, only partly visible in the shadow of a house, was Black Rope, the Apache they'd seen the first day at Fort Whipple.

As Cole made his furious way toward Martha, he heard her speaking. He couldn't understand the words, but he'd heard enough Apache to recognize it. Black Rope wasn't answering. When Cole got near them, Martha's words broke off, and she swung around to face him. Black Rope, still silent, walked away into the darkness.

Cole had never hurt a woman. He'd never wanted to so much before. "What the hell do you think you're doing?"

"We're leaving tomorrow. I thought he might know something about the people I'm looking for. It was my only chance to ask." She sounded shaky but defiant.

"That is crazy!" He'd almost said that she was crazy. Even in his rage, he remembered how she'd been treated and held that back. "Do you want to get to Fort Apache? Or do you want to stay in the Prescott jail? If that's your plan, I'm clearing out right now. I don't intend to spend time in the guardhouse here!"

"I overheard someone at the party say he'd just seen Black Rope. I left the general's quarters from the back way. No one saw me."

"Anyone could come along here. I saw you."

"You were looking for me," she protested.

"And a damned good thing I was. We're going back to the party. And we'll stay there until it's over. If you dance, you'll dance with me." He took her arm in a grip she couldn't break and started to turn around.

A blue-uniformed officer was coming toward them—Peter Dunham.

Cole checked his motion and made a rapid assessment. Peter probably hadn't heard them, but he could see them. Martha was slightly in front of Cole. He pulled her back against him and leaned down, nuzzling the side of her neck with his lips. He slid his hand up from her waist and cupped her breast.

Peter's "Ahem!" came at the same time as Martha's gasp, and covered it, Cole hoped.

"Mr. Baldwin. Mrs. Baldwin." Peter sounded slyly curious. "Getting some fresh air?"

Cole stepped quickly away from Martha. "Why . . . yes, sir. It gets warm inside."

"Not any warmer than out here, I'd say." Peter strolled on, the end of his cigar glowing and fading as he puffed on it.

After exhaling, Cole took Martha's arm again. Silently she walked beside him back toward the lights and music. In a corner of his mind, Cole recognized that she'd gone to find the Apache in spite of fearing him. At the moment he was too angry to give her credit for bravery. Angry because she was so foolhardy. Angry because he had to worry about what Dunham might have heard. And angry with himself because he enjoyed touching her breast too damned much. If they got out of this mess, he thought furiously, he'd be the luckiest man in Arizona. He planned to have a short career in the army, but he suspected it might seem very long.

9

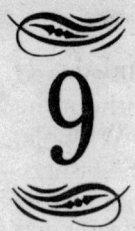

"Why, *Elizabeth*, you look positively peaked this morning," Alice said. They were standing in the staging area near the entrance to Fort Whipple. The familiar ambulance, which she and Martha would ride in to Fort Apache, was nearby. "Maybe you danced too much last night," Alice added in a wistful tone.

"Maybe I did." Martha chose not to explain that she hadn't fallen asleep until nearly morning. She'd lain awake, alternately angry at Cole for interrupting her conversation with Black Rope and at herself for being reckless. The Apache, she was certain, wouldn't tell anyone of her attempt to talk to him. But Cole was right. If Peter Dunham, or anyone else, had come along sooner, he'd have discovered her speaking to Black Rope. It wasn't fair to put Cole in jeopardy, at least not when her chances of success were so small. What if she had a really good clue to Pinecone's whereabouts, but also knew Cole would oppose her actions? What would she do then?

HEARTBREAK TRAIL 127

Cole and the other officers from C Company stood to one side, listening to Captain Fisher. Without the men from E Company who'd stayed at Fort Whipple, the column stretched only half as far. Only the Fishers' carriage waited in front of the single ambulance Martha and Alice would ride in.

Two laundresses were getting into one of the wagons. Martha didn't see Willie with them. "Where's Willie?" she asked.

Alice said in an irritated voice, "He's gone. Night before last he just disappeared. Fred looked for him, but of course he couldn't find him. Fred thinks Willie went into Prescott. There are Chinese families there who'll take him in." The annoyance in her face faded. "He wasn't much use, but I sort of liked him. I hope somebody is nice to him."

"Oh, yes. So do I." The last time Martha saw Willie he'd looked unhappy. Even his pigtail had hung sadly down his back. She hated the thought of the childish Willie separated from his own people. A Chinese family would be better for him.

Private Sperry came over from the ambulance where he'd been seeing to the mules. "Good morning, ma'am," he said, nodding in the general direction of them both. "Would you like me to help you inside?"

Alice got in, but Martha lingered outside, unwilling to leave the fresh morning. Sunlight had painted the pine needles silver-green, and its warmth coaxed the pine resin into releasing its pungent odor. Similar odors had surrounded Martha years before when she took her baby out into the woods to collect pine nuts. She remembered the way she had to stop him from putting the cones into his mouth. Her folly in seeking out Black Rope hadn't unmasked Cole and her, and this morning they were starting to the area where Pinecone might still live.

A whimpering sound came from the ambulance. Alice was giving in too much to her feelings, Martha thought a little impatiently. While she debated whether to offer more comfort, the whimper came again, not from inside the ambulance, but from underneath. She crouched down to look. Behind a clump of grass, she saw furry ears and a sad pair of golden eyes. A short brown nose thrust through the grass. After a moment, a fat puppy wriggled a short distance toward her.

"Private Sperry," she called. "Come see what's under the ambulance." When he came and crouched beside her, she pointed to the puppy, who had stopped and lay watching, as if waiting for an invitation to join them.

"It's a pup from a litter at the barracks," Private Sperry said. "Took a fancy to me. Must a' followed me this morning. Come on out, pup."

When the puppy stayed where it was, Private Sperry reached between the wheels. The puppy backed up, just out of reach. Private Sperry stood up. "Guess he'll have to stay there till we move out. He'll go home then."

"But he might get run over," Martha protested. "Or kicked by the mules."

Sperry shook his head. "A dog that don't git broke to mules don't last long anyways, ma'am."

After Sperry went back to his mules, Martha stayed crouching down, looking at the puppy. His tail was moving, making little puffs of dust behind him. "Come on, now," she coaxed. He took another tentative wriggle forward, then stopped again. She got down on her hands and knees and crawled under the ambulance. One knee pressed down on a sharp rock, and she gave an involuntary cry. The puppy's head came up, but he didn't retreat. She put out her hand and let him smell it. After several sniffs, he gave a tentative lick. She reached for him and got her hand under his body. Cautiously she held on to him and backed out.

"What are you doing?" The unfriendly voice was Cole's.

She looked up. The sunshine was behind his head, and his silhouette appeared eleven feet tall. As gracefully as she could while holding the puppy, she stood up. The dog snuggled against her, tucking his soft, furry head under her chin. With Cole's face visible now and his height reduced to only a head above hers, she said, "This is . . ." She thought of where she'd found him and finished, "Whipple. He's going with me."

Cole studied her for what seemed a very long minute. "I'll take care of him," she said.

"That's a better occupation for you than some I can think of."

It was his first acknowledgment of her blunder since last night, and made without anger. She smiled happily at him. "Whipple will be no trouble, and neither will I." Cole's eyebrows went up a fraction, as if he weren't completely convinced, but he said nothing.

She turned toward the ambulance to find Alice looking out the back window with an appalled expression. "You surely don't mean to bring that animal in here!"

Martha held Whipple hard enough against her that he gave a small whimper. In a few minutes he had become essential to her, but she couldn't explain to Alice that the way his soft body rested against her reminded her of a baby. "I'll hold him. And make sure he doesn't bother you," she promised.

Alice's face set in a stubborn expression. "Elizabeth, what can you be thinkin'? That dog most certainly has fleas, and you know he'll make a mess."

Cole put his hand on Martha's shoulder. It felt marvelously comforting. "Wait a moment," he said. "I think I can work out something."

Martha sat down on the step beside the ambulance and petted Whipple. Behind her Alice said plaintively, "You've been such a comfort to me, Elizabeth, but I just can't abide a dog in here." Martha didn't answer. Alice was right; she shouldn't have to share the ambulance with a puppy. *But,* Martha said silently to Whipple, *don't worry. I'll walk with you all the way to Fort Apache if I have to.*

Cole came back with Harriet Fisher, who went over to the ambulance and poked her head in. "Alice, Mr. Baldwin tells me you've not been feeling well. You should have said something before this. I'd welcome the company in my carriage, and you might have an easier ride that way."

After Alice expressed her gratitude and Cole helped her down, she went off with Mrs. Fisher. Martha smiled gratefully at Cole. "Thank you."

"Better walk him now. We're starting up shortly." He scratched Whipple once behind the ears and left, a jaunty swing to his step.

A grinning Private Sperry appeared with a piece of rope. "You can tie this around the pup's neck for now," he said. "I'll scare up a piece of leather strap for a collar later on. And I'll see he gits broke to the mules." Just before the signal to move out, Sperry brought her the bottom half of a keg. "Here, this will do to carry him in."

Martha scrambled down and pulled up several clumps of grass for lining. After the ambulance started up, she settled Whipple in it at her feet.

During each of the hourly rest stops, she got out and walked the puppy. Half the time, Cole came back and walked with her. The first time she protested. "You don't get any rest this way."

He shrugged. "I get all I need."

She didn't object again, grateful that the puppy had eased some of the tension between them.

When they stopped to camp that night, Private Sperry said, "Best if I learn Whipple about mules right away." Martha handed the puppy over reluctantly.

As she watched Sperry lead the puppy away, Cole said, "Dogs make good friends, but they can't always protect themselves in the wild."

She didn't want to hear the warning. "I'll take good care of him," she vowed. Cole went off to see to his men without answering. Belatedly she realized that he recognized how easy it was for her to become attached to a young, helpless creature. And that a loss would be particularly painful to her. It was more sensitivity than she would ever have expected from the man she'd found chained in a shed.

When Cole returned, Peter Dunham, carrying his folding camp chair, was with him. "Lieutenant Dunham's taking his meals with us for this leg of the march," Cole said.

"Lieutenant Brown's messing with the Fishers," Peter explained. "He's senior to me, so he eats with them now that General Porter isn't here. And I get to try Lane's cooking."

"How can Lieutenant Brown be senior to you, when you're both first lieutenants?" Martha asked.

"It's date of rank that counts," Peter said. "That's the date an officer receives his rank. What's the matter, Stephen, haven't you told your wife you're the junior officer in the company?"

"I have," Cole said, "but she doesn't believe anyone else is more important than I am."

Martha smiled. "I don't listen carefully to everything Stephen says."

After Martha sat down, Peter and Cole settled on their camp chairs. "You'll find out about rank when we get to Fort Apache," Peter said. "The most junior officer gets the last choice of quarters. If an officer comes along who outranks you, he can take over your quarters. You have to move out and find something else."

She didn't care, but Elizabeth would. "It sounds dreadful," Martha said.

"It's called 'ranking out.' I've seen posts with a new colonel where everyone had to move. Each one ranked out the officer next down the list. My wife hated it. That's one reason she's back in New York." Peter said this last nonchalantly, apparently untroubled by his wife's absence.

Lane called them to the meal set out on the mess chest lid. After they finished eating and were sitting around the campfire, Martha studied Peter curiously. He could be concealing his feelings, or he might not miss his wife; maybe he had a mistress. Peter's face was handsome enough to attract women. Even so, Martha decided, his looks didn't appeal to her. He was almost too pretty. Cole's face was more interesting—stronger, more used looking. The firelight on the two men just then brought out more differences than Cole's beard and Peter's clean-shaven jaw. Peter's features were smooth and regular. Cole's face had a slight

HEARTBREAK TRAIL

irregularity to his nose and definite cheekbones.

Startled, she realized that she was looking at Cole with a sense of connection—of pride. She hadn't felt connected to anyone for a long time. It was a good feeling, but unsettling.

"What do you know about General Crook's trail over the Mogollon Rim?" Cole asked.

"Only what Captain Fisher said. It's the shortest route to Fort Apache."

"Won't that be difficult for wagons?" Martha asked. "How will they get up and down the steep canyons?"

Peter's puzzled expression brought Martha up short. "You see," she said, "I did listen to my husband when he talked about Arizona."

"I didn't know you'd been in this part of the country before," Peter said to Cole.

"I haven't," Cole said easily, "but I have a good map." From the way he carefully didn't look at her, she guessed he was angry.

"My map's not worth much," Peter said. "If you don't object, I'd like to see yours."

Cole did look at her. His expression was outwardly amiable, except for his eyes. "Where is the map now, Elizabeth? You asked me for it yesterday."

"I, uh, well . . . I'm afraid it was in my bag, and when I was getting something, it fell out. Whipple chewed it." With wifely apprehension she didn't have to pretend, she added, "I didn't want to tell you."

After an uncomfortable moment of silence, Peter Dunham said, "Who or what is Whipple?"

"My puppy." She smiled at Peter. "I think from his appetite he may be part goat."

He didn't mention the map again. When he picked up his camp chair to leave, he said, "Anyone who eats

Lane's cooking is lucky. I'm glad I'll be at your mess every night the next couple of weeks." The smile he gave her had an edge of slyness to it. Not exactly flirtatious, but a little conspiratorial, as if he and she shared thoughts they shouldn't express in front of Cole.

"You're welcome here, of course, Lieutenant Dunham," she said in her most formal voice.

"Why don't you call me Peter during the evenings?" he said. "Then I'd feel right at home." Turning to Cole, he added, "And you, too, Stephen."

It was easy to figure out Peter expected her to suggest he call her Elizabeth. She didn't wait for Cole to respond. "That's gracious of you, Lieutenant Dunham. It's up to my husband what he does, but I mustn't forget my lesson about rank."

Peter's smile thinned, but he nodded and walked off.

The candle had been lit in the tent. After Martha made her brief excursion into the woods and returned, she found an unsmiling Cole inside. There was a new addition to the tent's equipment, a small iron stove that gave off more warmth than Cole's expression. It seemed a safe topic of conversation. "I didn't know we'd have a stove in the tent."

"Nights get cool in the mountains. But you already know that. I must have told you."

Talking about the stove wasn't safe after all. She sighed. "Yes, I slipped up. I'm sorry. It was a mistake."

"So was hunting up Black Rope," he retorted angrily. "We can't afford mistakes. And Peter Dunham took in both of them. Dunham isn't stupid, though you seem to think you can keep him happy."

She preferred responding to Cole's last accusation to apologizing again for her errors. "I'm not trying to make anyone happy. I can't help it if Lieutenant Dunham is having meals with us."

"If you hadn't been so good at getting his attention, maybe he wouldn't have decided on us."

He was glaring at her, and she returned the glare just as fiercely. "All any woman has to do to attract his attention is be a female. When Whipple is older, he'll be the same as Peter Dunham."

Cole's anger retreated into an expression that gave away nothing. She wished she hadn't spoken so hastily. "Don't you ever make mistakes?" she asked quietly.

"Plenty," he said, "and I know what they cost."

"I'll be careful," she promised, and added stubbornly, "But I haven't tried to make Peter Dunham take an interest in me."

Cole's expression softened a little. "I believe you."

The stove made the tent comfortable, but it reduced the space for moving around. Cole waited outside while she undressed and put out the candle. Some light seeped out from around the stove lid, outlining Cole as he came back in. It seemed only fair that he have the privacy he afforded her, so she closed her eyes. From listening to him undress before, she knew that he took off his outer clothes and left on whatever he wore under those. This time something sounded different, like another garment being pulled over his head. She couldn't resist looking.

He had on light-colored underwear from his waist down to his calves. In the faint light his bare chest and shoulders looked golden brown. Dark shadows of hair trailed down his chest to his waist. From the first day at the stage station she had noticed that his movements were smooth and easy. Now, in the single revealing garment, he looked graceful, as if he were thoroughly comfortable with his body. It reminded her of Apache men, the only men whose bodies she'd seen revealed in that almost proud way. Hard bodies, toughened by their strenuous life, yet fluid in movement. It reminded her of Sharp-Knife's body.

The memory brought a rush of feelings that she'd thought she would never experience again. The longing for touch, for warmth, for passion. With Cole those feelings had been slowly awakening, and they were dangerous. She clamped her eyes shut, but that didn't stop her thoughts. Had Cole ever been in love? He hadn't mentioned a woman when he told her about himself. But a man that masculine must have made love to a woman, probably to many women. From the way he'd looked at her a few times, she was convinced he felt desire for her. With a sense of shock, she realized where her thoughts were taking her. She was more interested in whether he had loved a woman than whether he'd murdered someone.

The stove lid clattered as Cole damped down the fire. The camp cot next to her creaked with his weight. His movements as he settled down jostled her cot ever so slightly, but each one was like a tremor along her nerves. She opened her eyes and stared up into the now dark tent. Sleep, that was what she needed. And to keep her mind on the image of her dark-haired baby.

Cole also was having difficulty relaxing enough to sleep. Doubts unsettled him. Maybe he'd been unfair to Martha about Dunham. She'd spotted him for what he was—a horny bastard. She could have accused someone named Cole Wingate of the same thing. He was plenty horny around her. And she seemed to know a lot about how men felt. Learned from her Apache husband?

Christ! Why couldn't he get that image out of his head? It stuck there—Martha, lying with the Apache. The two bodies, one pale and the other darker. Hands on her breasts.

Cole almost groaned aloud. From what he'd learned, the march to Fort Apache was tough as hell. Men and animals worn out at the end of the day. A good thing, he decided. Maybe that way he'd get some sleep.

By the third day of the march, the wagon road climbed through oaks and cedars at lower altitudes and pines and ash farther up. It began to seem more appropriate for mountain goats than vehicles. The heavily loaded freight wagons often lagged behind the troops and lighter carriages.

At the bottom of a steep pass, Mrs. Fisher's carriage and Martha's ambulance pulled to one side and halted. "Why are we stopping?" Martha called up to Sperry.

"Wagons got to go first," he replied as he climbed down from his driver's perch.

He set out the step and helped Martha, who had picked up Whipple, get out. She set the puppy down and kept a tight hold on the leather leash Sperry had provided. To the left of the narrow road an almost perpendicular rock wall rose to a level area high above. A few tiny pine trees grew out of the rock near the top. On the right side the land dropped off in similarly precipitous fashion to a wooded gorge. The track the wagons must ascend looked narrower than the space a brace of mules needed for their feet.

"Will the wagons be able to get up that?" Martha asked Sperry.

"Never been this way before. But I expect we'll manage."

Alice and Mrs. Fisher descended from the Fishers' carriage, and Martha went to join them. They all watched as the wagons arrived at the bottom of the ascent. Sperry helped hitch six of the extra mules to make up a team of twelve mules for the first freight wagon. The teamster for the wagon began to crack his whip and curse, singling out each mule in turn for an oath. Slowly, to the screeching of axles, the snaps of the whip, and curses, the wagon moved. At first it hugged the trail next to the mountain wall so closely it looked as if the wheels would be rubbed off. Then it swerved toward the drop on the opposite side. Martha held her breath in fear that mules, driver, and wagon would go crashing over the edge. At what seemed the last moment, the wagon lurched back to the left. It continued its swaying path to the top and around a bend out of sight.

Martha heard Alice's and Harriet Fisher's gasps of relief at the same time she let out the breath she'd been holding.

"I can't stand to look," Alice said. "I'm goin' to get back in the carriage."

"Walking up might be easier than riding."

Alice shuddered. "No, I want to be where I can't look." She went to the carriage and climbed inside.

After the second wagon made its lurching way up the pass, a third wagon pulled up to have its team augmented. The two laundresses Martha had seen when the company left Fort Whipple got out of the wagon, followed by a third, who climbed down awkwardly. She was far along in a pregnancy. She stood, rubbing the small of her back.

"How difficult the ride in the heavy wagon must be for that woman," Martha exclaimed.

"Yes, probably so." Harriet Fisher's voice was cool.

By the time the last wagon had made its precarious ascent, the first men of the rear guard detachment had come up. Martha looked for Cole, but he hadn't arrived. Harriet Fisher rejoined Alice in the carriage, and Sperry pulled the ambulance into line. The three laundresses still stood beside the road, along with the soldiers. Martha went to the front of the ambulance and said to Sperry, "Whipple and I will walk up with the other ladies. Can you wait for us at the top or will that hold things up?"

"We all got to wait, ma'am, till the wagons git down the other side." He looked as if he were going to say something more to her but then changed his mind. Slowly, the ambulance moved out after the carriage.

After the dust settled, Martha waited for the laundresses or the soldiers to begin walking. No one moved. Finally a corporal took off his cap, stepped over to her, and said, "We'll be following right along behind you, ma'am."

"Oh, thank you, corporal. I didn't know you were waiting for me." Feeling like a clown who'd been thrust into position at the head of a holiday parade, she tugged on Whipple's lead and started up the road.

Off to the right she could see across to mountains with swaths of dark green pines mixed with lighter green ash. She would have enjoyed the walk immensely, except for Whipple. The puppy didn't understand that they were leaders and must walk briskly. He investigated each rock or mule dropping, and Martha had to yank him along. Her contest with him slowed her down so that the laundresses and soldiers had to stop and wait. She picked him up and carried him, but soon she realized that he was too heavy to carry continuously.

This is ridiculous, she thought. She turned to the women directly behind her. "I apologize for my dog's manners. I'll have to let him down part of the time, so I may be slow. Please, go on ahead."

The three women looked at each other. Finally one, a sturdy middle-aged woman, said, "I'll spell you carrying him. He looks like he weighs a bit."

"Thank you. That's a very kind offer." She handed over the puppy.

Managing Whipple broke the ice. Soon the women responded to Martha's comments about the view. The two younger laundresses looked Mexican, which was confirmed by their soft accents. The pregnant one had beautiful dark eyes and a smooth, glowing skin. Her name was Soledad. She stoically kept up with the rest in spite of her heavy body. She was like Apache women in that, Martha thought, but Soledad must be feeling some strain from the exertion.

When they arrived at the top, they found the ambulance and wagons waiting along a stretch of level trail that ran through a meadow. Martha couldn't stand to see Soledad get back in the freight wagon. By now there were lines of fatigue around the beautiful dark eyes. "Please," Martha said to Soledad. "There's room in the ambulance for one more person. I'd like very much for you to ride there with me." The three women looked at each other in embarrassed silence. "It would be a help with my dog."

Finally the middle-aged woman spoke. "Soledad, if you can serve the lieutenant's lady, it's all right."

Martha didn't want to be served, but she decided to

accept what she'd won. As they walked to the ambulance, they passed Harriet Fisher. After a startled glance at Soledad, Harriet's face settled into disapproving lines. Once inside the ambulance Soledad took Whipple up into what was left of her lap and sat silently.

The image of Harriet Fisher's chilly expression remained with Martha. Though she wasn't sure why Harriet disapproved, she knew Cole wouldn't be pleased. She could only hope the ambulance gave Soledad a better ride than she would have had in the freight wagon because Martha suspected she'd done again what she'd promised Cole to avoid. She'd called attention to herself by her unorthodox behavior.

10

The marchers and the carriage and ambulance arrived at the evening's camp spot long before the wagons. When their ambulance stopped, Soledad gave a quick *Gracias* and disappeared. Martha let Whipple run before giving him to Sperry for the night. Since Cole was with the rear guard that day, she didn't see him until after the freight wagons had reached the camping site and their tent was up, its flaps tied back, and the tent chairs set out in front. He arrived at their camp looking tired. Concerned, she said, "You must have had a hard day."

"Not bad," he said. "Mrs. Fisher just gave me a message. She'd like you to go to talk to her. She didn't look too happy. What's this about?"

"I don't know." Martha was afraid she did know, but she hoped she was wrong. Harriet Fisher must remember what pregnancy felt like. That was something no woman forgot.

When Martha arrived at the Fishers' campsite, Harriet was waiting. "Please sit down," she said, indicating Captain Fisher's chair and taking the one opposite. She barely paused for Martha to sit before she began. "I realize that you are new to the army, Elizabeth, but it is your responsibility to know and follow the rules."

"I didn't know I'd broken any rules," Martha ventured.

"Not all rules are in the Army Regulations," Harriet said tartly. "The army has its ways, and it requires that officers *and their wives* maintain a proper distance from the enlisted ranks and their families. An officer cannot be soft. In battle discipline is essential. In order to succeed and for the safety of all the men."

"Yes, I understand that," Martha said as amiably as she could. "But I don't understand how that affects wives, who aren't in battle."

Harriet frowned. "Only the strict habits of daily life off the battlefield can achieve this discipline. If enlisted men see their . . . wives encouraged in familiar behavior toward the wife of an officer, they lose respect for that officer. That leads to breaches of discipline."

Martha wanted to protest that showing compassion ought to command more, not less, respect. But she repeated only, "Yes, I understand." She did know the army must have discipline. And so must she, she thought unhappily.

Harriet's expression relaxed from disapproval into patience. "In the army, Elizabeth, our husbands don't question decisions made by wiser and more experienced men. Our place as wives is to do as much." She leaned closer and whispered, "These women who travel with the enlisted men may not even be wives."

She rose, the picture of a headmistress who has finally gotten through to an especially dense student.

"I'm sure you have a very kind nature, Elizabeth. But let your husband direct you in these matters."

Martha almost choked on a smile, but she managed to get out the words. "Thank you, Mrs. Fisher, for your concern." She and Cole had enough problems without adding censure by the commanding officer's wife. Since she was clearly dismissed, she nodded and started back to her camp. Just as she reached it, Peter Dunham caught up with her.

"Elizabeth Baldwin," he said, "you're an unusual woman. I think that what you appear isn't all there is to you. Are you sure you're just an ordinary wife?"

Martha's heart felt as if it momentarily forgot to beat. Then she laughed. "Who would come to this wild country except an ordinary wife following her husband? Especially when the road is like the one today."

Cole came out of the tent, his hair wet, a basin of water in his hand. "Has anyone told you about your wife's traveling companion?" Peter asked.

"No," Cole said calmly. "If it's interesting, she'll tell me later." He went off to toss out the water from the basin.

Peter looked disappointed. He needn't be, thought Martha. He'd been successful in exacerbating trouble. She wasn't going to repeat Peter's remark; he had to be only flirting. She could easily be formal enough to discourage him. But she would have to tell Cole exactly why Harriet Fisher wanted to talk to her. That would be bad enough.

Cole was quiet during the meal. Peter was especially talkative, but he didn't bring up Martha's indiscretion with Soledad. She wondered how he knew about her activities when Cole didn't. It might be that he was more interested in what she did than Cole, except that

Cole had a major stake in her activities.

After dinner, the Fishers' orderly came to say that they were invited to the campfire at the commanding officer's tent site. On the way Alice and Fred Collins joined them.

At the campfire they put down their chairs and accepted cups of coffee that the Fishers' striker passed around. Captain Fisher greeted Martha with a touch of frost in his manner. He was warmer when he spoke to Cole. Probably pitied Cole for having a foolish wife, Martha thought.

By contrast, Harriet Fisher seemed delighted to see Martha. "How is your puppy getting along?" she asked.

"According to Private Sperry, Whipple is learning to stay away from the mules. And he's been very good in the ambulance."

One of the scouts had seen a small group of Apaches that turned out to be a family traveling north. "Is it safe to be sittin' here?" Alice said.

"Apaches usually don't attack at night," Captain Fisher said.

Alice asked anxiously, "If Apaches don't attack at night, when do they attack?"

"Generally just before daylight," the captain replied, "so you can sleep comfortably."

"Sleep!" Alice protested. "Now I won't sleep at all. I'll be waitin' for daylight."

Captain Fisher frowned. "You don't have to worry, Mrs. Collins," he said reprovingly. "General Crook subdued most of the hostile Apaches two years ago before he left."

Alice still looked apprehensive, and Martha wondered whether any of the men were concealing nervousness. They were right to worry; Apaches attacked with great brutality. But the Apaches also feared white men, and with equally good reason.

Before long Harriet Fisher stood up, the signal for dismissal. Martha would have been happy to linger around the fire, to postpone answering Cole's questions about her talk with Mrs. Fisher. The walk back to their campsite felt shorter than the same distance earlier. Fred seemed especially solicitous of Alice, assuring her that he would protect her from the Apaches. Who could protect her, Martha wondered, from her own impulsiveness and from Cole's anger? Yet if she saw Soledad in that situation again, it would be hard not to behave the same.

When the tent flaps closed behind them, she began before he could ask. "Mrs. Fisher wanted to see me because I behaved improperly for an army wife," she said, and went on to describe just what she had done.

Cole's expression didn't change during her recital. Finally he said, "That doesn't sound too bad."

Her confusion must have showed on her face because he sounded amused as he continued, "Harriet Fisher acted pretty pleased with you tonight. And helping the laundress was a kind thing to do." Then he added soberly, "It's having too much knowledge about the country and the Indians that can make the Fishers suspect us. But you didn't say anything tonight about Apache attacks. I know you wanted to."

Martha felt warm with pleasure. He'd understood how she felt, and he'd complimented her. Another emotion warmed her also, one she hadn't experienced in years—a feeling of sharing problems. Of comradeship.

He was studying her. "You look . . . I'm not sure. Did something nice happen I don't know about?"

"I thought we were going to have an argument. That you'd be angry about Soledad because Mrs. Fisher talked to me."

"Am I that hard to get along with?" He said it lightly, but she thought he sounded a little uncertain, as if her opinion mattered to him.

"Sometimes. You can be fierce when you're angry. I liked it just now when you approved of what I did. In the town where I was living with my grandmother no one I knew approved of anything about me."

"You were lonesome," he guessed accurately. "I was better off than that. Ira Gurnett, my father's friend in Tucson, believes in me. That means a lot."

"Yes. Tonight you seem like my . . . friend," she said, and then felt awkward.

"That's good." Cole seemed embarrassed also. Martha reminded herself that she and Cole had a temporary arrangement—if they got along better, that was temporary too.

Later, as they lay in their cots in the dark tent, he asked, "What will you do if you find your boy? Where will you go?"

"*When* I find him, I'll . . . I don't know, but I'll manage."

He was silent for several moments. "Lots of places a half-breed isn't welcome, especially when it's his mother who's white and not his father."

"My family has money. I can find a place to go." She knew she was avoiding reality. For so long she had clung to the image of the toddler instead of the boy who would be a stranger to her. If she thought about where they would go, she had to picture the boy. And money—what about that? Martha Turner, as far as anyone knew, was dead, cut off from her family's wealth.

But there were ways. Other women managed, alone with a child. So could she.

Cole was also thinking about Martha and the child she hoped to find. The half-Indian child who was born because she lay with her Indian husband. Often he reminded himself that he wouldn't let that picture affect him. But lying beside her, night after night, he wasn't sure he cared about his motives. Even when they were quarreling, he felt the excitement between them. The stereotype of a white woman and an Indian man might be part of it, but his scruples were fading fast.

He was determined not to feel responsible for her. But the hell with all that. He wanted her—wanted to undress her, touch her breasts and the soft skin at the back of her neck. Spend himself inside her. She wanted him too. He could tell by the way she looked at him sometimes.

He couldn't see holding out much longer. One of these nights he'd be doing his damnedest to get her into bed.

The fifteenth day after leaving Fort Whipple, the march came down through a side canyon into a river valley with cottonwood trees marking the river's course. Word came back along the line that this was the north fork of the White River. Fort Apache was four miles to the south. Martha took Whipple and got out of the ambulance, then walked alongside. She was too excited to ride.

At the top of a small rise, she looked down on the moving column of blue-jacketed men. They had almost reached a fork where the White River came in from the east. Along the far bank of that river she glimpsed a single row of log cabins set among medium-size trees. A large open area beyond with a flagpole had to be the parade ground. More buildings of varying sizes lay at the far side and end of the parade ground. Though not as large as Fort Whipple, Fort Apache was larger than Camp Mojave or Fort Yuma.

Martha picked up her puppy and said excitedly in his ear, "Look, Whipple. That's where we're going to stay for a while. It's big enough that no one's going to pay attention to what I do. At least, not much, I hope."

Sperry called to her. "Ma'am, we'll be fording the river. Best git inside before then." When she reached the wagon, he added slyly, " 'Less you want to walk cross the bridge with the troops."

Clearly she'd already earned a reputation with Sperry for behavior that wasn't ordinary.

"Thank you, Private Sperry. I think I'll ride."

They passed gardens where two soldiers stopped hoeing to exchange shouts with the column and watch them pass. What had first appeared to be brushy mounds on the opposite side of the river from the fort turned out to look familiar. Martha clutched Whipple with excitement. "Wickiups!" she whispered to him. "Apache houses." She strained to see more. As the distance narrowed, she could see people near the wickiups and a few smaller figures. Children!

Whipple gave a protesting yelp and tried to squirm away from her. She relaxed her grip on him and soothed him with fingers that trembled. It was ridiculous to think that one of those children was Pinecone. Her search could end in failure. But the hope that had burned inside her since Cole had agreed to her scheme wouldn't subside.

They were close enough to the fort that she could

see women near the line of log cabins—wives out to watch the arrival of new troops, she guessed. Over the sounds of carriage wheels and creaking leather harnesses she heard the resonant ring of a blacksmith's anvil. The ambulance rumbled along until it reached a wide, shallow stretch of the river. A little farther downstream the last of the soldiers were marching across a wooden bridge. Ahead the Fishers' carriage made its cautious way through the water and pulled up onto the opposite bank. Sperry shouted and slapped the reins over the mules' backs. As if they sensed an end to their labors, they started forward enthusiastically.

Martha's heart felt as if it filled her chest. She didn't want to nurture false hope but she somehow believed that here she'd find what she sought.

11

Private Lane's usually genial expression was glum. Cole noticed it as soon as the striker had looked around Cole's and Martha's newly assigned quarters. It amounted to a single room, half of one of the log houses in officers' row, with a kitchen shed in back. It also had a wide hall running from the front to the back of the building. The hall was shared with the tenant of the other side, the post surgeon.

"I think I can find a dining table, Mrs. Baldwin," Lane said in an unhappy-sounding voice. "Do you want me to put it in the hall?"

Cole waited for Martha to respond to the striker's question, but she was looking out a window. "Elizabeth," he finally said to her, "Lane needs your answer."

She turned around partway, as if she were attached to the window and couldn't move farther. Her face was bright, her blue eyes animated and her skin flushed. Cole thought she'd never looked prettier.

"I'm sorry, Private Lane," she said. "What did you ask me?"

He repeated his question, and she said, "Yes, thank you. That seems to be the only place we can eat." He nodded morosely and left.

Before she could look outside again, Cole said, "You need to act interested in our quarters. Lane expects it."

"Oh, dear. Is that why he seems discouraged?"

"Probably he's unhappy because there's no place here for him to sleep. Besides the six dollars a month, a soldier takes the job of striker so he can have a room to himself. Lane will have to go back to the barracks at night."

"I'm sorry Lane's disappointed," she said thoughtfully, "but if he can't live here, that's better for us. I was trying to think of a way to let him go."

He could see trouble ahead again. "Wait a minute. Remember, you're Elizabeth. She might do some naive things, but no woman like her would turn down a servant."

She sighed, but it wasn't a sad sigh. "Why must you be right so often? It's ungentlemanly."

"I never said I'm a gentleman." He intended to be stern but didn't make it. "Look, will you promise something?"

"What?"

"If you want to do anything . . . say, a little different from what other army wives do, talk it over with me first."

A small frown dampened Martha's cheerful expression. Finally she said, "I know what I do affects you. So I'll talk to you if I can."

Her eyes had lost their excited sparkle and Cole felt guilty. "Come on. We can't unpack until Lane collects furniture. I don't have to be on duty today. Let's find someone from the cavalry and get a tour of the post."

She smiled happily, and he felt rewarded. "Oh, yes. I'd like to do that. I'll get Whipple."

After she brought the puppy from behind the quarters where he'd been tied, they went out through the front hall. The row of houses for the officers faced the parade ground. Their half-house was at the opposite end from the much larger quarters of Fort Apache's commanding officer. When they reached the boardwalk that ran in front of the row, Martha immediately looked off to the north, across the river toward the wickiups.

"Do you know who has the other side of our house?" Cole asked.

She turned to him. "Don't you know?"

"Yes, but you haven't asked. Aren't you interested?" He had her attention now. "Please tell me."

"The post doctor has the other half of our house. He's not here right now, but he's due back soon. His name is George Lawton."

"Have you learned anything about Fort Apache?"

"It was set up in 1872." It occurred to him that five years ago would be about the time her brother had ransomed her. "We're relieving a couple of Eighth Infantry companies."

"Just C Company, by itself, taking the place of two other companies? If Alice knows that, she'll worry about Fred."

"C Company is a hundred men—full strength," he explained. "The ones we're replacing have lost a lot of men."

"In fights with Indians?"

"More soldiers die from getting sick than are killed by Indians. And lots of soldiers desert."

She looked concerned, but he wasn't sure what bothered her, soldiers dying or Indians dying.

A second lieutenant from the Sixth Cavalry came out of the adjutant's office, directly across from the end of the row. He had a freckled young face, sandy hair, and a mustache that made him look like a boy trying to appear grown-up. "Hello," he said when he saw Martha and Cole. "I'm Albert Parker. You're from the new infantry company."

"Yes," Cole responded. "I'm Stephen Baldwin." After he presented Lieutenant Parker to Martha, Cole said, "We're out to see something of the post."

"Let me show you around," Lieutenant Parker offered.

He turned out to be a thorough guide, starting them out past the quartermaster's office and storehouses and the adjacent stone guardhouse. From there they turned along the edge of the parade ground and went past the infantry quarters, which were small separate buildings, the flagpole, and a large barracks for cavalry troopers. "Those," he said, gesturing to three long, narrow buildings near the quarters, "are the kitchens."

"What are those small cabins in a row behind the kitchens?" Martha asked. Cabin was too dignified a name for the haphazard mixture of canvas, stone, adobe, log, and slab shelters.

"That's where the laundresses live," Lieutenant Parker responded. "When you want to have some washing done, send your striker and he can arrange it."

"How convenient," she said with a pleased smile. Cole guessed that her real interest was in seeing what happened to the pregnant laundress she'd befriended.

"What else would you like to see?" Lieutenant Parker asked. "We're not close to a town, but we have most everything we need—carpenter, blacksmith, stone quarry, sawmill." He laughed, a cheerful, boyish laugh. "I guess those don't interest you, Mrs. Baldwin. You'll want to know about the post trader. He's out east of the corrals. The schoolhouse is out that way too. But I guess you're not interested in that either, unless you have children."

"No children," Cole volunteered.

"What are those round things that look like big piles of mud and sticks?" Martha asked. "The ones across the river from our quarters. I saw Indians around them."

"Those are called wickiups," Lieutenant Parker said. "The Apache scouts live there." He pointed to a large building directly ahead at the far end of the parade ground. "That's the new hospital. The old hospital is behind it."

Whipple, whom Martha had restrained to a dignified walk, started pulling her in the direction of the hospital. When Cole saw two Apaches sitting on a bench in front, he suspected Martha was letting the dog drag her toward the Apaches. He reached over and took the leash, halting the puppy in midstep and tumbling him over. "Whipple needs to learn more manners," he said to her. "Maybe we'd better head back and tie him up now."

She gave Lieutenant Parker a sidelong glance, then said, "Yes, perhaps we should."

Just as they started across to the row of officers' quarters, a detachment of troopers in dusty pants, flannel shirts, and campaign hats rode past. The handkerchiefs around their necks fluttered like miniature jaunty flags. "They're going out to check up on the Apaches over in the bottomland," Lieutenant Parker explained. "The Indians grow some food there."

"Are there many Apaches living close by?" Martha asked.

"Three bands."

"Do they come to the fort?"

"Yes, once a week on ration day to get their food. But don't worry, we keep them in good order. You might like to watch when they come in."

"Yes, I would," Martha said. Cole had to admire her control; she sounded only mildly interested. But then she asked, "What days will that be?" a little too eagerly.

A large black dog ran by, and Whipple began to bark furiously. Cole let the pup carry on for a minute before he stopped him and said, "I think we'll definitely take this dog back and tie him up. Thanks, Mr. Parker, for the tour."

After Martha added her thanks, they left the lieutenant and headed toward the far end of officers' row. Martha picked up Whipple and carried him, giving Cole a rebellious glance. "It wouldn't have hurt to look at those Apaches by the hospital," she protested. "Or to ask Lieutenant Parker more questions."

"You'll find out plenty by listening or asking questions later. If you did run across an Apache you recognized, he might know you. That could cause us a hell of a lot of trouble."

Her face grew sad, and she said quietly, "I'll be cautious, but no one will recognize me. I'm just a white woman now."

Cole wasn't sure what she meant. Again he had the feeling he hadn't learned much about her. Not nearly enough.

Martha saw Cole's troubled expression and guessed that he was perplexed by her changing moods. She didn't understand herself either.

When they arrived at their quarters, she went around to the back and tied up Whipple, then looked across at the wickiups. Under the shade of an open brush-covered *ramada*, two Apache women were tending a cooking fire. Martha realized that a chasm greater than the river canyon with its steep banks separated her from those women. Time stood between them and her—time and the person she'd become.

After a few pats to console Whipple, she followed Cole inside. Lane was there. In their living-bedroom, new canvas, nailed down, covered the scarred floorboards. Two iron cots, a small table, and their folding camp chairs gave the room a surprisingly homelike appearance. Martha could smell fresh straw, and when she stepped on the canvas, it had a spring to it and gave off a faint crunching sound. Lane had put straw down under the canvas. "How did you manage all this?" she asked him admiringly.

His black mustache quivered with a pleased smile, showing his missing tooth. "Friend in quartermaster," he said.

"I'm sorry there's not a room for you here."

"That's all right, ma'am. Assignments to quarters can change mighty quick. We'll get the kitchen fixed up tomorrow." He said this last eagerly. Clearly he enjoyed his reputation as a good cook.

Soon after Lane left, a note arrived. The officers and wives already at the post were inviting the new arrivals to dinner that night in the old hospital building. "When we arrived at each of the army posts so far,"

Martha said to Cole, "someone entertained us. Is this what usually happens?"

"I think so. Army people look out for each other."

She felt a little guilty. The other army families believed that she and Cole were like them. "They're very generous."

"Once we're settled in here, you'll have your share of looking after people who pass through."

"Yes," she said thoughtfully. "I suppose that's so. You're already doing Stephen Baldwin's job."

Cole sat down in one of the chairs and leaned forward, his hands resting on his knees. "What's the trouble?"

She felt a burning behind her eyes and realized, astonished, that it was the beginning of tears. "It's foolish," she said slowly, "but I hadn't expected to 'settle in' here. I guess all I thought about was reaching the White Mountain Apache area."

"We're here. No one's caught on to us yet. So what's wrong?"

His quiet question was forcing her to face a hope, so secret she hadn't admitted it to herself. "I think I was expecting to return to the past. Somehow when I got here, I imagined Pinecone would magically appear." She rushed on, before he could say it. "I know, it was crazy. I didn't even know that was how I felt. Your question about whether an Apache might recognize me—well, it made me think how everything's changed. And I realize how impossible my fantasy is."

"Now you're not sure you'll find your child?"

Immediately she was wary. "Is that what you'd like—for me to give up looking?"

A half smile acknowledged her right to be suspicious. "I admit I've had that thought a few times."

"Well, I won't give up!" she said fiercely.

"Just so we agree on what we're doing." He was serious again.

"I already promised I'd talk things over with you."

"I expect you to keep that promise. I'm keeping mine."

When she didn't respond, he got up. "There's a water barrel outside. I'll bring in whatever you need for washing up. I can use the post bathhouse. Then we'll have to get over to the old hospital and make sure everyone takes us for Elizabeth and Stephen Baldwin."

As he left Martha thought that they were back to where they'd always been. Conspirators who were also in some ways contestants. No, that wasn't true. In the beginning she would never have told him any of her thoughts. She'd just admitted some very private ones.

When Cole had put on his dress uniform and Martha a rose silk dress, they went to the adobe building that was the old hospital. Tables were set for dinner in what must have been a ward. Harriet Fisher came over to greet them. "Please join the other officers of C Company. My husband will introduce you to the fort commander."

Soon afterward Lt. Col. Richard Stratton and his wife arrived. The colonel was a slender man with thinning gray hair, large ears, and a white mustache that spread out in a fan and concealed his mouth. Martha decided she liked his face. His wife looked much younger than he. Her dark brown hair, piled up and curled around her face, had no gray, and her face was smooth.

Captain Fisher began his introductions with his

most senior officer, Vernon Brown, then went down the line, introducing Peter Dunham and next Fred Collins. Finally he said, "And I wish to present Stephen Baldwin, our newest officer."

Cole saluted. Colonel Stratton returned the salute and repeated the formal words he'd used for each man, "I'm pleased to welcome you to Fort Apache."

At dinner Martha was glad to find Lieutenant Parker next to her. "Never short of fresh meat here," he said. "The hunting keeps us supplied with deer and wild turkey. Your husband will love it." The speed with which his generous portion of turkey disappeared suggested that the fort needed lots of hunters.

Martha realized she didn't know whether Cole liked to hunt. Since she'd never heard of a man who didn't, she said, "Yes. He'll be pleased about that."

"Good fishing, too. Do you like to fish, Mrs. Baldwin?"

She remembered a time when she'd liked to fish because she liked to eat, not for the pleasure of it. Here it would be a way to explore outside the fort. "Yes, I do."

"Mrs. Stratton will be happy to hear that. She loves to fish, but none of the other ladies here cared for it."

Alice Collins, who was sitting across from them, said, "Is it safe to go fishing? What about the Indians?"

"We send an escort when any of you ladies go outside the post," Lieutenant Parker assured Alice.

Martha felt a sharp moment of disappointment when she realized she couldn't roam through the reservation by herself, even as an army wife.

"The quartermaster can get you ladies good horses to ride," he continued.

Riding! That was a way to range good distances.

Martha said eagerly, "That will be wonderful."

After dinner the men went outside to smoke. When they returned, Cole and Lieutenant Parker joined Martha and Alice. Lieutenant Parker listed more advantages of Fort Apache—the clear air, the pleasant climate, good hunting. "And if you don't want game, you can order beef and mutton from the contractor in Tucson."

That seemed a curious arrangement to Martha. "Can a contractor afford to ship meat all the way out here?"

"Oh, yes. Selling to the army is good business. They supply rations for the Indians too. Contractors that service the army posts and reservations in Arizona make good money. Some of the Indian agents think the contractors get too rich." He shrugged. "It's probably the same around all army posts."

Cole said, "You say the contractor is from Tucson?"

"Yes, I think so. Lieutenant Young, the quartermaster, can tell you for sure."

Cole didn't ask anything more, and the conversation turned to hunting. Lieutenant Parker described his favorite route and offered to show it to Cole, who agreed. The two men excused themselves and went outside. When Cole returned, he joined a group of officers that included the quartermaster.

While Alice and one of the cavalry wives talked, Martha half listened. She was more intrigued by Cole's interest in the quartermaster. Ned Young was a chunky, clean-shaven first lieutenant with a fringe of hair around his shiny head. He appeared to be telling stories. Cole was laughing with the others, but she could tell by the way he stood, shoulders square and back straight, that he wasn't relaxed. She and Cole were beginning to know each other well. She could tell quite a bit about his mood from watching him. He was becoming adept at judging her in the same way.

Harriet Fisher came across the room, bringing one of the two infantry wives who was leaving soon. Reluctantly Martha returned her attention to the conversation around her. The departing wife, a Mrs. Kendall, explained that she didn't plan to take all of her household items with her. "We're to be stationed in San Francisco for some time," she said happily, "so my husband and I will have an auction before we leave."

After Mrs. Kendall walked on, Harriet Fisher said, "It's hard to get along on an officer's pay. And on isolated army posts it's difficult to get things you need. We all help each other."

The army, Martha decided, was like a club, with rules and obligations, and also loyalties. She and Cole had a membership that didn't belong to them. Her feelings about what had seemed a daring but simple idea were becoming more complicated all the time.

Colonel Stratton looked around with the air of a man who wanted to leave. The married men began breaking away from their groups and seeking out wives. Cole had just reached Martha when a man she hadn't seen before entered. He had thick white hair and a weary, aristocratic face that contrasted with a drab civilian suit. Surrounded by men elegant in gilt-trimmed blue and scarlet sashes, he looked like an aging duck with the head of a swan.

Lieutenant Parker said, "That's George Lawton, the post surgeon."

"He has the other half of our quarters," Martha said.

"Dr. Lawton's been around here a long time. He can tell you more about Fort Apache than anyone else."

Movements toward departure stopped while Dr.

Lawton apologized for coming in so late. "I've been at the San Carlos reservation," he said. "Too many Apaches from different areas, all crowded together. Makes for lots of sickness and problems. Some of the warriors have been leaving."

Major Owens, who commanded one of the two cavalry troops, said angrily, "The Interior Department with their crazy removal policy is to blame. Just wait. Those warriors will be raiding. There'll be settlers murdered. We'll have every trooper out chasing the hostiles. Then the editors of the *Citizen* will sit in their office down in Tucson and blame the army for not doing its job."

Colonel Stratton said sharply, "That's enough talk for now." The major subsided, but his bushy blond sideburns still quivered like the ruff of a dog.

Distressed, Martha wished the major hadn't been cut off. A copy of the *Arizona Citizen* she saw during the stage stop at Tucson reported that conditions were fairly stable and peaceful on the reservations. The doctor's report sounded alarming. Trouble from Apache raids could make searching for her son even harder.

The fort commander and his wife left. Others began to depart also. After Alice and Fred said good night, Lieutenant Parker took Cole and Martha over to George Lawton. The doctor put down a large glass half full of whiskey. He responded politely to Lieutenant Parker's introductions, but Martha had the impression he preferred his drink to meeting his new neighbors.

She longed to ask him more about conditions on the reservations, but she knew this wasn't the time. "I hope we'll have a chance to get acquainted soon," she said.

"Yes, that will be pleasant," he said with more ritual than warmth. "I'm sorry I wasn't here to welcome you.

I take mess with the adjutant, so I won't be in your way, Mrs. Baldwin. I'll see you tomorrow, Mr. Baldwin, when you bring over your medical records."

"I'm afraid I don't have those," Cole said.

"You haven't heard about Mr. and Mrs. Baldwin's adventures," Lieutenant Parker said with what sounded like envy.

George Lawton smiled, which only added to the weary lines of his face. "I can write to Washington for a copy of your records, Mr. Baldwin. They'll send them on."

The doctor's words hit Martha's ears like the urgent clanging of the fire bell in her Texas town. How quickly could records arrive—records that wouldn't fit Cole?

Except for a tiny line at the corner of each eye, Cole looked undisturbed. "I'm healthy," he said.

Dr. Lawton sent a sidelong glance in the direction of his half-finished drink. They all exchanged good-byes. As Martha and Cole were going out the door, she looked back. The doctor had finished the rest of his drink.

Outside on the walk, to still her growing alarm, she said to Cole, "Maybe the doctor drinks so much that he wouldn't notice or care what Stephen Baldwin's medical records say."

"Not likely. Some men can drink a lot and still do as well as most anybody else sober. If George Lawton's been here a long time, he's probably that kind of drinker."

"But the medical records—what can we do?"

Cole walked a few minutes without answering. No one else was nearby, and silence of the night was like a sound itself. It seemed peaceful, but Martha didn't feel at peace.

Finally Cole said, "I don't know. I'll have to figure out something. Maybe find out how mail comes in and make friends with the people who handle it. If I'm very lucky, I could get hold of the records myself."

"You mean steal them? That would be terribly dangerous!"

Cole said sardonically, "What we're doing isn't exactly safe. Stealing mail won't add much rope to the one they can hang me with. Anyway, we can't do anything about it now."

His composed voice steadied her, and she felt ashamed for letting her feelings get out of hand. She'd survived far worse situations than this.

They reached their quarters and went about their rituals of getting ready for the night. After Martha was in bed and Cole returned, he moved his bed away from Martha's. "I'll put it back in the morning, before Lane gets here," he said.

He snuffed the candle. A moment later she heard him bang into the edge of the metal cot, and then an explosive "Dammit!" was followed by muttered words that were probably obscene.

His reaction seemed out of proportion to the sound of the blow. "Are you hurt?" she asked.

"No!"

The rustling of the straw bed sack under his mattress told her he was finally settled. Now she could relax and sleep. But all her muscles were tense, and she found it hard to breathe. It must be the unsettling news she'd heard at the party that was bothering her. Potential trouble with the Indians. The threat of the medical records.

No—that wasn't the whole reason for the way she was feeling. It was also being here, in this room, with

Cole. They had shared closer quarters than this in the tent. But those had been temporary. Here they would "settle in," and each night would be followed by another that was the same. Each night she would listen, as she was doing now, to his breathing and, without thinking, match her breaths to his. Along with the odors of fresh straw and canvas she recognized the scent that was particularly his. It seemed like part of hers. He stirred, and she felt the movement.

Remember! she told herself. *Remember how you thought you couldn't love an Apache husband, but you did. Remember how painful it was when he died. Remember your son and why you're here. Don't fall in love with Cole.*

She hoped her advice wasn't too late.

12

When trumpeter's assembly call sounded the next morning, Martha barely roused and went back to sleep. At the bugle call for reveille fifteen minutes later, she stirred lazily. Cole would be dressed and gone, but she didn't feel like getting up yet.

There was a creak and then a rustle from the other bed. Startled, she sat up. Cole was just throwing back the blanket. He stopped in midmotion and looked at her. Tousled dark brown hair fell across his forehead. His eyes had faint lines under them and were decidedly unfriendly. His beard didn't conceal the tight line of his mouth. She'd seen pictures in post offices of outlaws who looked less intimidating than he did.

Maybe he was sick. "What's wrong?" she asked.

"Nothing," he snapped.

"But you're usually dressed when I—"

"Today I'm not," he interrupted. "I can't arrange everything I do to suit you."

She continued to stare at him, taken aback by his rude tone.

He scowled at her. "Do you mind if I put my clothes on now? Or are you planning to watch?"

"Of course not." She lay down and turned so she faced the wall. The noises from his movements were abrupt. When he put on his boots, the heels hit the floor loudly enough to waken the doctor in the other side of the house.

When the door finally banged behind Cole, Martha felt as out of sorts as he sounded. He had looked tired, as if he hadn't slept. She hadn't slept well herself. She'd stayed awake, mooning over him, imagining she might fall in love with him. How ridiculous!

She got up and dressed. Something was bothering Cole, but he wouldn't be so silly as to stay awake thinking about her, she decided a little wistfully. In the first weeks they'd known each other, there had been times she was sure from the way he'd looked at her that he desired her. The same feelings she'd felt stirring in her. But not lately. Not, she realized, since she'd told him about Sharp-Knife and the baby.

Cole had seemed to accept her story without the disgust she'd feared, but he must have kept it hidden. Even her brother hadn't been able to conceal his dismay at having a sister so degraded. It was unfair, but she'd cried too many tears over that in the past. Eventually she had learned not to let Benjamin's opinion bother her. She could ignore Cole's too.

She undid her nighttime braid and brushed her hair with determined strokes. Last night's folly and this morning's clearer understanding should be a reminder that she and Cole had different lives, different interests, different futures.

HEARTBREAK TRAIL

On her return from the privy behind the house she realized that Lane would be arriving and that Cole hadn't pushed the cots back together. When the cot did budge, it left a mark on the canvas that Lane could clearly see. She decided it didn't matter. The striker could think that she and Cole had quarreled, like a real married couple.

When Lane arrived, another soldier helped him carry in two large trunks and a chest. Martha recognized the chest; it held the supplies she'd bought in Camp Mojave. But she didn't see the barrel of purchases from Yuma, and she didn't recognize the trunks. After the second soldier left, she said to Lane, "Are you sure these are our things?"

"If you're looking for the missing barrel," he replied gloomily, "it broke loose from the ropes on one of the wagons and went down a mountainside."

"Oh, dear," she said and tried to remember what was in it. Yuma seemed a lifetime away. The barrel, she finally recalled, had held tinware and dishes. They didn't seem really important, but cooking and eating had to go on. A solution occurred to her. "One of the women I met last night said she planned to sell some household goods."

Lane looked more cheerful. "Well, now, ma'am, I'd say that's lucky. And it was a smart thing you shipped your trunks to Yuma. Those thieves that stopped that stagecoach might've wrecked them."

So, Martha realized, that accounted for the strange trunks. "Yes, we were fortunate."

"I'll just see about fixing up the kitchen shed," he said. "It'll take a while."

As soon as he left, she inspected the trunks. They were metal, held together by bands of wood, with brass corners. One, which had Stephen Baldwin's name on it, looked worn. The other gave off the smell of new leather. Stenciled on the wood slats of the top was *Mrs. Stephen Baldwin, care of Second Lieutenant Stephen Baldwin, Fort Yuma, Arizona Territory*. Elizabeth must have purchased it for the trip, or perhaps it had been part of her trousseau. Its unused appearance seemed to Martha like Elizabeth's hopes—new and shining—and its construction sturdy enough for a long life. Sadly Martha found the keys that had been in Elizabeth Baldwin's purse.

The second one she tried opened the trunk. A tray held small articles of clothing on one side: soft ivory leather gloves, two embroidered collars, a rolled up corset, and lace-trimmed camisoles and shifts. Photographs were neatly stacked in the opposite side. Martha spread them out, and put together a family. A middle-aged woman with hair severely drawn back from a plain but kind face must be Elizabeth's mother Mrs. Polk. Mr. Polk was beside her, looking proudly at the camera. Others were of children in different stages of growing up. Tears filled Martha's throat. She was glad the family still had other daughters.

Sorting through the photographs gave Martha a strange feeling. She had never seen these people and they would never meet her. Even so, she felt a connection, however fraudulent, to them. Reluctantly she set aside all the pictures that included Elizabeth after she passed the baby stage. Those would have to be destroyed.

Underneath the tray she found several wrapped bundles. A very lumpy one was a new dress helmet, its plume carefully protected with stiff paper. Perhaps, Martha thought, it was in Elizabeth's trunk because she intended it as a gift for her husband. Cole would look very handsome in it. Another bundle held a woman's hat, a small yellow straw to perch daintily on top of piled-up curls. Martha hadn't felt giddy enough for a hat like that since she was fourteen. As she opened other bundles she found dresses that were more daring than any she'd owned—with low necklines and tight waists, meant to be worn with the corset. She stroked the silks and soft muslin and felt as if she were being offered a carefree, frivolous time that had been taken from her when she was forced to become a woman before she was ready.

The last bundle was like a misshapen ball. She unwrapped layer after layer of soft, worn flannel and uncovered a deep blue porcelain teapot. It was short and round, with a wide band of gold around the pot just above the spout and lacy whorls of gold dripping from the band like fringes on a shawl. Tea had stained the rim and bottom of the white interior. Martha set the carefully secured treasure on the little table Lane had brought in the previous day. It was a gift to her from Elizabeth. Martha was astonished at how much she liked it. Is that what she wanted, a home, with a teapot to use over and over again?

Carefully she stored the pictures she must destroy in the bottom of the trunk and placed clothing over them. She put on her own hat, a brown straw, and went out to the back. Lane had found lumber and was putting up shelves in the kitchen shed, whistling a cheerful tune while he worked. "I'm going to see Mrs. Kendall," she said to Lane, "about buying dishes and pots from her."

Whipple ran a little circle around her, barking. "No, Whipple. You can't go with me. I'll take you out later and let you run." Lane restrained the dog while she left. As she walked, she speculated that having to chase after a puppy could be useful. He'd be her excuse for going outside the boundaries of the post.

Mrs. Kendall greeted Martha pleasantly. Martha explained about the loss of their barrel of dishes and pots. "I'd like to buy some dishes now," she said.

Martha chose enough dishes for four people, a coffee pot, and two pans. When she paid for them, she mentally counted the money she had left. When she'd been an Apache wife, she'd had Sharp-Knife's family to rely on. It seemed strange to think she'd been better off in that way as a captive than she was now. Three hundred dollars in gold had seemed like a fortune, but it could go quickly once she found her son. Cole was right that she might have to go far away to escape the stigma of having a half-Indian child.

When Martha arrived back at her quarters, she told Lane, "I purchased dishes from Mrs. Kendall. Would you please go and get them?"

"Yes, ma'am. And, ma'am, I found this photograph on the floor." He held out a picture of the Polk family, with Elizabeth seated prominently in front.

"Oh, no! How could I be so careless!" She didn't need to pretend to be appalled.

"Now, ma'am," Lane said, sounding almost as distressed as she was, "the picture isn't damaged."

She took the picture. "Yes, I see it isn't. Thank you, Lane."

"Is it your family? I hope you don't mind that I looked at it."

"No, of course I don't mind. It's my family, but I'm not in the picture."

He smiled. "I didn't see anyone who looked like you."

"I take after my grandmother, who lives in Texas."

He straightened up, as if she'd called him to attention. "Then she must be a handsome woman, if you don't mind my saying so, ma'am."

"Thank you for the compliment."

Lane set off for Mrs. Kendall's, and Martha hastily searched to make sure no other picture had been left out. When she was satisfied, she hid the photograph carefully away in her trunk.

When he arrived back at the house with the dishes, Lane put up a shelf in their living room. After she arranged the dishes along with the teapot, she felt better.

The outside door opened, and Cole came in. She told him about the Baldwins' trunks and pictures, and Lane's discovery.

"Sounds as if you handled it well," he said, and she felt as if the weather had changed from cloudy to sunny.

He looked around. "I see you're getting settled."

She explained about the missing barrel and buying dishes from Mrs. Kendall. "We need to work out something about money."

"I'll find out when I get paid. Does Lane have the kitchen ready?"

"He's working out there. You can ask him." Cole's interest surprised her. "Why do you want to know?"

"We need to invite people here for a meal. We'll get acquainted that way. Find out more about what goes on."

His explanation reminded Martha of a question she had intended to ask him the previous evening. "I'm guessing that the first person you want to invite is Lieutenant Young, the quartermaster."

"Yes. That's right."

"Why are you so interested in him?"

After the barest moment of hesitation, he said, "On an army post, the quartermaster is a good man to know."

That was probably true, but she didn't believe it explained Cole's special interest. As he started back outside, she said, "Don't you want to look in Stephen's trunk?"

"Later."

She was trying to decide where to store clothing when an invitation arrived from Lydia Stratton to go on a picnic. The wife of a junior officer didn't refuse a suggestion from the fort commander's wife. Glad to get out, she sent back an acceptance. Lane offered to show her the way to the quartermaster's corral, and they set out. When they passed the guardhouse, she heard a mournful singsong chant. A confusing mixture of memories rushed over her—she'd heard that music at early, frightening times, and later more serene ones. "What is that?" she asked Lane, though she knew.

"Somebody who got drunk last night, most likely."

"It doesn't sound like songs that soldiers sing."

"If you want to wait a moment, ma'am, I'll find out."

He spoke to someone on guardhouse detail, then returned and reported, "One of the Apaches from down in the bottomlands. He got into a ruckus."

So the Apaches were jailed here, along with the soldiers. But the Apache had their own ways of punishing troublemakers. The families involved took care of problems. Here apparently the army had taken over that role. The Chihinne must resent that. Startled, she realized that for the first time in years she had thought of the Apache as they thought of themselves—as Chihinne, the People.

Lane left her at the quartermaster corrals, next to four cavalry stables. She was disappointed to find they would use an army ambulance instead of riding. However, she was happy to see Alice, who greeted her warmly. Harriet Fisher was with Lydia Stratton, as well as two cavalry officers' wives Martha had met at the party.

After a mounted escort of four soldiers assembled, they started out, taking a wagon road that went east. Lydia Stratton identified the buildings as they passed. Farther on a large tank wagon drawn by six white mules passed them going into the post. "That's the water wagon," Lydia Stratton said.

Just past a brickyard and a sawmill, the river curved around, and the ambulance splashed across, its four mules pulling it easily up a shallow bank on the opposite side. At the top of the rise beyond, Mrs. Stratton had the driver stop. "From here you can see the fort quite well," she explained.

Martha scrambled down and looked back. The east fork of the White River crossed their road and curved around between the fort and the scouts' wickiups. Beyond the ford Martha's gaze retraced their path to the corrals and on to the building-ringed parade ground. There the flagpole thrust up its symbol of the authority that the United States boldly proclaimed. When she had lived in this wilderness, the Apache had not accepted that authority. They appeared to accept it now. She wondered what bloody events had changed their minds. Or was it a pretense of change?

"The Apache," she said to Lydia Stratton. "Are they really subdued?"

"General Crook, who commanded the Military Department of Arizona from 1871 to '75, made peace with most of the Apache tribes."

Martha thought she knew how the army made peace.

As if Lydia Stratton read minds, she added, "The Apaches trusted General Crook because he respected them and kept his word."

"I see," Martha said, and admonished herself not to judge before she knew more.

The road went gently upward through stands of mixed pines and cedars. Though Martha watched intently, nothing looked familiar. Finally they stopped and got out at a small meadow. When Lydia Stratton opened the picnic hampers, Martha smelled the odor of chilis and cumin. "Mexican-style food," she exclaimed in delight.

Lydia looked pleased. "So you like Mexican food, Mrs. Baldwin. I wasn't sure about those of you who are new to Arizona. I have a marvelous cook who came with us from our last post. Where did you learn to enjoy Mexican food?"

Where indeed! Elizabeth Baldwin was from St. Louis, not Texas. Quickly she chose part of the truth. "I lived with my grandmother in Texas for a while, and she had a Mexican cook."

Alice had been listening. "That explains the way you talk sometimes. Once in a while you sound more like folks from Texas than Missouri."

Martha smiled, but underneath she was appalled that she hadn't considered her speech. To avoid more discussion about herself, she said to Lydia Stratton, "Where was your last post?"

"Fort Lowell, just outside of Tucson. We liked it there. People from the town were very friendly."

Alarms sounded in Martha's mind. "When were you stationed there?"

"Until two years ago."

Before the trial. Martha's worry diminished, but the tortillas with beans and chili didn't taste as good to her as they had smelled.

After lunch, Martha was glad to start back to the fort. She wanted to see Cole, and also to find an occasion to talk to Dr. Lawton about Fort Apache.

When she reached the quarters, Lane greeted her before she could go inside. "Come out back and see the kitchen," he said proudly. The shed had been transformed, with an old zinc-topped table, an ugly black cookstove, and pots big enough to hold stew for twenty men.

"This is wonderful! Is it all from the quartermaster?" Martha asked.

Lane grinned in answer.

After further congratulations, she went inside and found Cole there. He was sorting through Stephen Baldwin's trunk. "Did you know," she said, "that the Strattons were at Fort Lowell before they came here two years ago?"

He put down a bootjack and gave her his attention. "No, I didn't."

"Mrs. Stratton said they got to know people in Tucson. Do you think—"

A sudden gesture of his hand stopped her. He motioned toward the wall that separated their room from the other half of the house. She listened, and heard the sound of someone moving around. "Well," she said lamely, "that would be different—to be stationed near a town."

"What I think, Elizabeth, is that we're here and probably will be for a while." He sounded like a husband chiding his frivolous wife. Martha felt her face flush. She deserved the scolding—not for what Dr. Lawton next door might assume, but for carelessness. Still, she didn't like it. If so much weren't at stake, she could wish that Cole would slip up occasionally.

"Fort Lowell," he said thoughtfully. "I wonder if anyone else besides Colonel Stratton has been stationed there." At least he appreciated the information.

Among the equipment scattered around the trunk was a riding crop. It reminded Martha to ask, "Are horses available from the stables?"

"Officers have to buy their own mounts. I'm planning to buy one and a saddle from Lieutenant Kendall. The post trader will give me an advance against my pay."

A good horse plus a saddle would cost fifty dollars of her dwindling money. Even so she said, "I'll need a horse too. Please arrange it for me."

His gaze fixed on her suspiciously. "This is Apache country. You can't go riding alone—Elizabeth."

"All right," she conceded, but only reluctantly. "I'll wait for you to ride with me—Stephen."

On the other side of the house a door shut. Bootheels sounded in the entrance hall, followed by the bang of the front door. She looked out the window and saw Dr. Lawton walking toward the hospital.

Cole gathered up the clutter around him, pushed some of it under the cot, and tossed the rest back into the trunk. "I have to go back to the barracks. I'll see about the horses."

"Lane has the kitchen fixed up. Do you want to ask someone for a dinner?"

He paused by the door. "Not yet. There's a game at the post trader's most nights. It's a good place for hearing talk."

"And the quartermaster usually plays there?"

"Yes." His tone of voice said he wouldn't volunteer more. Whatever interest he had in the quartermaster, he still wasn't telling her.

After he left she noticed that someone, Cole or Lane, had put up clothing pegs and a shelf. Happily she started shaking out clothing and putting her everyday apparel on half of the pegs. When Cole relaxed, she thought, he was more than handsome. His smile could charm her into forgetting why minutes before she'd resented his telling her what to do. His smile made a warm spot in her chest and a shiver over her skin. If they had horses and rode together, what would it be like? The two of them would be alone, away from the fort. In spite of knowing they were together only because of bizarre circumstances—and only temporarily, she longed to find out.

Outside, Cole headed across the parade ground toward the infantry barracks and mulled over Martha's information. So Colonel Stratton had been at Fort Lowell. That made the conversation at the fort trader's nightly card game more important than ever.

There was another good reason for joining the game. He needed more sleep than he'd managed the previous night. Coming back to the room late, he'd be tired.

Enough, he hoped, not to care that Martha was sleeping near him.

At first she'd struck him as an unattractive woman. Too cold and proper. He tried to recapture that impression. It wouldn't come. Instead he pictured her face, a faint sheen on her skin, her lips moist and pink. Even the hair that drifted across the nape of her neck was made to be brushed aside. When she walked, her body swayed with sensual motion that excited him. On top of that, he'd seen her in different moods. Fierce and determined. But soft and tender too. Vulnerable, needing protection. And too damned often he wanted to protect her. Just like a husband, for God's sake.

What the hell! Why didn't he just let it happen? His scruples about leaving her alone because of her past were crazy. But he couldn't forget a sentence that his father had drummed into him. A man's not a man unless he can control himself around women. Cole almost groaned aloud.

He'd better get his mind off Martha. And remember what he was at the trader's game for—information about the contractors who sold supplies to the reservations. Information he hoped to use to ruin Harvey Lippincott.

In Tucson that May evening a lantern burned later than usual in one of the boxlike adobe buildings on Ochoa Street. Inside, Harvey Lippincott sat in front of a large, almost bare desk. His black suit looked fresh and his hair carefully combed. Only his expression, as he listened to the man who sat behind the desk, lacked its usual smooth geniality.

Where Harvey was soft and round, Sidney Hubbard

was tall and so thin as to make observers question whether he ever ate. He had a long jaw that gave him a slight resemblance to a horse, a comparison most men feared to point out. "Dammit, Harvey," Sidney was saying, "you better be a hell of lot more careful."

"What are you talking about?"

"Buying a cheap brand of flour instead of the brand the army ordered. Then sealing them in bags marked with the expensive brand." Sidney shook his head, as if he couldn't believe what he was describing. "If you'd transferred the flour, it would have worked. Leaving the original bags inside the fake ones was God-damned stupid."

Harvey's ears burned, but he abandoned the pretense that he hadn't been responsible. "So someone complained. Nothing will happen in Washington. You'll fix it up."

Sidney leaned back in his chair, his eyes hard. "We're partners, Harvey, but that doesn't mean I'll make up for your mistakes. My connections in Washington can't take care of everything. You go too far and nobody there's going to help us. Word of something like this flour business leads to talk about a Tucson Ring of contractors. Accusations of influence getting contracts, then cheating the government. I don't like that. It makes all of us look bad."

"I'm not responsible for everything some army officer complains about," Harvey protested.

"If it causes problems, you damn well will be. Stick to the simple things, Harvey. Charge the army for blankets that you sell to the post trader. Or get some more of the scales fixed up so they weigh in our favor. I'll take care of the complicated deals." Sidney took a paper from the pile on his desk and began to add a column of figures. It was an obvious and insulting dismissal.

Harvey left, his thoughts feeding a burning resentment. Because Sidney had married a woman from an old Mexican family, he thought it made him aristocracy. Harvey had a few ideas of his own that didn't need permission from anyone.

13

"Mrs. Baldwin."

Lane's excited call reached Martha in back of the house before he came around the corner. "What is it, Private Lane?" Martha asked, as she pulled back on Whipple's leash to keep him from jumping on Lane.

"Someone just spotted the mail rider coming in." He turned and went back around the house. Martha tied up the dog and followed.

This was the first arrival of the mail in the four days since C Company had reached Fort Apache. All along officers' row, women emerged from the houses. A corporal with a detail of soldiers drilling on the parade ground called his men to a halt. Several officers were already gathered on the veranda of the adjutant's office.

Across the parade ground she saw Cole come out of the sergeant-major's office in C Company's barracks. He was the officer of the day, so she hadn't seen him since the previous afternoon. That was hardly different from the other days, though, because he'd spent his evenings gambling in the back room at the post trader's store.

At the west end of the fort a rider on a mule trotted in past the hospital. A dusty canvas sack was tied to the saddle behind him. As he rode by, the waiting women started toward the adjutant's office.

Martha joined the others. Medical records couldn't arrive this soon. But it had been almost two months since the stage station had burned. Though Elizabeth's and Stephen's families wouldn't know about that, there might be letters sent to them care of the regiment. If there were, she and Cole would have to decide what to do about answering. That would be a reason for him to spend an evening with her. The nights had been lonely. On the march she'd become used to being with him—to the mixture of attraction to him and resistance to those feelings.

The mail rider gave the sack to the sergeant on duty, who took it inside. Alice, her face flushed with exertion, came up beside Martha. "If I don't get a letter from Mama, I'll just die." She hurried on.

"Mrs. Baldwin." It was Peter Dunham's silky voice. She turned around and found him smiling at her in a faintly insinuating way, as if they shared a secret.

Instantly alert, she said, "Good morning, Lieutenant Dunham."

Her unfriendly tone didn't seem to discourage him. "Waiting for letters from home?" he asked.

Since it was obvious that the reason for being here was the mail arrival, his question didn't make sense. "Just hoping, like everyone else."

"And where will those letters come from? Shall I guess?"

Her heartbeat speeded up, and her throat felt dry.

HEARTBREAK TRAIL

Nevertheless she managed a condescending smile. "That wouldn't be much of a guess since you know we're from St. Louis."

He studied her for a moment. "Yes, I suppose that's just what I might say." The inference—that he might not guess St. Louis—hung in the air between them.

Her heart was racing now. She tried to remember everything she'd heard about him. He'd been with C Company in Wyoming and had arrived in Yuma by way of San Francisco, along with the Fishers and Vernon Brown. She was sure none of them had been in Arizona before. If he did know something, why would he speak to her and not to Cole? Maybe Peter had noticed the traces of Texas accents in her speech that Alice and Lydia Stratton had picked up.

As if it were unimportant, Martha said, "If my grandmother were alive to write to me, it would come from Texas. Then you'd guess wrong."

"Of course." He nodded as if he were pleased. "A grandmother in Texas. That's logical."

The sergeant from the adjutant's office reappeared. Martha was delighted to turn her attention to him. He gave sacks to men waiting from the infantry and cavalry units and then announced names of officers. She heard "Lieutenant Brown." "Lieutenant Dunham" came shortly after. Peter took a violet-colored envelope and stowed it in his pocket without looking at it. He didn't leave, but stayed, watching Martha. Nervously she thought that if he felt so indifferent to a letter from his wife, he probably was just flirting. "Mr. Collins" was followed by Alice's exclamation of pleasure.

"Mr. Baldwin," the sergeant called out. Martha quickly went up the four steps onto the veranda and received two letters. A precise handwriting had addressed one to Elizabeth Baldwin, care of Lieutenant Stephen Baldwin at Fort Yuma, with a request to forward. The other had a more girlish handwriting, with curlicues and flourishes; it was also sent to Yuma for Elizabeth Baldwin. Illogically, Martha felt relieved that they both were postmarked St. Louis. Peter Dunham's insinuations had unnerved her.

She turned the envelopes over and checked the return addresses. The precisely written one came from Mrs. Lysander Polk, Elizabeth's mother. Miss Myra Baldwin had written the other. Martha saw Cole approaching and waved to him. "Look, Stephen," she said, loudly enough that Peter could hear, "two letters from home. One from Mama and one from your sister Myra." Peter gave her a sidelong glance and went inside the adjutant's office. Martha breathed more easily.

When Cole reached her, she handed him the letters. He glanced at them. "Both to you," he said. "Myra knows you'll be the one answering."

How neatly he made that her job, she thought.

Cole considered her a moment, then said softly, "Something wrong?"

"No, nothing." She wasn't sure what to say about Peter. Or whether to tell Cole anything at all.

He returned the letters to her. "I have to get back to the barracks. You can give me the news later. I talked to Lieutenant Kendall about horses. He said we can arrange something. I'll see him when I'm off duty."

When Cole was a short distance away, Peter came out of the adjutant's office and increased his pace to catch up with Cole. Martha looked after the two men uneasily. If Cole thought there was a real danger of their identities being discovered, the only sensible thing would be for him to disappear. A promise to her didn't bind him to keep up this impersonation under all circumstances. But, she argued with herself, very likely Peter was just making an opening for a flirtation. She was reading danger where none existed. There was nothing, she convinced herself, to tell Cole about.

Back inside her house she sat down and held the unopened letters. She'd never opened someone else's mail, though why she balked at that when she'd appropriated Elizabeth's identity didn't make sense. Many of her reactions didn't make clear sense any more, such as her confusion about the way she felt around Cole. She opened the letter from Myra Baldwin reluctantly.

Accounts of dances and parties and picnics were written with sentences all running together, as if Myra had never heard of punctuation. At the end Myra complained, *Mama and Papa are ruining my life they refuse to even think about letting me visit you and Stephen they are so unfair I know I'd have all kinds of beaux there*. Alarmed, Martha decided an answer would have to portray life at Fort Apache as both very dangerous and painfully dull.

It was a relief to open the second letter and read Mrs. Polk's calm sentences. She wrote of ordinary family activities. The letter ended with: *I pray that you and Stephen are well and that the change of climate will have the effect you are hoping for*. A clear reference to the greatly desired pregnancy. Martha couldn't offer news of that sort when she wrote to Mrs. Polk.

When she wrote—but how could she? Her handwriting would give away the fraud! She stared at the creased sheets of paper with dismay. Why hadn't she thought of that before? But she had to write. Otherwise there would almost certainly be the risk of inquiries from St. Louis.

An idea came to her. She opened the trunk and

examined the worn gloves in the tray. Satisfied, she took out writing supplies she'd purchased in Camp Mojave and wrote, *Dear Mother.*

The words were stark and chilling on the paper. She'd never written those words to her own mother—and she had no right to them now. But she couldn't turn back. She took up the pen again.

"Please excuse my writing. I have a new puppy. While I was playing with him, I broke two bones in my right hand, so I'm having to use my left hand." She stopped and reread her effort. The words sprawled awkwardly over the page. They didn't resemble her own handwriting; surely Elizabeth could as easily have written them. She was taking a chance that Elizabeth was right-handed, but the odds were in her favor. The right-hand glove was more worn than the left.

Stephen, she continued, *has been worried. He helps me when he can, but he doesn't have time to write letters. He's too busy hunting the Indians who have been raiding regularly.*

She offered a silent apology to the Apaches who had accepted General Crook's peace. It also bothered her to make Mrs. Polk anxious. But she didn't know how closely the Polks and the Baldwins kept in touch with each other. And Myra, or at least her parents, had to be convinced that Fort Apache was no place for a young girl to visit. *Stephen,* she continued, *is going to buy horses for us, but I'm not sure how much riding we will do, because of the danger of meeting hostile Indians. So we live very quietly.* She concluded with a wish to give her love to all the family. Her letter to Myra was essentially the same, except that she added, *My hand keeps me from doing needlework, which is the favorite activity of the women here.*

She reread both letters; though readable, they were close enough to illegible to be anyone's handwriting. Her device pleased her. In subsequent letters she could add convincing details about problems caused by the hand she couldn't use. If she really had such an accident, she wasn't sure Cole would worry, but he would have to help her with things she couldn't manage. Such as braiding her hair. If she didn't do that at night, it became impossibly tangled. Cole might brush and comb it, lift it off her neck, separate the strands and weave them together. And then undo it in the morning.

A quiver ran across her skin, as if Cole were there. She couldn't seem to stop her imagination. She could almost feel the tug on her hair and his fingers brushing the back of her neck. He might have to help her undress—unfasten her clothes. Would he be content to do only that, or might he want to touch her, run his hands over the skin of her shoulder, touch her breast? Her breasts were aching now, and excitement was building low in her abdomen.

Remembered glimpses of him returned to fill out her picture—of Cole, his chest bare, a line of tan where his collar stopped. The dark brown hair across his upper chest dwindled to a narrow band that disappeared under the top of his trousers. She might touch him, and then he'd pull her close against him—against his bare chest and the hard strength of his body.

Martha jumped up from her seat at the little table, shocked at the vividness of her imagination, at how clearly she had observed physical details about Cole. Agitated, she walked around the room and stopped beside the iron cots, pushed together from their night-time separation. When she was first a captive of the

Apaches, she'd refused to cry and show her terror. Sharp-Knife told her later that one of the reasons he'd wanted her for a wife was her bravery. She wasn't brave now.

Her grandmother's friends had labeled her a sinner; maybe they were right. She wanted to lie in Cole's arms. To see his naked body and feel it next to hers. To experience again the pleasure she'd learned with Sharp-Knife. Fear kept her from letting Cole know that's what she wanted. Fear of the pain of eventual separation from him. Fear she would be diverted from her goal of finding her child. Fear that because of Sharp-Knife, Cole would reject her.

But she might never find Pinecone. And the pain of parting from Cole might be no worse than regret that she'd been too much a coward to let him see how much he attracted her. But Cole, she reminded herself, hadn't behaved recently as if he desired her. Still, he seemed to be a man of strong passions; she could revive his desire if she were willing to try. If. Too many ifs!

She put her replies into unsealed envelopes. It was only fair to let Cole read them. Would he notice the phrase about helping her and picture what that meant? No—she wouldn't think about Cole any more. Whipple needed a walk; that was an uncomplicated thing to do.

Outside, Whipple rewarded Martha by circling frantically in greeting, his yellow-brown ears flopping and his long yellow tail whipping around him. By the time she and the puppy reached the commanding officer's house, Whipple had resigned himself to walking with only modest sideways forays and she felt calmer. They continued to the edge of the bluff that dropped steeply to the river. She stopped beside the sentry post.

The sentry said, "Afternoon, ma'am. I wouldn't advise walking beyond here."

"Yes, thank you, Private." Ahead, the road going west out of Fort Apache descended through a cut in the bluff to the bridge. Beyond that, she knew, lay flat bottomland where some of the Apache bands attached to the fort planted their crops. She longed to be out there.

A large crow swooped down to investigate something in the trail. Whipple gave an excited bark and strained on the leash. Purposely, Martha let the leather loop on the end slip through her fingers. The puppy fell forward on his face and stayed a moment, as if shocked by the sudden freedom. Then he recovered and made a dash for the bird, which rose in a flapping of wings. Martha picked up her skirts and ran after the dog, shouting, "Whipple!" As she'd calculated, her voice sent him scampering on ahead. Together they raced down the slope to the river. Then, instead of crossing on the bridge, Whipple veered off to the left, running in among the weeds growing beside the water. In dismay Martha stopped, panting, and watched as the tip of his light yellow tail marked the errant puppy's progress.

Behind her the sentry called, "I can't leave to help you with the dog, ma'am."

"That's all right. I'll get him," she called back.

Splashing sounds alerted her that someone was fording the river. George Lawton rode toward her, dismounted, and doffed his broad-brimmed hat. "Good afternoon, Mrs. Baldwin. If you'll hold my horse, I'll see if I can retrieve your dog."

"Thank you, Dr. Lawton. I don't want to trouble you."

"No trouble." He gave her the reins of his horse and started after Whipple.

Martha sighed. Her chance to get across the river was gone for that day. Whipple managed to elude the doctor for several minutes. Finally the puppy became so interested in sniffing under an old log that the doctor grabbed the leash. Well, she thought as he picked up the puppy, who tried to lick his captor's face, this was her chance to get better acquainted with the doctor.

"Thank you, Dr. Lawton," she said when he deposited Whipple in her arms. "I apologize for bothering you with him."

"Glad to help." He took the reins for his horse from her but didn't remount. "If you're going back to your quarters, I'll walk along with you."

She smiled at him. "I would like that very much. I've been wanting to ask you about Fort Apache. Lieutenant Parker said you know about its history."

He looked pleased. "There's not much history in seven years, but I've been here."

Whipple wriggled and she let him down. Her firm hand on the leash allowed him only modest attempts at taking his own route. "Was this a reservation then?" she asked.

"No. Just an army post when it was established in 1871. The next year the first commander, Colonel Green, negotiated with Cochise, the Chiricahua leader, to bring his people here. Have you heard of Cochise?"

She'd seen him once, a proud, handsome man. "I read about him in a magazine."

Dr. Lawton snorted. "Probably made him out to be some kind of a devil. He was a great war leader, no doubt about that. But he was no bloodthirsty monster, the way the Arizona newspapers would have you think."

"Did he come here when the commander negotiated with him?"

"No. Colonel Green tried, but he didn't have power to provide the supplies he promised Cochise, and the War Department wouldn't back him up. So Cochise went back to raiding in the southeast. Other Indians did settle here."

"Which groups were they?"

Dr. Lawton looked at Martha curiously. "Most people who first come west think Indians are all alike. They hardly know that Apaches aren't the same as Navahos. You seem to know there are different Apache subgroups."

"Magazines have so many stories about Apaches," Martha improvised, "because they're so fierce and still not all subdued. Since we were coming to Arizona, I was especially interested in them."

"I see. Good, but stop me if you get tired of the details."

They had passed the sentry and the hospital and were starting along officers' row. Dr. Lawton went on speaking, his face and voice animated. "Most of the Indians who came when this area was designated as a reservation were moved to San Carlos in 1874. The Apaches left here are mostly White Mountain bands."

"Dr. Lawton, sir." Martha and the doctor turned around. A hospital orderly was hurrying toward them. He nodded in greeting to Martha, then said to the doctor, "We have a sick trooper. His bunky just brought him in. Says he drank two bottles of hair tonic. It looks serious."

Dr. Lawton said, "I'm sorry, Mrs. Baldwin. It's an emergency. I hope we can continue our talk another time."

"I hope so too," Martha said. She was sorry for the sick soldier, but she wanted to cry out in frustration. The doctor went off, leaving her with the question she longed to ask: what groups had been sent to San Carlos, and which ones remained here? She consoled herself that there would be an occasion for them to talk again; she would see to that.

Discouraged, she walked on. What if she learned that her son was likely to be at the San Carlos reservation? According to the map posted in the adjutant's office, the San Carlos reservation adjoined the Fort Apache reservation. However, it was about forty miles to the agency. Too far to get lost out riding and end up there, so getting to San Carlos would be difficult. Cole could well object to any attempt she'd make. In any case, until she talked to Dr. Lawton again, it was useless to worry.

Late that afternoon Cole returned to their quarters, and Martha showed him the letters and her replies. He sat down in a chair and read through them. She watched his face, but he didn't show any emotion. When he finished, he said admiringly, "You handled that very cleverly."

"Thank you." She silently chided herself for an unreasonable disappointment. He'd passed over her sentences about helping her without any reaction.

Cole had noticed the intimacy the letter suggested, but he had schooled himself to indifference. At least on the surface. He could see that something was troubling Martha, but he didn't know what. "If too many problems like this crop up," he said, "we may have to decide whether we can keep on with the impersonation."

"What else can we do?"

"Disappear so the army thinks we're dead."

His proposal challenged her; her whole body radiated resistance. As when she seemed vulnerable, he felt a strong attraction to her.

"I can manage problems," she said sharply. "I don't think you give up easily. You want to see it through too."

"But not against impossible odds," he cautioned.

He didn't want to dispute what were impossible odds, so he said, "I've made the arrangements about the horses. I have to see the post trader and get a loan against my pay. Since tomorrow's Sunday, we can go riding then."

"I'd like to." She went to her trunk and took out a small taffeta purse. "How much is my horse?"

He started to refuse and changed his mind. It would be acting too much like the husband he wasn't. "Forty dollars. That includes the saddle and gear."

He took the two twenty-dollar gold pieces and put them away in a corner of his trunk. "It would look strange to pay for your horse with gold and mine with greenbacks from the post trader," he explained.

As he was leaving, she asked, "Will you be gambling tonight?"

Card games. He'd never thought he could get so tired of them. But he was picking up good information that way. And it kept him out late. "It's Saturday night. The best poker night of the week."

A flicker of something sad in her eyes almost changed his mind. He left, knowing what he really wanted, but not sure whether to get off the track he'd set himself on.

On Sunday the morning shed its chill early, charging on into the warm day ahead. In the old hospital a visiting chaplain, making the rounds of isolated garrisons, prolonged his sermon unmercifully. Martha, sitting beside Cole, was thinking of the newly purchased horses. Today she and Cole planned to ride out to explore the nearby country. And they would be alone, away from Dr. Lawton next door. If they wanted to talk freely, they could. Or do anything else, an insistent voice in her head added.

As they left the old hospital, Harriet Fisher said, "Captain Fisher and I are expecting you and Mr. Baldwin for dinner, now. It's a Sunday custom in C Company."

Martha smiled and said untruthfully, "What a lovely custom. It's good of you to be so hospitable."

The Fishers' warm intentions didn't make the meal go faster or compensate Martha for waiting when she longed to be out riding. Finally Captain Fisher said, "If we're going hunting for wild turkeys, we'll have to get started. Lieutenant Brown, you're coming along, I believe. What about you, Lieutenant Dunham?"

"Yes."

"Mr. Collins? Mr. Baldwin?"

Martha held her breath.

"Yes, certainly," Fred Collins said. "Nothing I'd like better."

"Thank you, sir, for the invitation," Cole said. "I'll have to pass it by today. I promised Mrs. Baldwin that we'd try out the horses we just bought."

From the slightly amused glances Vernon Brown and Peter Dunham exchanged, Martha guessed they were thinking that Cole still put his wife's desires first, but she didn't care. After they said their good-byes and started back to their quarters, Peter Dunham said, with a touch of cruelty in his voice, "Be sure to take your pistol along, Stephen."

Cole smiled. "I'll remember."

Cole lingered with Whipple in the yard while Martha changed into a gray riding dress. Then she waited for Cole to change his dress uniform for field clothes. After tying up the dog, they walked to the quartermaster's corral.

Cole introduced Martha to Henry Thompson, the sergeant in charge of the stables, who led out a piebald Indian pony. "Indian ponies are good, tough mounts," Sergeant Thompson told her. "This one's larger than most, and he'll treat you right. If you need him to, he can run fast as a deer. And he's broken to weapons fire."

"I'm delighted with him." Martha stroked the nose, admiring the well-shaped head. "Do you know where Lieutenant Kendall got him?"

"Yes, ma'am, that I do. Bought him from a half-breed horse trader who came through here two years ago."

"Then he was an Apache horse?"

"Yes, ma'am. His name's Skinny. He was thin then, but not now."

Martha ran her hand over the black-and-white flanks and felt the muscles ripple under her fingers. An Apache-trained horse would have been firmly but never cruelly broken. Maybe her son had seen this horse—a farfetched possibility, but one that immediately endeared Skinny to her. She leaned her forehead briefly against the horse's soft nose.

When Sergeant Thompson helped her mount, Cole was already mounted and waiting. His horse, a large palomino mare, snorted and tossed its head so that its silver mane whipped like a banner. Cole easily controlled her, but Martha guessed that an indifferent rider would have trouble with so large and spirited a horse. "Meet Buttermilk," he said as they started out of the corral.

They took the road heading east and were almost to the ford of the White River when Peter Dunham, riding a black roan, overtook them. He looked as precisely turned out when he was riding as at a party. "I decided not to go hunting," he said. "Mind if I join you?"

Anger, disappointment, and alarm mixed and grew into a core of fury in Martha's stomach. She tried vainly to think of a reason to refuse. When Cole said amiably, "Fine. Glad to have you," she could only ride quickly on.

Beyond the ford a trail branched off from the road and followed the river. Martha took it, not waiting to consult with Cole whether that's the way he wanted to go. Behind her the men were talking of fort activities. Her anxiety diminished, but she kept ahead. Cole could stay back there and spend the whole afternoon with Peter Dunham for all she cared!

The trail split off again and climbed up into piñons and then taller pines. Martha began to listen for the myriad sounds: the bubbling of the creek, the caws and trills of birds.

Several miles up the creek the trail leveled and came out of the trees into an open meadow. To the right the meadow ended at the foot of a bluff. At intervals, paths marked the steep slope. Martha's heart began to pound. That bluff, with its animal trails—she was sure she'd seen it before. At a particularly sharp incline one of the paths cut back and forth instead of going straight down, making a giant Z. She stared at it. If she was right, a little farther on around a bend there would be a large, square boulder at the top with a pine tree growing out of a crack. Almost afraid to go forward, she held Skinny to a slow walk.

Around the bend she looked up—and didn't see the boulder. Despairingly she studied the bluff and saw two jagged pieces of granite halfway down the slope. At the top a large pine tree grew next to a rock shaped like a half-dome. The boulder *was* there! The roots of the pine tree had split it, and two sections had fallen away. She had been here before.

Martha began to tremble and tears formed in her eyes. As if alarmed by her mood, Skinny began to back up in little sideways steps. A hand reached out and took the reins. It was Cole, blurry through her tears. "What's the matter?" His voice was sharp and concerned.

"I . . . just . . . would you help me dismount, please?"

He tossed his reins to Peter, just behind him, and was off his horse and at her side within moments. She kicked her left foot out of the stirrup, and he reached up and lifted her down. Her legs felt as liquid as her tears, and she clung to him.

Cole didn't understand what had upset her, but he felt fiercely protective. He held her close, sheltering her in his arms, cherishing the feel of her rounded body against him. "Tell me," he said urgently, "what's wrong? Are you hurt?"

"No," she said into his jacket, "I'm so happy to be here."

Cole heard the muffled "No" clearly, but he wasn't sure he'd made out the rest correctly. He tilted her face up. "I couldn't hear you. What did you say?"

Tears still ran down her cheeks, but she was smiling. "I said I'm happy to be here."

It wouldn't make sense to anyone else, but he was sure he knew what she meant. Delight in her joy welled up in him. Gently he took her face in both hands and used his thumbs to wipe away her tears. At that moment resolutions about control meant less to him than the elation he shared with her. To hell with Peter watching. Cole leaned down and touched her mouth with his.

Her lips felt the way he'd imagined for weeks. Soft and yielding. The kiss deepened, and he didn't know if it was from her eagerness or his. Her lips parted, inviting his tongue to find the inner softness of her mouth. Every muscle in his body felt taut with desire.

Reluctantly he broke off the kiss and thought he heard a soft sigh from Martha. He hoped it was the same disappointment he could feel all the way down into his gut. He looked into her eyes. She gazed steadily back at him, and he knew that she was offering him what he wanted. If only Peter Dunham weren't along. . . .

"Ahem." It was Peter, politely blank-faced. "Is everything all right?"

"Yes, fine," Martha responded, wiping her damp cheeks with her fingertips. "I get emotional sometimes when the landscape is so beautiful."

Cole didn't look to see Peter's reaction to her thin explanation. "Maybe we'd better start back," he suggested. "It'll be close to dark by the time we reach the fort."

He helped Martha mount, letting his hands linger around her waist, and then remounted Buttermilk. They turned back the way they'd come. After a few minutes, Cole took the lead. He'd found that if he wanted to ride comfortably, he had to be ahead where he couldn't watch Martha. Let Peter watch, but he'd be the one going to bed with her. And as quickly as they could manage it.

Evening was softening the outlines of the fort when they splashed through the east fork of the White River and started across to the corrals. Partway along they met Lieutenant Brown riding toward them. An Apache scout and several mounted enlisted men from C Company were following him. Cole stopped and saluted. Lieutenant Brown hastily returned the salute and said, "I'm glad you're back. We're on our way to look for Mr. Collins. During the turkey shoot we all separated. He didn't join us on the way back. We expected to find him here, but he hasn't returned. You both can come along."

"Yes, sir," Cole responded. "With your permission, I'll see my wife to the corral and catch up with you."

Peter wheeled around and joined the other men. Cole put his horse into a trot and Martha followed alongside. "I hope Fred's all right," she said in a distressed voice.

No use reassuring her. She knew the hazards of the area better than he did. "We'll find out."

At the corral one of the enlisted men on duty bustled out to help her down. When she'd dismounted, Cole leaned down and said, "I'm sorry." It was all he could say. He meant it as sincerely as he'd meant anything in a long time.

She held out her hand as if she were going to touch him, then let it drop back. "I'm sorry too." He hoped she was. And that before long he'd learn how much.

14

As night deepened over Fort Apache, lights appeared in the barracks windows. Across the river gorge in the Apache scouts' camp, only the cooking fires confirmed the existence of invisible wickiups.

Inside the Fishers' living room, Martha sat on a couch and held Alice's hand. Harriet Fisher had insisted they come to her quarters while they waited for the searchers to return.

Tears filled Alice's eyes. "I want to be a good army wife, but I'm afraid. I'm not brave like you, Elizabeth."

"You're acting very brave," Martha said and hugged Alice. "If Stephen were lost, I'd be afraid too."

The truth of her own words echoed in Martha's head. At that moment, she realized, she wasn't playing the part of Elizabeth. If Cole were the one who hadn't returned, she would be terrified. Not just for herself and her precarious situation. For him. She would fear for the counterfeit officer who had kissed her that afternoon and with his caress made a promise that she wanted him to keep.

The outer door opened and Captain Fisher came in. Lieutenant Brown and Peter Dunham followed, but not Cole. Martha rose and Alice stood with her, clinging to Martha's hand. "Mr. Collins has not been located yet, Mrs. Collins," Captain Fisher said gravely. "However, the search will continue at daylight."

"Thank you, Captain Fisher," Alice said in a slightly trembling voice.

Martha's concern for Alice and Fred didn't obliterate another question. "Is my husband back?" she asked.

Captain Fisher frowned and said stiffly, "Mr. Baldwin didn't wish to give up the search. Lieutenant Brown gave him permission to continue."

A knot lodged in Martha's stomach. "He stayed alone?"

"Yes," Captain Fisher snapped.

The knot grew until it seemed to press against her ribs and constrict her breathing.

Lieutenant Brown said, "Mr. Baldwin agreed that he would remain close to the area where we left him. He'll be able to signal and listen for any responses from Mr. Collins."

Alice's lips were trembling. "Thank you, Mrs. Fisher," Martha said, "for your kindness. If Alice wishes, we'll go to my quarters and perhaps be able to sleep for a while."

Alice's tense and quick agreement told Martha she'd rescued them both just in time. Lieutenant Brown offered to escort them to Martha's quarters, and she accepted, grateful that his offer precluded one from Peter Dunham. The night had exhausted her ability to deal with more than the worry about Cole and Fred.

When they reached the small end house, Martha took Alice inside, then went back to thank Vernon Brown. He said softly, "No need to tell Mrs. Collins this yet, but we found Fred's mare coming back to the fort. She'd pulled her reins loose from a bush, and she had claw marks on her from a mountain lion. When Stephen wanted to stay, I didn't refuse."

"Yes, I see why you wouldn't. Thank you for telling me," Martha said.

Back inside Martha pulled off Alice's boots, then held her until the pent-up sobs diminished. Drained, Alice lay back on Martha's bed. Martha took off her own boots, unpinned and braided her hair, then blew out the lamp and lay down on Cole's bed.

His scent—a faint mixture of pine-tar soap, pipe tobacco, and something she could only call maleness—surrounded her. It was on the pillow and on the blanket she pulled over herself. She lay, staring up into the darkness.

Where was Cole, and what was he doing? If he were out searching and calling, he might have no more protection than Fred against a mountain lion. She offered a silent prayer that he and Fred would return safely.

Alice turned over restlessly. Martha said, "Try to sleep if you can." She put her hand across and grasped Alice's.

"I'll try," Alice quavered. After a while her breathing sounded steadier, as if she'd exhausted herself enough to doze.

Martha tried to take her own advice. She forced herself to blot out the present and think of the day just past. Immediately her mind went to its two extraordinary moments: she found the proof that she had been in this very area, and that meant her son might still be here. The other moment had been when Cole kissed her.

A kiss could mean nothing, but their kiss was between a man and a woman who had grown more aware of each other every day. She knew the pattern of his breathing, the timbre of his voice when he was angry, and the sound of his laugh. Without conscious thought, she'd learned how the hair grew in tight whorls at the back of his neck. And how the skin at the corner of his eyes tightened when something alarmed him. Their kiss had felt like a lighted match, ready to set a blaze that would flame a hundred times brighter.

She would never sleep unless she could banish those provocative images. Uneasily she remembered that the minister of her grandmother's church had said Martha was depraved to honor a union with an Apache man by seeking to keep the son. He really meant that she was depraved to have lain with a "savage." She understood his message and resented it fiercely. But how could she defend herself from that accusation now? She wanted to lie with Cole as with a husband.

If sharing Cole's bed—no, more than that—if loving him without being married was wicked and depraved, then she was. Just let him be safe!

Cole laid more branches on the fire and went back to cutting narrow strips from the horse blanket and tying their ends together. He'd circled as far as he could and still keep track of the firelight. Without moonlight, he could easily lose his bearings. Now with extra rope he'd borrowed from the scout and an extension of improvised rope from the blanket strips, he could go farther and still find his way back to his horse. Maybe a futile effort. But he had a gut feeling that Fred was hurt badly. Finding him before daylight could make a difference.

Because of his responsibility to Martha, he might not have volunteered to do this for someone else. But Fred had never treated him with the subtle—and not-so-subtle—contempt of some of the others. Stephen Baldwin wouldn't have had an easy time of it, getting a commission through political pull. Cole admired and liked Fred's decency.

When he'd reduced the blanket as much as he could and still shield the horse, he fastened the end of his rope to a tree. He held a resinous pine branch in the fire until it flared up into a torch and started out on the first leg of his search pattern.

He walked into the forest, climbing over tree stumps and boulders, keeping as much as possible in a straight line. As he went he unwound his extended rope, periodically calling and firing his pistol. When he reached the end of his line, he retraced his route and went in a different direction. By the fifth trip out and back, he decided a sensible man would give up. A sensible man wouldn't be in his situation to begin with. Doggedly he started out on another spoke of the wheel.

On the seventh trip, he had reached the end of his guide rope when he heard a shot in response to his own. Exultantly he fired his own pistol again and listened. Nothing. He left the rope and started along a ravine through which the sound of the pistol shot had come.

Scrambling down the sides of the ravine, Cole barely managed to hang on to his lighted branch. At ten-minute intervals he fired his pistol and listened, but he heard only the wind. When he was down to his last cartridge, he stopped and slumped down, panting, onto a fallen log. Maybe he'd gone in the wrong direction; in unfamiliar country he couldn't figure the tricks wind and echoes could play. If a mountain lion had mauled Fred, it could still be around. One bullet might not finish off a large cat.

Discouraged, he rose and let out his frustration in a bellow. "Fred, you bastard! Where the hell are you?"

From farther down the ravine came a faint, "Here."

Jubilantly Cole shouted, "I'm coming!" and plunged ahead.

He found Fred lying on a blood-soaked patch of pine needles. "Lion jumped me," Fred managed. "My fault. Stupid. Fell. Did something to my ankle. Fired at the cat. Scared it off. Then only one shot left."

"Don't talk now," Cole ordered. The amount of blood on the ground and on the right shoulder of Fred's jacket meant he'd lost a lot. "Are you in much pain?"

"Don't feel anything, except cold."

A bad sign. Cole opened his canteen and gave Fred all the water he could drink. After lighting a new branch, he took off his shirt and tore part of it in strips. From the rest he made a large pad which he slid under Fred's jacket and bound to the mangled shoulder. He put his jacket on Fred, his larger coat easily fitting over Fred's smaller one. By the time he finished, Fred was unconscious.

There was no way Cole could carry the burning branch and Fred too. He'd have to take his chances on making his way in the dark. At least it was straight up the gulch to where he'd left the end of his line. If he made it back to his horse, he could let her find her way back to the fort. After smothering the flame, he waited until his eyes adjusted to the dark, then hoisted Fred onto his shoulders and started back up the ravine.

Martha got up as soon as she could see gray encroaching on black sky outside the window. Her eyes ached with fatigue. Alice seemed to be asleep. Quietly Martha pinned up her braid, pulled on her boots, and smoothed at her wrinkled dress. Putting a shawl over her shoulders, she eased open the front doors and went out onto the porch. One dull yellow light glowed in the adjutant's office and another in a guardhouse window. The barracks were completely dark. She wanted to shout, prod the men awake.

Farther along officers' row, a light flared out onto a porch. She counted—four houses over. That was the one Vernon Brown and Peter Dunham shared. Surely that meant Vernon was getting ready to leave again. She waited, hardly breathing, watching the patch of light. When it went out, she thought she couldn't bear her disappointment. But then a dark figure came out, followed by another. They started along the boardwalk, coming in her direction.

She left the porch and went out to the walk. When they came close, she saw that Peter was with Vernon. This time she was glad to see him; he was one more searcher.

The two men stopped. In the pale light they seemed drained of color, similar in their grayness. Vernon said softly, "We're on our way to collect men for the search detail. We'll let you know as soon as we find anything."

"Thank you." Please, please, she added silently, don't waste time.

Vernon started on. Peter hung back and said, "Don't worry. We'll bring your husband back. If that's what you want."

Martha was too incensed to answer, and after a moment he followed Vernon. Too bad, she thought, Peter wasn't the one who was lost.

The two men were crossing in front of the adjutant's office when a soldier ran around the corner of the guardhouse. He skidded to a halt with a hasty salute to the two officers. Gulping to catch his breath, he said, "Excuse me, sir. Have to get the doctor. Mr. Baldwin just came in with Mr. Collins. They're going to need Dr. Lawton at the hospital."

Martha didn't wait to hear a reply. She ran back to the house, into the entrance hall, and pounded on Dr. Lawton's door. "Dr. Lawton! It's Mrs. Baldwin. A soldier says you're needed at the hospital."

A muffled voice responded, "Yes. I hear you."

She went outside just as the private arrived. "I've roused the doctor," she told him. "Is Mr. Baldwin all right?"

"I couldn't tell you that, ma'am."

From inside, Alice called, "Elizabeth, where are you?" She sounded frightened.

Martha hurried back to her room and found Alice sitting up in bed. "I'm here," Martha said. "A soldier just came. Stephen and Fred are back."

"Is Fred all right?"

No point in mentioning the urgent summons for the doctor until she knew more. "I'll go find out."

Alice started to get up. "I'm going too."

"No, please don't." Martha pushed her friend gently

back down. "You have the baby to think of. I'll come back as quickly as I can."

"All right."

As Martha closed her door behind her, Dr. Lawton emerged from the other room. He acknowledged her with a nod and hurried out and toward the hospital. She followed him outside and was starting in the same direction when she heard voices from the parade ground. There was enough light to see soldiers carrying a litter but not to see who was on it. Her stomach knotted again with fear until she saw among the men following one whose stride she recognized. It was Cole.

Uncaring what was suitable for an army wife, she picked up her skirts and ran. She stumbled once on a clump of grass and slowed to a rapid walk, reaching the soldiers just as they neared the hospital. Heads swiveled toward her, but she saw only one weary face. Cole reached out an arm to her, and she went into his embrace as a bird to its nest.

For a moment all she knew was that he was real, and there. But that wasn't enough. "Are you all right?" she asked. At the same moment she realized that under his jacket his chest was bare, his skin icy to her hand. In the growing light she saw dark stains on his jacket. "That's blood!" she exclaimed.

"Fred's, I'm afraid," he said. "He's bled a lot."

She turned, still in the crook of his arm, and they walked together after the litter. "Will he be all right?"

"Dr. Lawton will have to say." She could hear the weariness in Cole's voice. "I'll see him and report to Captain Fisher. Then I hope I can clean up."

"I must go back to Alice."

Reluctantly she pulled away and started back. She had gone partway when Peter Dunham appeared. "You gave our new hero a warm welcome," he said.

Fatigue eroded her caution about Peter. "Of course," she snapped. "Why do you think I wouldn't?"

"You misunderstand," he said smoothly. "That's exactly what I would expect you to do."

His voice suggested he meant something more. She regretted her impulsiveness. Even if it were wise, she wasn't up to confronting him this morning. "Excuse me. I must go."

When she reached her quarters, she glanced back. Peter still stood where she'd left him, watching after her. With a shiver, she went inside to Alice.

"Fred's hurt," Martha said as gently as she could. "A mountain lion attacked him. Dr. Lawton's tending to him now."

Alice listened calmly then agreed that Martha go with her to the hospital. When Dr. Lawton appeared, he was reassuring. "Mr. Collins will be all right. He's weak because of the bleeding, but Mr. Baldwin found him in time."

At this news, Alice's shaky control dissolved. Dr. Lawton and Martha took her back to the Collins's quarters where the doctor gave her something to make her sleep. After he left, Harriet Fisher arrived. "I'll stay with Alice now," she told Martha.

Gratefully Martha hurried back to her house where she found Cole and Lane. One of them had started a fire in the stove. Cole had on a fresh shirt and pants, and his hair was still wet from bathing. He was describing the previous night's events to Lane. Martha insisted he begin again.

When he finished, Lane said admiringly, "That was mighty good work, sir. The company will want to hear all about it."

"Thank you, Lane. Right now, I have the day off," Cole said, "and I plan to sleep for a while."

After a grinning Lane left, Martha found it suddenly difficult to look at Cole. Feeling awkward and shy, she straightened her bed. When she came to his, she hastily smoothed the covers. She was behaving more like a thirteen-year-old girl than a twenty-five-year-old woman, she scolded herself. But the scolding didn't slow the rapid beating of her heart or prevent her chest from feeling tight with anticipation—or maybe apprehension. She wasn't sure which.

"Martha." Cole's voice was soft but compelling.

She looked at him. A slight flush darkened his skin; tension showed in the small lines around his dark eyes. "Do you know that coming back to the fort yesterday, the only thing on my mind was making love to you?"

Her heart gave a sudden, enormous thump. "Yes," she whispered.

"After the stagecoach attack, we made a bargain. You said we had an agreement, nothing more. Do you still feel that way?"

"No." One-word answers seemed to be all that would come out, but this one was enough.

He reached out and pulled her close. Through the shirt his chest felt warm now; she thought she could feel his heart beating. With fingers that were as gentle as they were strong, he touched her cheek, then traced the line of her jaw and finally her lips. When he lowered his mouth to hers, his kiss felt like answers for all the questions she had been asking of herself, and of him too.

But as her kiss responded to his, those answers weren't enough. Caressing her neck, then slipping to her shoulders, his hands softly brushed her breast. Low inside her, urgency built for the special knowledge that a man and a woman discovered together.

He pulled back and looked down into her face, as if he too had questions that needed answers. His eyes changed, desire clear in them, and he reached for the line of buttons on the front of her dress. In the midst of her longing, shyness intruded again. It had been so long since she had known a man intimately. Nervously she stopped his fingers with hers. "It's daytime. Will someone come looking for you?"

"Not today. Unless the fort's attacked."

When she didn't release his hand on the buttons, he used the other to pull the pins out of her braid and let it fall down her back. It reminded her that she hadn't washed since the night before. "I . . . I slept in my dress last night."

"Then let's take it off."

"But," she began, and didn't know just what she wanted to say.

He took her face in both hands and gazed down at her.

"Do you want me to let you do it yourself?"

Again he'd understood how she felt. "Yes. I do."

He released her and stretched out on his cot, resting his head on his folded arms. "I plan to watch," he said, in a voice that was as much teasing as passionate. She had a perverse moment of regret for the change.

She poured water from the pitcher into the china washbasin, then turned her back and unbuttoned her dress. Keeping her back to him, she stepped out of it. He said, "Very nice," and her heart did several turns. Even the skin of her arms and shoulders warmed at his tone.

After she washed her face and neck, she hesitated, then slipped the lacy straps of her camisole off her shoulders and let it fall around her waist. She waited. He said, in a blurred voice, "Ah, beautiful Martha has a beautiful back."

Hastily she finished and unbraided her hair. Then, boldly, not attempting to cover her breasts, she turned around.

Cole lay on his bed, one arm still behind his head, the other hanging down off the cot. His eyes were closed.

Surprise, disappointment, and laughter all struggled for expression. While she'd been marshaling her courage, he'd been trying to stay awake. She went closer and tenderness subdued other feelings. He looked so young and weary. No wonder.

He opened his eyes and tried to shake himself awake. "No," she said softly, "we'll wait."

When he started to protest, she put her fingers across his lips. "I'm tired too. It's better to wait until after we've slept."

He sighed, and his lips moved against her fingers in a kiss before his eyes closed again.

Gently she lifted the fallen arm back onto the bed. He turned a little, pulling the other hand from under his head, settling himself. "Sleep well," she whispered.

She adjusted her camisole up over her shoulders again and lay down on her cot. Next time, she wouldn't hesitate so long.

As she felt herself falling asleep, she reached across and touched his hand. He stirred, and she started to draw back. "No," he muttered, and held on to her hand. "Sorry," was the next mumbled word before he slid back into sleep. She lay and felt more complete than she had in years, comforted by the hand grasping hers.

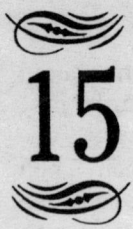

15

Martha stirred, coming awake slowly, briefly confused by the sunlight coming through the window. She must have slept several hours. Then she felt a touch on the side of her face and turned her head. From the cot beside her, Cole leaned across, resting on his elbow, his face close above hers. "I thought you were going to sleep all day," he said softly. His eyes revealed that sleep had only interrupted his desire to make love to her.

He leaned over farther, one hand holding her face, and his lips touched hers. Beneath the brush of his mustache, his mouth moved against hers, opening, tasting, sending excitement through her. It was the sensation he'd stirred in her in the desert when she trimmed his hair and beard. That first effect had been subdued, a suggestion of the possibility of desire. This was the same feeling, magnified many times over.

When the kiss ended she felt breathless with anticipation and vulnerable at the same time. She thought of

Discover a World of Timeless Romance Without Leaving Home

GET
4 FREE
HISTORICAL ROMANCES
FROM HARPER MONOGRAM.

JOIN THE TIMELESS ROMANCE READER SERVICE AND GET FOUR OF TODAY'S MOST EXCITING HISTORICAL ROMANCES FREE, WITHOUT OBLIGATION!

Imagine getting today's very best historical romances sent directly to your home – at a total savings of at least $2.00 a month. Now you can be among the first to be swept away by the latest from Candace Camp, Constance O'Banyon, Patricia Hagan, Parris Afton Bonds or Susan Wiggs. You get all that – and that's just the beginning.

PREVIEW AT HOME WITHOUT OBLIGATION AND SAVE.

Each month, you'll receive four new romances to preview without obligation for 10 days. You'll pay the low subscriber price of just $4.00 per title – a total savings of at least $2.00 a month!

Postage and handling is absolutely free and there is no minimum number of books you must buy. You may cancel your subscription at any time with no obligation.

GET YOUR FOUR FREE BOOKS TODAY ($20.49 VALUE)

FILL IN THE ORDER FORM BELOW NOW!

YES! *I want to join the Timeless Romance Reader Service. Please send me my 4 FREE HarperMonogram historical romances. Then each month send me 4 new historical romances to preview without obligation for 10 days. I'll pay the low subscription price of $4.00 for every book I choose to keep – a total savings of at least $2.00 each month – and home delivery is free! I understand that I may return any title within 10 days without obligation and I may cancel this subscription at any time without obligation. There is no minimum number of books to purchase.*

NAME_____

ADDRESS _____

CITY_____STATE_____ZIP_____

TELEPHONE_____

SIGNATURE_____

(If under 18 parent or guardian must sign. Program, price, terms, and conditions subject to cancellation and change. Orders subject to acceptance by HarperMonogram.)

GET 4 FREE BOOKS
(A $20.49 VALUE)

TIMELESS ROMANCE READER SERVICE

120 Brighton Road
P.O. Box 5069
Clifton, NJ 07015-5069

AFFIX STAMP HERE

the window and said, "Do you think anyone can see in?"

For answer he rose and pulled the faded red cotton curtains across the windows. Hastily he returned to the cot, half falling with unaccustomed clumsiness over one of the folding canvas chairs. She moved over, making room for him. He lay on his side facing her and kissed her again, gently at first, then with hungry insistence. The hot flicker of his tongue parted her lips, and a flame of arousal raced across her skin until she glowed with warmth. Eagerly she reached up to him and returned the kiss.

His hands moved to her neck, tangling in the hair at her nape. She ran her hand across his chest, feeling the hard muscles through his shirt, and touched the soft chest hair where the top buttons were undone.

"Martha," he murmured, "why did we wait so long?"

"I don't know." In a recess of her mind she did know, but at this moment she didn't want to remember why. With his kisses he traced a line from her lips to the corner of her mouth to her eyelids, and then to her lips again. Urgently he caressed her, inviting her to respond more boldly. She did, thrusting her tongue into his mouth, savoring the sweet, salt taste.

She turned so that they lay facing each other. He pushed aside the blanket covering her and drew her against his chest. She felt the brush of his beard against her face, his heartbeat in agitated rhythm with her own. Her inner being responded to the warmth of his mouth, the touch of his hand, caressing her shoulder, the growing ache that began in her abdomen and spread to her breasts. His fingers slipped underneath the lace edge of her camisole.

The rush of his breath when he found her nipple told her that the touch affected him as much as it did her. Lightly he stroked, leaning over her, slipping her camisole aside, and catching the crest in his mouth. His tongue felt like rough velvet, sending bursts of heat through her. Pleasure captured her in powerful bonds.

His caresses played on her tender skin and all her senses. He seemed completely male, with a male's power to reach deep inside her. His erection thrust against her hip. She felt a clutching in her belly that made her want to press even closer to him and feel his hard body against hers.

She thought she'd experienced passion but she was unprepared for her overwhelming need. Sharp-Knife had been considerate and loving, and she'd had pleasure in his arms. But he taught her only part of what she was already discovering with Cole—the urgency of the feelings that were sweeping her along.

"Martha," he breathed. "Let me look at you."

A fleeting thought about the daylight made her hesitate, but only for a moment. She sat up and raised her arms for him to pull the camisole over her head. He didn't stop with that but crouched beside her, lifting her hips and slipping off her pantalet.

Separated from him, without the heat of his body next to hers, she felt chilled.

His next words warmed her. "God, you're beautiful. I guessed you were, but not clearly enough."

Boldly she reached for the opening of his trousers. "Now you," she said.

As he stood and stripped off his shirt and pants, she looked with wonder at his naked body. Below his broad chest, his flat belly and lean hips emphasized the muscled power of his thighs and legs. His penis, springing erect from the dark hair at his groin, was part of that masculine beauty. Impatient, she wanted to feel his naked chest and stomach and thighs against hers. She reached out to him, and he lay down again beside her.

Despite the force of his passion, Cole wanted somehow to find the restraint to go slowly. He must let her savor the building of pleasure so that she would be eager and ready. Another thought was there too—he wanted her to learn that he was a better lover than her Apache husband.

He discovered that the ache of delay was also a special pleasure. Her gasping response as he caressed her breasts and kissed her nipples to tautness intensified his. The fire in his groin built as he slid his hand over the faint roundness of her stomach.

Though her feelings were sweeping her along, Martha was aware of the muscled plane of Cole's chest, the rigid cords in his arms, the pressure of him against her thigh. She ran her hands across his back, reveling in the feel of the taut muscles. When she touched, then stroked his erect penis, he shuddered.

"Martha, I don't think I can wait. I want you, now. Are you? . . ."

She could barely gasp, "Yes."

He moved above her, his weight bringing him into that world with her. His hands held her face, his mouth captured hers, and she felt his rigid shaft pressing into the emptiness that had to be filled.

He began to push against her, gently, then retreating and pushing again. Tension shivered through her in waves. He lifted her hips, fitting her to his accelerating rhythm. She gripped his shoulders, moving with him.

A final thrust, and he filled her with himself. For a moment he lay, his head beside hers, and she shook with the beat of his heart. Then he raised his head and kissed her urgently. Her pulsing blood knew she couldn't bear any more or she would explode. She was wrong.

The excitement widened, but he was with her, moving within her, easing back and thrusting again. At each movement she wanted even more. The rhythm he created pushed her upward, receding and building again until she reached a crest, and spasms shook her. She heard his gasps and felt him shudder with the same wrenching release. As tension slowly drained away, he held her tightly.

When Cole could breathe again, he lay, cradling Martha's head on his shoulder, and stared up at the ceiling. He'd wanted her pleasure to be greater than she'd ever had before. What he hadn't expected was that she would give him more sexual fulfillment than he could remember. He'd lost himself in her, and her response had increased his enjoyment beyond any he'd known before. Was it some particular way she moved, or the intensity of her passion? Something she'd learned from her Apache husband? No. It had been just a long time since he'd bedded a woman—that must be it.

But there was tenderness in his feeling for her at this moment, and he gave himself to it. He turned to her again, kissing her eyelids, her forehead, the side of her mouth. Strands of hair trailed across her face, and he brushed them aside and captured her lips for a lingering kiss, and another, and still another. She responded eagerly, and then stopped him, sounding almost shy as she asked, "Was it worth the wait?"

"God, yes. You don't know how hard it's been—sleeping next to you for so many weeks, and not doing anything more."

"Yes, I know," she said, and blushed a deep rose, delighting him.

To make up for so many lost nights, he began to caress her again, intimately, knowing now just how to awaken her desire. She responded with her own passionate embraces. Finally he sheathed himself in her tight heat until she cried out her shuddering pleasure, then spent himself again inside her.

Kissing her, he pulled the blanket over them, then settled her into the curve of his body. "You've worn me out more than hunting for Fred last night," he teased her.

Her "Mm" sounded sleepy and satisfied.

When Martha woke again, the room was dark except for the faint glow around the edge of the stove lid from the embers. She lay on her side, with her back to Cole. One of his arms was around her, with his hand resting on her breast. It felt warm and secure to lie so close to him. Too secure.

She had hoped to recapture the pleasures that she'd known as Sharp-Knife's wife. But they were pale memories next to the passion Cole had aroused in her. She wouldn't call it love—that was too dangerous an idea. Whatever it was, together with this feeling of safety in his arms, it might weaken her resolve for finding her son. That mustn't happen.

Cole's breathing sounded steady, but when she cautiously started to pull away, his hand tightened on her breast. "Don't get up yet," he said.

"I have to." She pulled away and sat up. "I'll be right back."

He turned over and stretched. She got up and felt along the foot of the cot for her chemise.

"Wait, I'll light a candle," he said. From the half-laughing tone of his voice, she suspected he wanted the candle, not so much for her to find her way as for him to see her.

He lit the candle, and from his expression, he wasn't disappointed. Then another spurt of shyness overcame her and hurriedly she pulled on her pantalet and found her camisole. It was halfway over her head before he caught her hands and stopped her.

"It's a shame to cover this up," he said, and lightly touched one pink nipple. The effect was a tiny explosion in her breast that radiated into her body. Astonished and disconcerted that after so much lovemaking he could arouse her so easily, she stepped back and pulled down the camisole. She could see that his gesture had affected him as well. Without looking at him again, she took her dress from a peg on the wall and, with her back to him, put it on.

As she started toward the door that led outside at the back, he said, "You'll need a light." When she turned, he had his back to her, lighting a small square lantern. His back muscles narrowed to tight buttocks and strong thighs and calves. He turned and handed her the lantern, and she thought how beautiful he was. She couldn't tell him so in words, but her face probably had. She fled outside.

The chilly air cooled her heated face, but it didn't calm her thoughts. Cole had shown her a sensual side of herself she only partly knew existed. In most other people's eyes, she'd been disgraced before she knew him. If making love with Cole confirmed the accusations that she was wicked, it didn't matter. Her newly discovered self didn't care.

Whipple came out from his corner beside the kitchen shed, and she remembered she hadn't fed him. When she found his bowl, it had been used. Lane had looked after the puppy. Inside the kitchen a covered plate sat on the zinc-topped table. The smell told her it held biscuits and that she was hungry. The stove was still warm, and a pot of coffee sat on the back. Lane must have come to the kitchen sometime while she and Cole were inside. Had he guessed what they might be doing and not knocked on their door? In spite of her conclusion that she didn't care what others thought, she felt herself blushing.

Guessing that Cole must be hungry too, she stirred up the stove and added enough pieces of kindling to heat the coffee. In the cooler she found cheese and sliced it, then put everything on a board Lane used as a tray.

"I wondered why you were out here so long." Cole stood in the kitchen doorway, dressed again in his light blue pants and wool shirt. "I like you better without clothes," he said.

Smiling happily at him, she said, "Lane left us some food."

"Good. I'm hungry."

They carried the food inside and ate at the rickety table in their room rather than at the larger table in the entrance hall. There had been no sounds from Dr. Lawton's side of the house, but without discussing it, they agreed that they didn't want to talk to him just then. Eating alone together seemed a part of their new intimacy. When they finished, Cole took their dishes back to the kitchen.

On his return, he stood looking down at the stove, which he'd already replenished. His eyebrows slanted down in the beginning of a frown. "I know it's late to bring this up," he said, "but I should have been more careful. Stopped sooner, or done something else."

She felt as uncomfortable as he looked, but she couldn't be less forthright than he was. "You mean—so there's less risk of having a child."

"Yes. We don't want that to happen."

"You're right," she said, because that was what he expected her to say. The feelings that rose in her were so strong, so confused with images of a black-haired infant nursing at her breast, that she forced them back again. Later, when she was alone, she might examine them to find out why the necessity of preventing another child was so painful.

Cole waited a moment as if expecting more of a response, than went on. "I could say today won't happen again, but I'd be a liar." He grinned, more openly and boyishly than she'd ever seen before. "What I'd like is for it to happen as often as possible."

Grateful for his lighter mood, she said, "Apaches practice abstinence to limit babies." Only when she finished did she realize she had in effect brought up her past sexual experiences.

For a moment his face clouded, then he said easily, "I've heard some of them have two wives. That must be why."

The sound of the outer door was followed by a knock on their door. Cole opened it to George Lawton. "I saw your light," the doctor explained, "and thought you'd want to know about Mr. Collins."

"Yes, we do," Cole said.

"Fred won't look as handsome to his wife, but he'll be all right."

"I'm so glad," Martha exclaimed, aware that she hadn't thought about Alice since that morning. "Please, Dr. Lawton, come in. Would you care for coffee?"

The doctor shook his head. "No, I'm going to get some sleep." As he turned to go into his door, he stopped and swiveled back to face Martha. "By the way, tomorrow is ration day when the Apache bands come in for their supplies. Since you're interested in the Apaches around here, Mrs. Baldwin, you'll find it enjoyable to watch."

When both doors were closed, Cole said, frowning, "Let's walk over to the hospital. I'd like to have a word with Fred if he's awake."

"Yes, and I'll stop and speak to Alice." Martha guessed that Cole also wanted to say something to her that he didn't want to chance the doctor overhearing. While she found her shawl, he put on his coat and field cap and picked up the lantern.

Outside the air felt chilly. Martha shivered with the contrast between the cold and the warm intimacy of the room they'd just left. Once they were on the walk, Cole said, "I didn't know you'd been asking Dr. Lawton about the Apaches in the area." His voice had an edge to it.

"We met the other afternoon, and I told him I was interested. I think that's natural curiosity," she defended herself.

"True. But as for going out to watch them, that's something else. You know now that you've been in this area before. One of the Apaches might recognize you."

"No one would expect me to return as an army officer's wife," she protested. "People usually see what they expect to see."

"Maybe, but not always," he said sharply. He stopped, and they faced each other in the path, the lantern lighting his beard from below but leaving his eyes in shadow. It gave him a sinister appearance. For the first time in weeks the effect reminded her strongly of the convicted murderer she'd unchained. "I think," he went on, "you should stay out of sight tomorrow."

Stubbornly she insisted, "Dr. Lawton will be looking for me."

"You can spend ration day with Alice. She'd like that. There are other ways to ask around about the Apaches who took your son."

As they walked on toward the hospital, Martha thought sadly that none of the differences that divided her and Cole had changed because of their new intimacy. She intended to watch the Apaches come in for their rations. Cole was wrong to think he could convince her to stay away. But he was right about something else: As long as they shared the masquerade of husband and wife, the physical attraction between them was strong enough that they would lie together again. She didn't know how much that would affect him. She did know she would pay for those pleasures with pain at their inevitable separation.

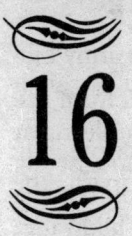

16

In the bedroom of the Collins's two-room quarters, Martha finished brushing and pinning up Alice's blond hair. She had arrived early that morning to relieve a weary Harriet Fisher, who had stayed with Alice overnight.

"There," Martha said. "Now you're ready to visit Fred in the hospital."

Alice gave a distraught smile. "Thank you, Elizabeth. You'll go with me, won't you? I just dread goin' over there by myself."

Martha was dismayed at perhaps missing the Apaches coming for rations, but she couldn't refuse. "Yes, of course I'll go with you."

"Oh, Elizabeth," Alice said gratefully, "You're a real friend." Her face brightened. "What shall I wear?"

After a yellow dress was finally chosen and Alice was fussing over a missing earring, Martha said, "I'll wait for you outside." She put on her shawl and a straw bonnet, one she'd bought in Yuma for the trip but never used, and stepped out onto the porch.

Rations for the Apaches were distributed from the quartermaster's storehouse, a long adobe building at the east end of the parade ground. Martha thought she saw more soldiers than usual going in and out, but she didn't see any Apaches. Perhaps the guards hadn't let them into the fort yet. If Alice were content to sit with Fred by herself at the hospital, Martha planned to observe the Apaches. To her relief, Cole had left for duty earlier that morning without asking her what she intended to do.

The issue of whether to stay out of sight as he asked had been on her mind the previous night. She thought it was on his, too, because he hadn't suggested making love again. But, she reminded herself, they'd made love thoroughly enough during the afternoon that perhaps Cole needed to recover. That train of thought led to remembering exactly what they had been doing.

"Elizabeth, you are positively glowin'," Alice said from the doorway. "You look like the cat that licked up all the cream."

"Oh, it's a pleasant morning. And Fred is going to get well." Truth, but only a tiny part of it.

They started along the boardwalk toward the hospital. Alice glanced sideways at Martha and exclaimed, "My goodness, I've never seen you wear a bonnet before."

"Well," Martha said, improvising, "the sunshine's brighter now. A bonnet will keep me from getting too brown." It would also shade her face better than a hat, a precaution she'd decided on in deference to Cole's warning.

"That's very sensible," Alice said approvingly. "I was

just surprised because it doesn't seem like somethin' you'd pay any attention to."

Quickly Martha reviewed how Elizabeth might answer. "I've been a little careless since we've been here. At home in St. Louis, Mama wouldn't let my sisters and me go out without bonnets."

"Good morning, ladies." The voice behind them was Peter Dunham's.

Alice stopped, and Martha reluctantly did the same. Peter was his usual carefully groomed self, looking as if he were only temporarily inhabiting his field uniform. Martha could imagine his dress uniform, standing in a corner of his room, waiting impatiently for Peter to return.

"Good mornin', Lieutenant Dunham," Alice said, brightly. "We're on the way to see my husband. Won't you walk along with us?"

"Thank you, I'd be delighted." He held out an arm to each woman. Martha couldn't see any way to avoid him.

"Mrs. Baldwin, did I hear you mention the name of my home town?"

An edge of apprehension tingled up Martha's spine. "I don't believe I know what that is."

"Did I forget to tell you?" He paused, then like a politician scoring a particularly enjoyable point over an opponent, said, "I was born in St. Louis."

Martha stumbled over an uneven board in the walk and had to clutch Peter's arm to keep her balance.

"My goodness, Elizabeth," Alice exclaimed, "are you all right?"

"I'm fine," Martha said, hoping her agitated breathing wasn't obvious. "I just didn't watch where I stepped."

"Did you twist your ankle?" Peter asked in a voice that was too solicitous. "Let me rotate it for you, and you can tell me if it hurts."

He was already starting to crouch down before Martha stopped him with a sharp, "No. It's all right."

She couldn't, however, refuse to return her hand to his elbow as they walked on. Deciding she didn't dare ignore his challenge, she said, "You were born in St. Louis?"

"Yes."

Boldly she pursued him into enemy territory. "I'm surprised you haven't mentioned it before. I don't remember a Dunham family, but then we didn't know everyone in the city. Did you live there long?"

He looked at her with what appeared to be admiration. "Only three years, but I have cousins on my mother's side who are still there."

They had passed the commanding officer's house and were nearing the hospital. "Elizabeth, maybe you shouldn't go into the hospital with me," Alice said, and added forlornly, "It isn't very pleasant."

"I want to see Fred." And get away from Peter Dunham, Martha hoped. She needed time to think about his belated revelation.

"Then I'll leave you ladies here," Peter said. Martha had seldom been as glad to say good-bye to anyone as she was to him.

Inside the hospital, they found Fred sleepy and feverish. He held out his hand first to Alice, and after she kissed him, to Martha. "Thank you, Elizabeth," he began in a weak voice.

"Please," she interrupted, "don't talk. Just get well."

She left Alice and went back to the entrance and sat on a wood bench. Immediately her mind began searching for clues to Peter Dunham's behavior and how much danger he posed. If he suspected something about her and Cole's identity—which would explain some of his remarks—why hadn't he said anything? Why had he waited until now, instead of mail day, to say he was born in St. Louis? He acted as if he knew some secret about her. But what? And how did he expect to use it?

He clearly enjoyed making her uneasy; maybe he hoped for intimacy with her. If that were his purpose, her best response was to discourage him, but just enough to keep him expecting her to change her mind. At any rate, she must tell Cole. It wasn't fair to keep silent about something that could jeopardize him as well as her.

A sobering assessment occurred to her: In her eagerness to find her child, she had dismissed anything that suggested her scheme might not succeed. Seizing the chance to come back to the place she'd been a captive had been bold. She was still convinced it was the right thing to do. If she saw her Apache brother- or sister-in-law today, what would she do? Even though a hundred different things could happen, she must have some kind of plan, not go on trusting to luck. The problem with Peter Dunham showed that luck could go against her as well as with her.

Alice came out from the ward room with Dr. Lawton. He smiled when he saw Martha. "Good morning, Mrs. Baldwin. Are you and Mrs. Collins going to watch when the Apaches come in? They should be starting about now."

"I hope so. Alice, remember earlier, I was telling you about ration day? Since you don't need to stay here, let's both watch." Shaken by the encounter with Peter,

Martha was ready to heed Cole's warning. She wouldn't stay away, but two women would make each one less conspicuous.

"I'll go along with you to the adjutant's office," Dr. Lawton said. "You'll get the best view from there."

Outside, Apache men and women were walking up from the river crossing at the west end of the fort. Some carried babies in cradleboards on their backs, but Martha noted with disappointment that none had older children with them. When Martha, along with Alice and the doctor, reached the adjutant's office, a line had formed that stretched halfway from the quartermaster's storehouse to the office.

The contrast of that line with the Apaches as she had known them struck Martha. She hadn't thought about what a ration line meant. Though the men and women in line were laughing and talking, Martha felt sad for them. A proud people, they'd sometimes had a precarious living, but they'd never existed on white men's charity. These lands had been theirs, until white men appropriated them.

At the office veranda Lieutenant Parker greeted Alice with sympathy and good wishes for Fred's recovery. With youthful envy in his voice, he said to Martha, "You must be very proud of Mr. Baldwin."

"Yes, I am," Martha said.

The end of the ration line was getting closer to the adjutant's office. Martha, with her heart beating painfully fast, stood beside the wall, where the veranda roof shadowed her but she could easily watch the Apaches.

Some of the clothing looked the same as she remembered. One older man wore a long-sleeved buckskin shirt and skin breechcloth above moccasins that came halfway up his thighs. Most of the other men had on long red or gray cloth shirts over cloth drawers that reached to their knees, with the upper part of their moccasins rolled down below the knee, forming pockets. Sharp-Knife had carried a small knife in his. A few men wore denim shirts, something new from when she lived among them, and one had on a black derby hat. The garments of most of the older women were buckskin tops and skirts. Younger ones wore full skirts of brightly colored cloth and high-necked long-sleeved blouses of calico and other colorful prints. Martha could remember only a few women wearing cloth blouses and skirts. The pendants and ornaments made from shells and stone, worn by men and women alike, were the same as before.

Soon newcomers joining the queue were close enough that Martha could hear bits of their conversation. She recognized a few words and phrases, but most passed her by too rapidly to catch their meaning.

"The band chiefs actually collect the rations," Dr. Lawton went on. "They make the distribution to the families in their groups."

"Who are the band chiefs?" Martha asked, and waited tensely for the answer.

"Miguel, Pedro, and Diablo."

Disappointingly, the names meant nothing to Martha, but they were Spanish, probably given by the Mexicans and adopted by Americans. One of the band chiefs might be from the family group of her son.

The Apache women waited in line, but some of the men wandered around or gathered in small groups, talking. "Are they allowed to go anywhere they want to?" Alice asked in an apprehensive voice.

"On ration day they pretty much have the run of the

fort," Dr. Lawton said. "You shouldn't worry, though, Mrs. Collins. The White Mountain Apache are perhaps the most peaceful toward whites of all the Western Apache groups. They used to make a few raids into Mexico, but even before we came, they got most of their goods by trading with the Zunis. Not like the Chiricahuas. That's a different story."

A middle-aged Apache with receding hairline and a stern expression walked past. His forehead and the right side of his face looked battered, as if he'd suffered many old wounds. Alice moved closer to Martha and gripped her arm.

The doctor glanced at Alice and said reassuringly, "That's Miguel, from the Carrizo band. He and some of his people were imprisoned in '64, apparently just to warn any other White Mountain people to keep the peace. They were kept jailed for a year. When he was released, he worked to get the rest of his people freed and didn't seem to hold it against the army for what was certainly unjust treatment."

Alice said suspiciously, "So there hasn't been trouble here since the reservation was established?"

The doctor's face took on a resigned expression, as if he'd concluded that no matter what he said, Alice was determined to worry. "If you listen to visitors from Tucson, the White Mountain Apaches pass along guns and ammunition they get from the Zunis. Maybe it's true. A band chief isn't like a general. He can try to persuade his group, but he can't tell the other men what to do. There are always a few young hotbloods, eager to prove their courage."

The phrase that alarmed Martha wasn't the one about young men wanting to fight. "Do visitors come here from Tucson? It's such a long way."

"About a hundred twenty-five miles, by way of Fort Thomas and San Carlos. No one comes during the winter, but in another month or so, when it's hot there, we'll have a few visitors."

Finally Dr. Lawton had said something to make Alice look cheerful, but it had the opposite effect on Martha.

Miguel, the Carrizo band chief, had stopped in front of the old adjutant's office, a small adobe separated from the new one by the commissary office. Two Apache men joined him, and Dr. Lawton pointed them out. "Those are the two other band chiefs. Pedro is the one in the middle. Diablo has his back to us."

Pedro looked the oldest, a thin man with a serious mouth and sad eyes. From the back Diablo appeared sturdier and his movements more youthful. He turned partway around, and Martha almost gasped. A profile jumped out at her from her memory—prominent nose, steady eyes under heavy brows, determined mouth and jaw. The thick black hair, parted in the middle and cut to blunt ends, might be any Apache man, but few faces had that distinctive look of quiet power. Until Sharp-Knife married her, she had been so confined that she saw none of the men and women of consequence. Afterward she had gained status and participated more in the life of the band. There had been a leader—a proud man, somewhat vain—who could have been Diablo.

Forgetting about remaining in the shadows, she stepped forward to the edge of the veranda. From the closer distance she could see an earring in Diablo's left ear. Sunlight glinted on a silver circle and caught the bright yellow of a dangling feather. It fit with her memory. She was sure. Diablo was the leader of the band to which Sharp-Knife's sister-in-law and brother belonged. In her nervous excitement Martha gripped the oak post at the corner until her fingers hurt.

Alice said, "Elizabeth, I'm going back to the quarters. Are you coming?"

Reluctantly, Martha looked away from the three chiefs and glanced over the line of Apaches that now reached back to the adjutant's office. The puzzled gaze of a middle-aged Apache woman standing near the veranda caught hers. For a moment she and the woman stared at each other. Trembling, Martha turned quickly so that she faced Alice, with her back to the Apache queue. "Yes, I'll go with you," she said, and was astonished that she sounded normal.

Somehow she managed thanks to Dr. Lawton and a good-bye to Lieutenant Parker. All the time her tumultuous thoughts whirled around the question she couldn't answer: She didn't remember the woman in line, but had that woman recognized her?

Martha's heart was still pounding painfully when they reached the first house on officers' row. After agreeing to return for dinner, Alice announced she was going on to her own quarters to take a nap. Martha felt relieved; she needed to be alone to sort out all that had occurred that morning. But when she went inside, she found Lane waiting, an eager smile on his face.

"Mrs. Baldwin, two of the cavalry officers are moving on, leaving tomorrow. I believe, ma'am, that you and the lieutenant can move to half of Major Owens's quarters."

"Oh." It took a moment for her to readjust to thinking about something as ordinary as where she lived. Then her first reaction was that she didn't want to move—to leave this room where she and Cole had made love. "I'm not sure. You did so much work fixing up this room, and the kitchen. It seems a shame to give them up."

Lane beamed. "Don't you mind about that, ma'am. I like fixing things up. I'll have the new quarters just the way you want them in a jiffy."

She remembered that larger quarters would mean a room for him. "As long as it isn't too hard for you, that's fine."

"If you don't mind the suggestion, ma'am, the lieutenant best see about quarters right away. Before some other officer comes along who ranks you out."

Clearly, a larger place was worth the risk to Lane of being ranked out later. "All right," she said. "I'll ask Stephen to inquire immediately."

It occurred to her that not long before she'd worried about having Lane where he could observe Cole and her often. Now she liked the idea, even though they would have to be cautious about talking. The prospect of demonstrating that she was Elizabeth, Stephen's loving wife, produced quivers of anticipation in her stomach.

Cole came in soon afterward, and Lane told him about the possible move. "Sounds good," Cole said when Lane finished, "I'll go to the adjutant's office and find out about it."

After Lane left to report to his barracks, Cole said heatedly, "I noticed that you and Alice Collins were watching the ration line this morning."

"I was careful. I wore a bonnet and stayed mostly out of sight." She hoped he would leave it at that.

He didn't. "Did you see anyone in the ration line that you recognized?"

"Yes, I think so. One of the band chiefs, the one

named Diablo, looks like a man who was a leader of the group of my husband's brother and his wife."

"The ones who kept your son?"

"Yes." She had to say the rest. "One woman looked at me as if something about me puzzled her. It could just be that she was interested in my dress or bonnet."

"Or she might have recognized you," he said grimly.

"If she did, she wouldn't say anything to anyone here," Martha justified herself. "Apaches don't trust white people that much."

"But she might tell your brother-in-law?"

Reluctantly Martha said, "That's possible. But I don't know if she did recognize me. And by watching I saw Diablo. That was important." She had no way to balance the result now—could only hope it was in her favor.

After Cole had seen about the vacant quarters, he and Martha looked at them. They would have half of a six-room house with the front room large enough for both a living room and dining room, leaving two bedrooms.

"If you're interested," the departing wife offered, "I'd be happy to sell you most of the furnishings."

"Yes, we'd like that," Martha agreed, hoping it wouldn't take too much money. When she and Cole left Fort Apache, it might be in the middle of the night—hardly a couple moving on who could resell their possessions. Her reluctance lessened when she saw the double bed that would be part of the furnishings, and she guessed from Cole's expression that the same thoughts occurred to him.

By the time the arrangements were completed, Cole went to collect Alice for dinner with them. Afterward came a final visit to the hospital and reassurance to

Alice that Fred really would be all right. At close to midnight they left her at her quarters.

When Martha and Cole arrived back in their room, he had his jacket and shirt off and was unfastening the buttons of her dress before she could speak. No resolution that she must talk to him withstood the passion he aroused, first with his eyes, then with his hands and mouth.

Their joining began tentatively, like a small stream that twisted around barriers and merged with other streams to make a lake behind a dam. When the dam broke, the stream had become a torrent of feeling that rushed along in a great flood. Their lovemaking reached an impossible height, fusing them into a single being—and then she floated slowly back to the surface in his arms.

He brushed hair away from her face and kissed her gently. "Martha," he murmured, "I love . . . to make love to you."

She ran a finger along the edge of his bearded mouth, feeling suddenly shy. "And I love the way you do it—the way we make love together."

Long, peaceful minutes followed with Martha close in his sheltering arm, feeling the steady heartbeat from his chest underneath her cheek.

Finally the reality of the outside world couldn't be postponed longer. Reluctantly she pulled back from him. "Cole, I must tell you something that happened today."

Cole was half-asleep, content with the lingering touch of her skin. The delight of caressing her and being caressed in return had been even greater this time. Underlying his pleasure was the belief that she couldn't have responded more fully to any other man. Talking didn't appeal to him, but he said, "You mean besides the Apache woman in the ration line?"

"There are two other things. Peter Dunham was born in St. Louis."

He sat up, completely alert now. "How did you find that out?"

"He told me today." She continued with an explanation that included previous remarks Peter had made, ones she'd never mentioned to him.

He lit the candle beside the bed. "Why didn't you tell me this before?"

"It didn't seem important—just Peter's way of rather obnoxious flirting. The first time it happened, we did talk about it."

"Yes, I remember something along the trail. Peter could be a problem, depending on what he knows. But maybe not much, or he'd have said something before this." He ran over the possibilities in his mind and came to an uneasy conclusion. "It's not reason enough to change our plans—at least not now. I'll watch him and try to figure out what he's doing. What's the second thing?

"Dr. Lawton said that in another month or so, visitors may come up from Tucson. A sort of excursion, it sounds like."

"Christ! Visitors from Tucson could finish us."

"How well do people in Tucson know you?"

"It's not a very big place. My family's well known." Bitterness flared, raw and burning in his gut. "The only son turning out a murderer got plenty of attention."

She leaned forward, her soft brown hair falling across the golden skin of her shoulders. "I don't believe you're a murderer," she said softly.

"Thank you. You and Ira are the only ones. Even if

someone who came along agreed, they'd still report me as an impostor. I'll have to think about this. And be ready to run if we have to."

"But not yet. Surely, we're safe enough for now."

"I guess so."

Cole snuffed the candle and lay back, staring up into the darkness. If he had any sense, he'd get out of here. Insist she go too. But she wouldn't. He was sure of it, and that changed things.

Besides the threat of what she'd learned today, something else bothered him. Why had she waited until now to tell him? Why pick this time, when she probably knew he wouldn't feel like arguing with her about anything? Damn, he didn't like the idea she might be making love to get her way, playing on his feelings.

He thought of moving back to his cot, but he knew he couldn't. Not after finding out what making love to her was like. And tonight he hadn't given her a chance to tell him anything before he'd rushed her into bed. But he'd better remember that finding her son came first with her, and be a little wary.

His resolve didn't make him feel easier. Instead he felt sad, as if the danger weren't to his safety, but of losing something valuable. He'd almost said he loved her. Was it true? Along with the other things he hadn't figured out, he didn't know that either.

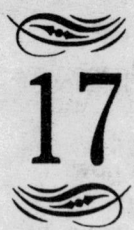

17

"You don't have a duty detail this morning?" Martha asked Lane when he appeared the next morning.

"No, ma'am. Just to get you packed up so we can move tomorrow." He went outside where Martha could hear him whistling and speaking in cheerful tones to Whipple.

She was trying to decide what to pack first when Cole returned. He had left soon after reveille, and she hadn't expected him before midday. "I'm leaving on a special detail," he told her as he took his carbine down from a wall rack. "Some trouble north of Show Low. A couple of Apaches and some miners. We're to settle things down and bring the ones involved back here."

He stuffed an extra shirt and his flat campaign hat into a canvas bag and put on a broad-brimmed Mexican straw hat. She had seen the cavalry officers wearing these instead of regulation headgear when they were leaving the fort. Obviously Cole expected to do a lot of riding.

She wanted a promise he'd be safe. Instead she asked, "How long will you be gone?"

"I don't know. It depends on what we find." Cole stood, his bag and carbine in hand, and regarded her soberly. "You and I have a lot to talk about, but it'll have to wait. Will you stay away from any Apaches who come into the fort while I'm gone?"

His risks on army duty were because of his promise to her. "Yes, I will."

The tense lines around his eyes relaxed a little. "One good thing—Peter Dunham and I are both on this detail. I'll see whether he says anything suspicious."

Peter with Cole—another thing to worry about.

Cole put down his bag and carbine to take her in his arms. His hat fell off, but he didn't seem to notice. She welcomed his arms holding her, and his body against hers. He kissed her and rubbed his hand along her spine. "And Peter won't be here to bother you. That's almost worth the assignment."

Giving in to her emotions, she said, "I wish you didn't have to go."

"So do I," he responded. But he picked up his bag and carbine, put his hat back on, and went out the back door. She followed and heard him say to Lane, "I count on you to look out for Mrs. Baldwin while I'm away."

"Yes, sir. I can make room to sleep here in the kitchen tonight."

She expected him to tell Lane that wasn't necessary. But he said, "Very good," patted Whipple, and strode off in the direction of the stables. She watched him go, his back straight and broad, the hat slanted just enough to give it a rakish air. Not so long ago she'd been completely looked after by her grandmother, and had felt imprisoned. Now she felt cherished. It almost made up for the anxiety that would stay with her until Cole returned.

Lane mustered two other soldiers and had the household moved before noon the day after Cole left. By the time Martha added their few things to the purchased furnishings, she was astonished at how familiar the rooms looked. Except for a Navaho rug and several Apache baskets hanging on pegs over the fireplace, she could have been in one of the modest houses of her grandmother's friends.

The bedroom was plain, with a washstand, one chair, the small table from the previous quarters to hold a candle, and the double bed. After Martha spread out the blankets over a bed sack stuffed with new straw, she lay down and imagined Cole coming back, perhaps that night, and joining her there. The familiar and decidedly pleasant tension began building and hurriedly she got up.

After an offer to help Lane settle pots and supplies in the kitchen lean-to had been refused, she went to the hospital. She found Alice with a clear-eyed, smiling Fred. "My shoulder is sore," he said in response to her inquiry, "but I'll be fit and back to duty in a day or so." Soberly he added, "I don't think I could do what Stephen did. And I'll never be able to repay him for saving my life."

"If you're out of the hospital soon, he'll be rewarded," Martha said.

As she left, she wondered how Alice and Fred

would feel if they knew the truth about Cole.

When she got back to the new quarters, she met Major Owens. He stopped and said cordially, "I'm glad you and Mr. Baldwin are sharing the house."

"We're happy to have it." Despite her misgivings, she must offer hospitality. "We'd be pleased if you took meals with us, Major Owens."

"Thank you, Mrs. Baldwin, but I have someone who cooks for me." He nodded and went off toward the cavalry stables.

Martha remembered a glimpse of a young Apache woman when she and Cole had looked at the new quarters.

Lane was still happily busy in the kitchen. She was too restless to stay inside, so she put Whipple on his leash. "Do you know where in the laundresses' houses I can find Soledad?" she asked Lane. "I'd like to arrange with her for doing our laundry."

He looked as if he wanted to object, but he said, "I think it's the third house from the west end."

Determined not to be deterred, Martha thanked him and started off. As she walked around to the other side of the parade ground, she kept a tight rein on Whipple. It was tempting to try letting him run again, but she'd promised Cole to avoid Apaches while he was away.

The dwellings for the laundresses were not much more than huts. The roofs of tree branches surely dripped water and mud in wet weather. By comparison, Cole's and her half of a log cabin was luxurious.

When she found Soledad, the pregnant woman's appearance further unsettled Martha. Soledad's skin had lost its olive glow, and her lustrous eyes looked dull and dispirited. Her strained smile as she said, "Please come in," only made her unhealthy pallor more apparent. After Martha tied Whipple outside, Soledad showed her to the only chair and seated herself on a stool.

"How are you?" Martha asked.

"I am fine," Soledad said stiffly, reminding Martha of the social distance between them.

"That's good," Martha said, though she didn't believe it was true. She knew she couldn't ask anyone who looked so ill to do laundry for her.

"I need someone to do laundry. Can you suggest someone to ask?"

"Mrs. Bowen would like the work."

"Where can I find her?"

"If you send your striker," Soledad said, "he can bring her to your house." It was a reminder that she knew proper behavior, even if Martha didn't.

Martha got up. "Thank you. I'll send Private Lane to see Mrs. Bowen." At the doorway she stopped, not able to leave without saying something more even if it were out of character for Elizabeth. "If you should find you aren't well, Dr. Lawton at the hospital might be able to help you."

Soledad looked shocked. "I could not go to see a man."

"Yes, I just thought . . . well, good-bye."

After retrieving Whipple, Martha walked unhappily along the row of houses and back across the parade ground. She remembered that when her son was born, two old women had helped her, and the shaman had waited outside, offering prayers. She hadn't needed the herbs that were given to women having difficult labor, and she didn't know how well they worked. But she wished she had herbs for Soledad. She looked as if she would need more than ordinary help for the coming birth. Prayers too.

Cole didn't return that night, or the next. By Friday afternoon, Martha was anxious. She had fussed over the new rooms until she decided that she was too caught up in domesticity. When she realized how much she thought about Cole, especially after she went to bed, her fears returned that making love might weaken her resolve if they disagreed about how to search for her son.

The arrival of the mail rider provided a diversion. Though she didn't expect letters, she joined the group of officers and wives at the adjutant's office. Dr. Lawton was there, talking to Lydia Stratton, the fort commander's handsome wife. Martha believed Cole's reassurances that records from Washington couldn't be requested and returned in this length of time, but a shred of uneasiness remained. How she would know whether Dr. Lawton received any official mail she wasn't sure, but if they included records for Stephen Baldwin, she hoped he'd mention it. Then she and Cole could figure out what to do before the doctor made comparisons. As the mail was being passed out, Martha observed that Dr. Lawton received one letter of ordinary size—not official looking. There was nothing for the Baldwins.

"The rider actually reached us a day ahead of schedule," Lydia Stratton said. "We should have a dance to celebrate. We'll use the ward room in the old hospital again." She smiled at Martha. "Elizabeth, even if Stephen doesn't return in time, you must come to the dance anyway."

"I was wondering if I should," Martha said. In her grandmother's town, a married woman didn't go to a dance without her husband.

"Oh, my, yes," Lydia assured her. "Sometimes our husbands can be away for weeks at a time. On an army post, especially one as isolated as this, the officers and their wives are like a large family. You're part of our family."

Martha felt warmed, and not so fraudulent as she had in the past. Elizabeth's identity felt more genuine all the time.

That night anxiety about Cole kept her awake. If Peter accused Cole of not being Stephen Baldwin, what would happen? Cole might come back a prisoner. She didn't know the punishment for impersonating an officer, and she certainly couldn't ask.

Stop, she told herself. Worrying wouldn't bring Cole back sooner or more safely. Instead she must make more specific plans for finding her son. It was unlikely that group members linked by close family ties would be separated. So if Diablo was the man she was almost sure he was, Pinecone was with that band. If she approached anyone in Diablo's band, it might be someone who recognized her. The best strategy would be to make friends with someone in one of the other bands, Miguel's or Pedro's. Then, cautiously, when she was sure she had the person's confidence, she'd inquire first about her brother-in-law's wife. That name Martha would never forget.

She tried it out on her tongue: Tsalbe-stiine. She-Sticks-to-Her-Cradle. Though Martha had never forgiven She-Sticks-to-Her-Cradle for taking her son, it had consoled her a little over the years that he was being cared for by a woman who loved children.

Somehow she must gain the confidence of someone who could help her. Though any Apache woman would be loyal to her people, she would also understand a mother who wanted at least a glimpse of her child.

It all seemed complicated and dependent on chance. Martha went to bed feeling frustrated and discouraged, and frightened. She must try, otherwise this would all be for nothing. No—not for nothing. She ran her hand over the space waiting beside her. No matter what the future held, the masquerade with Cole was definitely not for nothing.

When Cole didn't return that night either, Martha passed beyond anxiety to numbness. She spent Saturday morning helping Lane make shortbread. The samples, hot from the oven, tasted better than biscuits. Whipple gladly cleaned away any crumbs that fell and begged for more.

She was licking her fingers when she heard footsteps on the veranda. Whipple sniffed, gave a yip, and raced around the side of the house. Cole! She wanted to race after the dog. Instead she hurried as fast as she modestly could through the back door. By the time she reached the front room, he was inside. She surrendered her pride and ran into Cole's arms.

He lifted her against him, bringing her mouth up to his. She could feel his kiss scorching her from her lips along the length of her body to her dangling feet. His lips gentled, inviting her to return the kiss. Tentatively she tasted his mouth, then opened hers to his eager tongue. Finally he lifted his head and let her slide down against him. Through her clothes she could feel the firm plane of his chest rubbing against her breasts and his erection pressing her abdomen. Her legs didn't want to hold her up when her feet touched the ground, but it didn't matter because his arms supported her.

At the sound of footsteps, she pulled back. "You've been gone three days."

His eyes still caressed her. "A long time. Too long."

At Lane's knock Cole turned and opened the door. After the exchange of salutes, Lane said, "Welcome back, sir. I hope your trip was a good one."

"The prisoners are in the guardhouse, so I guess it was. You and Mrs. Baldwin have done well here, I see."

Lane beamed. "Thank you, sir."

The next ten minutes she and Cole followed Lane while he showed off the details of the new quarters. When she and Cole were finally alone, with both Lane and Major Owens gone, they sat in the living room. Cole told her about his trip. "We had a little trouble. Three miners got into a fracas with a couple of young Apaches."

Alarmed, she asked, "How young?"

"Fifteen or so—older than your son. One of the miners was killed and the other two injured. We rounded them up pretty easily. Taking in the two Apaches was harder. The scouts with us finally persuaded them to surrender."

"What will happen to them?"

"They'll all go to Tucson to be tried in the court there."

"Tried in court!" she exclaimed indignantly. "But how can Apaches get a fair trial? When a white kills an Apache, he's defending himself. When an Apache kills a white, it's called murder. I'm astonished they surrendered."

"The scouts explained. The young men who raid and get into fights endanger the peaceful ones. Too many problems and the whole band suffers. So the older Apaches put pressure on these young men to give themselves up." He looked at her quizzically. "I'm surprised you still defend them, after what happened to you and your family."

"I don't forgive that, but I learned they have reasons for what they do. Their homelands were stolen. Now they live on reservations, not as their right, but because the army lets them." Other things were on her mind too. "What about Peter? Did he say anything unusual to you?"

"Nothing. He treated me the same way as always. I'm a political appointee instead of a West Pointer. So with him I rank below a good corporal."

"Does that bother you?"

He shrugged. "Not much. Whatever Peter thinks he's doing, he's not tipping his hand now. So it seems to point to interest in you, but not me." His face hardened into a scowl. "All we can do is to pretend what he says doesn't affect us. And wait and see. What about you? Anything happen here?"

"You're really asking whether I stayed away from the Apaches, aren't you?"

A teasing grin replaced the scowl. It made him look younger, almost boyish. "If I knew just what to expect you to do when I'm not here, I'd rest easier."

His expression reminded Martha of the way he looked sleeping, and a feeling of tenderness warmed her—a pleasurable but tricky emotion. "I didn't go near any Apaches. I spent most of my time right here, being very domestic."

He looked around the room and said, "I like the results."

His approval felt good, and for a moment she let herself enjoy it before she went back to reality. "The mail came again. Nothing for the Baldwins. Dr. Lawton didn't get anything that looked official. I hope you're right that medical records couldn't arrive yet. Have you found out what chance there is for you to get hold of mail from Washington before Dr. Lawton does?"

"Not too good," he said. "The mail isn't always handled by the same person. But I'll keep working on it."

She took a breath and plunged into the problem that had been most on her mind. "You asked me to stay away from the Apaches, but I have to do something about finding my son. I'll avoid anyone from Diablo's band, but I'll have to try to make friends with someone to find out where he might be. If you know some of the scouts, maybe you could get some information."

For a moment Cole's expression reminded her of her father's when he was about to do something her mother wouldn't like. "Maybe later. When I reported in, Captain Fisher told me I'll be part of the detail that takes the prisoners to Fort Lowell outside Tucson."

"You're going to Tucson?" It was bad enough that there might be visitors later on, but this was disaster. "How can you get out of it? Can you be sick?"

Tiny lines of tension appeared around his eyes. "I plan to go."

She stared at him, too shocked to answer until anger freed her voice. "That's insane! You said the trial attracted notice. Someone will recognize you."

"I started growing a beard very early. Nobody's seen me without one for years. So I'm going to shave off my beard. Nobody's going to know me. Remember what you told me about the Apaches recognizing you—people see what they expect to see."

"What if you're wrong?"

"I've thought about that." Cole's voice was pained. "I don't expect to be caught. But if that did happen, you must say I threatened you—made you come with me. That you were afraid to tell anyone."

"No one would believe that."

"Colonel Stratton would at the least be uncertain long enough that you could get away."

Despairingly she pleaded, "But why are you going? I don't understand."

"It'll give me a chance to talk to Ira Gurnett. He'll help me hunt for the witnesses I need and get me information. At the post trader's games, I heard about the corruption with supplies for the reservations. The army wants to nail the people involved. I want to make sure they get my stepfather, Harvey Lippincott." Cole spat out the last name as if he couldn't tolerate the taste of it in his mouth.

Appalled, all she could think was that he risked everything, just when she was getting closer to finding her son. "Do you resemble your father? And your voice—it will sound the same."

"I don't look a lot like my father. I used to wish I did, but now it's good I don't. I can disguise my voice."

"How can you explain shaving off your beard just before you go to Fort Lowell? Won't that seem strange?"

An ironic grin twisted his mouth. "I'll say you don't like the beard because it scratches your skin. That you've been after me a long time to shave it off. They all think I'm so crazy for you I do anything you ask."

The silence hung between them until the lines of his face softened. "If people watch me around you, they'll believe that. I can hardly keep my hands off you. Right now I'd like to be in the other room in bed with you. I guess you know that."

Her heart responded with hope before she could settle it down. "But you're going to Tucson."

"Yes. I have to."

There was one more thing she had to know. "If you found a witness, someone who could clear you, what would you do? Would you come back here?"

A long moment followed. He had to be weighing a terrible choice. "Yes, I think so."

Before she absorbed the pain of his uncertainty, he asked, "If you found your son and saw a way to leave, would you? Or would you wait for me to come back?"

"I'm not sure." It was a choice she couldn't make yet.

When they arrived at the ward room that evening, a murmur spread around the room. The men looked surprised, the women fascinated. After looking through Elizabeth's trunk, Martha had chosen a peach-colored silk dress that showed more of her breasts than any gown she'd worn before. But her appearance, she was sure, wasn't what caught the attention.

Fred, released from the hospital but confined to a chair, said, "Stephen, is that you?"

Alice was more forthright. "I declare, Stephen, you hardly look like yourself."

At least Cole was right about the extent of the difference shaving off the beard made.

No one else mentioned Cole's missing beard except Peter Dunham. He studied Cole a moment, then said, "If you hadn't been with your wife, I'd have expected an introduction."

The music began and in Cole's arms Martha felt as if she were dancing with a stranger. She should have expected the force of the jaw and the strong lines of his mouth. Even so, the clean-shaven face shocked her. The marked difference in his appearance should have reassured her as well, but she was too apprehensive about his trip to take much comfort from it.

For the first several dances Cole either kept her as a partner or maneuvered her to the opposite side of the room from Peter.

She sat for a time with Fred until Captain Fisher asked her to dance. He danced carefully and precisely, making a duty out of it, and left her beside Fred—and Peter. Before Cole could politely leave Harriet Fisher, who had been his partner, Peter bowed. "May I have the pleasure, Mrs. Baldwin?"

She had to say, "Yes."

The music slowed to a leisurely waltz. Peter said, "So your husband shaved off his beard to please you. Were you showing me your power over him?"

Martha gave Peter a deliberately puzzled glance. "Lieutenant Dunham, you're being ridiculous. Stephen is considerate of my wishes, but he does what he wants." That was true enough. "If I did have 'power' over him, I wouldn't care whether you knew it or not."

He smiled in the enigmatic way she detested. Fortunately it was a short dance, and Cole claimed her again. Soon afterward the party ended.

When she and Cole reached their quarters, he asked, "What did Peter say to you?"

"Something silly. The usual party talk." There was no point in having him worry more.

When they went to bed, Cole turned toward her and caressed her arm. "I know you're unhappy about my decision. I'm sorry about that. If I could change lots of things, I would. What I don't want to change is the way I feel when I touch you. The last three nights I thought about making love to you. Let's not lose tonight too."

She reached out to him. He kissed her, promising that their embraces would drive away unhappiness. With his hands and mouth he aroused her until every nerve in her body begged for release. When he reached the same pitch of intoxicated desire, he entered her, filling her with excruciating pleasure that was at the same time wild discontent. With each thrust her need grew until in his explosion her passion too was satiated and the promise of his earlier kiss fulfilled.

As she lay in his arms, her apprehension about the days ahead gradually returned. When she was a young girl her family had gone to Galveston and seen a circus there. One girl had walked on a high wire, capturing Martha's breath at each tentative step. Now Martha felt as if she were that performer, balanced precariously on a thin wire. But she couldn't imagine a triumphant bow for her at the end.

18

Tucson, May 25, 1877

By noon the sandy surface of Tucson's Congress Street glittered in the hot sunshine. Small barefoot boys, darting across between horses and wagons, lifted their toughened feet with unusual speed. One, dodging a rider, barreled into a man in front of the Congress Hall Saloon. The boy took a quick look at the man's angry face and dashed on, scooting around the wagons parked outside the Lord and Williams store.

"Look out, there!" Harvey Lippincott shouted. He brushed angrily at a dusty swipe left on the sleeve of his black coat. "Hellions," he muttered. "Shouldn't be allowed to run the streets." When he was poor and barefoot, he hadn't run wild. He'd got out and found work to do—a man's work in the mines, and damned hard work it was. Harvey took off his black derby hat and used his handkerchief to wipe away a line of perspiration that had collected along the edge of his silvery hair. After he carefully folded his handkerchief and resettled his hat, he went into the saloon.

Inside, the night's coolness lingered, contained by the adobe walls. An American flag hung on each side of the clock over the polished wood bar. The atmosphere of patriotic luxury soothed Harvey's irritation. He saw Elias Wilson, a reporter for the *Tucson Citizen*, across the room, and made his way through the tables, nodding with restored good humor at men he knew.

When he reached Elias, the reporter waved a welcoming hand. "Greetings, Harvey." As Harvey sat down, Elias signaled to the shirt-sleeved waiter collecting empty glasses on a tray. "A whiskey for Mr. Lippincott."

"No whiskey," Harvey called to the waiter. "I'll have a sarsaparilla." To Elias he said, "Doc Handy tells me I have to cut down on the drinking. Some damn fool thing about my heart."

"Well, you tell Mrs. Lippincott to take good care of you, so you're around for a long time."

Harvey said, "I'll do that," and thought sourly that Elias's advice was wasted. Emma was still too busy moping about her precious son's death to take a decent interest in her husband's needs.

"How's the freighting and contracting business?" Elias asked.

That topic suited Harvey much better. "The army and the Indians on the reservations still have to eat. So do their animals."

Elias gave a knowing smile. "The Indians off the reservations are mighty good to you too. The longer the Apache wars last, the more soldiers are stationed here, and the better your business is."

Harvey glanced around to make sure no one was in

hearing distance. "A few more articles about how the army's interfering with the contractors will help. But I hear that some of the Indian agents have been making charges again about spoiled beef and short weights. Now, that kind of irresponsible charge doesn't belong in your paper."

Elias leaned back, sloshing the last of his whiskey around in the bottom of his glass. "Well, now, that's a little tricky. Folks like to read about something that sounds a little scandalous."

"It will be to your advantage," Harvey promised. "Remember when the commander up at Fort Apache had the notion of letting the Apaches cut hay for the army? Even had them raising their own beef. Why, we'd have lost the meat and fodder business both. Some of you reporters were a big help in getting that stopped."

"That's right. It wouldn't have been so good for you, with all the cattle you run on the Wingate ranch."

Harvey had trouble keeping his smile in place. "We call it the Lippincott ranch now," he said. "I suggest you find something else to print. And stir up folks about why the army doesn't to stop the Apache raids. Say they should send more troops here. Leave the contractors alone."

Elias lifted his glass in a toast to himself. "I do what I can for my friends, especially the Tucson Ring."

The last of Harvey's smile disappeared. "You've had too much to drink, Elias. There is no Tucson Ring. We don't have that kind of influence in Washington. Those missionary types from the Dutch Reformed Church have too much imagination."

He left, not waiting for the sarsaparilla. As he headed north on Myers Street, he gave a disgruntled glance down Maiden Lane. That's where he'd like to be. Damned fool doctor, telling him to be careful of his heart. A visit to California Mary would do him and his heart more good than a dozen doctors. Sometimes he wasn't sure if having the Wingate ranch and mine was worth being so damned respectable. Now that Cole was dead, if Emma pined away, he wouldn't mourn long.

He stopped suddenly, then continued on slowly and turned along Pennington Street. Everyone knew Emma had put as much store in Cole as she had in his father. What if she got so despondent that she wasn't in her right mind? Women in that state had been known to take too much laudanum.

What if he helped her along?

The thought pursued him all the way to the Cosmopolitan Hotel where he was to meet Emma. Outside Harvey stopped, as if he were considering what to do, and gave himself time to think. No, he decided, there were too many past events he didn't want questioned. What he'd been contemplating was too dangerous.

Inside the Cosmopolitan Hotel Emma Wingate Lippincott perched nervously on a sofa in an alcove off the lobby. Ira Gurnett sat across from her, his tall, thin frame folded into a small chair. When she'd run into Ira, she hadn't been able to resist inviting him to sit down. He eased her craving to talk to an old friend who had loved Cole as she had. At the same time she dreaded Harvey finding her with Ira.

"I don't believe Cole was guilty," Ira was saying. It was an old conversation, repeated each time they met because of her passionate wish to hear it. "Men gone in drink do things they wouldn't when they're sober. But murder just wasn't in Cole's nature."

"But the evidence—it was his gun. There were witnesses who'd heard him swear to get Luther's murderers."

"Yes, I know. I heard him myself. But he meant legal justice. He was too much like Luther to take the law into his own hands."

Though Ira knew Emma needed his reassuring words, in his own mind doubts lingered about the truth. In the years between Emma's remarriage and Cole's return, the once happy boy had become a man as toughened in mind as in body. He'd vowed to get revenge, and Ira wasn't so sure he hadn't killed the man he was bringing back to Tucson. But Cole was dead now; Emma might as well have what comfort she could find.

Ira looked across the lobby and saw Harvey Lippincott come in. Harvey's smile, Ira decided, was like his hair, very carefully tended. Even his slight paunch made him look comfortable, a man easy with the world. In Ira's opinion it was all a front. Inside was a man as mean and angry as a gunfighter. Emma wouldn't get comfort there.

Still, Ira didn't want to make trouble for her. He rose as Harvey approached. "Good afternoon, Harvey. My wife asked me to remind you and Emma that it's been a long time since we've seen you. Olive wants you to take supper with us soon. How about Thursday?"

As Ira expected, Harvey said, "We'd enjoy that very much, but there's a meeting I have to go to."

"Then, Emma, you come see Olive, most any day you can."

"Yes, Ira." She glanced nervously at her husband. "I will, someday soon."

Ira left, knowing she wouldn't. He thought that if Cole were alive and saw how his mother's spirits had diminished, he'd likely hate Harvey Lippincott even more.

Coming over the pass in the mountains northeast of Tucson, Cole reined in to let Sergeant Briggs catch up. Partway across the desert plain was a cluster of what looked like flat brown boxes.

"That must be Fort Lowell ahead," Cole said to Sergeant Briggs.

"Yes, sir. Looks like it."

The Fort Lowell Cole remembered had first been a supply depot and then a regular army post in Tucson. He also vaguely recalled that a new fort was being constructed out of town about the time he'd come back home from his wanderings, but then he was off in pursuit of his father's murderers. So this fort was unfamiliar to him. As for his appearance—the eleven days' riding had tanned the lower part of his face so that he didn't look as if he'd just shaved off his beard. If luck were with him, he'd get away with this. Muscles tense and heart beating, he started his horse down the trail toward Fort Lowell.

Another hour of riding took them to the corrals on the north side of the fort. Cole left the four prisoners for the sergeant and five men of his detachment to guard while he reported to the adjutant's office. After the prisoners were delivered to the guardhouse and the C Company men settled in barracks, Lieutenant Faust, a pleasant man with glasses and a beard beginning to gray, showed Cole around the post.

"Once you've taken care of business," Lieutenant

Faust said, "there are plenty of things to do in town."

"How far is it into Tucson?"

"Seven miles. The Sixth Cavalry band is giving a concert at Levin's Park in town tomorrow evening. Most everyone from the post is going. Like to have you join us."

Tomorrow. Saturday, June second, 1877. Exactly ten years from the day his father was murdered. A ten-year-old grief that still ate at Cole. "Yes, thanks, I'd like to go." But not to the concert, where too many people might know him.

In the bachelor officers' mess he listened and learned that relations between the town and the fort were unpleasant when soldiers got drunk and shot inhabitants' pets. When the railroad arrived, the wealthy freight-and-supply contractors, who were not popular among the officers at Lowell, might not prosper so much. At this last bit, Cole thought with pleasure of Harvey Lippincott and hoped the railroad arrived soon.

That night he lay on a cot in Lieutenant Faust's living room and tried to plan how to get into Tucson without attending the band concert. Instead his unruly thoughts kept returning to Martha. He missed her company and her passionate responses when they made love, and he wished he knew what she was doing.

The 125-mile trip from Fort Apache to Fort Lowell should have taken no more than a week, even with a wagon. But they'd been delayed at San Carlos by a disagreement. The Indian agent had expressed at length his opinion that they had no right to take the two Apache prisoners in to the civilian court in Tucson. Finally Cole insisted on going ahead, but it had added an extra four days getting there. He didn't like being away longer than he had to, especially with Peter Dunham left at Fort Apache.

He returned to the question of the band concert. One excuse that the other men would accept occurred to him: He'd say he wanted to find a woman. Whatever else changed about Tucson, the sporting district on Maiden Lane would be there. He wondered how Martha would feel about his excuse—and realized he was thinking like a husband again! To hell with that. He needed sleep.

He settled into a more comfortable position and closed his eyes. Thoughts of Martha didn't fade, but eventually he managed to drop off.

The next morning Cole learned from the adjutant that an officer and men from one of Fort Lowell's companies would take the prisoners to the jail in Tucson on Monday. It was a relief that he wouldn't be delivering the prisoners into the town. Although he'd assured Martha that he wouldn't be recognized, he wasn't completely confident. If he was lucky enough to find Ira right away, his men could rest Sunday, and they could start back to Fort Apache on Monday.

That evening when Cole joined the Fort Lowell officers for the ride into Tucson, they were all in dress uniforms. It gave him the opening he wanted. "I think I'll skip the concert," he said to Lieutenant Faust. "I'd make Fort Apache look pretty shabby, turning up in my field uniform."

"That doesn't matter," the lieutenant assured him. "If it bothers you, we can go back and scare up a jacket you can wear."

"Well, to tell the truth, with just a night or two down this way, I'd rather spend my time with a woman. There must be some in Tucson who are . . . friendly to strangers."

Lieutenant Faust's smile acknowledged that he understood. When they reached the outskirts of Tucson, he told Cole, "Just follow Stone Avenue to Maiden Lane and go right. I think you'll find what you're looking for."

Cole said, "Thanks," and fell behind the others until they turned to go toward the old presidio. He continued south on Stone Avenue past Maiden Lane and took Church Street. From there he cut across Church Square, letting his horse slow to a walk in front of San Augustin's Church. Its low tower and cross made a familiar outline against the night sky. He remembered afternoons he'd hung around the square, waiting for the girls to come out of the convent school next door.

No time for reliving memories. Ira's wife, Cole remembered, liked concerts, but Ira didn't. If his luck held, he might find his father's friend at home alone. When he reached Myers Street, he put his horse into a steady trot going south.

The Gurnetts lived on the edge of town in a rambling adobe that had been built for a large Mexican family. Ira and Olive had wanted children but never had any. Cole thought that probably explained why Ira had taken so much interest in him. Over the years that concern had been important to Cole, and never more than now.

When he approached the house, he reined in to take a look. Three carriages stood with their horses hitched to the railing, along with two saddle horses. The rooms along the front were all lit. He swore under his breath. The Gurnetts were entertaining.

Nothing to do but wait. There'd be a servant or two

in the house, but on Saturday night none of the hands who worked outside would be around. Cole made a wide circle to the back and dismounted beside the corral. His horse champed restlessly, perhaps because he smelled the fodder in the barn. Cole patted him on the neck. "Sorry to make you stay out here," he said softly. "I promise you a good rubdown when we get back to Lowell."

Soon afterward he heard voices from the front of the house and slipped around where he could see what was happening. Guests were getting in carriages and onto horses. From the conversation he could hear, they were heading for the band concert. To his disgust, he saw Ira help Olive into one of the carriages and get in with her. Damn! Why the hell did Ira have to take up music now? When the sounds of hoofbeats and creaking wheels died away, Cole went back to the corral to check on his horse and find a place to settle down for the next several hours.

As at other quiet times since he'd left Fort Apache, thoughts of Martha surfaced. It still surprised him that a woman who'd first appeared so proper was so bold. More than bold—reckless. At times he was furious with her. Probably he'd be angry more often except that he understood the thrill of challenging danger. That feeling of excitement was one of the reasons he was in Tucson now.

The rattling of wheels interrupted his thoughts. He listened, and when the sounds stopped, he rose and went around far enough to see. It was Ira alone. He got out of his carriage but left the horse hitched up and the carriage lantern on. Elated, Cole guessed Ira had taken Olive to the concert and would go back to pick her up when it was over. That should give a couple of hours when Ira would be alone except for the servants. The gods, Cole decided exultantly, were still with him.

He didn't have time to intercept Ira before he went inside, so he stayed motionless in the shadows. He'd wait to make sure Ira would be alone before revealing himself. A few steps took him to the wall beside the recessed window of the office, Ira's favorite place to sit and read. He heard Ira say to someone, "No, don't wait up." Then came the sound of footsteps entering the office. In a moment the glow of a kerosene lamp sent out a square of light onto the sandy ground beside the house.

A door banged farther away. That would be the servant going to one of the rooms across the back of the central patio. Cole waited another five minutes, then stepped cautiously to the window and looked in. Ira sat reading in a familiar old leather armchair. *This is it*, Cole thought. He tapped on the glass.

Ira looked up and stared at the window. Cole moved closer so that the light shone on his face. He tapped again. The book fell from Ira's lap as he grabbed for a gun on the table beside him.

"Ira!" Cole spoke carefully so the sound would carry through the glass without rousing anyone else in the house. "It's Cole."

Ira leaned forward, gripping the gun. Even through the distortion of the wavy glass, Cole could see Ira's face become almost as white as the walls. Ira rose and came slowly to the window and opened it.

"Cole?" His stunned voice sounded old and uncertain.

"Yes, I'm alive." The reassurance seemed necessary. "I don't want anyone to see me. Is it all right to come in?"

In reply Ira put down his gun and reached out a hand. Using it as leverage, Cole boosted himself through the window and found himself in a bear hug. When he was released, he saw tears in Ira's eyes and felt the beginning of tears in his.

"My God, Cole! You scared the shit out of me." That sounded more like the Ira he remembered. "You're lucky I didn't shoot you. You don't look like yourself without the beard. What happened? Why are you in an army uniform?"

"You probably won't believe it. Sometimes I don't, myself."

"We got word you'd been killed in a raid. There's an inscription for you on Luther's tombstone."

His father's tombstone—those words robbed Cole of his euphoria at being with Ira. "That's why I'm here, to talk about my father's death and all the rest."

"Then sit down and start talking."

"All right, but first—how's my mother?"

"Unhappy about you. Otherwise she's getting along all right."

That wasn't the most satisfying report, but he needed to get on with his story.

When he finished, Ira sat quietly for a moment, then said, "Do you know the risk you're running coming back here?"

"Yes, but I had to talk to you. I didn't kill Sam Weaver. I was bringing him back to testify against Harvey. Judging from the way Harvey operates, he probably hired someone to kill Sam for him. I need your help to find that man."

Ira shook his head. "You're likely right about what happened. But the man Harvey hired probably got out of the Territory."

"Maybe. But then again, the killing would give the man a good source of money blackmailing Harvey. I'd bet that whoever Harvey hired comes around to get more money out of him. You know people here. I'm hoping you can find out something for me."

"That's possible." Ira sat, rubbing his knuckles. "Of course I'll help you if I can. But what if you never find this man? He could be dead. What would you do then?"

Cole stood and walked restlessly around the room, looking at the familiar objects. Finally he faced Ira again. "I just have a feeling that I'll find that man. If I don't, Harvey still has to pay for my father's death."

"That means you intend to kill him?"

"Yes."

Ira stood and put his hand on Cole's arm. "I believe you're not a murderer. I don't want you to be one. Be patient. I'll do my damnedest to come up with some information for you."

"Thanks, Ira. I was counting on you. Now I'd better get away before you have to go back to pick up your wife." Cole found paper and pencil on Ira's desk and wrote down Stephen Baldwin's name and company. "Here's the name you can use to get in touch with me. You better make up a name for the return address."

Ira grinned. "You mean, like the señorita you visited tonight?"

Cole said, "No," a little more sharply than he intended.

Ira looked at him carefully. "What about this Martha, or Elizabeth—whatever you call her? Can you count on her?"

"She has as much at stake as I do." He and Martha were co-conspirators, but they were more than that now. He wasn't sure just how much, but enough that he had another request of Ira. "If I should be recognized, would you go to Fort Apache and see what you can do to help Martha? I know it's a big favor, but there's no one else I can ask."

"Of course I'll go. She means a lot to you?"

Cole hadn't been ready to answer that question for himself, but he owed an answer to Ira. "Yes, she does."

Sunday at Fort Lowell Cole felt more relaxed than he had since he left Fort Apache. Aside from some sly comments about his lack of interest in music, no one cared what he'd been doing in Tucson. There was time to rest and see that his men and animals were ready to start back to Fort Apache. And to look forward to being with Martha.

Early Monday as he was closing his saddlebags, a summons came from the adjutant's office. When he arrived there, the harried-looking adjutant returned his salute and said, "Mr. Baldwin, arrangements for the disposition of the prisoners have changed. You and your men are to deliver them to the Tucson jail and turn them over to the civil authorities."

Cole's pulse began to drum. "But, sir, my orders were to turn the prisoners over to you. My men are waiting for me to leave."

"Then tell them they're not going yet," the adjutant snapped. "These are your orders now. You will have your detail at the guardhouse immediately after morning parade."

As Cole walked away, he thought grimly that if he liked danger, he should be delighted now. He wasn't.

Lieutenant Faust explained. "There's been a lot of

trouble between the military and civilian authorities over who should try Indians, with the Indian agents mixing in too. Here at Lowell we get complaints all the time. I'm guessing the CO decided to let you take in the prisoners so that if someone's unhappy, you'll get blamed. He can say we're not involved."

The explanation made sense, but it didn't ease Cole's renewed anxiety. So much for his belief that the gods were smiling on him. For a while they just hadn't been looking.

He took the papers he'd happily turned over to the adjutant on Friday and met Sergeant Briggs and his Fort Apache detail at the guardhouse. The prisoners were already in a wagon. The Apaches looked defiant, the miners uneasy. Cole was about to start out when he realized that he shouldn't know where to go. "Better tell me where the jail is, corporal," he said to the soldier on duty at the guardhouse.

"Yes, sir. It's back of the courthouse. On Church Avenue, just south of Cemetery Street, next to Leatherwood's Corral."

"Thank you, Corporal."

They left, and Cole mentally castigated himself for almost slipping up. He couldn't afford mistakes like that. As he rode he flexed his muscles, trying to ease them, but by the time they reached the outskirts of Tucson, his neck and shoulders felt encased in iron. As an officer, he could let the sergeant and men take the prisoners into the cells. The only person he'd have to see would be the head jailer. It might not even be the same man. Anyhow, he'd been in enough tight places that he could count on his hands being steady to hand over the papers.

When they arrived at the back of the courthouse, he

dismounted and waited by his horse. After the prisoners climbed down from the wagon, Cole told Sergeant Briggs, "Go on inside. I'll be in the jailer's office."

The sergeant went about seeing the prisoners inside, and Cole went up a single step into the office. He stopped at the door and took a breath, then went in.

The man at the desk looked up, and it was the same ruddy face, even to the small scar over one bushy eyebrow. Dan Jackson was still the jailer. Cole walked over to one side of the desk so that the light from the window was at his back. Making his voice as gruff as he could, he said, "Here are the papers for the prisoners from Fort Apache."

"Thank you, Lieutenant . . ." Jackson looked at the papers. " . . . Baldwin. If you don't mind waiting, I'll check these." He left and went through an inner door. Before it swung shut after him, Cole glimpsed the iron bars of the first cell.

He stood with his back to the window and felt sweat trickle down from his collar. By the time Jackson returned, the whole back of Cole's shirt was wet under his wool jacket.

"All settled, Lieutenant Baldwin." Jackson sounded friendly, something Cole had never heard when he was on trial for murder. "Your first trip to Tucson?"

Conversation was about as appealing to Cole right then as an encounter with a scorpion. "Yep. Nice place."

"Where you from, Lieutenant?"

"St. Louis." Sergeant Briggs appeared outside. "I see my men are ready."

The jailer's bushy eyebrows went up. Cole hoped it was in surprise that he wasn't more friendly. He didn't wait to find out.

Though the air was already warm outside, it felt chilly to Cole. "Let's go," he said to Sergeant Briggs, and swung up onto his mount. From the resigned looks of his detail, he guessed they would have liked to linger in Tucson. He didn't give them the chance. Nudging his horse in motion, he rode north on Church Avenue and felt as if he were leaving the devil at his back.

Harvey Lippincott paused in front of Leatherwood's Corral and stared at the army officer riding the gray gelding. When the officer came out of the jail, something about his walk seemed familiar. The blue stripe on his pants indicated he was an infantry officer, and Harvey couldn't think of any infantry officer he knew. But that walk was familiar in some way. Suddenly, it struck him that Luther Wingate had had that same kind of arrogant swing to his stride.

A pleasant thought occurred to Harvey. Wouldn't it be a great joke if Luther had a by-blow? An illegitimate son he could tell Emma about, to let her know her precious Luther hadn't been such a saint after all.

Harvey walked on to the jail and went into the office. After he exchanged greetings with Dan Jackson, he said, "By the way, who was that officer who was just in here? I think maybe I know him."

"A Lieutenant Baldwin, from Fort Apache. He brought some prisoners in."

"Did he happen to say where he's from?"

"Yes, matter of fact he did. Comes from St. Louis."

Luther had never been in St. Louis. Harvey said his good-byes and left. Too bad, he mused. He'd have loved seeing Emma's face when he told her about the

Wingate born on the wrong side of the blanket.

The idea still pulled at him. A woman could have met Luther and then gone to St. Louis to have her child. It was a farfetched notion, but appealing. Harvey thought idly that it might be worth following up on that officer if he had a chance.

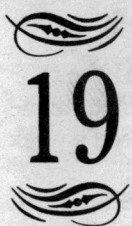

19

Fort Apache, June 7, 1877

Martha looked out the front window for the hundredth time and saw Dr. Lawton heading for the hospital. Quickly she put on her hat and went outside. She arrived at the boardwalk just as the doctor passed.

"Good morning, Dr. Lawton."

"Mrs. Baldwin." He smiled warmly. "I've missed seeing you since we don't share quarters."

"Yes, I too. I'm out for a walk because it's such a pleasant morning. Do you mind if I go along with you?"

"I'd be delighted."

As they walked, the doctor remarked on the patches of phlox and purple lupine that were brave enough to spring up on the parade ground. When they had almost reached the hospital, Martha got around to the question she hadn't asked anyone for fear the extent of her anxiety might show. "How many days does it take to get to Tucson and back?"

Dr. Lawton gave her a sympathetic look. "Someone with prisoners in a wagon would probably need a week each way, if everything goes smoothly."

If everything goes smoothly—frightening words.

"You're missing your husband, I'd guess," he added.

"Yes, I am." More than missing him. As each day passed, her apprehension built. Now she was terrified for him. She was less fearful for herself. If something happened, she hoped she could escape into the wilderness and at least have a chance. In the Tucson jail, he wouldn't have any. "I'm frightened," she blurted out.

Dr. Lawton's eyebrows went up a fraction. "Forgive me for my frankness, Mrs. Baldwin, but you seem to be a woman who is seldom frightened. That's what makes you different from most of the young wives who follow their husbands to army posts."

"Thank you for the compliment, but I worry the way any other wife does."

"I assure you, Mrs. Baldwin, that there's little reason. For some time the Apaches have been quiet all along that route. Your husband strikes me as a resourceful and capable man. Save your worrying until there's more cause."

He had no idea how much cause there was to worry, but she did feel calmer. She smiled at him gratefully. "Thank you, Dr. Lawton. I'll try to follow your advice."

They reached the hospital and exchanged goodbyes. As Martha walked on, she thought how easily she identified herself as a wife. Did that mean she loved Cole?

She stopped at the edge of the bluff near the ford, staring down at the river, but not seeing it. Love wasn't part of their bargain, and both their tasks were unfinished. But that's what had happened—she loved him.

Though she'd told Cole many things about herself, she wouldn't reveal her love to him. It might seem she was trying to bind him to her beyond the conclusion of their bargain. She sealed it away in herself.

A rider splashing through the ford distracted her. It was the mail carrier, bringing along with the mail the worry of medical papers from Washington. She followed the others to the adjutant's office, searching in her mind for a better way than looking over Dr. Lawton's shoulder to find out if Stephen Baldwin's records had arrived. At least Peter Dunham was out on patrol for two days. She was especially glad he wasn't around for mail delivery.

Dr. Lawton hadn't appeared to get his mail when Martha heard Baldwin called. Again there were two letters, one from Elizabeth's mother and the other from Stephen's sister. After a glance to identify them, she lingered, pretending a great interest in the cavalry drill on the parade ground. At last Martha saw Dr. Lawton coming for his mail. She continued watching the drill but from the corner of her eyes kept track of the doctor as he went inside the adjutant's office. When he came back out, she intercepted him. "Dr. Lawton," she said softly, "I've been a little concerned because Stephen is often so tired. I keep wondering if there's something about his health he hasn't told me. Can you find anything to explain it in his medical records?"

He frowned impatiently. "I don't have Stephen's records yet, but I'm sure they will show him to be as healthy as he looks. Maybe he isn't sleeping enough. I'm sure you can see that he gets more sleep, Mrs. Baldwin."

His voice was bland, with no suggestive edge, but she felt her face heat up. Still, it was worth the discomfort to know the medical records hadn't arrived. She smiled and said, "Thank you, Dr. Lawton. I'll remember your advice."

She walked back to her quarters and resolved to subdue her fears for Cole's safety. Nothing she did would affect the outcome of his trip; she must get on with living Elizabeth's life. To begin with that meant reading and answering the letters; it should keep her mind occupied.

Myra Baldwin's letter began with a brief inquiry about the broken hand and quickly went to a passionate denunciation of her parents for refusing to let her visit Arizona. Martha was pleased that her descriptions of the dangers had been so effective. A disquieting note came at the end, however. In her unpunctuated style Myra wrote, "I haven't given up hope tell Stephen he should write to papa and say I should visit."

Martha sat down at the table and took up the pen in her left hand. *Dear Myra, Thank you for your letter. I'm sorry that Stephen cannot write to your father because he is away. Most of the officers of the post are gone on patrol.* She studied what she'd written and frowned over the words, *your father*. What would Elizabeth call her father-in-law? Should she rewrite her paragraph and make it Father Baldwin? No, she'd leave the phrase as it was. Sighing, she took up her pen to continue with a brief but dull description of Elizabeth's life.

She finished the letter to Myra and opened Mrs. Polk's. It expressed sympathy and concern for her hand and included advice for soaking it in hot salty water and then rubbing it with grease. She read on through the account of family activities to the affectionate closing.

Another sheet of paper followed, with the notation at the top that it was for Elizabeth alone. "I am alarmed," Mrs. Polk wrote, "that you are allowing Stephen to persuade you to go riding. Since you have never cared to ride, he should accept your refusal. I realize that conditions in Arizona are different from St. Louis, and also that it is very important that you please Stephen. But remember what is *essential*, for Stephen's family as well as for him. You *must not* risk anything that might prevent your conceiving a child. You may believe, Elizabeth, that the past is past, as perhaps it should be. But that is not often the case."

Puzzled, Martha reread the separate note again. Clearly the last advice was to be kept from Stephen. The irony of it struck her—she was impersonating a woman who had secrets too.

Awkwardly Martha wrote, *Dear Mother, Thank you for your letter and your good advice. I will follow it carefully.* She finished with the same routine account she had given Myra Baldwin. As she sealed the envelope, she hoped she wouldn't have to receive and answer many letters. Already Martha felt a connection to Elizabeth's mother who still would have to go through the loss of her child.

A knock on the door forced her to compose herself before she opened it to Mrs. Bowen. She had a worn face and reddened hands that testified to the privations of her life on frontier posts. She held a bundle of clean laundry she was bringing back.

"Please come in, Mrs. Bowen," Martha said, then noticed that the laundress's eyes were swollen and teary.

If there was a protocol that prohibited an officer's wife inquiring into the personal affairs of an enlisted man's wife, Martha didn't care. She drew the other woman inside and said, "I think something bad must have happened. Do you object to telling me about it, Mrs. Bowen?"

The tears surfaced. "It's Soledad. Poor thing, she's dead in childbirth this morning, and the babe too. May God protect her soul and the soul of the little one."

Soledad dead! Martha felt a pain that was part sorrow and part self-blame, and she wept along with Mrs. Bowen.

After Mrs. Bowen left, Martha decided she must see Alice, who might be apprehensive if she knew about Soledad.

As soon as they'd exchanged greetings, Alice said, her voice trembling, "Did you hear that a laundress died this morning? In childbirth."

"Yes, I did hear."

"Elizabeth, I'm frightened."

Martha took Alice's cold hands and rubbed them. "It's natural to be frightened. It's also natural to have babies. Most babies and mothers get along fine." She longed to reassure Alice with her experience and chose the next best way. "My sister was afraid too, and she had a healthy baby with no problems."

Alice calmed down enough to take out an unfinished baby quilt. Martha spent the afternoon helping with the sewing. At suppertime Alice asked Martha to spend the night. "Fred's away, and so is Stephen. Please, Elizabeth, stay."

In the middle of the night Martha wakened to Alice's moans and cries. As soon as she saw the blood, she knew what was happening. Frantically she propped Alice's hips up and used towels to try to stop the bleeding. Then she threw a shawl over her nightgown and said to Alice, "I'm going to get Dr. Lawton."

"No," Alice panted, "I don't want a man here." But she screamed again.

Martha grabbed a lantern and ran to the doctor's quarters. She pounded on the door, calling, "Dr. Lawton. You must come!" The doctor appeared, his white hair disheveled. "Alice is having a miscarriage."

Seeing that he was getting into motion, she ran back to Alice's quarters. Dr. Lawton arrived a few minutes later, but as Martha feared, there was nothing he could do. When it was over and he had given Alice laudanum, he said, "I'll rouse Harriet Fisher. She'll want to know about this."

Later, when Harriet had insisted she would take a turn staying with Alice, Martha walked back to her quarters. The post lay quiet, clinging to the last of the night's sleep. Pink-tinged light barely showed above the flat-topped mountains to the east. Dejectedly Martha went up the walk to her house, then paused to look again to the east. That light promised a new day, but in the previous one, Soledad's unfinished life and two unlived ones had been lost. What did it mean? As she watched color spread across the sky, determination grew in her. Life could be too easily destroyed. Cole might not return, and while she waited for him, a chance for her to regain her child might be lost also. If there was any kind of opportunity, no matter how slight, she must seize it.

Two days later after the Sunday morning Bible service, Harriet Fisher announced there would be no midday dinner for C Company officers and wives. "It doesn't seem appropriate when Mrs. Collins has suffered such a recent loss. And the sad events yesterday." There had been a simple burial service for Soledad on Saturday. "Several of the officers and their wives are planning to visit one of the Apache camps," Harriet continued. "You have spent too much time with Alice, Elizabeth. Now that Mr. Collins is back, I think you should get out with the others. Lieutenant Brown can tell you about it."

"Thank you. I'll speak to Lieutenant Brown." Though Martha tried not to get too excited, anticipation began to build. She would have to find out which encampment they would visit. If it were not Diablo's, she would go. She saw Vernon Brown ahead of her on the boardwalk and hurried to catch up with him.

In response to her question, he said, "It's Miguel's camp. Or I should call it a ranchería, that's the term here. We're going to ride out in three quarters of an hour."

"Where are the other bands camped?" she asked.

"Diablo and Pedro have their rancherías along creeks east of the fort. Miguel's is west. I hope you'll join us, Mrs. Baldwin."

"Yes, I'd like to."

She hurried to her quarters and changed into a riding dress. In Elizabeth's trunk she found some heavy black veiling and pinned it to a small black hat, then put the hat on. As long as she kept the veil in place, the woman who looked back at her from the oval mirror on the bedroom wall would be impossible to identify.

Martha arrived at the cavalry stables early. The horses were still tethered on the picket line, being groomed. She spotted Skinny and went to pat his neck.

"Are you joining us for the ride?"

Dismayed, she turned to face Peter Dunham. As usual, he had on a perfectly turned out uniform and a smile to match. She looked at him warily and reconsidered whether to go. Behind him she saw Vernon Brown and decided. "Yes, I'm interested in seeing an Apache ranchería." She would stay in Vernon's company.

The encampment was a few miles from the fort, on the west side. Several Apache women were hoeing in a field along the river. One had a boy of about eight or nine with her. Though Martha knew she wasn't apt to see her son there, she let her horse lag behind while she studied the boy. He and the woman looked completely unfamiliar. Disappointed, she urged her horse to a trot and caught up with the others.

After about an hour, they reached the ranchería. These wickiups were different from the ones Martha had lived in. Those had been covered with buckskin. Most of these had canvas over them. But the *ramadas* looked the same—like rooms with roofs made of leafy branches, and no walls, only corner posts. The smell of corn and beans cooking, the dogs barking, and the black-haired children laughing—these impressions took her back vividly.

The scout went forward to greet Miguel, who welcomed them. Now and again Martha understood a word but caught only a little of the meaning. Her ear wasn't tuned to the whole phrases necessary to make sense out of the Apache speech.

After the riders dismounted, Martha walked to an area where young boys were playing hoop and pole. As each boy took his turn at throwing a hoop and then a pole to fall where the hoop would land on it, she remembered Sharp-Knife talking to their infant son, promising he would teach Pinecone to be the champion hoop-and-pole player. The bittersweet memory was so sharp that she had to turn away from the game.

As she walked around the ranchería with the others from the fort, she began to feel discouraged. She couldn't envision how she would get to know one of these women, much less become friendly enough to make inquiries about her son. How could they talk when, even as she remembered the language, she couldn't use it? Then she thought of the young woman she'd seen going into Major Owens's half of the quarters. The major must use some language to speak to the housekeeper. Arizona had been a Mexican territory until midcentury. Spanish might be the key. Martha decided she would try speaking to Major Owens's housekeeper. It distressed her that she hadn't attempted it before. She'd let Cole's prohibitions constrain her too much.

On the ride back, Vernon lagged behind with the scout, and Peter moved up to ride behind Martha. She didn't like the feeling of his being at her back. When they reached the stables, Peter said, "Mrs. Baldwin, is your horse lame?"

She was sure Skinny wasn't lame, but Peter's question alerted the private at the stables who considered Skinny his particular charge. While she waited for his inspection, Vernon walked around restlessly, obviously anxious to go. "I don't mind waiting for Mrs. Baldwin," Peter told him. "Then I'll escort her to her quarters."

"Fine," Vernon said, and started off.

Martha gritted her teeth and turned her back on Peter.

"I can't find anything wrong, ma'am," the private said.

"I didn't think you would," she said. "Thank you, though, for looking."

Still angry, she walked with Peter as far as the edge of the parade ground, then said, "I prefer to walk back to my quarters by myself, thank you, Lieutenant Dunham."

"Oh, but I told Vernon I'd be your escort."

Exasperation and a measure of apprehension put an edge on her voice. "That doesn't oblige me to walk with you." Turning, she started toward officers' row, only to find him following after.

Martha thought they must look ridiculous, walking in two-step like a comedy team, but she kept on. She was behaving exactly as a wife should with a man not her husband. Peter apparently wasn't worried, because he followed her to the front of her quarters.

She stopped and faced him then. He wouldn't try to go inside with her, not when anyone could see. "Goodbye, Lieutenant Dunham," she said.

Before she could turn away, he said softly, "It would please me very much if you were at home this evening. I'd like to stop and see you."

An undertone to his voice warned her not to obey her first impulse—to go inside and slam the door without answering. "Lieutenant Dunham, my husband is not at home, but he is expected at any time. If he is here, he will be too tired to have visitors. If he isn't home yet, it would be improper for me to receive you."

"But you haven't always worried about what's proper, have you, Elizabeth?"

His use of her first name was an affront, but Martha was too alarmed now to react to that. She spoke quietly but forcefully. "Lieutenant Dunham. *You may not visit when my husband is not home.*"

"I think it's the other way. I wouldn't want to visit if Stephen were home. You see, Elizabeth, I've noticed things about you, and I think you'll want to discuss them with me. Just today I saw the way you watched the children."

He paused, as if enjoying the effect or perhaps waiting for a comment. Martha's throat was too dry to talk, and all her effort concentrated on not showing fear.

"Anyone watching you," he went on, "would say it's a shame you don't have children. But then, is that true? Can you truthfully say you've never had a child?"

For a moment longer he stayed, his gaze fixed on her.

Fury helped overcome fear. "I have a gun. If you dare to come here tonight, I'll shoot you."

Briefly he looked taken aback. Then his confident smile returned. "I don't think so. You don't have the stomach for it. And I think you want to hear what I have to say. I'll see you this evening." He gave a mocking bow and left.

20

Martha grabbed for a sheet of paper as it fluttered off the table in the front room. It was Myra Baldwin's letter. She tossed it aside and resumed her frantic hunt for the extra note from Mrs. Polk. Where could it be?

Ready to scream with frustration she stopped and stood back to look. A corner of white showed where the edge of the table rested against the wall. She pulled at the corner and an envelope came up. Mrs. Polk's letter must have slid over the edge and caught there.

She gave her shaky fingers time to recover before she opened the envelope and found the extra page. After she reread it twice, she put it carefully away in Elizabeth's trunk, then sat down to think.

Elizabeth had a secret, Martha concluded, that concerned a child. Or at least a pregnancy. The secrecy of Mrs. Polk's letter implied that Stephen wasn't the father, and probably didn't know about the pregnancy. Something had happened to the child. Maybe a miscarriage. Perhaps the child had been given up for adoption. Or there were dangerous things desperate girls and women did to themselves.

Trying to remember everything Peter had said, Martha decided that somehow he knew enough about Elizabeth's past to think he could use the information. One of the cousins he mentioned could have been a close enough friend to know about Elizabeth's troubles. Elizabeth must have gone away, which would account for Peter's remarks about mail from someplace besides St. Louis.

If Peter didn't know that she wasn't Elizabeth, it would explain why he hadn't dropped hints to Cole. He wasn't threatening to expose the masquerade. He was threatening to tell Stephen about Elizabeth's pregnancy in order to blackmail her, for sexual favors.

It was impossible to sit, and Martha rose and paced nervously around the room. What if she were wrong about Elizabeth's past? If Peter knew something different that she had no clue about, he might guess the truth. Oh, if Cole would only return!

She heard the sound of the front door and then Lane's footsteps going to the back room. In her worries she'd forgotten him. Here was her answer—make an excuse to keep him about. Peter couldn't let the striker see him here with Cole gone. She took several deep breaths to restore her outward composure, then went along the hall and knocked on Lane's door.

When he opened it, she said, "Private Lane, I don't want to impose on you, but I wondered if you could help me this evening. The . . . ah, light for reading at night isn't good. Would you mind helping me try the furniture in different places?"

Lane looked distressed. "I'm sorry, ma'am. I can't.

HEARTBREAK TRAIL

I've just been put on guard duty for tonight."

"That's too bad," she said, trying not to sound as upset as she felt.

"I don't feel easy about it, most particularly because Major Owens is officer of the day. Lieutenant Baldwin wouldn't like me leaving you alone in quarters. I tried to get out of it, but the sergeant said they needed me."

Strikers escaped many of the regular details. Had Peter arranged for Lane to get duty? "Please, don't worry about me," she said, managing somehow to sound unconcerned. "Stephen might even return by tonight."

Lane's unhappy expression eased a little. "Yes, ma'am, I surely hope he does."

Martha's next thought was to visit Alice and Fred. Maybe they'd invite her to have supper with them. Possibly, if she sounded lonesome enough, she'd be asked to stay overnight. She walked quickly along the boardwalk as the afternoon was almost over. She didn't have much time left.

Fred let Martha in with a polite greeting but he lacked his usual cordiality. To Martha's surprise, Alice was sitting in a chair with a blanket over her knees. After Martha gave Alice a hug, she said, "You must be feeling better to be up out of bed."

Alice sent her husband an angry look. "No, I'm not. But Dr. Lawton thinks I should be up. Of course Fred agrees with him."

Fred flushed. "I just feel we ought to do what Dr. Lawton advises."

"He doesn't know what's best for a woman, and you don't either," Alice said sullenly.

"Would you like me to make some tea?" Martha asked.

"I just want someone to pay attention to what I think." Tears began forming in Alice's eyes.

Martha put aside her troubled thoughts to do what she could to soothe Alice. By the time she made tea and they drank it, Fred didn't object when Alice insisted that Martha help her back to bed.

"Thank you, Elizabeth, for coming," Fred said when Martha came out of the bedroom and closed the door. "I wish I could invite you to stay longer, but, well, it's hard to get Alice to do what Dr. Lawton says unless we're alone."

Martha knew she couldn't impose on Fred and Alice now. "I understand," she said. "Alice will surely feel better soon. This is just very difficult for her now."

Once outside, her own problems returned to her full force. It was no use wishing for Cole. She must decide for herself about Peter.

She reached her quarters, and thought of another worry. If anyone saw Peter arrive, her reputation would be jeopardized. Questions would be asked about Cole and her. But surely Peter would be careful not to be seen. He ran a risk too. It probably didn't matter that he was married. But an officer was supposed to respect the wife of another officer. She could threaten him with reporting his attentions. It would be a bluff, but he wouldn't know that.

The most frightening uncertainty had to be considered. What if Peter knew the truth about Cole and her? If he threatened to reveal their masquerade? She imagined how Peter's mind might work. He chose to threaten her because she was a female he could make use of, but he left Cole alone because he was afraid of what Cole might do. Afraid Cole might kill him.

The words circled around in her head: kill him. Terrible, horrifying words.

She shuddered. Images of death returned to her—of her parents and brother slaughtered beside the trail. Sharp-Knife's lifeless body, carried back from a raid.

There were bolts on the door; she could refuse to let Peter in—but that would only postpone another set of threats. Everything suddenly seemed clear. The thing to do was to confront him and deny everything. But she must be skillful, let him make accusations so that she could judge how much he knew.

Could she lie with Peter to save herself and Cole? A chill ran through her body. First she would pray to God, to all the Apache deities, and to her own wits to keep her safe from that.

When it was dark, Martha drew the heavy curtains and turned the kerosene lamps low. She thought over her conclusions again, but nothing new occurred to her. Outside a dog howled and others took up the mournful chorus. The sound seemed to reflect Martha's anguished frame of mind.

Restlessly she made a path from the front room into the bedroom and back again. She'd chosen a dress with long sleeves and a high neckline, relieved only by a small lace collar. It was the kind of apparel her grandmother had worn, and Martha associated it with an imperious woman who dominated the others around her. Putting it on had been donning a kind of armor. She had pulled her hair back into a tight bun. Peter Dunham would find a woman who looked forbidding.

She opened the tray of her trunk where she kept the derringer and looked at it and the cartridges beside it.

Finally she took it out and put it in her pocket, unloaded.

When she thought she couldn't endure the waiting longer, a soft tap sounded at the outer door at the back. Her heart gave a tremendous beat, driving breath out of her chest. Then it settled down into a strong, steady rhythm that let her breathe freely. Hoping she had the strength she needed, she went to the door and let Peter inside.

He looked ready for a general's inspection, the three creases in his jacket sharply defined. Martha had a moment's conviction that he couldn't possibly intend anything so untidy as bedding her. The anticipation in his blue eyes and smile dispelled her hope.

"Good evening," he said.

She turned and walked back along the hall to the front room without answering. This wasn't a social evening, and she wouldn't pretend it was.

When they were inside the front room, he put his hat on a peg beside the door, then studied her. "You look very lovely, Elizabeth," he said, with a slight stress on her name.

Her hope that he didn't question her identity faltered. Still, there was nothing to do except keep to her planned defense. She held her head rigidly erect and imitated her grandmother's most chilling voice. "You do not have permission to use my Christian name, Lieutenant Dunham." With an imperious gesture toward a chair, she said, "Please sit down, Lieutenant. It's time for our discussion."

Peter smiled, looking amused and confident. "You're not the commanding officer, Elizabeth. Do you think we really need to talk? That's not what I'm here for." He reached out and touched her cheek.

She slapped his hand away. "Don't touch me! This afternoon you said you have things to discuss with me. That's the only reason I let you in."

He laughed outright. "My, you are fierce. All right, we'll talk for a while." He sat down and settled himself comfortably, as if he anticipated a friendly chat. "What do you want to talk about?"

She took the chair opposite him, not relaxing her rigid stance. "You are the one who said we had something to discuss."

"Yes, but I let ladies go first." He was playing games again, circling around her like a strong animal wearing down a weaker one.

For a moment she let him wait, then said, "Blackmail."

His eyebrows rose a little, but she hadn't disturbed his composure. "That's an unpleasant topic."

"I believe it accurately describes what you've been attempting. Almost since Stephen and I met you, you've been hinting that you know something about me. Something that I wouldn't want known." Her stomach was like a cold rock and her palms were damp. But she pushed on. "Say plainly what you think you know."

Peter didn't answer. He leaned back, as if thinking, but his eyes betrayed his enjoyment. She didn't delude herself that he was reconsidering his threat—he was prolonging the entertainment. The torture.

There had been a few people in her life she'd hated, but not with the degree of hatred Peter aroused at that moment.

Finally he spoke. "I know that you have had a child, and—" He stopped, eyeing her.

She waited, still in limbo, to hear the rest.

"And I know that it wasn't Stephen's." He smiled, an expression of satisfaction.

Nothing about an impersonation!

In her relief, Martha laughed. For the first time since he'd arrived, Peter looked taken aback, his confidence not quite so complete.

"That is not true," she said. "It's ridiculous."

"If it's not true, why did you let me in tonight?" he challenged her.

"Today you threatened me. I don't like that. I decided the way to put an end to your threats was to talk to you." She stood up and went to the door. As if no question remained whether he would do as she asked, she said dismissively, "Good night, Lieutenant Dunham."

The ploy didn't work. He rose also, but he didn't move toward the door. "No, I'm not leaving. We haven't settled this yet."

She leaned against the door a moment, gathering strength. "You're wrong about me. What more is there to say?"

"If I'm mistaken, why did you put up with what you call my insinuations so long? Why didn't you complain to Stephen about me?"

"I'm surprised you don't understand," she temporized and groped for an answer.

His satisfied look returned. "No, I don't. Tell me."

"I hoped when you saw how foolish you were being, you'd leave me alone. Stephen is new in the army. Some of the West Point officers hold it against him that he received a political appointment. I didn't want to make more trouble for him by telling him about you. If he knew, he'd be furious."

Any pretense of amusement or amiability disappeared from Peter's face. A ruthless purpose glared at her from his eyes. "More angry than if he knew that you had deceived him?"

Her stomach knotted again and her hands felt damp and cold. "He'd know you are making up lies."

"Not lies. You didn't make a trip to Texas, or wherever you said. Or maybe you did go, but not to visit any grandmother. You'd been having yourself a good time and you got caught. So you went away to have a child."

Contempt seemed the best response. "Are you finished with this insane story?"

Peter moved closer. The look of anticipation had returned, and she guessed that he'd been saving something he thought would win whatever he wanted. "Not quite. The father of your child just happens to be your mother's brother. I don't know what happened to the child. It must be around somewhere. Stephen Baldwin may think he married a pure young girl, but he didn't. He married a woman who seduced her own uncle. The army might be interested in that."

Thoughts raced through her mind, but she couldn't seem to gather them into a coherent pattern. All she could pluck out of them was a single conviction: The army must not look into Cole's and her affairs.

As if he sensed her hesitation, Peter grabbed her and pulled her roughly into his arms. Before she could evade him, he captured her mouth with what might have looked like a kiss but was really a punishment. She wrenched her head to one side and jerked back. "Let go of me!"

He laughed. "You're a hot one. Your uncle probably wasn't the first."

Furiously she pushed back and reached for her derringer. In her frantic movement, the gun caught on the edge of her pocket. Peter grabbed her wrist, and with the other hand wrenched the gun away. "Well!" He held it a moment as if testing its weight. "So it's not loaded." He tossed it onto the floor where it slid under the table.

She twisted in an effort to free herself. As she did, her heel caught against the leg of a chair. It threw her off balance and Peter picked her up and held her pinioned against him as he half carried, half dragged her, into the bedroom and across to the bed. She struggled and got a leg free enough to kick at him. The result was to knock him off balance so that they fell together onto the bed. His weight on top of her pinned her there. He gripped both her wrists with one hand and her chin with the other, panting from the effort to hold her down.

"Damn you," she hissed. "Let me go!"

He smiled, back in control again. "I'm going to make you happier than any of your men did."

She tried to free her hands, but his grip was too strong. He let go of her chin and pulled at the front opening of her dress. The first button gave, then the second, and finally the row, like stitches of old thread bursting open. He pushed at the fabric, but the dress was belted too tightly at the waist for him to get it down. With a growl of frustration, he leaned to one side and reached down. Getting a wad of material, he jerked at her skirts.

In a panic she cried out, "Cole will kill you."

Peter hesitated, and his grip on her hands loosened. She pulled one hand free. With all her strength she lashed out at his face. Her blow landed on his nose.

He gave a sharp cry and covered his nose. With her

freed arm she shoved her elbow into his ribs and pulled loose. Scrambling across the bed, she crouched on the floor on the other side, gasping for breath.

Peter's face was an explosive red except for a white streak across his nose. The streak turned red and the surrounding color faded. Then she noticed his eyes, which had a wary look. At that moment she realized what she'd said. The anger that fueled her struggle to free herself turned into a sick dread.

"I mean it," she said. "If you don't leave, I'll tell Lane you tried to rape me and he'll find some way to kill you."

"You're bluffing," he said sharply. "No soldier's going to risk hanging for some officer's wife. Not even a striker, unless maybe he's been sharing her."

Genuinely shocked, she said, "You have an evil mind."

"Is that what Lane's doing—taking turns with Stephen? Maybe that's something else Stephen ought to know."

Still trembling, she got up. He seemed to accept her substitution of Lane for Cole. Boldly she said, "Stephen knows everything about me."

Peter gave her a glance of disbelief and his earlier confidence resurfaced. He turned his back and went over to her mirror where he straightened his jacket and smoothed his hair. While his attention was on his appearance, she slipped around the bed and back into the front room. He followed but didn't attempt to approach her.

Apparently willing to settle for threats, he said in a mean voice, "You mean Stephen knows you lifted your skirt for every boy around and had a kid by your uncle?"

The moments between the bedroom and front room had given her brain time to function. "Think of this, Lieutenant Dunham. If you told Stephen such lies, it would make him furious. Not at me. At you. I haven't seen Stephen really angry very many times, but I'm positive that you don't want to see him that way."

Peter stared at her for several long moments. She prayed that he would go without more questions. Finally he picked up his hat and went to the door. With his hand on the latch, he turned and said, "You must think you're the belle of the post. This was a game, to amuse myself. But I'm not sure you're worth this much trouble."

She waited until he'd left through the back door before she picked up the derringer and went on trembling legs back to the bedroom. Numbly she put the gun away, then took off her damaged dress and folded it into the trunk. She found an old worn shift, its familiarity providing comfort. After she put it on, she crawled into bed, not caring that she hadn't braided her hair. She lay, exhausted, while tears ran down the sides of her face, washing away some of the bitter taste of the evening.

When the tears stopped, she lay awake, unable to dull her thoughts. Her strongest desire was for Cole to return safely. She prayed that Peter Dunham would never again approach her. And that he was so disgruntled that he wanted to forget the night's events—and never realize that in a moment of terror she'd said Cole and not Lane. Just before dawn exhaustion finally overcame fear and regret, and she fell asleep.

* * *

The last miles of the trail to Fort Apache seemed as long as the rest of the way from Tucson. Cole restrained his impulse to put his mount into a gallop. The horse was tired; it wouldn't be fair.

Behind him his men slouched or dozed in their saddles. He'd overheard some grumbling when he'd had Sergeant Briggs roust them out at three that morning. They wanted to arrive at Fort Apache too late to be put on a fatigue detail. But Cole needed to get back and see Martha, to let her know he hadn't been recognized, and make sure she was all right.

By the time they reached the post, morning parade was over. After leaving his horse at the stables and sending the men with Sergeant Briggs, Cole headed for the adjutant's office to report in. As he rounded the corner of the guardhouse to walk across the east end of the parade ground, he looked toward officers' row, half hoping to see Martha out watching for his arrival. She wasn't in sight.

"Lieutenant Baldwin!" It was Lane, calling from the guardhouse door.

He stopped and walked over to Lane, who saluted and said, "Glad to see you're back, sir."

"Thanks, Lane. Glad to be here. I see you pulled guard duty."

"Yes, sir. Something a little extra last night." He shrugged. "Can't expect to miss it all the time."

"Everything go all right here while I was gone?" Cole asked.

"Fine, sir. I think Mrs. Baldwin will be happy to have you back. She was sounding pretty lonesome last night."

It was a personal comment for a private to make to an officer, but strikers developed a degree of informality with families they served. Cole grinned and said, "That's good. I wouldn't want her to be happy because I'm away."

At the adjutant's office, Cole finished his report and was relieved from duty for the rest of the day. At their quarters, to his disappointment, Martha wasn't in the front room. He considered looking for her, then decided he'd clean up first, and went into the bedroom. He found Martha there, asleep.

She lay on her side, her legs slightly bent, one hand nestled under her cheek. Her hair spilled out around her head in a golden-brown fan. She stirred and turned over onto her back, pushing the blanket aside. Through the thin white material of her shift he saw the swell of her breast and the pink circle of nipple.

He could feel the beginning of an erection. He hadn't wanted to get back to Martha solely to find out what happened to her. He'd wanted to see her, to touch her, to love her until she cried out with pleasure, and then spend himself inside her.

Let her sleep a little longer, he decided. Quietly he collected his bathing things and went back outside. A visit to the officers' bathhouse would feel good. And getting rid of the smell of sweat and horse ought to make him a more appealing lover.

The hand caressing the side of her face seemed to Martha like a dream. Then the events of the past evening intruded into her sleep and fear rushed over her that somehow Peter had returned. She opened her eyes and at the same time jerked away from the hand. It took a moment staring up at the man sitting beside her on the bed to come fully awake.

Cole!

The relief was so great that sobs started deep in her chest and exploded into weeping. She scrambled up and propelled herself at him. His arms met her and enfolded her close against him, giving her safety.

"Martha! What's wrong?"

She couldn't answer, only cling to him. He stroked her tangled hair and held her until she got out between sobs, "I thought . . . I was afraid . . . you weren't coming back."

"I'm here. No trouble in Tucson. Everything's all right."

She couldn't stop crying, and he sounded more urgent when he repeated, "What's wrong? Tell me!"

"It's Peter."

Cole's arms tightened around her. "All right. I'm here. I won't let him hurt you." He shifted so that he leaned against the bedstead, still keeping her close in his arms. When her tears finally stopped, he said, "Now tell me. Start at the beginning."

She pulled away a little so that she could see his face, and began with the trip to Miguel's encampment. Cole frowned at that. "Cole," she said, "I have to do something to find my child. I can't just stay here forever, playing house! That could last months. You don't want that."

He hesitated a fraction of a minute. "No, of course I don't. But don't take chances like that again. We agreed that I'll see what I can find out." She wasn't content to leave that up to him, but she didn't argue.

When she told him her conclusions about Mrs. Polk's note, he nodded. "It sounds as if you've probably got it right." He was silent as she recounted Peter's charges, though his jaw clenched. She didn't mention the struggle or Peter's attack in the bedroom, but when she finished, Cole said furiously, "You should never have let the bastard come here. You should have told him I'd take care of him when I got back."

Her temper flared also. "But, Cole, I didn't know whether you'd be coming back here or going to prison. I had to find out what he knew. The only way to do that was to talk to him."

Cole glared at her. "Talk to him! It sure as hell isn't talk that Peter wants."

Something must have shown in her face that Cole pounced on. "It wasn't all talk," he insisted. "There was more to it. Dammit, tell me what happened!"

Reluctantly she said, "He tried to kiss me. But I pushed him off."

Cole wasn't letting her go with that. "So, you pushed him off. That doesn't sound like a kiss."

"All right. He tried to touch me, but he didn't actually hurt me." Now came the difficult part, the mistake she must confess. Looking at Cole's angry face, she almost ended the story there. Bravely she went ahead. "He did frighten me, and . . . I told him to stop or you would kill him. That's not the worst part. When I said it, I used your name. I said Cole, not Stephen."

The skin around Cole's eyes tightened. "How did Peter react to that?"

"I don't think he noticed. He was . . . well, excited."

That wasn't the word to use to dampen Cole's anger, but he said, "What's done is done. I'll find him and see how he acts."

"As soon as I realized I used your name, I said something more about Lane, as if that's what I'd said before. That diverted Peter and he made some remark about Lane sharing me with you."

"That sounds like something that son of a bitch would think of," Cole said, with such rage that Martha was glad Peter wasn't there to be confronted.

"Wouldn't it be better if you acted the same toward Peter as always? That we pretended I hadn't told you anything about it? He'll think he's right about Elizabeth. Maybe he is. Then he won't be asking different questions about us. You tell me to be careful not to do something to make people notice us. Fighting with Peter would get everyone's attention."

She saw Cole damp down his fury to a containable level. "Yes, you're right. Peter is safe from me for now."

"You matter to me, Cole. Not just because I need you, but because you're the man you are."

His face softened. "You're important to me too." He pulled her back into his arms and began to kiss her, at first softly, then insistently. "I couldn't wait to get back here—to make love to you. But if you don't feel—"

She put her fingers up to stop him. "That's what I want too."

Under a swiftly discarded robe he was naked, his arousal obvious. His body seemed more magnificent in its masculine beauty than she remembered. As he pulled her close again, she clung to him, her heart racing, her breath coming in sharp gasps. They parted for him to slip off her shift, then he leaned over her, and traced the contours of her face with his lips. Greedy now for the feel of him, she pressed close.

"I imagined this a hundred times," he said softly, rubbing his thumb gently across her cheekbone.

"I did too."

All was new, and yet familiar in taste, in the feel of skin and muscles, in the scent that was unique to him. Her center throbbed with readiness, and she arched her back and hips to meet his touch. When she stroked him, he gasped. His voice came out in a muffled cry, "Martha, I can't wait." When she felt him fill her, her spiraling excitement began, the pulsing waves of sensation building, until he cried out and shuddered with the release of passion.

She clung to him, searching for her own crest, still caught in unfinished desire. Lying above her, he buried his face in her neck and groaned. "Oh, God. I'm sorry. I wanted you so much."

Though she still felt her need, his words gave her a different kind of pleasure. "I know," she whispered. "I wanted you too. But it doesn't matter." His rasping breath told her how intense his desire had been, and knowing that she had caused both passion and satisfaction gave her a new contentment.

He raised his head and said softly, "We'll have to wait a bit for me to recover." Then he held her close and slowly, tenderly, he proved that waiting could be as much pleasure as fulfillment. Soon, she entwined her legs around him and together they reached the climax that had eluded her before.

As she lay in his arms, she thought that it wasn't the passion of his kisses that meant the most to her this day. It was their sweetness, and the safety of his embrace. The feeling of being treated as if she were precious both aroused and satisfied her desire. More words hovered near the surface, words that included love. But she wasn't sure how much love mattered, and there were things she wanted to know.

Reluctantly she sat up. "You haven't told me what happened in Tucson."

"Now?" he protested lazily. "Your breasts are much more interesting." Her tangled hair had fallen forward over her breasts. He pushed it aside and touched one nipple.

"No, Cole. I want to hear about Tucson."

To prevent distractions, she found her discarded shift and a robe and put them on. Cole got up and provided her a pleasurable view of his naked body as he pulled on pants and a shirt. She went into the front room and opened the curtains a little.

When Cole came out of the bedroom, she said, "You were away so long. I was afraid you were in jail there."

"I was in the jail, but not as a prisoner. If that happened, you'd have heard it from Colonel Stratton." He went on to describe the delays reaching Tucson, getting a promise of help from Ira, and taking the prisoners to the jail.

"And you're sure no one recognized you?"

"The jailer didn't, and I didn't see anyone else I knew. So it's all right. Now we'll get on with finding your son, and we'll go about it discreetly."

"Yes," she agreed, and silently vowed to heed his warning as much as possible. She hoped she didn't have to decide who was more important to her, Cole or her son.

21

"*Damn,*" *Martha muttered* to herself. That was the third time she'd knotted the thread in the tablecloth she was embroidering. She looked up and saw Cole hurrying across the parade ground to their veranda.

"I thought you'd like to know," he said softly, "that Peter volunteered to take a detail going up to Holbrook to check on some missing supplies."

"I'm glad," Martha said, relieved. "Do you think he's avoiding you?"

"He should!"

Alarmed by Cole's grim expression, Martha said, "Remember, we agreed you'd act the same as always."

"Yes," he said grudgingly. "If he's gone a while, maybe I can ignore the bastard when he's back."

Cole left and she went back to the sewing that gave her an excuse to watch for Major Owens's Apache housekeeper.

The woman didn't appear that day, or the next. But

on Saturday Martha heard a door closing in the major's half of the quarters and then the sound of the door from the hall out to the back. She'd heard Major Owens go out earlier, so she quickly walked outside. The Apache housekeeper was just inside the open doorway to the major's kitchen shed. She turned around, and Martha realized that she was more a girl than a woman. Though she wore her long, straight hair loose in the fashion of married women, she didn't appear more than fourteen or fifteen years old. Her blue gingham blouse was belted over her full skirt by a wide leather belt studded with bits of turquoise.

Martha had rehearsed how to begin. She smiled and said, "*Buenos dias. Habla español?*"

The girl hesitated, as if not sure whether to answer or run away. Finally she said softly, "*Si, señora, poco.*"

A little Spanish was all they needed, Martha thought, delighted. In her simple Spanish, she explained that she wished to learn some Apache ways of cooking.

That appeared to startle the girl, who asked, "*Cocimiento Apache?*" as if she couldn't believe a white woman really wanted to learn how she cooked.

When Martha insisted that she did wish it, the girl smiled, then broke into giggles. After she recovered, she gestured an invitation into the major's kitchen. Martha followed and introduced herself, using the Spanish for Elizabeth. "*Me llamo Isabel.*"

In turn the girl said, "*Me llamo Dulcita.*" That surprised Martha. She couldn't imagine the rather vulgar Major Owens naming the girl Little Bonbon. Maybe she'd misjudged his feelings for this pretty Apache.

Martha watched while Dulcita ground up walnuts and a piece of dried, roasted mescal, the sweet tuber of the maguey cactus. That had been Sharp-Knife's favorite dish, and Martha felt a little sad, remembering his enjoyment.

As their exchange of limited Spanish continued, Martha learned that Dulcita had been at Fort Apache for several months. They shared the Apache food, and Martha savored the familiar taste.

When she was about to leave, Dulcita said softly, as if speaking to herself as much as to Martha, "*Me llamo* Na-li kide-ya." Startled, it took Martha a moment to translate to herself that the Apache meant Maiden-Who-Walks-on-a-Ridge. It was surprising that Dulcita mentioned her Apache name at all. Ordinarily names were used only in times of danger. Dulcita must be very lonely and wanted someone to know her name. And of course she didn't expect Martha to know that using her name was unsuitable, or what the name meant. Martha left, pleased by their encounter for her own sake, and also drawn toward the young Apache.

In the next days Martha concentrated on winning Dulcita's confidence. It chafed her to refrain from speaking Apache, but she didn't dare proceed too quickly. Still, each evening she could report progress to Cole. Her hopes for Dulcita kept her from being too disappointed when another ration day passed and she recognized none of the families gathered to be counted and receive their rations.

The mail often arrived on Friday, and so did Martha's anxiety about Stephen Baldwin's medical records. That morning she reminded Cole, "We've been here six and a half weeks. That's long enough for medical records to get here from Washington."

"Only if Dr. Lawton sent for them right away. He's a good doctor, but he doesn't get around to the records very fast. Al Parker told me about a private in his cavalry company. The man's been waiting since February for a certificate that a back injury is serious enough he can take a medical retirement."

Exasperated that Cole didn't seem as worried as she was, she asked, "Do you know who sorts the mail?"

"It's not the same person all the time." He put on his uniform jacket and cap and fastened his belt.

"Is it the same person most of the time?"

Stopping in front of her, he said softly, "Martha, you are beginning to sound like a wife."

He tried to kiss her, but she dodged, so furious that she was on the edge of crying. "Cole! This is a serious threat!"

A frown creased his face. "I know it. But I can't do anything more until the records get here. I'm so damned nice around the adjutant's staff now that they're probably taking bets on which man I'm going to ask for a walk in the woods. There are a couple of corporals who handle the mail most of the time. I've left hints that I'd as soon official letters to the doctor got delayed a little. That's the most I can do now." His expression gentled. "It doesn't do any good to worry, Martha. I know my neck's at stake. But if I'm going to hang, I'm sure as hell going to enjoy myself now. Like this."

She didn't evade his kiss, nor the caresses that went with it. He expressed regret for both of them when he finally said, "Damn! Have to go."

Refusing to worry sounded fine, but as the morning went on, Martha kept watching for the mail rider. It kept her enough on edge that when Whipple got into the way while she and Dulcita were cooking, she scolded him severely.

"Please," Dulcita protested softly in Spanish, "he is my friend. He is a puppy and he wants a taste." She gave him a tidbit of venison, and he looked up at Martha with such a satisfied expression that she had to laugh.

The mail rider arrived just after noon mess call, and people left their meals to go to the adjutant's office. The corporal gave Martha one letter, for Stephen Baldwin. To her alarm, it came from Tucson. The sender's name was identified only as Ramirez, and the rounded handwriting looked feminine.

Alice had come up, with Peter Dunham just behind her. "What's the matter, Elizabeth?" she asked. "You look upset."

"No, not upset. I'm just surprised." With Peter listening, Martha decided on apparent candor. She kept the letter where he and Alice could see it. "Stephen doesn't know anyone in Tucson who would write to him. Unless he met someone when he was there."

Alice looked at the letter and giggled. "Maybe he got acquainted with a senorita who wanted his address."

To her chagrin, Martha felt her face flush. "I'm sure he'll tell me all about it," she said.

"Yes, he probably will." Alice giggled again and gave Peter a conspiratorial glance. She was obviously enjoying her suggestion that Cole had strayed, and was inviting Peter to share the entertainment.

Annoyed, Martha was debating whether to reply when she saw Dr. Lawton coming down the adjutant's office steps with several pieces of mail in his hand. One was a large, official-looking envelope. Whatever hints Cole had given about delaying the doctor's mail hadn't worked. Or else they had and the delay was over. Concealing her agitation, she said to Alice,

"Excuse me. I want to tell the doctor what I've been doing."

The doctor saw Martha and greeted her warmly. As they walked toward the hospital, she chattered on about learning to cook Apache foods from Dulcita, hardly knowing what she was saying. She got a glimpse of the return address on the large envelope. It was from army headquarters in Washington! Her chatter must have made sense because he said approvingly, "The Apache have an interesting culture, but most of us don't bother to learn about it. You're an unusual woman, Elizabeth. I wish there were more army wives who thought like you."

There was no time to worry about being unusual now. They had reached the hospital entrance, and she must not let him get away with that letter. "Do you have a few minutes more?" she said. "There's something I'd like to ask about."

"Yes, fine. Please come along inside."

He escorted her into his office, a small room off the hall. Cole seemed to be right about the doctor's haphazard record keeping; stacks of papers covered the desk, an extra table, a chair, and a set of bookshelves. He balanced the new mail on top of a stack on one side of his desk.

After he cleared off a chair for her, he sat down behind the desk. "How can I help?" he asked.

"I'm . . . worried about Mrs. Collins."

As he started to reply, an orderly said from the open doorway, "Dr. Lawton, sir, may I speak to you?"

"Excuse me," the doctor said to Martha, and her already rapidly beating heart speeded up even more. If he left, she would take the letter and hide it under her skirt.

Martha rose, as if too agitated to sit, and stood beside the desk, within reach of the Washington letter. But the doctor went only as far as the doorway where he listened to a few words from the orderly, said, "That's fine," and turned back.

Seeing her chance disappear, Martha pretended to stumble, and fell against the desk. As she did, she threw out her arm and knocked against the papers. The entire stack quivered and toppled onto the floor. The newest mail slid the farthest, fanning out between the desk and the wall.

"Oh, Dr. Lawton," Martha gasped. "I'm so sorry!"

She bent down and started gathering up the papers.

Dr. Lawton came over beside her. "No need to do that, Mrs. Baldwin. I can get them."

"No. It was terribly clumsy of me, and I should pick them up." She reached out quickly and grabbed the Washington letter and two other envelopes.

"Not your fault. I shouldn't let them pile up this way. I hate keeping records. A failing of mine. One of these days soon I'll get to them." He crouched down and started picking up pieces of paper that included unopened mail as well as reports and other official looking correspondence.

With the doctor so close, it was impossible for her to conceal the official envelope under her skirt. She did the only thing she could think of. As she stacked papers, she put it on the bottom and the rest of the new mail on top.

"There, that's enough," the doctor said, collecting the last paper from the floor. He piled his accumulation on top of Martha's stack, apparently not noticing or perhaps not caring that he was covering up the latest mail. Martha breathed a little more freely and took her seat again.

Dr. Lawton resumed his place behind his desk. "Now, what were you asking?"

"I was concerned about Mrs. Collins," Martha repeated.

"She's looking particularly well to me. Better than any time since she's been here. Lots of women out here don't welcome children. It's hard, bearing them and taking care of them on an army post." He looked at Martha speculatively. "Is that's what's worrying you—that you might have a child out here?"

"No, Dr. Lawton, but it's kind of you to ask." She rose. "Thank you for listening to me about Mrs. Collins."

On her way back to her quarters, she thought about the doctor's remarks. Except for the first time she and Cole made love, they had been careful; it was finding her child that concerned her, not the prospect of another. She must move boldly before Dr. Lawton decided to catch up on his records.

When Cole got off duty that evening, she told him about the letter from Washington. "Since it got to the doctor, I'll have to retrieve it," he said.

"How can you?"

"Steal it." That seemed riskier and far less certain to Martha than Cole's cool voice made it sound. "We may have extra time," he went on. "The doc likes his whiskey. I hear that every so often he takes off and goes on a bender. He was away on one when we got here. Six weeks is fairly long between sprees. The chances are good he'll go away soon for a week or so. I could probably get into his office then."

She didn't like it, but Cole's idea was the best they could do unless something else came up. "There was a letter for you," she said, and gave him the Tucson envelope.

He looked at the outside and grinned. "Ramirez. That's good."

"Alice thinks it's from some woman you met there."

As he tore open the envelope, he explained, "That's what Ira wants it to look like." After he read it, his face lit with an exultant grin. "I was right! Harvey Lippincott is part of the Tucson Ring. Ira's working on finding the man who killed Sam Weaver, and he thinks he has a lead." In his exuberance, he lifted Martha and swung her around once before he put her down. "I'm angling for duty with the quartermaster. That will put me in a position to get evidence about the contractors who sell to the army. Maybe everything will come together before too long."

She made up her mind. "I'm going to talk to Dulcita." He frowned, but she didn't let him speak. "I have to do something. You may not be able to get the medical records back. If Ira finds your man, you'll probably want to go to Tucson and do something about that. I won't tell Dulcita who I am. I'll say someone asked me to look for a child in Diablo's camp."

"I guess you haven't heard."

"Heard what?"

"Word came today from headquarters at Fort Whipple. The agent at San Carlos wrote to General Kautz charging that an officer here had bought an Apache girl and forced her to become his mistress. Supposedly he's holding her captive in his quarters. The newspapers picked up the story too. Major Owens was on the carpet."

"But Dulcita isn't a captive, and I don't believe Major Owens bought her!"

"You're probably right, but Dulcita is gone."

Martha sat silently, staring at Cole, a sick sensation in her stomach. With Dulcita gone, there was only one course to take. "Then I'll go to Diablo's camp myself."

"You can't do that! You said someone recognized you."

"I wasn't sure anyone did."

"If someone does," he argued, "they'll probably take your son off someplace where you can't find him."

Stubbornly she persisted. "I'll wear my hat with the thick veil and some extra clothes to make me look heavier. I have to do something!"

"You can be patient a little longer. One of the scouts is pretty friendly with me. A few more contacts and I think I can trust him enough to ask him to help. We're fixed here. Everyone accepts us. It's a base of operations we can count on a while longer."

She didn't say anything, but her mind was made up.

On Sunday when the afternoon ride was being organized, Martha said to Vernon Brown, out of Cole's hearing, "We haven't ridden east for a while. It's pretty out that way."

"That's a good suggestion," he responded, and went about his customary arrangements.

Cole didn't learn where they were going until they were at the stables and mounted up. "This was your idea?" he asked Martha in a soft, chilly voice.

"Yes," she snapped, loudly enough for Alice, who was nearby, to raise an eyebrow.

Several miles along a creek that branched off from the river, the group stopped to rest the horses. Martha wandered off and Cole followed. He said in a low voice, "I think I know what you want, and it won't work. There's no way I'll let you persuade them to go there."

Martha and Cole were still close enough for others to hear if she raised her voice. She turned on him and said loudly, "Yes, and I suppose that explains why she sent you a letter."

He looked genuinely bewildered. "What are you talking about?"

"No woman is going to write to you from Tucson unless you gave her reason to," Martha said as furiously as she thought a jealous wife would. She ran across to her horse, which she'd left conveniently by a log, and mounted. Skinny leapt forward into a fast departure. Behind her she heard Cole shout something, but she didn't catch the words.

She raced out of sight and a good distance along the trail that led east before he caught up with her. Expecting anger, she had a rebuttal ready—a visit to Diablo's camp was essential.

As Cole slowed Buttermilk to a walk beside her, he said, "That was neatly done." He sounded disapproving but not furious. A quick sideways glance confirmed his resigned expression.

"I'm glad you understand," Martha said.

At that moment Cole didn't feel understanding, but he'd realized that she was determined to go. Better that he be with her than to stop her now and have her try it later by herself. This way he could impose some conditions. "When we get there," he said, "you stay back, on Skinny. And keep your veil in place. Since it's Sunday, one of the scouts may be there. I'll go into the camp and make whatever excuse you probably have figured out."

Protest flared in her eyes, but after a moment she said, "I'd thought of asking the way back to the fort."

"Won't do. I've been out on enough patrols to know the area." He wasn't willing to look that stupid.

"Then we'll just stumble onto them. They move their ranchería often enough to make that plausible."

"No. This one's been in the same place quite a while." He thought over the possibilities. "What might work is to ask about Dulcita. Do you know what band she belongs to?"

"She didn't say, and I couldn't think of a way to ask her."

"I can say she helped you and you're worried about her. But you don't know where to look for her."

Martha said excitedly, "Yes. I do want to know what happened to her."

Her veil had come loose. He almost reached across to tuck it back in himself. Christ! They were about to get into a situation where he'd need all his wits. And what was on his mind? Touching her. Disgusted with himself, he said roughly, "Fasten your veil," and put Buttermilk into a lope.

After several miles, the trail left the forest and entered a meadow. Stopping just before they reached the edge of the trees, Cole looked at Diablo's camp. It resembled the other rancherías around—brush and canvas-covered wickiups next to open *ramadas*. The dwellings were scattered across the upper side of the meadow, beside cornfields that bordered a stream. "What are the Apache names of the man and woman who kept your son?"

"Apaches don't use names in talking to each other, so you probably wouldn't overhear anyone using those names."

"Tell me anyway, just in case."

"Sharp-Knife's brother is Na-ho-kuse, Big-Dipper in

English. His wife is Tsalbe-stiine. That means She-Sticks-to-Her-Cradle."

"And your son? You told me his name in English is Pinecone, but I don't remember the Apache."

"Nilchi Bidahsaa," she said wistfully.

"Is there any way I could identify any of them?"

Martha didn't answer immediately, as if she were studying the images in her mind. "Big-Dipper is unusually tall. He has a thin face, and a bad scar on his right hand. I think She-Sticks-to-Her-Cradle is ten years older than I am, so she'd be about thirty-five. She's not pretty, except for her eyes. Sometimes they're beautiful. Sometimes they're very cruel."

That wouldn't help him. Most Apache women looked alike to him anyway, with their bulky clothing and long hair that often concealed part of their faces. "What about your son?"

Martha's eyes looked misty. "Pinecone is eight years old now. He's probably tall for his age like his father and uncle."

Not much to go on, but time to try. "Wait here. I'll look for someone I can talk to."

Buttermilk had taken just a few steps when Cole heard shouting from the camp. He reined in and rose up in his stirrups to see past the branches of the tree in front of him. From behind him, Martha said, "What is it?"

"Just a couple of boys wrestling." Nine or ten children were gathered around two boys in front of a wickiup. Martha rode up beside Cole and pushed aside a pine branch to see.

The boys circled each other, calling out words that had the sound of taunts. The children around them jostled each other, laughing and yelling. One boy struck out at the other and was tripped in return. The one who'd been tripped shouted something—a harsh, angry word. The watchers stopped laughing. In the center the two boys circled each other again. They weren't playing now. However it had started, it had turned into a fight.

One boy lunged and knocked his opponent off his feet. The boy on the ground grabbed the leg of the one still standing, and they were both down, rolling over each other. Then one threw the other off and got to his knees. He picked up a small rock. Someone screamed, but before anyone could reach the kneeling boy, he smashed the rock against the prone boy's head. There was silence, then one of the children ran screaming to a nearby *ramada*. Several women came running and gathered around the boy on the ground.

"That boy!" Martha exclaimed. "He's hurt!"

Before Cole realized what she intended, she had spurred Skinny around him and into a gallop down the trail into Diablo's camp. Swearing to himself, Cole started after her.

By the time he caught up, they were halfway to the first wickiup. Three men stood waiting for them. Cole recognized one of them as Smiley, an Apache scout who lived in the wickiups north of the fort. Smiley spoke only a few words of English, but like many of the scouts, he understood quite a bit more. The other two were strangers to him, one young and one old, but neither was tall. Cole silently thanked God for that. "Remember," he said softly to Martha, "you stay back, and *you don't say anything!*"

"All right, but ask about the injured boy."

Cole and Smiley exchanged greetings, and Cole

explained that his wife was concerned about Dulcita. When he mentioned the name, the scout's expression lost the habitual smile that had earned his army name. He consulted briefly with the other two men, then shook his head. "No. Not here."

"Would anyone in your village know where she is? I'd like to ask, if that's all right."

Smiley frowned. "No. Not here." He and the other two men waited, and they didn't invite Cole and Martha to come into the camp.

Cole wouldn't give up without at least finding out about the injured boy. "We saw the trouble," he said. "Is the boy all right?"

Smiley glanced at the group of women, and the others did the same. As they looked, one of them raised the boy up, letting him lean against her. Smiley said something to the older man with him. The man looked uncomfortable, but the young one and Smiley laughed.

"Is the boy all right?" Cole persisted. He had to forestall any more rash moves by Martha.

"Yes. All right." Grinning, Smiley gestured toward the older man. "His son. Needs learn fighting."

The women who had surrounded the boy were looking at Cole and Martha. Cole could feel goose bumps on his neck. It was time to go, before the women or anyone else came any closer. "Thanks for letting us know Dulcita's not here," Cole said to Smiley. "If anyone sees her, please tell her my wife was asking about her." Judging by the reception her name got them, he was sure no word would be passed on.

He wheeled Buttermilk around, getting her between Skinny and the camp. Martha had no choice but to turn her mount and start up the trail. Cole knew each day without news added to her desperation. Would he have to lock up Martha to keep her from trying it again by herself?

22

An enormous fatigue overcame Martha, so that she wakened in the morning too tired to plan her next move. She sensed that Cole was on guard, waiting for her next impulsive action. He didn't need to worry. During the days after their visit to Diablo's ranchería, she kept to being Elizabeth Baldwin, army wife, quietly absorbed in domestic duties. Lane got into a fight with a corporal from one of the cavalry companies and was put on the wood-cutting detail and confined to barracks. She did the cooking but she followed the striker's recipes, indifferent to trying Apache foods. On ration day she got out the binoculars, but she used them without expectation of seeing anyone she recognized except Diablo.

The explanation for her lassitude was partly clear to her. With Dulcita's disappearance, she had to recognize that the difficulty of finding her son was enormous. Two pieces of extraordinary good fortune—the so-far successful masquerade and being assigned to the White Mountain area—had lulled her into expecting success. After being barred from Diablo's camp, she couldn't think of how to proceed.

The only thing she stirred herself to do was to waylay Major Owens one morning when he was leaving his quarters. "I became fond of Dulcita," she said. "Do you know what happened to her?"

"I don't have any idea," he said stiffly.

One afternoon in early July, Cole came in from duty with a jubilant smile. "A dispatch rider just got in. Remember the Indian agent at the San Carlos reservation who wanted Major Owens court-martialed? He just resigned."

Martha's hope revived. "Does that mean Dulcita might come back?"

"No chance of that," he said sympathetically. "Colonel Stratton's going strictly by regulations about officers keeping women now." Then enthusiasm relighted his eager expression. "The agent resigned because of an order stationing military officers at the Indian agencies as inspectors. That means I may be able to get definite information about the crooked contractors."

She subdued her disappointment in order to be pleased for him. "Will you be an inspector here?"

"Not as an assignment. But I might get the job until someone arrives. And make friends with the man who does." He walked around the room as he talked, his voice excited. "This means another opportunity. A new agent at San Carlos won't know the ropes. The suppliers who cheat the army and the Indians will make the most of it. After that's gone on for a while, there are bound to be records to use against them."

Uneasily she considered what he was saying. "That means the Indians at the agency won't get the food and supplies they need. Can't something be done now to protect them?"

"Maybe, but the point is for the contractors to get in deep. That takes a little time."

She understood why he was so pleased, but she wasn't. "If you're assigned there, you don't intend to stop any fraud! You *want* the Indians to be cheated."

"No, I don't," Cole protested. "But there has to be something to charge the contractors with."

"You told me that there's evidence now of cheating by the contractors." As she thought about it, her anger grew. "You want to wait until you find something to charge your *stepfather* with."

Cole's expression grew strained. "You're right. That's what I want. The investigation doesn't depend on me, but if I get a chance to delay things until the right time, I will. And I won't do anything to make anyone suspicious of us here before I can collect evidence. I don't have a witness for the murder I didn't do. Maybe I'll never find one. But Harvey Lippincott's going to pay. This could be one way."

Revenge. She understood its power even though long ago she'd lost the desire to avenge her parents' deaths. Warily she watched Cole. He had a stillness about him that sounded a warning. "There's something else," she said.

"Yes," he acknowledged. "You won't like it. Two ranchers on spreads north and west of San Carlos have been killed and their stock run off. General Kautz is sending details out all over the area. So tomorrow I'll be off chasing hostiles."

"Hostiles! From what I know about San Carlos, it's a terrible place. It's hot. There's no place for decent farming. Different Indian groups are crowded in together."

"Now, wait a minute." Cole put his hand on her arm.

She shook it off angrily. "Because of the cheating you don't want to stop," she charged, "they may not get enough to eat. If some of them do raid, it's because they want to stay alive!"

"So do the men in my command." He spoke as hotly as she had. "It's our job to protect the people of the Territory."

"The Apache were the people of this Territory before Mexicans or Americans heard of it! They have the most right to be here. But you think more of soldiers you've known only a little while."

They were squared off now, like the Apaches and soldiers they were defending. "Yes, I do. They have a hell of a hard job. I respect them and I owe them loyalty."

It was an impasse they didn't know how to resolve.

That night when they went to bed, they didn't touch. Martha lay in the dark and thought of her son. Even if she never saw him again, his welfare mattered more than anything else. But as she listened to Cole's breathing next to her, her emotions waged a painful war inside her.

Ten days later the detachment returned at nighttime, men and animals exhausted. Martha concealed her relief that the pursuit had been futile, and she and Cole greeted each other without the anger of their parting.

The next morning, Cole was summoned to the adjutant's office. When he arrived, he found Lieutenant Parker, officer of the day, his face flushed with excitement. "Smiley just brought two squaws in. They say they can tell us what direction the hostiles headed. The ones you were after. Colonel Stratton is on the way over, but I thought you'd want to be here."

The two Apache women sat on a bench at one side of an inner room. They appeared to be mother and daughter. Smiley stood leaning against the wall. He and Cole greeted each other. Since the day at Diablo's camp, Cole had taken pains to be friendly with the scout. The two women looked at Cole, but they didn't speak. Cole went with Parker back to the front office and said, "Smiley is trustworthy, but why would two women come and tell us how to find men of their band?"

"Smiley says the son of the older woman was badly injured by one of the hostiles. They want the men brought back so they can get justice."

It sounded plausible. Colonel Stratton arrived and listened to Smiley's translation. He believed the story enough to order the detachment, with Smiley accompanying them, back into the field. He took the precaution of detaining the two women, who protested angrily after Smiley told them they would be locked up at the fort.

When Cole arrived back at the quarters, he explained the situation to Martha, who looked tired and discouraged. "I'm sorry to go off again so soon," he said. "Will you be all right? If you get a chance, go see Dr. Lawton. Take a look at his desk." That wasn't the only reason he suggested seeing the doctor, but he didn't know how she'd respond to the idea that he was worried about her. He wasn't sure how he felt about that himself.

"Dr. Lawton isn't here," she said. "You were right about him. It seems it was time for him to go off somewhere. He left three days ago. I made an excuse to go by his office after he left. The door was locked."

"Then his mail is safe for now."

"I've been trying to think of a way I could get into his office while he's gone," she said.

"No! If the men we're looking for are where the women said, I'll be back in a couple of days. I'll do something then."

He took her into his arms and smoothed her hair, then kissed her. She returned his kiss, and he liked the way it tasted. "I've been getting along well with Smiley," he said softly. "We'll find your son."

An hour later Cole rode north with the detachment. At the top of a rise, he reined in the sorrel gelding he'd drawn for the detail. Looking back, he could see Fort Apache spread out across the low mesa, its boundaries defined by the two rivers that met at the northwest corner. With his final words to Martha, he'd made the job of finding Pinecone his job too.

He turned his horse and set it into a gallop to catch up with the line of soldiers, mules, and horses moving up the trail in front of him. He'd made an earlier vow to avenge his dead father. And he had a tie to that motley, underpaid, sometimes brave, usually obscene bunch of men in front of him. Right now they came first. He'd sort out the other loyalties later.

* * *

As she had been doing frequently, Martha took Whipple for a walk. He was happily uncomplicated, delighted with attention from her, willing to go anywhere she went without questioning whether it was prudent. She thought of going to the hospital and trying to get into Dr. Lawton's office. Cole's order forbidding it could be ignored. But she couldn't summon the energy necessary for the effort. Instead she walked out toward the stables where Whipple had learned the exact distance to stay behind the mules in order to bark and make them kick their heels without his getting hit.

In the next two days while she waited for Cole to return, she spent most of her time with the dog. Brushing his yellow-brown fur and playing with him was a pleasant, mindless activity that soothed her spirits. The second night she felt particularly restless, and she took him out for a walk. It was late enough that the sky had lost its blue, and buildings and trees were fading to soft browns and grays. After she and Whipple returned to her quarters, she went around to the back and sat down near the top of the river gorge. Soon campfires flared beside the wickiups of the scouts, and she could hear an occasional laugh. At dusk like this, she imagined Pinecone at one of those fires and felt closer to him.

When her imagination wore out the pleasant pictures, she called Whipple from the edge of the gorge and started inside. At the back door she waited for him. He ran as far as the major's kitchen, then swerved off to sniff around it. "Whipple, come!" she said sharply. Instead of obeying, he whined and jumped at the closed door of the kitchen shed. "There's nothing inside for you to eat," she said to him crossly. Since

Dulcita's departure, Major Owens ate at the bachelor's mess, and his kitchen wasn't used.

Whipple wouldn't leave. He whined again and pawed in the dirt at the bottom of the door. Impatiently Martha went back. "All right," she said to him. "I'll open the door and let you see for yourself that you won't get any tastes here."

When she swung the door open, Whipple almost knocked her down rushing inside. He launched himself into the far corner with the high-pitched bark of welcome that he used when Cole or Lane returned to the quarters. A gasp came from the corner. There was only one person Whipple would be so eager to see who might be in this kitchen.

"Dulcita?" she whispered into the dim shed, then added in Spanish, "Don't be afraid. Please come out."

Dulcita came slowly out into the light. She looked like a frightened child. Martha repeated, "Don't be afraid."

At that moment Martha made up her mind to abandon caution.

She said in Apache, "Maiden-Who-Walks-on-a-Ridge, I must speak with you. Will you come and sit with me by the riverbank?"

Dulcita gasped again, and clapped her hand over her mouth. She stood, silent, staring with wide eyes. Martha waited, her chest painful with anticipation. By using Dulcita's Apache name, Martha hoped Dulcita would recognize both an affinity between them and the importance she attached to her request.

Finally Dulcita stepped cautiously forward. Martha turned and walked down to the edge of the river gorge and sat down. Here the water made enough noise that if they were close together, they could talk but their voices would be lost in the rushing sound.

Dulcita sat down. "How do you know my language?"

"I once lived with the Apache many years ago."

"Why are you here at Fort Apache now?"

"I will explain it all to you, but first please tell me why you are here and how I can help you."

For several minutes there was nothing but the sound of the river. Finally Dulcita said, "I came to see *el mayor*. My people will not let me stay in the village. I hoped *el mayor* would help me."

"Major Owens cannot do anything for you. He has been in trouble over keeping you here. Do you want to stay with your people or do you want to go someplace else?"

"I want to stay. But they tell me I am not loyal to them, that I am like the white man now. My father hates the white man. My mother would let me stay, but my father will not."

Martha knew she had gone too far to turn back now. "There are two Apache women who came to the fort to tell where some of the men had gone. Do you know about them?"

"Yes, I know. My sister still talks to me, and she said I should have gone with those men. She said they will get away, that the women came to give false information so the men will have more time to get into the mountains."

"The women are still here. The commanding officer decided to keep them. He will be angry when he finds out their story isn't true. They are locked in a room. If I help you get them free, would that convince your father to accept you back?"

Dulcita was silent, and then said with more animation in her voice, "I do not know, but I think so. If I could do a good thing for these women, my mother would talk to him."

Martha had tried to contain the trembling in her chest. "If I help you, I want you to do something for me. Something that must not be told to anyone. Apache or white man. Will you keep my secret?"

"Yes. I will keep your secret."

"When I was about your age, Apaches attacked my family." Martha went on to tell of her captivity and of her lost child.

Dulcita listened silently. Finally she said, "I know of Big-Dipper and She-Sticks-to-Her-Cradle. I think that they have a boy who is younger than their daughters."

"Is he called Pinecone?"

"I don't remember his name. They are not at Diablo's camp now. Some of the people from the camp have gone to Flute Mountain. I think they will be back before Big Harvest."

Martha's emotions careened between despair and hope. Flute Mountain was miles to the north. Big Harvest was September. Not so long.

She got up. "There's probably a lock on the door of the room where the women are. I'll find some kind of tool to use. Then we'll go to the room and see what to do." Planning might be better, but the detachment could return at any time. Then the women might be put in the guardhouse. It was almost dark. Best to act now.

Among Cole's things she found a bootjack and in the kitchen shed a heavy knife and a screwdriver. All clumsy tools but perhaps sturdy enough to force open a lock. She carried them outside to where Dulcita and Whipple waited. "Follow me along the edge of the bluff," she told Dulcita, and started off.

Skirting along behind officers' row, she saw no one before they reached the last house. Having stayed there, Martha knew just where to look to see through the entrance hall without being seen. A latch with a padlock had been added to the door that went from the hall into the room where the women were held. The wood of the door, she remembered, was old and hard, but the lock was substantial. It would take too long to get out the screws that held the latch. She decided to look at the side window. It was fairly low to the ground and partly concealed by a clump of small, brushy cedars.

Martha had Dulcita go into the old kitchen shed and keep Whipple quiet while she edged along the side to the front and peered cautiously around the corner. A private sat on the front veranda, his chair tilted back on two legs, his slouch proclaiming boredom. She retreated back to the window. Two nails had been driven in at the corners so that it couldn't be opened from the inside. Using the heavy knife and screwdriver, she worked at the nails. Perspiration began to dampen her back, and her fingers ached, but the first nail began to give. She got it out and flexed her fingers, then began on the other. When it finally loosened, it slipped free with a jerk. The screwdriver banged against the window glass.

Martha crouched down, her heart beating so hard it seemed as loud as the river. She waited, but the guard didn't appear. When her heart slowed, she slipped back to the kitchen shed.

"Dulcita," she whispered. "I am going to take Whipple and do something to get the guard's attention. As soon as you hear him leaving, go into the window and call the two women to open it and climb out. Then run away however you can."

Dulcita whispered, "I will come to tell you when I hear more about your son."

Martha took Whipple by his collar with one hand and held his muzzle shut with the other. He squirmed, but she held on. She pointed to the window, then pulled Whipple to the edge of the river. At this spot the river had once undercut the bank but then changed its course, leaving the steep bank and a large thicket of willow at the bottom. She looked down into the darkness and almost drew back. But desperation left her no choice. Silently she cried an apology to Whipple and pushed him over the edge.

He fell in a cascade of yelps and landed in the tangle of willow. She knelt on the edge and screamed, "Whipple!" He set up a monumental howling, and she screamed again.

Feet pounded behind her, and she turned to see the private from the front veranda. "It's my puppy," she said frantically. "He fell over the edge. I think he's hurt."

Whipple's howls gave substance to her statement. The private knelt beside her, peering into the dim gorge. When he started to get up, she cried, "Can you see him?"

"No, ma'am, I can't," he said, but he delayed to peer down into the darkness again.

"What shall I do?" She clutched at his arm. "He's just a puppy. I should have been watching him better."

After another look, the soldier got up. "Well, ma'am, I'm sorry I can't help you. I'm on duty here."

"Isn't there anyone who can help?" Her anguish over Whipple gave authenticity to the hysteria in her voice.

"Yes. Likely there's somebody at the adjutant's office. It's close."

"Whipple," she cried. "It's going to be all right. I'll find someone." He reacted to her voice by howling even more loudly.

The sound of commotion must have reached the adjutant's office, because a corporal she'd seen there appeared out of the growing dark. The private guarding the house went back to the rear entrance, but she could see that he was looking her way instead of inside. "I'll get a light and a rope," the corporal told her. "We'll have your puppy up in no time."

By the time the corporal returned with another soldier and a rope, Martha didn't have to pretend hysteria. The guard hadn't raised any outcry. All she could hope was that the spectacle she and Whipple were making absorbed the guard's attention so much that he wasn't noticing anything else.

With the other soldier holding the end, the corporal used the rope to lower himself down the bank. At the bottom he called up, "I have him, ma'am." Several more soldiers arrived, and together they hauled him up.

Martha seldom wept, but when the corporal put Whipple into her arms, she began to cry. "I don't think he's hurt much. Just scared," the corporal said anxiously.

"Yes, I'm sure you're right," she said shakily. "I do thank you so very much."

"Oh, my God!" It was the shocked voice of the

guard. "Corporal Wiggins. A window's open. The Apaches are gone!"

The soldiers deserted Martha for the guard. She sank down onto the ground and clutched Whipple in trembling arms. While the soldiers fanned out in a hasty search, she ran her hands over him, checking that he wasn't injured. When she could control her legs enough to get up, she waited in the shadows, too anxious to leave until she knew whether any of the women would be discovered.

The officer of the day appeared, a cavalry lieutenant whom Martha barely knew. Incredulous questions turned into angry accusations. Phrases such as "allowing prisoners to escape" and "dereliction of duty" brought home to her something she hadn't considered. A new anxiety kept her lingering on the sidelines: What would happen to the private who had been on duty?

The officer snapped, "Private Flynn, you are on report." Stricken, she hastily moved forward to the group of men standing in the entrance hall of the house.

"Excuse me, lieutenant. I'm to blame for the trouble. When my dog fell into the gorge, this soldier came to see what was wrong, but only for a moment. I'm sure anything that happened is my fault, not his."

"Thank you, Mrs. Baldwin, for volunteering that information," the lieutenant said stiffly, "but this is a matter for me to settle. If the colonel wishes to hear what you have to say, he will be in touch with you." He turned to the corporal and said, "See that Private Flynn is confined to barracks." To one of the other soldiers, he said, "Please escort Mrs. Baldwin to her quarters."

Holding Whipple, Martha started toward her quarters. As she walked, her anguish about what might happen to Dulcita and the two women was increased by guilt about the soldier on report. The effect of her scheme on him hadn't occurred to her. Cole would be furious.

23

After a week of futile scouting Cole and his men returned to Fort Apache. During the patrol it had become obvious that the runaway Apaches had not been in the area reported by the women. On the way back to the fort, Smiley's face was gloomy. When they splashed across the ford and pulled up at the guard post, the sentry on duty saluted and said to Cole, "Sir, one of your scouts, Smiley, is under arrest."

"On what charge?"

"You'll have to speak to the adjutant about that, sir. My orders are that he's to go to the guardhouse."

Reluctantly Cole had Sergeant Briggs assign two men to take an unresisting and morose Smiley away. Cole left the sergeant to take care of his horse and dismiss the patrol while he went to the adjutant's office.

As soon as he reported in, he asked the adjutant, "What's this about Smiley?"

"Somebody helped those two Apache women escape," Lieutenant North said. "Smiley's from their band. He stays in the guardhouse until this gets sorted out."

"Why the guardhouse?" Cole protested. "I'd swear he expected to find the hostiles where the women said they'd be. He was taken in like the rest of us. That's humiliation enough."

Lieutenant North shook his head. "If Smiley does a stint in the guardhouse, the rest of the scouts will check out the stories they hear more carefully first. You can take it up with the CO, but it's my guess it won't do any good."

"I'll do that." Cole started for the door.

"You better hear what happened first," the adjutant said.

Something in North's voice warned Cole he wasn't going to like what came next. Slowly he turned around to face the adjutant. "So how did the women escape?"

"Your wife," North began uncomfortably, "was walking her dog."

Martha! Cole listened, but he didn't need the details to know what he hoped Colonel Stratton didn't suspect. The only thing he was unsure of was just how she managed it, and why. At the end he said, "Thanks for letting me know."

When he left, he decided to see the CO before he heard Martha's explanation. His reactions might be more convincing if he didn't know the truth, and anger about her activities was real enough.

When he reached Colonel Stratton's office, the aide informed Cole that the commanding officer was out. As Cole left the office, Lydia Stratton stopped him in the entrance hall. "I thought I heard your voice, Mr. Baldwin." Her smile had its usual cheerful warmth. "The colonel will be back soon. I'm just having tea.

Please, have a cup with me while you wait."

Cole said, "Thank you, Mrs. Stratton, but I haven't had time to clean up since I got in from patrol."

"That doesn't matter a bit," she said generously. "I'm used to it."

"Then I accept."

They spent a quarter of an hour drinking tea and making inconsequential conversation before Cole heard the front door and the colonel's voice. He put down his cup and rose. "Thank you for the tea, Mrs. Stratton."

She rose also, her eyes sympathetic. "I like your wife, Mr. Baldwin. Spirited young women like Elizabeth have a little trouble getting used to army ways, but they make the sturdiest wives over the long term."

The long term wasn't part of his and Martha's plan, but he appreciated the kindness of Lydia Stratton's words. "That's a generous thought, Mrs. Stratton."

Back in Colonel Stratton's office, Cole guessed from the commanding officer's frown that he didn't share his wife's tolerant view of impulsive behavior. As soon as salutes had been exchanged, Cole said, "With your permission, sir, I'd like to say a word about the Apache women who escaped. I'm convinced that Smiley did not know that they were offering false information. I'm sure he believed it. And he was angry and upset when we could see we had a false lead. His loyalty and credibility have never been in doubt before."

"Yes, I'm aware of that," Colonel Stratton said. "Well, we can't question the two women now. Though God knows we get little enough information when we do."

The colonel didn't have to say more. Best, Cole decided, to face his disapproval headlong. He spoke rapidly, hoping to stall off a reaction until he could finish. "Lieutenant North told me that someone took advantage of a commotion caused by Mrs. Baldwin and her dog and helped the women escape. It was unwise of my wife to be walking with her dog that time of day, and near the place where the women were held. I'm afraid, sir, that she doesn't consider the security problems of a wilderness garrison—that someone might be watching for just such an opportunity. I feel responsible for the problems the escape caused Smiley and Private Flynn. If there is anything I can do about the trouble they're in, I want to."

Colonel Stratton's unhappy expression didn't moderate. "Regardless of the reason, Private Flynn was the one who left the prisoners unwatched. As to Smiley, I'll consider your point." He paused, as if to give weight to what he planned to say next. "Speaking quite privately, Mr. Baldwin, I recognize that wives have ways of influencing their husbands. It's up to the husband to maintain a perspective on how far he lets that influence affect him."

Cole could feel the heat creeping up his neck and spreading to his ears. "Yes, sir," he said to the wall behind the colonel, hoping that was all.

"Frankly, a reputation for paying too much attention to your wife preceded you here. However, from Captain Fisher's reports and what I've observed, you are a good officer. You might in time be a superior one. Perhaps you need to see that your wife understands this."

"Thank you, sir. Is that all?"

"Yes."

His gut churning with angry humiliation, he saluted and left.

* * *

Martha waited in the front room of their quarters. Her palms were damp and her throat dry. Lane had told her about Cole's return, and then tactfully announced that he had duties at the company barracks that would keep him busy until late afternoon.

She was grateful for his understanding. Like everyone else, he knew about her excursion with Whipple and its dismal consequences for Private Flynn. He was assuming that she'd want privacy for the explosion when Cole returned. Lane didn't guess her real apprehensions.

Though she regretted the consequences for the soldier in trouble, she felt justified in helping Dulcita. Surely Cole would understand when she explained. What she really dreaded was telling him the other news—the news she could no longer conceal from herself. She was pregnant.

For five days she'd stayed at her quarters. Whipple was nursing a sore paw, and she spent a lot of time guiltily fussing over it, assuring him she hadn't intended to hurt him. Also, she wanted to be there in case of word from Dulcita. Keeping to herself gave her lots of time to think, and to recognize the signs of pregnancy she remembered from nine years before. The realization delighted her—and frightened her. For months she'd felt as if she were two people, and now she was even more divided. One part of her longed for a child who might take away some of the pain of losing Pinecone. In that, she was like Elizabeth, who had so much wanted Stephen's child. But the real Elizabeth would have been a married woman who had the real Stephen, a husband who loved her and would love and help care for a child. Martha's frightened side hoped that Cole loved her, but she knew that she had no right to count on him.

She had proposed—insisted on—the arrangement that had put them in this situation. If she feared that a new child could ruin her efforts to find Pinecone, Cole would have the same fear for his plans. And they couldn't keep up the masquerade forever. Someday they would have to disappear. She'd considered not telling him but dismissed that thought. He must know, just as she did but had ignored, that being careful didn't prevent all conceptions.

The time for painful thinking also made her recognize how much she loved Cole. Not more than her son. Not more than she would love his child. But more than she had known a woman could love a man. Much more than her feelings for Sharp-Knife. Somehow her love made it even more important that Cole understand she wasn't asking for a commitment from him. That she hadn't been secretly trying to tie him to her. So she waited with painful anticipation for him to arrive.

When he appeared in the doorway, she could see from his expression that he was a volcano about to erupt. He threw his campaign hat onto the table and put his pistol down beside it, as if he couldn't trust himself to keep a weapon close at hand. He stood, legs apart like a fighter, and said, "I want to know what happened."

"Last Thursday about dusk I was out walking Whipple—"

"The most notorious dog at Fort Apache," he interrupted coldly.

Anger began to displace distress. "If you want to

know what happened," she snapped, "then you'll have to listen."

In the face of Martha's anger, Cole realized he must rein in his temper or they'd be shouting. "All right," he said, "I'll listen." He sat down and waited.

By the time Martha finished with, "I feel bad about Private Flynn," his anger had cooled off. It still stung when he thought of the dressing down he'd had from Colonel Stratton, but he could understand her motives.

"Have you heard from Dulcita?"

"No, but she might have trouble coming back. I guessed that the sentries would be extra careful now, and I couldn't think of a way to go out of the fort."

"Thank God for that. Dammit, Martha, you'll have to let things ride for a while. Stay close. Act like a wife who wouldn't think of doing anything unusual. Give Dulcita a chance. If she's going to warn your brother-in-law, she's probably already done it."

"I don't think she'll warn anyone."

"Then be patient. Don't lose everything now. Is Dr. Lawton back?"

"Yes, he came back yesterday. He looked awful, and I think he's staying in his quarters. At least, I haven't seen him go past."

Suddenly his clothes felt as if they were stuck to him with dirt and sweat. He got up. "I'm going to get a bath. Later I'll see if there's anything I can do about Private Flynn. And I'll stop by the hospital and check the doctor's desk if I can. If we can hold out a little longer, I have a good chance of working with the suppliers." He gave her a rueful grin and ran his finger along her cheek. "The colonel will want me around here where I can keep an eye on you."

When he was halfway to the bedroom, Martha said, "Wait. I need to talk to you about something else."

Startled at the urgency of her tone, he stopped. "What else?"

Her face had lost its earlier color, making her blue eyes look even more intense than usual. She opened her mouth as if to speak, then closed it again.

"What is it?" he asked, truly alarmed.

"I . . . we are going . . . that is, I'm pregnant."

He stared at her, confused feelings whirling inside him. She was waiting for him to say something. All he could draw out of the confusion was, "Are you sure?"

"Yes."

She was still waiting for his reaction. But how could he respond when he didn't know what the hell he felt? He looked down at his hands, which were clenched at his sides, and loosened them. Gradually emotions he could recognize surfaced. Pride, and dismay. He'd be a father. But he hadn't avenged his father's death. Or cleared his name. If he had a child, he wanted one who could look up to him. "How can you know for certain?"

"I remember from the first time."

The first time. The reminder of her Apache husband prodded at forgotten jealousy. How did she feel? Would another child mean as much to her as the first one? It was a question he couldn't ask. "We've about run out our string here anyway," he said slowly. "The thing to do is figure out how to get away. Make it look as if we just disappeared. Plenty of soldiers desert. Not officers that I've heard of, but that has to happen too. We can—"

"No!" Her eyes flashed and her voice was fierce. "This is the closest we've come to doing what we started this for. Dulcita won't betray me. She'll come back and let me know how to find my son. You're in a position to get information you need about your stepfather."

"And what about my child?"

"You don't have to worry about it. I'll take care of both children."

"A baby, carried with you God knows where, while you're finding a place that won't run you and a half-Apache child out?"

"I can manage."

She'd answered his unspoken question about which child was more important. "Apparently you don't expect me to take any responsibility for my child," he said, and heard in his accusation hurt and anger he hadn't intended to reveal. "A child deserves two parents. We can leave now. Go someplace where we're not known. Probably a long way from here. We can make a new start. Get married."

Her eyes held a flicker of something that could have been joy. But it vanished so quickly he wasn't sure he'd seen it. "That wouldn't work," she said flatly. "We'd both regret it. I'd always wish I'd found my son. You'd be unhappy about your stepfather and end up wondering if I'd trapped you into marrying me."

Because he suspected in some portion of his mind that she might be right, that added to his anger. "Did you? Was that what you had in mind? Another father to take care of a new child—along with the one you really care about?"

It was full battle now. "If I wanted to pick out a man to be a father for another child, I wouldn't have chosen the murderer I found in the shed that day."

Feelings he hadn't known he had were being torn

apart. "Maybe I'd have been better off going to Yuma Prison. I'd have a chance to escape from there and I wouldn't have to guard my back all the time because of you."

Martha said coldly, "I'll behave like the perfect wife while you're doing something about the medical records and getting your information. I won't go to Diablo's camp again yet because I think Dulcita will come back soon. If my son isn't there, I may have to go somewhere else on my own. Then we can be rid of this farce and each other."

They'd used too many words that couldn't be retrieved. He turned and left. As he headed for the post bathhouse, he thought how easy it was to say things that made saying anything more impossible.

That night Martha learned from Cole that the job of overseeing supplies for the Apaches left on the reservation had temporarily gone to Robert Morgan, the officer who was already in charge of the scouts. Cole began spending every evening at cards again. Since he and Martha exchanged only polite conversation, he didn't explain his reasons, but she'd heard that Robert loved to gamble. So did the post trader and the quartermaster. Cole was gathering information.

Five days later, after supper when Lane had gone to the barracks for the evening, Cole said, "A garrison court-martial is being convened for Private Flynn."

Guiltily she said, "I'm sorry."

"No—that's good. If he had to stand a general court-martial, that would be more serious. This means he'll probably get off with a reprimand and some time in the guardhouse."

It didn't sound good to her, but she'd finished making apologies for what happened. "Does it bother you, to hear that a man has to be confined in a guardhouse?" It was the most personal thing she'd said to him since their bitter words about her pregnancy.

"Plenty of men in jail belong there."

Venturing a little more, she said, "You didn't."

His stiffened face meant he hadn't forgotten what she said. "I thought you weren't sure about that."

"I am." She thought the line of his mouth eased a fraction. Her uncertainty hurried her on before she could be disappointed. "What about Smiley?"

"I've vouched for him, and he's cleared of charges. But it's crazy." Anger sharpened his voice. "An Apache scout shouldn't need the word of someone like me. He knows a hell of a lot more than I do about this kind of soldiering."

"You're a man and white and American and an army officer," she said, voicing her own bitterness. It was the wrong thing; it put them on different sides.

He stiffened again and said sarcastically, "Not quite all of those."

They finished their coffee in silence. As he started to leave for the post trader's nightly game, he said, almost offhandedly, "Dr. Lawton wants to see me tomorrow. He said we have something to go over."

She'd been waiting so long for this to happen that it had become a little unreal. It was as if she'd stepped away from the guillotine and was watching it fall on someone else. But the thud was there, in her stomach. "I suppose it's the medical records," she said, hoping he had some other explanation.

"I don't know, but that's likely."

"Why didn't you tell me this earlier?"

"He caught me just as I was coming in for supper."

Illogically, it enraged her that he'd eaten with good appetite. "But we have to think—decide what to do!"

"There's time for that. I'm Stephen Baldwin's build and coloring. Otherwise I wouldn't have gotten away with the impersonation this long. Tomorrow I'll see what Lawton has to say. Try to bluff him. I'm not going to spend time in a jail again. But we're getting too close here to run unless we have to."

He sounded and looked unbothered. She couldn't feel that way; she needed to at least have a plan. "I can get along in the woods if I have to. I remember enough, and it's summer."

His appearance of calm vanished. "No! You're not going anywhere by yourself. The Apaches haven't spotted you because you're a white woman. Remember *that*." More quietly he added, "After I talk to Lawton, we'll see."

He went out, leaving Martha certain only that she didn't know how things stood between them. Their quarrel hadn't destroyed the tie that had grown over these months, but their paths still led in divergent directions. Though she hadn't told him, she had been getting ready for his news.

Even before the night she helped the Apache women escape, she'd been collecting supplies that would be needed to survive if she and Cole had to disappear. On the excuse that she wanted to find out how soldiers had to live on long marches, she'd asked Lane to help. He went along with her request without surprise; her reputation for eccentricity was useful. Now she checked her storage box: canteens, a blanket apiece, hardtack, coffee, beans, bacon, two sharp knives, her derringer. Cole's rifle and ammunition and a change of clothing would complete all they could take with them, less if they couldn't get their horses. The lessons she'd learned living with the Apaches stayed with her still. She could manage, with or without Cole.

24

Cole headed for the hospital the next morning with muscles as tight as stretched rawhide. When he reached it, he walked past along the edge of the bluff, trying to work out more of his tension before he went in to face the doctor. Down below, the north and east forks of the White River met in a froth of bubbles and a friendly rushing sound. A peaceful vista, at odds with the violence that could break out in the contests for the land. The fort was here because of that violence, and so was he. But unless his skills at talk outmatched the doctor's perceptions, he wouldn't be here for long. A little more time—that's all he and Martha needed.

Dr. Lawton wasn't in his office. "He'll be along shortly, sir," the orderly volunteered.

"I'll wait."

The tottering stack of papers had shrunk to two moderately neat piles, one on each side of the naked-looking desk. Cole quashed the temptation to extract Stephen Baldwin's medical records. If Lawton were suspicious, the disappearance of records now would confirm his doubts. Instead Cole took a chair and settled himself in an unconcerned slouch. He corrected to attention when the doctor walked in, but not until he'd made sure Lawton had a chance to notice his relaxed position.

"That's all right, Mr. Baldwin." The doctor gestured for Cole to resume his chair. "No formality necessary this morning."

"Thank you, sir." Though the post surgeon was a civilian, he held informal rank higher than a lieutenant. Dr. Lawton didn't seem to care about having it acknowledged, but this wasn't a time to risk offense. "Late night at the trader's," Cole offered, as explanation for his earlier slouch, and as a bond of male fellowship. The doctor liked to gamble.

"Yes, well, this shouldn't take long." Dr. Lawton picked up the paper on top of one of the piles. From a drawer he took out a pair of steel-rimmed glasses and put them on. Cole had never seen the doctor wearing glasses, and the difference they made in his appearance was startling. Instead of the weary, sophisticated aristocrat who understood and dismissed the world's foibles, he became a pedant, searching out truth and error. The change sat uneasily in Cole's stomach.

"A copy of your medical records arrived," Dr. Lawton said, neatly ignoring the fact that it had lain on his desk for over a month. "I need to check them with you. Let's see—born in St. Louis, January eleventh, 1853. Makes you twenty-four."

He shot a glance at Cole over his glasses. Could he detect the four years' age difference? He went back to reading the paper while Cole's pulse rate edged up a notch. "Married September fourth, '75. So, you have a wedding anniversary coming up next month. Two years. Congratulations."

"Thank you." Dammit, why didn't he get on to the medical part?

"Hmm. This sheet's just basic information. The other one's here somewhere. I was looking it over Saturday. Washington likes to hide whatever you need," Dr. Lawton grumbled, inadvertently echoing Cole's impatience. He put the first sheet aside and looked at the next one. "Yes, here we have it. Measles, mumps," he read, "usual things. Smallpox. You're lucky you aren't scarred."

Cole relaxed a little. Despite Lawton's appearance in the glasses, he sounded fairly casual. Maybe there was nothing that could specifically identify Stephen Baldwin.

Lawton read silently a moment longer, then said, "Here's the part I need to ask you about. And I'd better check out the curvature of the spine. We can do it right here."

Cole's pulse zoomed again. He stood up and started to unbutton his jacket, wondering what the hell curvature of the spine looked like.

As Dr. Lawton came around his desk, he said, "How did you get the scar on your right thigh? Doesn't say on the information sheet."

Cole stopped, his jacket partway off his shoulders, and looked at Lawton with what he hoped was a bewildered expression. "Scar? I don't know what you mean. I don't have a scar on my leg anywhere. Are you sure that's what it says?"

Dr. Lawton looked back at the paper. "Yes. Listed under identifying marks: two-inch scar on right thigh."

"Something's strange about this. I wondered when

you said curvature of the spine. Nobody ever told me anything like that. I supposed the army doctor in St. Louis noticed something I didn't know about. And smallpox. I had chicken pox, but not smallpox. Maybe I said the wrong word when I had the examination. But the scar business—that's just plain wrong."

Dr. Lawton frowned and read over the paper again. "Your name's at the top. Stephen Baldwin."

"You can look, sir, but you won't find a scar. And I don't believe anything's wrong with my spine." Cole slipped his jacket off and then his shirt and turned his back to the doctor.

"You're right," Lawton said. "Spine's as straight as I've ever seen. Don't bother with showing me the leg."

Cole said, "Do you think some clerk started copying my records and then got them mixed up with someone else's?"

"I guess anything's possible in Washington," the doctor said, but it was a routine response, without conviction behind it. "I'll look you over right now. Get some sort of record started here and write to Washington again."

When Dr. Lawton finished his examination, he sat back down at his desk and picked up the offending sheet of paper again. "Well, you're healthy enough for the army, even if you're not the man described here."

As Cole fastened his jacket, he said, "If you're through, sir, I'd like to get back to duty."

Dr. Lawton looked up, leaning back in his chair. He still held the paper as if he were trying to make up his mind about it. "Yes, I'm through, for now."

* * *

Martha, practicing her role as well-behaved army wife, spent the afternoon at Harriet Fisher's. Along with several other wives, she helped piece squares for a quilt to send to the Fishers' married daughter. She'd been somewhat reassured by Cole's report of his visit to Dr. Lawton, but concern about the future dominated her thoughts. If her son were with the group Dulcita said would return in September, that was about four weeks off. In that time, Martha hoped, Cole would learn what he wanted about his stepfather. Provided that Dr. Lawton didn't make more inquiries, she would wait that long for Dulcita before acting on her own.

Partway through the afternoon Lydia Stratton came in, her dark eyes animated. "A message just arrived over the telegraph," she announced. "We're having visitors from Tucson. They'll arrive Saturday."

Martha's anxiety, which she had thought diminished, leapt into full life again.

Alice asked the question Martha couldn't get out. "Who's coming?"

"Five people altogether. I know one family well, Cecil and Dorothy Hays, and their daughter, Betsy. The wire didn't say who else is with them."

Alice clapped her hands. "Then we'll have to have a party."

Martha suddenly found her voice. "Let's have a masked ball."

"Oh, yes," Alice exclaimed, "let's do. We haven't had a masquerade since April. They're so exciting."

Not too exciting, was Martha's silent prayer. "How long will the visitors be here?" she asked.

"I don't know," Lydia answered. "Probably at least a week."

That night she told Cole about the visitors. His explosive "Damn!" expressed her reaction too. Frowning, he said, "Our luck's getting thin. That was a good move of yours about the ball." The frown gave way to a smile that wasn't quite a smile. "We could go as a gallows thief and a widow."

She laughed and felt a little easing of her pain. Bitter humor was better than tears.

"I'll have to see what I can do about a special assignment, away from the fort if possible. I can't wear a mask all the time."

"Maybe you won't recognize any of the people."

"That wouldn't mean they hadn't attended the trial. It was a popular event."

"I've been collecting things we can use if we have to get away in a hurry." She showed him the storage box.

"Good planning." He closed the lid with a bang. "But I'm not leaving until there's no other way."

When it was time for him to go to the post trader's game, he lingered, and despite the differences that separated them so profoundly, Martha felt a ripple of excitement. He looked at the clock several times, as if it were giving him an order he'd rather ignore. Finally he put on his jacket and left. Though Martha didn't doubt that he would keep to his course, his reluctance comforted the secret longing inside her that clung to the memory of nights of passion and love.

By Friday no assignment had turned up to take Cole away from the fort. One of the cavalry lieutenants was to be the officer of the day on Saturday, so there was no excuse for Cole to miss the masked ball. For the occasion, the largest room in the new hospital was made available as the ballroom. Its three occupants were moved temporarily to the ward room of the old building. The officers' wives pressed into service their strikers, a few extra soldiers, and the few enlisted men's wives on the post. Together they took over the kitchen and dining room for preparing and serving supper. Martha helped hang flags and arrange flowers while the soldiers polished brass fixtures and waxed the ballroom floor to a shine. Dr. Lawton's office was fitted up for a cloakroom. Martha looked into the office, but the desk and table were bare and the cabinets locked.

On Saturday the best that Cole could wrangle was to supervise the practice on the rifle range, which would keep him there most of the day. Martha hovered at her window until she saw the visitors arriving in the early afternoon. Lydia Stratton went out to greet a middle-aged couple and a young woman. That would be her friends, the Hays. The two others, who would stay with the Fishers, appeared to be an older couple. The man was tall and thin, with white hair, a contrast to the woman, who was short, dark haired, and quite plump. That was all Martha could see of them. She asked Lane if he'd heard who they were, but he didn't know.

The first test would come at the dress parade for retreat. This parade was held every day that the weather was good enough. Martha had hoped for a storm. During the morning, white, fluffy clouds piled up over the high mesas to the north, but they didn't move south. The afternoon was fine and clear.

Cole came in shortly before the drum and bugle call signaling half an hour to the retreat parade. As he changed into his dress uniform, he asked, "Did you see who came?"

"Yes, but I didn't find out their names. They look

ordinary, old enough to be parents of anyone our age. That's all I could tell."

Adjutant's call sounded ten minutes later, and Cole was out and gone. Martha followed as far as the walk in front. To her right she saw Lydia Stratton and Harriet Fisher in front of the commanding officer's house, along with their visitors. She hoped they were all shortsighted.

Captain Fisher marched C Company to the parade ground where they lined up in units. Captain Fisher gave the orders, which Cole and the other junior officers of the company relayed to the noncommissioned officers and on down the line to the soldiers, who went through portions of the manual of arms. The cavalry companies went through their drills. After roll call was taken and orders and assignments were read, the three companies were dismissed.

Martha had watched the visitors all through the parade. No one had appeared excited, at least not from that distance. Still, she found that her fingernails were digging into her palms, leaving red crescents. She released her fingers and went into the quarters. The supplies she had put aside were already packed into two knapsacks. There was nothing to do except dress for the ball and hope.

She and Cole had decided he would be a clown so that his face could be painted around the mask. When unmasking time came at midnight, the paint would still make a partial disguise. She wore a white cap and an apron over a skirt, pinned up to the daring length of three inches above the floor, and carried a pail. Milkmaids were so common at masked balls that she hoped to escape any special notice that could single out Cole as well. To ensure that someone else would be the center of attention, she had suggested to Alice that she dress as a gypsy fortune teller and pretend to read cards. Martha helped plan outrageous fortunes to tell that would keep everyone interested in the gypsy.

At nine o'clock Martha and Cole were ready. He had a wide red mouth over a dead white face and two blue spots on his cheeks. A loose shirt and pants that Martha had patched together from scraps of different colors hung shapelessly on his frame. "How do I look?" he asked her.

"Like anyone. Just a man."

"All right. Remember, if someone does definitely recognize me, leave, take your knapsack, and get off the post. On Skinny if you can. Go east. There's the best cover that way."

"No, I won't do that."

He frowned and started to speak, but she got in first. "How would it look if I ran off right away? It would mean an accusation was true. Surely Colonel Stratton won't accept someone's word without an inquiry. If I stay it will delay things long enough that you can get away too."

He studied her for a long moment. "What about your son? You risk jail if you're wrong about the colonel."

"I don't think it would turn out that way." She wasn't as sure as she sounded, but she couldn't run away without trying to save him.

"All right. But if it doesn't work the way you think, do what I suggested once before. Say I tricked you into helping me in the beginning and then threatened you. You were afraid not to go along."

"That would be another charge against you."

"They can only hang me once."

The thought didn't reassure Martha, but it was time to go to the party.

When they reached the temporary ballroom, Martha looked at the lanterns sending out a seductive glow over the veranda and heard music from inside—and wanted to turn around and leave. Cole took her hand and tucked it into the crook of his elbow. "Have to test this sometime," he said coolly, and started inside.

Once in the ballroom Martha was delighted to see that a circle of people had already formed around Alice. She was studying cards on a table. Sitting across from her was a sailor. Harriet had accidentally let slip that that would be Captain Fisher's disguise. "You'll be shipwrecked on a Pacific island," Alice was saying. "The three daughters of the king of the island will all fall in love with you. The king will make you marry all of them."

The laughter that attended that and the next fortune for a queen, who was Harriet, let Martha and Cole examine the guests unnoticed. Mr. and Mrs. Hays weren't wearing costumes. The girl with them, dressed as a Mexican senorita, had to be their daughter. "Do you know them?" Martha whispered to Cole.

"Not really. They look a little familiar, but if I ever met them, it was a long time ago."

Martha didn't see anyone who could be the other two guests. "Let's go to the refreshment table," she suggested to Cole. "It's in the hall." When she and Cole reached the door, she saw the other couple, also not in costume. At the same time Cole stopped, and his arm went rigid under her hand. She turned to go back into the ballroom, but Cole clamped his elbow next to his side, imprisoning her hand, and started into the hall. It was either break away, be dragged along, or walk forward as if she weren't marching to the gallows. She went with him.

Cole made for the refreshment table and stopped next to the couple from Tucson. Why, Martha screamed inside, did he have to challenge them so soon? He could test his disguise from a distance. "We're not supposed to make introductions until midnight," he said, "but that doesn't seem polite to visitors. I'm Stephen Baldwin, and this is my wife, Elizabeth."

The tall man smiled and put out his hand. "Pleased to meet you, Mrs. Baldwin. Lieutenant. I'm Ira Gurnett, and this is my wife, Olive."

Cole's friend! Martha didn't know whether to scream with relief or hit Cole for that ghastly walk across to the table. What she did was smile pleasantly and say, "I'm delighted to meet you, Mr. and Mrs. Gurnett."

After that it was as if a balloon of fear that had been in her stomach had burst. While Cole danced with Olive, she danced with Ira and exchanged polite and meaningless comments about weather and the history of the fort. Later she even stayed comparatively calm when Cole danced with Mrs. Hays. The daughter, Betsy, was sufficiently besieged by the bachelors of the garrison that Cole didn't have to partner her.

As midnight approached, the fear in Martha's stomach began to grow again until it was a physical pain. She and Cole had agreed that leaving before the unmasking would invite questions, so she concentrated on giving the appearance of having a good time.

For the last dance before midnight, the musicians outdid themselves in a slow waltz. Cole came to partner Martha, and she went into his arms wondering whether this would be the last time they would dance together. He didn't appear to have any such gloomy thoughts. Instead he grinned at her with his wide clown mouth and said, "Enjoying yourself?"

"Stephen Baldwin, I don't know a man who can be more exasperating than you are." It sounded wifely, and she was sure he knew that she meant something much stronger.

Midnight. Martha removed her mask with fingers that shook. Cole calmly took his off and said, "At last. That mask is hot." He wiped his forehead with a finger that had brushed the blue spot on his cheek. It left a smear across above his eyes and gave his face a further distorted appearance.

Quickly Martha said, "Stephen, you've smeared your face paint," and added to the mess with her finger. "Oh, dear. Now I've made it worse."

"Never mind." He grinned at her, his eyes inviting her to consider it all a game of chance. "Shall I get you some food?"

Eating was impossible but she said, "Just a little, please," because that was part of the game.

She was watching him cross to the other side of the room when a girlish voice nearby said, "Now I remember." It was Betsy Hays, with Peter Dunham.

"What do you remember?" he asked.

"That man in the clown suit. He reminds me of someone, and I just remembered who."

Martha knew she should do something to stop the conversation, but the words had paralyzed her.

"It was a murderer who was tried in Tucson last year. January, I think." Betsy giggled. "Mama didn't know, but twice I sneaked in to watch the trial. The clown looks a little bit like that man. What was his name? Cal, or something like that."

Peter broke into the flow of chatter. "Miss Hays, it's not kind to be talking about another man when you should be thinking about me."

She giggled again. "Why, Lieutenant Dunham, you mustn't be jealous. That man's dead, and you aren't."

Martha went to the door and intercepted Cole as he came in, two plates of food in his hands. "I'm feeling too warm, Stephen," she said. "Shall we go out onto the veranda?"

Outside they found a bench with no one close by, and Martha sat down and held the plate. In a soft voice she hoped was normal she said, "Betsy Hays thinks you look like a murderer she saw in Tucson."

"Someone handsome, then," he said, and incredibly began on a piece of turkey.

"I don't know. She says he's dead."

"Then I'm glad I'm not that man."

That silenced her, and she watched with unbelieving fascination as he finished the turkey and ate an oyster patty, a slice of melon, and a small square of pink-iced cake. He looked at her full plate and asked, "Aren't you going to eat?"

"No. I must have gotten too hot dancing. Would you like it?"

Under the paint, the skin she could see lost its color. "Thanks. I've had enough."

One of the sergeant's wives, who had been hired to help, came around collecting dishes. She looked disapprovingly at Martha's untouched food. Martha had to stop herself from apologizing and thought a bit hysterically how persistent habits are that she could worry about wasting food when her world might crash at any moment.

"Elizabeth," Cole said, just loudly enough for others to hear them, "I can't stand this paint. It's making my face itch. I'm going back to the quarters and clean up. I'll be back when I'm finished." His voice took on a suggestive timbre as he added, "Would you like to come along and help me? We won't be long, and then we can dance again."

She understood. He was using his reputation for not being able to keep his hands off his wife to get them away from the dance. "Yes, of course."

His purpose was even clearer when they reached the edge of the light from the lanterns on the hospital veranda. He stopped and pulled her into his arms. Anyone on the veranda could still see them dimly, enough to note the passionate kiss. At first her mind was on the audience and how convincing she and Cole looked. But as he held her, his kiss deepened, and what had been pretense became real. The red paint around his mouth tasted bitter, but she didn't care.

They parted, and looked at each other, then he took her hand and started along the boardwalk. He pulled her along faster and faster until they were running in the dark.

They reached the dark, silent house and didn't bother with a light. They didn't need to see to find each other's mouths. To know how to pull off each other's clothes. To fall naked on the bed together.

It was crazy, she thought fleetingly. They didn't know what would happen to them tomorrow, and all that mattered was the explosion of love and desire that obliterated everything but the two of them—touching, tasting, caressing, and finally joining together in a whirling spiral that seemed to bring the heavens down into their special space with them.

Gradually the real world came back. They washed off Cole's paint that covered almost as much of her. And with that came renewed passion and the world retreated again.

Only much later did he ask her about Betsy Hays. She had to tell him about the name that Betsy almost had right. "If Betsy says anything more to Peter, he might remember that the name I accidentally used wasn't Lane, but Cole."

"We're so close! If you're right, Dulcita will help you. And I know some things about Harvey Lippincott that ought to put him in jail. He's been greedy as hell. It's blatant enough that I hope something will happen."

"Cole, that's wonderful!"

"There's more. My mother told Ira that she's sure someone's blackmailing Harvey. That's why Ira and Olive are here. He didn't trust sending a message to me. The man may not stay around, though." He paused, and though she couldn't see, she could picture his face, dark eyebrows drawn together, eyes slightly narrowed, mouth a purposeful line. "I've got to get to Tucson. Ned Young and I have become friends. Thank God he's quartermaster. He's angry about the cheating. I think I can work something with him. Then when I get back, somehow we'll find Nilchi Bidahsaa."

She was less hopeful. A trip to Tucson had been dangerous before. If he was in town, hunting for a man, the chance of someone identifying him was even greater. She loved him for remembering her son's Apache name. Tomorrow would come, but for the night, she would lie close in his embrace and cherish each moment.

* * *

The next day Cole came back just before retreat, looking troubled. "Is something wrong?" she asked. "Has Betsy Hays said anything?"

"Not that I know of."

"Then what is it?"

"A detachment of infantry from C Company along with some of the Tonto scouts goes out on patrol first thing tomorrow."

"You've been ordered to go too?"

"That's my assignment."

"What about the man in Tucson?"

"I'll see if I can get out of going on patrol."

His apparent reluctance surprised her. "But I thought this was your chance to find that man. Isn't that what's most important?"

"Yes, it is," he responded, but without the conviction she expected.

Now she thought she understood. "You don't want to let your men go without you."

"I've worked with them. They're the best platoon in the company. I don't like sending them with someone else. But you're right about what's most important. After the parade for retreat, I'll speak to Ned and see what I can arrange."

Nothing was ever straightforward and simple. If Cole went either chasing Apaches or into Tucson, he'd be in danger. Should she wait longer for Dulcita? She wandered around the house and went out to visit Whipple.

Outside, she didn't see the dog. She'd taken him off the line because his paw was healed, but he'd been staying close by. Now he was gone. She was deciding whether to go out looking for him when the door to Major Owens's unused kitchen opened a crack and a voice whispered, "Her-Eyes-Blue. Here!"

Martha's heart gave a suffocating leap. Only Dulcita would be calling her Apache name. She looked around. No one else was in sight. She ducked into the shed and found Dulcita and Whipple.

"I have been waiting since before dawn. She-Sticks-to-Her-Cradle and Big-Dipper came back to the camp two days ago. Pinecone was with them."

Joy and relief poured over Martha with such intensity that for a moment she felt faint. Her son was alive and in Diablo's camp.

Dulcita said sharply, "You are not listening."

"I'm sorry. Go on."

"Pinecone is always with Crouched-and-Ready, the brother of She-Sticks-to-Her-Cradle. Crouched-and-Ready wants to marry Round-Maiden."

"That's the younger woman of the two we helped escape?"

"Yes. Last night he told her he has been talking with a Chiricahua, someone from the south, new in the camp. There is a plan for some of the young men to go on a raid with the Chiricahua. Crouched-and-Ready wants to go. Pinecone wants to go with him, and Crouched-and-Ready says he will take him. I think they will go soon."

Suddenly everything did seem simple. "As soon as it is dark enough, I will go to the camp. Can you get back out of the fort all right?"

"Yes."

"Then meet me a little way past the east fork. I will be there when it is almost dark."

Whipple and Dulcita stayed in the shed, and

Martha went inside the house. She watched retreat, as did the visitors, but again Cole was at the back. Betsy Hays appeared to be paying more attention to Lieutenant North than to the display on the parade ground. In addition, one of the cavalry horses appeared lame, which concentrated eyes on Major Owens, anticipating an outbreak of his well-known temper. Though the back of his neck became a bright enough red to be seen from a distance, the horse was taken out of line and nothing more said.

After retreat, twilight seemed to last forever. Cole came in only briefly. "It worked," he said jubilantly. "Ned got me the assignment for Tucson. I leave in the morning. Right now I have to see him again, to work out just what he wants me to do. It may take a while."

In his preoccupation, he didn't seem to notice anything unusual about her. When he left to go back to the quartermaster's office, she finished her preparation: making sure the knapsack was packed evenly to minimize the effort of carrying it. Getting the last of her gold and her derringer. Putting on her sturdiest clothing and boots. Writing a note to Cole.

The note was the most difficult. She thought of so many things to say, all of them futile. Finally she wrote, "Dulcita has come. She's seen my son. If I don't go now, I may never find him, so I'm going. I don't know what I'll find, so I don't know whether I can come back. If I can't, it will be difficult for you, but everyone knows what an irresponsible wife I am. I've been sleeping late, so Lane won't know I'm gone until he comes to cook dinner tomorrow. You'll be on your way to Tucson then, so it won't keep you from what you're doing. You can say that I ran off and you don't know where I've gone. That will be the truth." She put the note in the storage box. Cole would look there, but no one else would.

When it was almost dark, she took her knapsack and went outside to the kitchen shed. She tied Whipple back on his rope in the yard. He protested, and she knelt beside him, scratching behind his front leg and the top of his tail, and dripping tears on him. "Goodbye, Whipple," she whispered. "I wish I could take you, but I can't."

She wiped her tears and told Dulcita, "I'm leaving now. We'll meet in a little while."

Keeping to the back of the buildings, she headed for the stables. If possible, she'd take Skinny. Otherwise she'd walk. At the corner of the stables where the horses belonging to the officers were kept, she looked cautiously to see whether anyone was around. No one was there. She could hear Major Owens bellowing in the main cavalry area. His anger about the lame horse at retreat sounded in full force. He was shouting orders, which in turn were relayed to men with horses on the picket line. That could go on all night. No one would see that Skinny was gone.

She saddled her pony, then mounted and circled around past the empty schoolhouse. After that she took the edge of the gorge past the sawmill to a place that wasn't an ordinary ford. "Come, Skinny, you can do it," she urged.

He did, and wet but undetected, she arrived at the opposite bank. She kept him to a route among the trees at one side of the trail until she saw Dulcita waiting. At that point if she turned around in the saddle, she could look back and see the fort behind her. She resisted the impulse and rode on straight ahead.

25

It was almost midnight before Cole returned to his quarters. He appreciated Ned Young's cooperation in getting sent to Tucson to look into the supply situation. The quartermaster hadn't said so, but Cole had an uncomfortable feeling that Ned thought he was afraid to stay at the fort where he might have to chase Apaches. It galled him to be under that kind of suspicion.

He'd also been able to catch Ira out on an evening walk, and Ira had agreed to his suggestion that he and Olive say the altitude bothered her and they'd like to return to Tucson. Cole and his soldiers would be the logical escort. That would give them an opportunity to talk. Altogether, he thought as he went up the walk, a good evening's work.

When he reached the veranda, he noticed that there was no lantern burning inside. That surprised him; he'd expected Martha to be waiting to hear how things had worked out. She must have gone to sleep, though

Whipple was making so much racket that he didn't see how she could. Instead of going on in, he detoured around to the back. Whipple was tied up. Martha hadn't done that for a while.

At Cole's appearance, Whipple's barks changed to pleading yips. "Calm down," he told the excited dog. Better to let him run than for everyone on the row to listen to him the rest of the night. As soon as Whipple was free, he took one sniff at Cole, dashed to the gorge, ran along the edge for a few feet, then disappeared over the side. Cole heard dislodged rocks bouncing down, and then nothing.

It added up to something wrong. Cole charged into the back entrance to the hall, through the dark front room, and into the bedroom. He didn't need the lamp to know that Martha wasn't there, but he lit one anyway and looked at the empty bed. Had she left, just like that, without a word? No, he didn't believe it. He opened the storage box and found with a mixture of dread and relief that the box held one knapsack—and a note.

As he read, relief swiftly gave way to anger. Why would she light out for Diablo's camp at night, without waiting to talk to him? The hell of it was, he couldn't go after her. Not until he figured out what kind of a story he needed. This—just when he was on his way to Tucson. Martha had left him in an impossible situation.

There were two choices, as far as he could see. One was to go on to Tucson. The other to stay here, have some reason to explain her behavior, and look for her. It looked as if going to Tucson was best. If Martha didn't come back, someone from the fort would hunt for her. Since she'd advertised her interest in Apaches, they'd look at the camps first. The bands here at Fort Apache had been peaceful for several years, Diablo's in particular. She'd be safe enough with his band. For now, Cole decided, he needed the cover of his uniform to get to Tucson. And it would give him time to figure out a story, if she hadn't taken care of everything before he got back. Man or woman, she was the quickest person he'd ever known for thinking her way out of a situation.

It had to look as if he didn't know she'd left. He took gear for Tucson and went across to a section partitioned off at the end of one of the barracks. Since there were no bachelor officers' quarters, it was used for visiting officers. He spoke to the private on duty. "I'll be sleeping here tonight if anyone wants me. Have to get up early tomorrow. I don't want to disturb anyone at my quarters." A feeble excuse. The private would think he'd had a fight with his wife and wanted out of their house.

Riding double on Skinny in the dark slowed the progress of the two women. As the hours passed, Martha's fear grew. Would Pinecone and Crouched-and-Ready still be at Diablo's camp? It was a question too agonizing to think about. When they finally reached the edge of the camp, she guessed that the trip from Fort Apache had taken at least four hours.

Dulcita said, "You stay here. I look for Crouched-and-Ready." She slid from Skinny's rump where she had been riding behind and went softly toward the camp. Martha dismounted. Skinny wanted to get at the grama grass in the meadow ahead, and she kept herself occupied quieting him and listening uneasily for anything that could tell her what was happening in the camp. It had been too long since she had practiced Apache skills.

Despite Martha's watchfulness, Dulcita appeared without making a noticeable sound. "Did you find Crouched-and-Ready?" Martha whispered.

"I think he is not in the camp. I will find the one he plans to marry." Dulcita motioned for Martha to follow. Martha's disappointment was enormous.

Leading Skinny, Dulcita doubled back over the way they had come for a short distance, then set off in a wide arc that took them above the camp and to the opposite side. Dulcita said, "Wait." Cautiously she approached a wickiup almost at the end. In a few minutes Martha saw her coming back along with another woman. When they reached her, she saw that Dulcita had brought Round-Maiden.

Round-Maiden whispered to Dulcita, "You are sure the white woman can speak my words?"

"Yes," Dulcita whispered to her, then to Martha, "Round-Maiden says the men have not left. They are at a meeting spot. She thinks Pinecone is with them. Do you still want to see them?"

For a moment the earth whirled around Martha in a joyous, dizzying swoop. It righted itself and she said, "Yes, I do."

"She will take you to Crouched-and-Ready," Dulcita said. "I will go now."

"Thank you, Dulcita. I hope all is well with you."

"Yes. My mother has told my father I am their Apache daughter again, and he has listened."

After she left, Round-Maiden whispered nervously, "Are you sure you want to talk to Crouched-and-Ready?"

"Yes!"

"All right. You helped me escape from the fort. I will take you to him."

Round-Maiden motioned, and Martha followed with Skinny patiently trailing behind her. As she walked, she thought of the dangers. In any normal group of Apaches, she wouldn't fear rape. But a renegade who hated all whites—that was something to fear. Surely the other men would not condone such an action. And she wouldn't be staying with them, only taking Pinecone with her. What if they were not where Round-Maiden thought they were? Could she go after them, trailing a group of men on a raiding party? It had been years since Martha had kept up the grueling pace of Apaches on the march. And she was pregnant. If Pinecone was already gone, what would she do?

They went what seemed miles into the woods. An old moon had risen, giving light but increasing her anxiety about the time. Round-Maiden didn't speak. Martha stopped her once. "Who is the Chiricahua man Crouched-and-Ready is with?"

"He is called Haske-kilnihi."

As they walked, Martha had to think to translate the Apache name. When she did, her fear increased. He-Calls-Himself-Angry wasn't a reassuring name.

A form rose so suddenly in their path that Martha gasped. It was a man. He spoke in Apache to Round-Maiden. "Why are you here? Who is this white woman?"

"She is the one who helped me escape at the fort. I am here to repay her."

Her heart thundering, Martha said in Apache, "I am here to see the brother of She-Sticks-to-Her-Cradle."

"Who is this white woman who speaks the Chihinne tongue?"

"My Chihinne name is Her-Eyes-Blue. My husband's brother is Big-Dipper."

"Big-Dipper has no brother."

"He did once."

He was apparently considering this anomaly. Finally he said, "Come." To Round-Maiden he said, "You come too."

After a steep climb up the slope, they circled three large boulders and came to a level space. Horses were picketed in a small grassy area and several men sat around a tiny smokeless fire. She searched with her eyes among them. No young boys! A pain filled Martha's chest, so severe that she almost gasped aloud. Then she saw two forms, not bulky enough to be men, lying to one side wrapped in blankets. Men could stay awake, but boys needed sleep. Her heart began to hope again. Her impulse was to run to the boys, pull aside the blankets, and look at their faces. With great force of will she remained where she was.

The man who had led them here crouched beside a man who was sitting by the fire, polishing the stock of a rifle, and said something into his ear. He looked quickly at Martha. He rose, still carrying his rifle, and crossed to her, then stopped and studied her face. "You came to see me?"

This ought to be Crouched-and-Ready. Martha searched his face, but he didn't look like the boy of twelve she faintly remembered. He appeared to be the right age, about twenty. He was slight, with regular features and a wiry body. "I am looking for the brother of She-Sticks-to-Her-Cradle," she said.

While she had been studying him, his eyes had never left her face. "You are the white wife of Sharp-Knife," Crouched-and-Ready said. She must have changed less than he had. "What do you want?"

"I have come about my son." An almost invisible tightening of his facial muscles told her what she wanted to know. "He is here," she said confidently, "and I wish to see him."

"The boy with me is the son of my sister," Crouched-and-Ready said.

"He is the son of Sharp-Knife," Martha insisted, "and so he is my son."

Crouched-and-Ready scowled. "No longer," he said, as if that settled things.

Martha saw she must try a different way. "My son is only eight years old. That is too young to go on a raid. Did my husband's brother and his wife agree that he could go?" The scowl was fierce, but Martha sensed uneasiness underneath. "I think they did not agree. I will take him back to the camp."

"No." From Crouched-and-Ready's expression, she could see she had offended his pride. "I promised him. He goes with me."

Desperately she threatened, "If I tell your sister, she will be angry. She and her husband will not want my son to go."

A deeper, heavier voice intervened. "What is this white woman doing here?"

Martha turned to face a tall, broadly built Apache man. He had a heavy nose in a wide face and eyes that looked as if they had seen many painful things. The long black hair that hung down on either side of his face was thick. His turban, made of red and blue flowered calico, was pulled low on his forehead so that it emphasized the cruel look of his eyes. Only his full mouth suggested a man who might once have laughed and loved his children.

"She wants to see the boy who came with me," Crouched-and-Ready said in a deferential tone.

Martha's throat was so tight she could feel the cords along the side of her neck. This must be He-Calls-Himself-Angry, the Chiricahua who had enticed the young men from the villages. The name fit. Martha decided boldness was the only way with this man, as long as she didn't let him see how terrified she felt. "I have come for my son," she said.

He-Calls-Himself-Angry gave her a contemptuous look. He turned to Crouched-and-Ready. "Have your woman take her back when we leave. We will keep the horse."

Crouched-and-Ready hesitated, then said nervously, "If she goes back, she will talk to my sister about . . . the boy. I think we should take her with us."

A new fear engulfed Martha. Not a captive again!

Now the Chiricahua's contempt was for the younger man. "A woman will slow us down. And the white soldiers will follow us."

"They will follow us anyway," Crouched-and-Ready argued. "If we have the white woman with us, they will worry about killing her and hold back with their rifles."

"White women scream."

Despite her fear, she decided instantly. Better to go as a captive than give up after all this time. "I will not scream," Martha said, calling up more assurance than her trembling inside gave her the right to claim. "I learned Apache ways."

"If you scream, I will kill you," her opponent said matter-of-factly.

Terrified, she believed him. But with that threat he had also agreed to take her.

He looked at the sky and said, "It is time to leave.

Big-Coyote is not here. We will go without him. Tell your woman to wait here until the sun has come up before she returns to the village. You can ride the new horse."

Without Skinny she would never keep up. "No," she said. "That horse is mine."

He-Calls-Himself-Angry measured her again, then shrugged and paid no more attention. Maybe he respected her boldness. More likely he knew she needed the horse and had decided that she was useful. It didn't matter. She was going.

She turned to Round-Maiden. "I thank you for what you have done. You have already repaid me, but I wish to ask one more favor. Could you spare your moccasins? If you can, I will give you my boots in trade."

Without responding, Round-Maiden took off her moccasins and handed them to Martha. "Thank you," Martha said. "They will let me follow where I cannot go in my boots." She pulled off her boots and handed them to Round-Maiden, then put on the moccasins.

The men obliterated traces of the fire. Martha watched the boys. Crouched-and-Ready roused them, and they rose instantly. One boy was already getting broad—older than eight. The other was as tall as the older one and slender. He noticed her and looked at her curiously. His hair and eyes were dark—like the hair and eyes of all the others. Nothing in his face reminded her of the laughing toddler she'd searched for so long. Then one of the men spoke and the boy went to do some task. In the way he held his head and in the motion of his body as he walked she saw Sharp-Knife. It was Pinecone!

At the signal from He-Calls-Himself-Angry, she started down the slope leading Skinny. Ahead of her was her son with his father's body and motions. She should have been terrified, and she was. But she was also joyful.

In spite of his decision to go to Tucson, Cole hardly slept that night. He was awake and up well before reveille. As soon as assembly was over, he checked that his detail of four men was ready to leave and then reported to the adjutant's office.

Jonathan North was yawning and nursing a cup of coffee. He looked at the papers on his desk and said, "You're getting an early start. Are your men ready?"

"Yes."

"Oh, and here's a message from the people staying with the Fishers. Seems they want to go back to Tucson. So you'll be their escort."

"I hope they don't waste half the morning," Cole grumbled.

Lieutenant North snorted. "You know civilians. They think we're here to wait on them."

Cole stood, shifting his weight restlessly. He didn't have to feign impatience.

The outer door banged as Robert Morgan burst in. Cole had never seen the officer in charge of the scouts so agitated. "One of my scouts just picked up some information," Robert said, "about a Chiricahua who's been visiting some of the White Mountain camps."

"Someone we know about?" North asked.

"No, but the scout says the man was at San Carlos for a while. His wife and child died there. After that he left the reservation. The scout thinks maybe he was on a raid in February down in Sonita. Fifteen whites were killed and over a hundred horses stolen. Most of the people in the camps don't want him around. But he's stirred up some of the young men. A dozen or so of them left the reservation with him sometime before dawn."

Robert looked at Cole. "I think you better know, Stephen, that a woman and a couple of children were with them. The scout says from what he heard, the woman is white, and she had a horse that sounds from the description like Skinny. I checked, and Skinny isn't in the stables. Also, your dog was found wandering around Diablo's camp. Is Elizabeth all right?"

Cole said, "I slept at the barracks last night," and was out the door and on a run to his quarters. He didn't believe Martha had gone with the Apaches willingly. Unless Pinecone was with them and she couldn't get him away.

He took just enough time to get his breath and pick up Martha's note before he ran back to the adjutant's office. "She's not there. I'm going to see Captain Fisher."

"Hold on," Lieutenant North said. "The CO's on his way here. Talk to him first."

Cole's heart was pounding from more than the run. He saluted when Colonel Stratton entered and remained at attention while Robert repeated what he'd said earlier. The colonel turned to Cole and said, "What about your wife?"

"I believe she may be with the Apaches who left, sir."

"What!" The colonel's face looked concerned, but angry too. "Do you have any explanation for that, Mr. Baldwin?"

"May I speak to you or Captain Fisher privately, sir?"

The colonel considered, then said, "I'll hear what

you have to say in a minute." He gave orders for a detachment of scouts, troopers, and mounted infantry to make preparations to go after the departed Apaches. After that, he went into the inner office and motioned Cole to follow and close the door. He seated himself at his desk. "Your wife had some part in the escape of the two Apache women. And now this. What is your explanation?"

"Before that, sir, if Captain Fisher agrees, do I have your permission to go with the detachment in pursuit?"

"That depends on your explanation."

"Yes, sir. Perhaps you'd better read this first." He handed Colonel Stratton Martha's note.

The colonel motioned to Cole to be at ease and read the note over. When he finished, he read it again and said, "This doesn't make much sense."

"I'm afraid that's the point, sir. May I speak frankly on a private matter?"

At the colonel's nod, he continued. "Before Mrs. Baldwin and I married, she had a child. It was not mine. One of those things that happen. I understood, and though I know that some might think less of her, I did not."

The colonel didn't react, but his expression was less unfriendly. "The baby, a boy, was adopted by a family that was moving to California. Later someone suggested to her that the family had been attacked by Indians and killed. All but the adopted child. This preyed on her mind until she became convinced that it was so. Not only that, but when we arrived here, she decided that the baby was in this area."

"But this is not on the main stage route," Colonel Stratton pointed out. "If a family had been attacked on the way to California, it would likely be south of here."

"Yes, sir. I tried to make her understand that. But I'm afraid that on this, she's not quite sane. I think it has been worse because for some time she did not have the prospect of another child. Now, we are expecting one of our own—" At that point Cole found his voice choking up with an emotion he hadn't allowed himself to recognize until now. He had to wait to speak again. "Excuse me, sir."

"That's all right," Colonel Stratton said kindly. "I appreciate that this must be painful for you. Sit down, Mr. Baldwin, if you wish."

"Thank you. I'm almost finished. I had hoped that with a new child coming my wife would forget her obsession that her previous child was here. I was wrong. Mrs. Baldwin made friends with the Apache woman who was with Major Owens and talked with her in Spanish. I can't say whether my wife had anything to do with the escape of the Apache women. But I believe she has been in touch with the major's housekeeper and learned something that led her to go to Diablo's camp. Whether she went voluntarily with the Apaches who left I don't know. I don't need to tell you, sir, that I am gravely concerned about her. So you see, sir, that's why I am requesting an assignment to the patrol to follow the Apaches. It's my place to take care of her."

"Yes, I understand, but I'm not sure I agree." Colonel Stratton got up and went to the door and looked into the other room. "Captain Fisher, I'm glad you're here. Please come in."

When the captain entered, Colonel Stratton said, "Mr. Baldwin tells me Mrs. Baldwin may be the white woman who is with the Apaches who left the reservation. The reasons are personal, and we don't need to go into them. Mr. Baldwin wishes to be assigned to the patrol following the Apaches."

"Sir," Captain Fisher said in his manner that always sounded as if he were quoting a textbook, "Mr. Baldwin is to go to Tucson this morning on an errand of some importance for Lieutenant Young, who went to some lengths to convince me that Mr. Baldwin is the best man to send. There is the additional consideration that it is often inadvisable to send an officer on a duty when he has too much involvement in the outcome. It can affect his thinking and lead to unwise decisions."

"Yes, that's true," the colonel agreed.

"Then, sir, I urge that Mr. Baldwin go on to Tucson."

"Very well."

There it was. All Cole had to do was to accept the decision of his two commanding officers. He would be gone to Tucson and still have done what he could for Martha. But in the mixture of lies and partial truths he'd told Stratton, there was one true statement. Inside of him where the essence of his being lay, he did want to take care of her. He loved her and wanted her to be safe—and to bear the child that she was carrying now, his child. Harvey Lippincott could wait. Clearing his name could wait.

"Colonel Stratton, Mrs. Baldwin is in a difficult state of mind. I think I am the one who can deal with that best. I urge you to reconsider." He'd bypassed Captain Fisher, but he had to have that yes. Colonel Stratton was more likely to give it to him.

While he waited for the CO's answer, he came to another decision. If he could go with a detachment of soldiers and scouts, he would. Alone he was no match for the Apaches, not on their terms. But if Stratton refused, he'd go anyway.

The colonel finally spoke. "Captain Fisher, without going into the details, I believe Mr. Baldwin is correct. If you agree, we'll assign him as second-in-command to the patrol that leaves shortly. Someone else can make the trip to Tucson."

"Thank you, sir." Cole kept his voice formal—the relief he felt would be unmilitary to express.

Outside, while the last preparations were going on, Cole found Ira alone and explained.

"I'll do what I can for you in Tucson," Ira said.

"You've already done that," Cole assured him. "It's not your fight. And Harvey doesn't play fair. I'd appreciate it if you can try to keep track of the witness. Otherwise I want you to stay out of it. Will you promise that?"

"All right. I promise." Ira made a gesture as if to hug Cole, but they were where anyone could see. He said, "Good luck," and Cole knew how much affection that carried.

Less than an hour later Cole rode out with a detachment of twenty mounted infantry, nearly half of C Company's current strength, and eleven Tonto Apache scouts that included Smiley and Gopher, a scout who acted as interpreter. To Cole's disgust, the officer in command was Peter Dunham.

26

He-Calls-Himself-Angry and his followers headed north through the forests. Halfway into the first day of travel Martha was exhausted by the pace. Two things kept her up with the others: watching Pinecone, and the black looks the Chiricahua gave her from time to time. She hung on, dismounting when they did to lead their horses up steep slopes and across the arroyos that the streams cut into the plateau. When they finally stopped, she dropped down to the ground, unable even to look around at first.

He-Calls-Himself-Angry had chosen to stop in a deep canyon with openings at both ends so that escape was possible in either direction. Camp was set up in a spot with boulders to shelter behind. The men took their horses a little farther up the arroyo where there was some grass. As soon as Martha could move, she took Skinny and hobbled him with the other horses.

She looked around for Pinecone. He was not in sight. Alarmed, she searched quickly for Crouched-and-Ready and found him by the fire that had been started. "Where is the boy?" she demanded.

"He is learning what he came to learn," he growled. "Up there. At the top of the canyon."

So Pinecone was a lookout. Young boys often were given that job because their eyesight was keener than most of the men's. Knowing that didn't protect her from fear for him. "He is there alone?"

"He is with the lookout to learn what to do."

"When will he be here?" she asked. "I want to talk to him."

"No. That is not good," Crouched-and-Ready said.

"It is my right. He is my son."

Crouched-and-Ready frowned, but his expression wasn't one of complete refusal. She guessed that he wasn't easy about her position and didn't know whether she had rights that must be acknowledged. "The boy is not a white woman's son now."

His words hurt, and some of the pain came from her fear that he was right. The only visible sign of her blood was that Pinecone's skin, though tan, was lighter than most Apaches'. All the glimpses she'd had of him that day—the way he rode, the way he imitated the man he called his uncle, his eagerness to do whatever the older boy did—were of a boy who was Apache. "I want to talk to him," she insisted.

After a long pause, Crouched-and-Ready finally said, "If I let you talk to him, you must give your word that you will not say that you are his mother."

She didn't like being forbidden to do what should be her right, but for Pinecone's sake it made sense. He had looked at her curiously, but he was too busy acting like the men to pay much attention to her. To try to convince him that a strange white woman had a claim to him might alarm him and turn him against her. Besides, if she didn't promise, he'd probably be left on lookout all night. "I give my word."

"Tomorrow, then, you may talk to him," Crouched-and-Ready said arrogantly.

She seethed, but recognized that he was establishing his authority, showing the others that she didn't intimidate him. It was safer for her not to push any of them too far.

When she lay down to sleep, each muscle cried its complaint. It was evidence of how distant she was from Apache life—from Pinecone's life. That difference haunted her until finally exhaustion overcame her fears and she slept.

The next day was even more grueling than the first. Only her determination not to show pain kept her from crying out at every step she took on foot or every jolt when she was on Skinny. A new fear plagued her, that she might lose the unborn child she carried. But when she had been with the Apaches, she'd seen pregnant women in all kinds of punishing circumstances.

It was late, and the fire in another arroyo had burned down to coals before her opportunity to speak to Pinecone finally came. He approached and sat down beside her place, which was apart from the men. "My uncle says you want to speak to me."

It was a boy's voice. She grieved for all the lost years since it had been a baby's voice. "Yes. Please sit down."

He looked at her curiously. "How do you know to speak like the Chihinne?"

"I lived with the White Mountain people many

years ago. I knew your father." He might think she meant Big-Dipper, but she wouldn't say more about that now.

"Why are you here?"

"I wanted to talk to your uncle. He and I decided I would come with you. I would also like to know about you."

He was eyeing her warily. "What do you want to know?"

"The things you can do. Are you good at hoop and pole?"

The mention of the game boys and men liked best appeared to relax his guard. "Yes. I am very good." Hesitantly, then more easily, he went on to tell her about camp life. As he described the games and his practice for tracking and hunting, she pictured the camps she had lived in and substituted him for boys she had seen then. He spoke proudly of his accomplishments, and she shared his pride. She felt grief as well, for all she couldn't know.

Pinecone also talked of the time before his band had lived on the reservation, things he wasn't old enough to remember. Proudly he described being on forced marches to escape enemy war parties. "I smeared clay on my face so I would look like the ground. I moved so silently," he bragged, "that no enemy could find me. When I walk on my toes, the best tracker will not know where my feet have gone."

Martha listened, thankful that after Americans arrived, the White Mountain Apache had been a generally peaceful group and one of the earliest to accept reservation life. But it discouraged her that his band's history had become so much his own that he claimed it as if he had lived then.

When his uncle called, Pinecone got up to leave. Martha put out her hand and touched his arm. He drew back, startled, but her fingers still held the sensation of warm, smooth skin. Quickly she said, "Will you tell me another time about your camp?"

"Maybe," was his unsatisfactory answer. He ran off without looking back.

She stared longingly after him. He seemed so completely and happily Apache. If he had a choice, he wouldn't choose to go with her.

Later when he and the older boy had gone on lookout, she approached Crouched-and-Ready. He was sitting with a man who looked about his age, but the man seemed solemn compared to the others, not joking about how many horses and cattle they would take from the ranchers. He had a square, quiet face and a stocky build. Earlier, Martha had heard his name, Stirs-up-Earth. Not a warlike name.

"I wish to talk to you," she said to Crouched-and-Ready.

Stirs-up-Earth started to leave, but Crouched-and-Ready motioned for him to stay. "You are my good friend," he said to the quieter man. "Stay and hear what the one who was the wife of Big-Dipper's brother says."

So they were friends. Maybe that was why Stirs-up-Earth had come, and perhaps he would be a steadying influence. Encouraged, she began. "I wish to speak of the future of . . . the boy." It was hard not to call Pinecone her son, but she needed the goodwill of these men. "Many white people come each year to Chihinne lands. They believe that they have a right to the land because the Chihinne do not use it in the way of the whites."

Crouched-and-Ready looked disdainful. "I am teaching my sister's son to be stronger than the white people. He will learn to hunt and raid, and to make war. He will take what he needs."

"It will not be that way!" She waited, giving her agitation time to lessen. "You remember what Nantan Lupan told the people."

At hearing the Apache name for General Crook, Crouched-and-Ready scowled, but she hurried on. "He said that the peaceful ones would be treated fairly and given a chance to live on the lands set aside for them. But the ones who leave the reservations and attack the whites will be hunted down and killed or put in jail."

The black eyes looking into hers flashed with anger. "He did not speak the truth. The white men do not treat the people fairly. At San Carlos they must live together with their enemies. The red strata clan women and babies die from hunger and sickness. No warrior can let that go on. We will drive out the whites. The boy is learning to be a warrior."

It was useless to challenge him in an argument about the treatment of the people on the San Carlos reservation. "There will never be enough warriors to drive out all the white people. The people must learn to live according to white ways. If the boy comes with me, he will have more chance to learn those ways. His life will be easier."

Crouched-and-Ready jumped to his feet, his hands clenched. Stirs-up-Earth rose quickly and put his hand on the other man's arm. Then he spoke to her in a voice as quiet as his manner. "Does it matter if his life is easier if it is a bad life?"

"It doesn't have to be bad," she cried. "The Chihinne way is a good way. I know that. The people use the land wisely and they share among all. They respect each other's rights and punish only when they must keep their honor. But the Chihinne are few and white people are many. The white way will prevail." Her emotions broke through. "If my son is with me," she finished passionately, "at least he will be alive!"

Stirs-up-Earth said, "A man is not alive if he gives up the ways of the people. The ways of his father."

She wouldn't accept that. It was in her mouth to say that she'd given up the ways of her father when she was a captive. But she didn't, because she hadn't given up being white. For a time her ways had been taken from her, and she couldn't forget the bitterness of captivity. With Sharp-Knife she had achieved a kind of happiness and pleasure, but never real contentment. Would Pinecone feel that same way if he went with her? Was he so Apache that he was lost to her? The idea appalled her. He was young; he could change. She wanted to think that he didn't have to remain Apache. But she wasn't sure any longer.

"We'll speak about this again," she said, and retreated to her separate niche. She pulled her blanket around her and lay down. It was a long time before she fell into a restless kind of sleep.

Cole began to have doubts about Peter Dunham's leadership by the end of the first day's march out of Fort Apache. When the bugle call sounded to halt for the night, the detachment had covered less than the twenty-five miles specified by army regulations as the maximum for men on foot. Cole, who had been fretting at the rear all day, galloped forward and swung off his horse next to Peter, who had already dismounted. When Peter turned and looked at him expectantly, Cole gave the salute that was seldom required on campaign. "Why are we stopping?" he asked heatedly.

Two enlisted men, one of them Peter's orderly, were already erecting the large double tent used in the field when two officers were on a routine march. Peter said, "The water and grass are good here, and the men are tired. We'll get a fresh start in the morning."

"But the scouts are way ahead of us now. And there's daylight for another two hours." When Peter didn't respond, he snapped, "Dammit, Peter, my wife's out there."

"That's exactly why we're stopping, Mr. Baldwin," Peter said with a relish that suggested he'd been waiting for Cole to object. "You need time to calm down. I can't take the chance your feelings will get the best of you. It could get the whole detachment in trouble. The scouts will let us know when they spot anything."

There was some truth in what Peter said, but his patronizing tone infuriated Cole. "I don't think I can make trouble back with the rear guard," he ground out, and added a belated, "sir."

Peter turned to watch the progress of the tent, and Cole stalked off to where the horses were being picketed. Sergeant Briggs met him and asked, "Did Lieutenant Dunham give orders about how many guards to put out for tonight and where to put them?"

"No, sergeant. You'd better ask him." It was an order that should have already been passed on. But Cole was sure Peter wouldn't want to hear about it from him. Let Sergeant Briggs do the reminding. It was a hell of a situation when the commanding officer was more interested in showing his authority over his second-in-command than getting the job done. He'd act on his own if he had to.

After checking that his horse was being groomed and fed, Cole went back to the double tent to eat food that tasted to him like pieces of harness. He let Peter ramble on about the pleasures of New York City women with only an occasional "That so?" As soon as the meal was over, he said, "I'm going to see about Pease. The sergeant thinks he's sick."

"You take the men's complaints too seriously, Stephen. Lets them think they can get away with faking."

Cole just shrugged and left. After finding out that a groaning Pease had eaten a full meal, he left him to the unsympathetic attention of the sergeant and found a log where he could sit by himself. Where was Martha? Was she safe? After his father's death, Cole hadn't been able to put much stock in traditional religion. If there was a God who cared about humans, he hoped that God was looking out for Martha. If she was safe, he might even believe in something more than himself again.

The next day went much like the first, with the measured pace making Cole feel like a smoldering fire about to burst into flames. Four hours into the third day's march, one of the scouts reported finding a fresh trail, and the whole column speeded up. When word came back to Cole, he gritted his teeth and remained with his rear guard, cursing his position but knowing he couldn't abandon it. At least Peter was responding, though he wasn't pushing fast enough to suit Cole, who let his own men bunch up so that they were closer to the main body.

They had the rest of the column in sight following

one of the canyons that cut down from the Mogollon Rim, the edge of the high northern plateau, when one of the men came racing back. "Two hostiles sighted at the far end of the canyon," he reported. "Lieutenant says come up."

Cole put his horse into a gallop up the canyon, his men following just behind. He was almost up to the main body of horses and mules when, from along the right-hand rim of the canyon, sudden puffs of smoke were followed by the sound of rifle fire. Ahead a horse staggered, and then another as more shots came from above.

Without waiting for commands, the men in the bottom of the canyon scrambled from their mounts and scattered up the left canyon wall. Cole spurred forward to just out of rifle range. In one motion he grabbed his carbine and slid from his horse. A quick look behind him assured him that his men had followed suit. He ran until he was close enough to fire and took cover at the base of a boulder. He steadied his carbine along the edge, and waited for the next puff of smoke.

It came, but not from across the canyon. The shot rang out from the left rim, and a soldier sheltered behind a rock screamed and threw up his hands, staggered from the rock, and fell. His body rolled down and lodged against another rock. Cole swung his carbine around and got off a round at the next puff, but he couldn't tell whether he'd made a hit. More shots picked off another man caught in the crossfire.

A soldier let out a string of curses. "Red bastards must have Sharps or Henrys. Better rifles than ours."

Sergeant Briggs said roughly, "Shut up."

Cole didn't hear Peter's voice. Cautiously he rose up and spotted Peter down about fifty feet ahead, in the widest part of the canyon bottom. He must have been caught in the first fire, his horse shot from under him. With one arm he was struggling to get to his downed horse. One leg dragged uselessly. Bullets spit up dust around him. He jerked suddenly and rolled, grabbing his side with his uninjured hand.

Cole sprang to his feet. He shoved his carbine at the man closest to him. Then he half ran, half slid down the slope and along the canyon bottom. He could hear bullets spattering around him, but he didn't feel the hit his muscles expected. His sprint took him to the now motionless Peter. He leaned down and grabbed Peter under the arms. As he did, Peter screamed.

"Good," Cole panted. "You're alive. Now help me. Hang on."

Peter moaned, but he pushed up feebly with his uninjured leg. Cole got a better grip and staggered back toward his men. He could see flashes from the rocks there. His men were giving him what cover they could. In front of him a rock exploded, and he felt a fragment slice into his hand. When he was close to the boulder, Sergeant Briggs jumped out and helped him carry Peter farther back. "See what you can do for him," Cole gasped and grabbed his carbine.

At the far end of the canyon he saw dust. If it came from the movement of more hostiles, there were more of them than anyone thought. The dust divided into two lines, angling up the slopes. The scouts who had been ahead of the column had returned and were firing their rifles. By the time they were halfway up the canyon wall, the guns along the rim were silent. Cole guessed that the hostiles had fled. But by the time his men could follow, they would be on their horses and gone.

HEARTBREAK TRAIL 395

When the scouts came back to report that he was right, the toll of the ambush was counted. One man killed and four wounded. One had a superficial shoulder wound. Another had lost two fingers, and the eye of a third had been hit by a rock fragment, like one that caused the blood dripping down Cole's hand. Peter was the most seriously hurt. He'd lost a lot of blood from the bullet that had penetrated his side, and the bones in one arm and one leg were broken. By the time the fighting ended, he was unconscious.

Cole took stock with Sergeant Briggs and Gopher, the scout who was acting as interpreter. "How many hostiles?"

"Tracks of six," Gopher reported.

"Six men in the right position can do a hell of a lot of damage."

"That is not all of them," Gopher said. "The others must be ahead."

Was Martha with them? Cole wondered, and put aside the anguished question for then.

"Who's the best corporal to send back with the wounded men?" he asked Briggs.

"I'd say Jefferson, sir."

"Then have the men fix a litter between two mules for Lieutenant Dunham. The others ought to be able to ride. Send Corporal Jefferson and six men back to the post with the wounded. The rest of us will move on as soon as all equipment is checked. Put out four flankers. If the scouts can pick up a trail, we'll keep on it tonight."

"Yessir."

"And make sure horses are watered and canteens filled. We don't know where we're going."

"Yessir." The sergeant sounded approving.

Gopher gave Cole a determined look. "We will get a trail. This time we will find all of them."

"Good. But don't let them know you're there. And no firing on them until I get there." Cole had heard of scouts being so eager that they started shooting before the soldiers could catch up with them.

"Yes," Gopher said, but not as if he considered himself bound by it.

"You start shooting," Cole said softly, "and you won't have to worry about who's going to keep the fire going in your wickiup when you're old."

Gopher studied Cole. "We'll wait," he said, and this time he meant it.

As on the previous two days, keeping up the pace took all Martha's energy. Toward the end of the day, Crouched-and-Ready dismounted and started leading his horse up a mountainside. She slid awkwardly from Skinny and looked up at the rock-strewn slope he intended to climb. Just ahead of him she saw Pinecone clambering over and around the boulders as if he could go anywhere Whipple could. Grimly she grasped Skinny's leading rein and followed. She lagged farther and farther behind until Stirs-up-Earth was the only one still in back of her. Several times when she thought she couldn't possibly scale a rock, he went up before her and pulled her up. Then he let her get ahead again.

She had stopped, panting, when He-Calls-Himself-Angry and five other warriors came up from below her. They passed her without a glance, and she realized she hadn't seen them for several hours.

When she finally struggled to the top, she found they had made a camp on the mountaintop in an area that looked as if it had been sliced away. Even the August wind felt cold, and she shivered from the chill and fatigue. She lay down, putting her hands protectively over her stomach. In spite of memories of pregnant Apache women performing strenuous activities, the extent of her exhaustion frightened her. When there was no pain or sign of anything wrong, her fears that she was harming this new child eased. As soon as she rested a little longer, she intended to talk to her son again and to Crouched-and-Ready.

While she recovered, she watched hungrily where Pinecone sat. He and the older boy were gambling with pebbles, unnoticed by the men, who were talking excitedly. At first, engrossed in the laughter that made Pinecone's face look childish and dear, she didn't pay attention to the men. Then a phrase caught her ear.

" . . . hit the one down in the canyon. Three times." The bragging voice belonged to He-Calls-Himself-Angry. "They fell right into the trap when we let them see two of us. It was a good place for an ambush."

Ambush? Her tired mind leaped on the word. She strained to hear what they were saying.

"I killed the first horse," put in a very young man called Flies-in-His-Soup. "My uncle taught me. Kill the horses first."

"Horses are easy to hit. I would have done more than that if I had been there," Crouched-and-Ready grumbled.

The Chiricahua snorted. "You wanted to bring the white woman. Don't complain if you have to go with her."

What were they talking about? Who'd been shot? She had to know. Getting up cautiously, she moved nearer the group of men.

Flies-in-His-Soup laughed. "The scouts went far ahead. They couldn't find our trail."

Martha's heart began to race. When she had gone to Diablo's camp, all she'd thought of was finding Pinecone, not of other possible consequences. Scouts—that meant soldiers, probably from Fort Apache. He-Calls-Himself-Angry had said something about shooting a man three times. If the soldiers followed because of her, she might be the reason one of them was hurt or dead.

No—that was too terrible a responsibility to take on herself. Patrols went out from the fort whenever any special movement of the Apaches was reported. Even so, a cold guilt settled in her stomach—because selfishly, she also felt relief. Cole couldn't be the man who was shot. He was on his way to Tucson.

After more bragging about how successful the ambush had been, the question of moving on came up. He-Calls-Himself-Angry was for going north as soon as it was light. "I know where we can get good horses," he said.

"The soldiers will expect that," Stirs-up-Earth pointed out in his reasonable voice. "They will not look for us this near. And they will not track us over the rocks. I covered the marks of the white woman."

There was more discussion and general agreement on staying. He-Calls-Himself-Angry growled, "Only one more day here," then stamped off by himself. The others began gambling, apparently feeling secure. Martha thought they were probably right. The difficulty of the ascent and its closeness to the trail probably protected them. She prayed so.

When the gambling broke up, she approached Crouched-and-Ready. Immediately he ordered

Pinecone to join the man on lookout and then said to her, "The boy does not want to talk to you again. It would be better if you went away and left him alone."

It was true that Pinecone had not come near her except for their one talk the previous night. Stubbornly she insisted, "He is my son. I have waited many years and come many miles to find him. I will not give up."

"He is Chihinne. That is his way." Crouched-and-Ready rose and walked off.

She looked after him, then slowly went back to her belongings. It was cold; she must have some shelter. Wearily she moved her blanket and knapsack next to a rock that would cut the wind. She sat against the rock, waiting. Finally she saw Pinecone return. She watched him, memorizing his movements, trying to ignore the conviction that was becoming greater all the time—that Pinecone was lost to her. Finally satisfied that he was back in the safe area, she lay down and closed her eyes.

At a soft footfall, she sat up eagerly. But it was Stirs-up-Earth. He crouched down, resting on his haunches, and said, "The boy is clever. He will get along well."

"Tell me," she said, "is he good at tracking? He says he is."

Stirs-up-Earth smiled. "He should be more modest. Yes, he is skillful. He learns quickly. Someday he may be the best hunter in his band."

That was solace to Martha, but only a little.

Stirs-Up-Earth stood and looked down at her. He said, in a voice that sounded sympathetic, "Many children are lost. Their mothers weep for them, but that does not bring them back. My mother's sister lost a girl child to the white man's disease. She did not want to believe that her child was gone. She spent many years asking everyone where the girl had gone. Her other children cried for her but she did not hear them because she was always asking." He walked away then.

Martha pulled her blanket around her and lay down again close to the rock. She looked up at the stars and knew she must answer the terrible question Stirs-up-Earth had raised. Was she blinded by her longing for Pinecone?

For painful hours she followed the constellations moving around the sky as she wrestled with answers. For as long as she could, she repeated the reasons to herself why she must take Pinecone away. The future of the Apaches was very uncertain. He was her son, not She-Sticks-to-Her-Cradle's. But in the end she couldn't ward off the devastating conclusion: Pinecone was Chi-hinne in all his actions and feelings. Maybe Stirs-up-Earth was right. Maybe she had already lost him.

That decision wasn't for now. Her immediate task was to survive this march and see that Pinecone was safe with his band. Then she would—do what? She couldn't return to Fort Apache.

When she had been with Sharp-Knife, a woman had returned who had been captured by Mexicans and escaped from them. The woman had walked, alone, all the way back to the White Mountain area. If an Apache woman could do that, Martha resolved, she could go as far as Tucson, with or without Pinecone. In Tucson she would look for Cole. If he wasn't there, she would ask Ira Gurnett where Cole was.

Another search? Yes, to find the man she loved. More peaceful in her mind than at any time since she had left Fort Apache with Dulcita, Martha was able to go to sleep.

A man's voice roused her, calling loudly in Apache.

HEARTBREAK TRAIL

Instantly she was awake and grasping her derringer. "The soldiers are here," the voice said.

It had been more than six years since she had heard that voice, but she recognized it. Big-Dipper, Sharp-Knife's brother. He called again. "The soldiers are all around you. Put down your rifles and they will not harm you."

Terror sent her scrambling to her feet. Dawn was just turning everything from dark to light gray. She saw Pinecone, not far away, beside Crouched-and-Ready. Fear for herself made her draw back to the shelter of her rock. He-Calls-Himself-Angry had threatened to kill her if she screamed. He might do that now. She grabbed her derringer and cocked the hammer.

Another voice called, this time in English. "Elizabeth. Stay down."

It was Cole!

Across from her at the farthest edge of the circle she saw a forage cap she recognized. Cole had raised up enough that it showed. At almost the same moment He-Calls-Himself-Angry swung around and aimed his rifle at the cap.

She screamed.

27

He-Calls-Himself-Angry whirled toward Martha and fired. A loud report rang in her ears, and rock chips sprayed out from the boulder behind her. With shaking hands she pointed her derringer toward the Chiricahua and pulled the trigger. He didn't react; she had missed.

He dropped his gun and sprinted the few feet across to Crouched-and-Ready and grabbed for his rifle. Crouched-and-Ready held on. Martha heard Pinecone cry out and saw him start for the two struggling men. Instantly she ran after him, stumbling once, but not until she was close enough to grab him. Gripping him with her arm, she cocked the hammer of her derringer again.

He-Calls-Himself-Angry swung his fist against Crouched-and-Ready's head. As the younger man staggered back, He-Calls-Himself-Angry wrestled the rifle away. He cocked the gun and aimed for Martha and Pinecone.

Cole scrambled up over the rim. He-Calls-Himself-Angry swung around. Martha let go of Pinecone and fired her second shot. He-Calls-Himself-Angry's arm jerked once.

A single Apache leapt over the ring of boulders and down into the camp area. The Chiricahua spun farther around toward the new intruder. Before he could shoot, Crouched-and-Ready charged from behind. He-Calls-Himself-Angry staggered and recovered. He swung his rifle butt at the other man's head. Cole fired. In almost the same moment Stirs-up-Earth fired a single shot into He-Calls-Himself-Angry's back. He-Calls-Himself-Angry jerked and fell. Blood gushed out of his back and chest. He groaned once, and then was still. Martha, holding Pinecone, stared at the Chiricahua with mixed horror and relief.

Just visible around the top, soldiers and scouts appeared. Martha recognized the Apache who had come over the rocks. It was Big-Dipper. He called out, "Put away your guns. We will have no more killing. We will settle this by talk."

Cole motioned the scouts and soldiers back out of sight. Pinecone pulled away from Martha and ran across to Crouched-and-Ready. The rest of the Apaches, who had scattered around the area, came cautiously back to the center. They held their rifles in position to fire. Cole was the only blue-uniformed man left, and Martha waited with a fearful pounding in her chest. He looked across at her. She wanted to run to him, but she was afraid to move.

One of the Apaches pointed to Cole. "If the soldiers and the scouts stay away, we will talk with this white man."

"He does not speak our words," Big-Dipper said. "He will need Gopher."

The Apaches consulted briefly and agreed. A scout Martha concluded must be Gopher came down into the camp area. Cole said something to Gopher, who translated, "The white woman is to come here." Cole motioned to Martha.

Feeling like a doll painted to look real but actually made of sawdust, she walked toward Cole. His eyes held onto her, and when she reached his side, he gripped her hand once. Big-Dipper gestured that they should sit down. The Apaches sat uneasily, and Martha was shaking as she sat cross-legged on the ground.

"Are you all right?" Cole asked.

"Yes."

"Your son?"

"He's over there."

Cole glanced at Pinecone, then turned to Gopher. "Let them know that the scouts and soldiers are all around them. They won't come closer as long as we're talking. I'd like to hear first why they left the reservation."

After Gopher translated, the Apaches retreated and huddled together. Their words weren't audible, but their gestures looked agitated. Finally Stirs-up-Earth stepped forward and spoke to Gopher, who reported, "They say they came because of agents who cheat the Apaches. The new agent at San Carlos doesn't take care of people there."

Cole looked at Martha with a question in his eyes. She guessed he wanted to know if he was getting an accurate translation. She gave a faint nod.

He said to Gopher, "Tell them we don't control the agent there. But we'll work on it—try to see that conditions change. At Fort Apache they aren't cheated. That is their reservation, and they must return."

"What will happen to us if we go back?" Stirs-up-Earth asked.

Gopher relayed the question to Cole. "I can't promise what Colonel Stratton will decide. One soldier has died. But the man who was chiefly responsible is also dead. If they return and intend to live peacefully, I believe they'll be allowed to stay with their bands. They'll have to give up their weapons."

There was silence after the translation. Then Flies-in-His-Soup said, "I will go back. I will be a scout for the army."

Several others nodded, and they all looked at Cole. When Gopher reported this, Martha asked, "Is that possible?"

"Maybe. General Crook often recruited his most fierce opponents, the ones that were still alive. He said it gave the wild young ones a chance to be useful." Cole turned to Gopher. "Tell them I'll make the request."

Stirs-up-Earth announced the young men's agreement. "We will follow the soldiers," he said and pointed to Big-Dipper. "He will go with us. It will be his word that we are coming."

Cole shook his head to this report. "They can travel together, and if Big-Dipper wants to join them, that's up to him. But they go along with the soldiers." After more consultation, the young men agreed and started gathering their equipment. Cole called to Sergeant Briggs, who appeared, followed by the rest of the detail. The sergeant stationed them at intervals around the periphery. Big-Dipper took the Apaches' weapons and gave them to Cole. He handed them on to the soldiers, who surrounded the Apaches and started down toward the canyon bottom.

Big-Dipper approached Martha where she was waiting off to one side. He looked at her gravely. "Sister-in-law, I am told you came to see my nephew."

His use of the kinship terms encouraged her, and she spoke candidly. "Six years ago you took him away from me. That was not right. I came to take him back."

Big-Dipper looked troubled but determined. "I understand your anger. But you are white. Your brother was offering for you. He would have taken my nephew away from his people."

Martha started to protest that her brother didn't want a half-breed child. But that argument would only confirm Big-Dipper's ideas of the evil ways of white men. "He belonged with me."

"My brother was dead," Big-Dipper reminded her. "If your brother had not come for you, would you have stayed and lived as Chihinne?"

She couldn't answer. It was painfully impossible to know. "But he is not safe with you. The white people are taking the Chihinne land." She could see her argument wasn't making headway with Big-Dipper.

"He will live to manhood with us. We have learned to get along with the white people. We follow their rules."

"He wasn't safe on this trip. An eight-year-old shouldn't have been here."

"Yes," Big-Dipper acknowledged. "That is why I followed. My wife's brother will not make a mistake like that again."

Pinecone came over and stood close beside his uncle. He looked solemnly at Martha, and in his eyes she saw admiration that gave solace to her wounded spirit. "Are all white women brave like you?" he asked.

Her throat filled up with tears. She feared if she answered, they would spill out and disgrace her.

Big-Dipper answered for her. "No. But this white woman, who has lived with our people, is very brave."

Pinecone's face crinkled into a smile, exuberant and warm—a smile to treasure and cheer her through the time without him she knew was ahead.

She managed to say, "I think you are a very brave boy." His face sobered, as if he were trying to show how little her compliment meant, but the smile remained in his eyes.

Big-Dipper said, "We must go." Pinecone turned with him, and the man put his hand lovingly on the boy's head. Pinecone glanced back once, but didn't look again. Martha saw sadly that though he'd been curious about her, he was eager to return to his Apache family.

By the time the strange group of soldiers, scouts, and would-be scouts camped for the night, they were halfway back to Fort Apache. Two soldiers put up half of the double tent at a good distance apart from the rest of the camp. Once supper was over and they washed away some of the dust of the march, Cole and Martha had their first chance to be alone and talk freely.

To Cole, Martha appeared so exhausted that he worried she was ill. He insisted that, before they talk, she lie down on the cot. He sat on a chair beside her. "Are you sure you're all right?"

"You've asked me that four times today. Yes, I'm fine. Just tired. You haven't told me much about the patrol. He-Calls-Himself-Angry bragged that he'd shot a soldier down in a canyon bottom. Was anyone badly hurt or . . . killed?"

"One man died."

"Who was it?"

"A new man in the company. No one you know." It was no use to burden her with a name. "Three others were hit. And Peter Dunham was pretty badly shot up."

"Peter? He was along?"

"He was in command. He was caught in crossfire. After he was wounded, I sent him back to the fort. When we get there, we'll find out whether he survived."

"Sometimes I wished he would disappear. That's about the same thing as wishing he'd die. But I didn't want to be responsible for anyone's death."

"You didn't plan what happened. You're not responsible. Peter wasn't as careful with his command as he should have been." He might as well tell her the rest. Someone would. "After Peter was shot, I pulled him to safety."

She looked distressed. "In crossfire? You could have been killed too."

"Yes, it's strange. At times I felt like killing him. But I couldn't let him stay where he was and have the Apaches do it for me." Brusquely, because he'd been so worried, he said, "That wasn't the bad part. I didn't know whether you were safe."

"The march wasn't any worse than ones Apache women make. I guess women on wagon trains endure a lot too." She finally added what he wanted to know but had felt awkward about asking. "I haven't lost the baby."

He took her hand and lifted it to his lips. He turned her hand over and kissed the palm, then kept it in his own hands. "I know why you went to Diablo's camp. Why did you go with the men?"

"I didn't intend to." When she finished her explanation, he shuddered to think of the danger.

"Why are you here?" she asked. "Why didn't you go to Tucson?"

His explanations took longer than hers, because he had to describe first what had happened at the fort and also what he had told Colonel Stratton. "It was a wild story," he concluded. "I didn't like saying you were not quite sane, but it was all I could think of."

"Maybe I have been a little mad," she said unhappily.

"No, you're not mad. Well, maybe some of the things you do are. My story fit enough of the facts that the colonel believed me. And he let me come on the patrol to look for you."

"What do you mean that he let you? Didn't he order you to come?"

"No. He was going to send me on to Tucson. But I argued him into letting me on the patrol."

"But—the witness in Tucson. Didn't Mr. Gurnett say the man was likely to leave? And your stepfather. That's the most important thing for you to do."

He looked at her fingers, covered with abrasions she must have gotten on the rocks, and stroked them tenderly. "Finding you," he said softly, "was more important." He shifted to the side of the cot where he could look down at her better. "You know, don't you, that I love you?"

"Oh, Cole." With her free hand she reached up and touched his face. "I hoped you did. I wanted to think you did, because I love you. But the things we want—need—are different. It seems hopeless for us to be in love."

"How is it hopeless? I was sure this masquerade would be a disaster when you suggested it. So far we're still here. If we can do that, we can do anything."

He leaned over and kissed her to stop her objections. It aroused desire in him, but desire that was muted by her exhausted face.

"Tell me about Pinecone," he said. "I watched him when I could today."

"If you had to guess, would you know he was only half Apache? Would you guess he was my son?" An intensity in Martha's voice warned him that this was an important question. He owed her an honest answer.

"No, I wouldn't. He looks like the boys I see around the Apache camps. Maybe he'll look more like you when he's older." He added the part that was still uncomfortable to him. "Does he look like his father?"

She sighed, a lonesome sound, and he pulled her up into his arms, shifting so that she rested across his lap, her head against his heart. "Tell me what you're thinking," he said tenderly.

"Yes, he's like Sharp-Knife. When he's grown, he'll look a lot like his father." She stopped, then went on slowly, "He thinks and feels like his father, and like Big-Dipper. Pinecone is so Apache that . . . he'll never want to be anything else."

She turned suddenly, burying her face against him. Sobs shuddered through her, sounding as if each one were being torn out of her. He held her, wanting fiercely to protect her from pain, knowing he couldn't. Instead he smoothed her hair, and when her weeping finally quieted, he kissed the last of the salty tears.

When she spoke, her words trembled. "He belongs with his Apache family. Even if I could steal him away, he'd hate living with me. I can't take him away from the life he loves."

"But what about everything you've done—the risks to find him!"

She sat up slowly. "The search wasn't for nothing. I know where he is. I'll stay in Arizona. That way, I can keep track of his band. Steal him if I have to. Apaches captured me. I could do the same, to make sure he lives."

The fierce expression on her face softened and became uncertain. She leaned against him again and touched his hand almost shyly. "Pinecone isn't the only one who matters to me any more. I want to be where you are."

He strained her close and found her lips in a kiss that made remembering how tired she was more difficult.

When the kiss ended, she sighed. "We'll have a child to think about too. Can you live in Arizona, or will you have to go away?"

"I don't know. I've thought about that when I wasn't worrying about what was happening to you. I wouldn't give up you and my child so I could get revenge for my father's murder. A live child counts for more than a dead father."

"But clearing yourself—that's worth more."

"Sounds like we're arguing each other's case," he teased her.

She didn't smile. "There's the army to worry about. I've put us in a mess."

"Yes, but I wouldn't change it now. We may have to

disappear again. Probably for as long as the same regiments are stationed in Arizona."

This time she did smile. "You mean we'll have to be a third set of people? Another masquerade?"

"Whatever it is," he promised, "we'll do it together."

A kiss to seal the promise wasn't enough. "I want to make love," she said softly.

"Are you sure?" he asked, but she reached up to him and it didn't matter that they were tired.

They lay together, but he was still aware of all she had gone through. Their lovemaking began quietly. Then tenderly, lovingly they exchanged caresses that were familiar and yet new with understanding and love. With each touch and kiss passion grew. When they reached the tumultuous climax, it was like the midnight sky, exploding with stars it would take more than their lifetimes to count.

At dawn, while the men were getting ready to leave, Martha told Cole, "I must speak to Big-Dipper. Could you ask Gopher to send him here?"

"Why? I don't want the soldiers to hear you speaking Apache."

"Say that I want to thank Big-Dipper. I wouldn't need words for that. The Apache won't let on that I speak their language. They don't volunteer information to whites. And all the soldiers look too busy to pay attention to me."

When Big-Dipper arrived, Martha made sure no one saw or heard them. "I will not try to take Pinecone with me," she told Big-Dipper. "I see that he wishes to stay with you. But I intend to see him again. I'll find some way to visit the band. Will you promise that when he is older, you will tell him that I am his mother?"

Big-Dipper considered and finally nodded. "Yes, I promise. I will tell him you did this from love for him. And that he must respect and honor you."

"Thank you." Martha knew he would keep his word. It had become a matter of honor with him. As he walked away, Martha thought sadly that knowing Pinecone would eventually learn the truth wasn't much, but it was something.

It was almost dark on the second day when they arrived at Fort Apache. The march had been long, but everyone was eager to get back. Just above the junction of the two forks of the White River, Gopher came to Cole where he rode with Sergeant Briggs and Martha.

"The Apaches who left the camps do not want to go into the fort," the scout reported.

Cole thought it over. "Sergeant Briggs, do you have all their weapons?"

"Yes, sir."

"Leave a detail of men with them here until I can check with Lieutenant Morgan. If he's willing for them to stay with his scouts, they won't have to come into the post. Gopher, tell them I'm trying to work that out. But what happens after that depends on Colonel Stratton."

When they rode on into the fort, the sentry greeted Cole with special respect. As they went on, Martha heard the sentry say admiringly to Sergeant Briggs, "We heard what the lieutenant did."

"Yes," Sergeant Briggs said. "He had a fool's luck."

The sergeant sounded casual, but Martha glanced back and could see from his beaming face that he was taking pride in his lieutenant.

As they approached their quarters, Cole said, "I must see Colonel Stratton and Robert Morgan. Will you be all right here?"

"Yes. Just please see that Skinny gets plenty of attention."

"I'll see to that, ma'am," Sergeant Briggs volunteered.

When they reached the house and dismounted, from the back came a familiar barking that turned to frantic howls. "I forgot to tell you," Cole said, "that Whipple followed you to Diablo's camp. Someone must have brought him back."

Tired as she was, she couldn't go inside without greeting the wriggling mass of yellow dog. She imagined that his golden eyes looked reproachful, but his eager tongue welcomed her. She was equally delighted to see him. Cole left her there, hugging Whipple.

When she finally went into the house, it seemed unfamiliar, as if she had been away a month instead of less than a week. In a few minutes Lane arrived, out of breath. "The lieutenant says you're all right. I'm surely glad to know it."

"That's very kind of you, Private Lane." She returned his smile gratefully. It wouldn't have been surprising if he hadn't come at all. Striker to a mad woman—that couldn't be comfortable for him. Maybe Colonel Stratton was the only one who knew Cole's explanation of her disappearance, but from the way gossip circulated, she wasn't counting on that.

"Is there anything I can do for you, ma'am?"

"No, thank you. I just need to rest. There is something I'd like to know. The soldier who died—is there to be a burial service for him?"

"There was a service already, yesterday."

Martha felt sad, but relieved.

After Lane left, she lay down, expecting worry to keep her awake. But knowing that she and Cole would be together gave her the serenity to fall asleep.

Cole found Colonel Stratton in his office. The colonel waved aside the salutes and came around to shake Cole's hand. "Sit down," he said, and Cole took the chair gratefully.

When the colonel was again settled behind his desk, he asked, "Your wife? Is she all right?"

"Yes, she is, sir. Thank you for your concern. I need a decision from you about the Apaches who came back with us." He described the agreement with them and their desire to be scouts. "I told them, of course, that it depended on you."

Colonel Stratton pursed his lips. "Been reading about Crook's methods? Not a bad idea, letting them join the scouts, but there's our man who's dead and the punishment for that."

"Sir, if I may suggest—there's a balance of sorts here. The Chiricahua from San Carlos who stirred things up is dead. According to the Apache way of looking at things, that's a man for a man. And, I have to add, sir, that the Chiricahua did have legitimate grievances. That doesn't count for the soldier's life. But the men who want to be scouts would call this fair. It seems to me there's something on their side. I believe they'll make good scouts."

"Um, yes. You may be right." The colonel frowned.

"I'll leave them with the scouts for a day or so, with a detail to guard them, while I decide. I'll probably let them stay, but it won't hurt for them to wonder whether we're going to punish them. Tell the adjutant to send a detail to replace your men."

"Thank you, sir."

The colonel tapped his finger on a paper on his desk and said angrily, "You're right about San Carlos. There's trouble again. The new agent seems to be listening to the suppliers instead of to us. A bad situation. Lieutenant Young tells me you helped him dig up some information that might stop some of the cheating. It ought to put a few of the contractors in jail, but it probably won't."

Colonel Stratton rose and said formally, "I congratulate you, Mr. Baldwin, on your heroic action in saving Lieutenant Dunham's life."

Cole rose also. "Then Lieutenant Dunham will be all right, sir?"

"That's the word from Dr. Lawton. I'm sure Lieutenant Dunham will want to thank you as soon as you can get by the hospital to see him."

Maybe, Cole thought. "I'll stop and see him as soon as I make my report to the adjutant. With your permission, sir, I'll do that now."

They exchanged salutes, and Cole had started for the door when the colonel said, "Your wife, Mr. Baldwin, is she . . . well, I mean, did you work things out?"

"I believe so, sir. I hope so."

"A difficult situation," was the colonel's last comment as he sat down again, signaling that Cole could leave.

After Cole finished at the adjutant's office, he debated going back to his quarters. Reluctantly he started for the hospital instead. The corpsman on duty stopped him. "Sorry, sir. Lieutenant Dunham's been feverish today and he's asleep now. Maybe tomorrow morning would be better."

Relieved, Cole said, "I'll come back then."

As he turned to leave, he saw Dr. Lawton coming out of his office. The doctor paused, then continued on to greet Cole. "I didn't know you were back," he said.

"An hour or so ago. I was just here to see Peter, but he's asleep."

They went out onto the veranda. The sky was almost dark. Crickets chirped noisily, blending with the softer sound of the river. Dr. Lawton stopped, and Cole did the same. "My favorite time," the doctor said. "Not quite night but not day either. It's a good time to pretend things are the way I want them to be instead of the way they are." He laughed then, a mocking sound. "Also time for the first whiskey." In a more normal tone he asked, "How is your wife?"

"All right, I think."

"You'll be coming back to see Peter tomorrow?"

Cole's stomach did a sudden flip. "Yes, in the morning."

"Stop in to see me when you do. I have something to discuss with you." As the doctor walked off into the darkness, he looked as weary as Cole felt.

28

At Cole's knock on the doorjamb, Dr. Lawton looked up from his desk. In the morning light his eyes were bloodshot and his skin pale.

"Morning, Stephen. You already been to see Peter?" the doctor asked.

"Not yet. I came to see you first." The doctor's use of first names made the military formalities seem unnecessary.

The doctor started to get up, then slouched back into his chair. "Close the door, if you would, please. And have a seat."

After the door was closed and Cole sat down, the doctor shuffled papers around before finally choosing one. Cole had the strong impression that Lawton was as reluctant as he was for the interview to begin, and his hopes rose a little.

After some hard thinking, he hadn't told Martha about the doctor's summons. The claim that he'd originally forced her to go with him as a cover would protect her. That and the belief held by a lot of men that a woman was so weak that once trapped by a man, she would give in and say nothing. Not a very credible defense, but one that would get her off, especially since she was pregnant. The alternative—that he and she try to leave during the night—seemed to him now unrealistic. So he'd decided to take his chances with George Lawton.

Lawton pulled out his glasses and studied the paper in his hand. He took off the glasses, frowning at them as if they could answer a puzzle. Finally he looked over at Cole and said, "Who are you?"

Cole's midsection churned and then subsided. "Second Lieutenant Stephen Baldwin, C Company, Twenty-Fifth Infantry Regiment, United States Army."

A flicker of amusement lit the doctor's eyes and then was gone. "We both know that's not true. If it were, that would mean you'd grown an inch and a half between January when you got your commission in St. Louis and May when you arrived here. That's according to your enlistment record. Not the medical records you suggest a clerk copied incorrectly."

Cole couldn't think of a way to explain.

"Dammit," the doctor said, "I want an answer! If you'd skipped out with the company funds, it would make sense. But for the second time you're the post's favorite hero. At least among the people who think Peter's neck is worth saving. I want to know who you are and why you're here."

Now the doctor was beginning to make more sense. He wasn't outraged. He was curious. Cole's hopes grew stronger. "I was at the same stage station as Stephen Baldwin when it was attacked last March. He was killed and I wasn't. I took his identity."

"Why?"

"He was going to join his regiment at Fort Yuma. I was on my way to the territorial prison. As a convicted murderer. I decided it would be safer to be Stephen Baldwin."

"So what is your real name?"

"Cole Wingate."

"Wingate." The doctor looked thoughtful. "I think I recall. Something in Tucson. The murder of a man you were traveling with. Are you guilty?"

"No."

The doctor leaned back in his chair and folded his arms behind his head. It was the stance of a relaxed man, not one who was planning to order someone off to jail immediately. This interview was nothing like what Cole expected. "Dr. Lawton, I'd like to ask you a question."

"Go ahead. As long as you answer all of mine."

"You know that I've been impersonating an officer in the United States Army. I just admitted that I was convicted of murder, and you ask whether I did it. Why?"

"I suppose anyone can commit murder under extreme circumstances," the doctor said thoughtfully. "But you're not a man who's likely to do that. You keep your control too well. What about Elizabeth? How does she fit in?"

"Elizabeth Baldwin was killed along with her husband. My . . . this Elizabeth is really Martha Turner, the only other person besides me who survived."

"Then she's not your wife?"

"Not yet."

"Why did she agree to this impersonation? Did she know you in Tucson?"

"No, we were strangers." Cole did a rapid rundown of his story and decided it was still the best one. "I threatened her until she agreed to do what I told her to do. She's been afraid to say anything."

Dr. Lawton laughed. "If you told stories all along that bad, you'd never have gotten away with this. No one who's spent much time with Elizabeth would believe she's afraid to speak up. What I really want to know is how you persuaded a woman like her to go along with you."

The more relaxed and entertained the doctor looked, the more Cole's pulse accelerated. He'd resigned himself to the worst, and hope was more stressful than resignation. "That's not exactly the way it was. I didn't do the persuading. She did. More than persuading. I was a prisoner—chained to a post when she found me after the attackers left. I had to swear I'd do what she wanted, or she'd leave me where I was."

This time the doctor did look surprised, but he said, "The colonel told me that she had a child she thought might be with the Apaches."

Cole hesitated, and the doctor added, "The colonel was consulting me because he thought it sounded like a medical problem. Neither he nor I have talked to anyone else about it."

"The story about her is partly true. She can tell the rest if she wants to." Cole's sense of timing told him the entertainment was over. Now for the reckoning. "What are you going to do?"

Dr. Lawton fiddled with his glasses, started to put them on, then put them back down on the desk. With each movement Cole felt the spring that was lodged where his stomach should be winding up tighter. When it was about to snap, the doctor cleared his throat.

"I've decided," he said, "to recommend to Colonel Stratton that Second Lieutenant Stephen Baldwin be given an immediate discharge. Honorable, of course. The reason for it is the problem of his wife's physical and mental health. In most cases of ill health, officers send their wives home to families and remain in the service. I shall suggest that in Mr. Baldwin's case, this isn't advisable."

Cole was stunned. "Thank you."

Dr. Lawton smiled, his weary cynicism at its most evident. "Don't be too grateful. The army could be embarrassed if anyone knew it hadn't detected an impostor. Even I might feel embarrassed that I didn't check Baldwin's papers more carefully."

He got up and came around the desk. Cole rose also. The doctor's ironic smile was gone. "You have done well here. It's a shame you can't stay. Men who desert sometimes rejoin under different names. It's not uncommon. However, that's probably impossible for you because you've been an officer."

Cole put out his hand, and the doctor shook it. "I am very grateful," Cole said, "and Martha will be too."

The doctor was all business now. "I'll speak to the colonel this morning. I'll also tell him I'm recommending that you leave with your wife as soon as possible. So that she can seek additional medical advice."

As Cole started to leave, the doctor said, "And congratulations."

"Congratulations?"

"Not for being a hero. You're going to be a father. If you can put up with children, you'll be a real hero."

Cole was surprised enough to ask, "How did you know?"

"It's a look women get. Motherhood ruins a woman. The more babies they have, the worse it gets. I'll stand you a whiskey tonight. You can call it congratulations, or consolation."

Halfway down the hospital veranda steps, Cole remembered that he hadn't seen Peter. It was tempting to skip the visit, but at this point, he wanted to do everything according to Stephen Baldwin's character.

Peter was in a room by himself. His face still looked feverish, but he was awake. Cole looked at him and thought of the times he'd have liked to be the one who put this man in the hospital. "Hello, Peter. How are you feeling?"

"Terrible," Peter said glumly.

Cole didn't have to do much guessing to know that Peter hated being obliged to him. He pulled up a chair and sat down, when what Peter likely wanted from him was a salute. "Having much pain?" he asked.

"Not more than I can put up with." Peter seemed fascinated by a spot on the ceiling.

Cole waited.

Still looking at the ceiling, Peter finally said, "You probably saved my life. I'm grateful."

It was the most ungracious thank-you Cole had ever received. But he'd never relished one more. "That's all right, Peter. I would have done the same for any man in your fix."

Peter gave up the ceiling and looked directly at Cole. "I consider myself under an obligation to you," he said sullenly.

"No need to feel that way," Cole said and gave Peter his cheeriest smile. "But it's nice to know you appreciate me."

Even a fever couldn't account for the red color of

Peter's face. Cole stood up. "I don't want to wear you out," he said solicitously. He gave Peter another smile to infuriate him, and left.

Outside the hospital the August day was heating up, but it felt like spring weather to Cole. He was taking long strides toward his quarters when he heard a call. It was Ned Young.

"Congratulations on the patrol," the quartermaster said. "Did the colonel tell you? We sent word to Fort Whipple about that material you helped me turn up. Headquarters promised to pass it on to Washington, and to the governor's office."

"The colonel mentioned it."

"By the time I finished the list, we could document thousands of pounds of beef that was purchased and never delivered, and the same for all kinds of supplies." Ned shook his head in disgust.

"There's one name I remember," Cole said casually. "Someone who was cheating on beef deliveries, I think. Harvey Lippincott. Did you find anything more about him?"

"Lippincott. Yes. I heard about him from the quartermaster at Lowell. Lippincott was running government cattle on a ranch he owns near Tucson. Supposed to be keeping them until time for delivery. But that son of a bitch was putting his own brand on them."

"Has something been done about it?"

"Word went out. Probably nothing much will happen," Ned concluded gloomily. "Damned bastards get rich off the army and the Indians. If anyone protests, they pull strings in Washington and get away with it. At least we sent off a helluva good report."

"You did what you could," were Cole's parting

words. He'd work on his own brand of justice once he got to Tucson.

Why was Cole taking so long to visit Peter at the hospital? Martha pushed aside the letters from St. Louis that had come while she was gone. It was impossible to think about answering them until she saw Cole again. When he'd left that morning, something had made her suspicious—a tight set to his mouth as if he had a particularly unpleasant job ahead. It was something more than just visiting Peter.

She wanted to take a walk and look for Cole, but she was too uncertain of her position at the fort to do that now. Instead she went out to the back. Whipple greeted her happily, and she sat down on the step and hugged him. From the parade ground she could hear the shouted orders of morning drill. Across in the scouts' camp smoke from the cooking fires drifted up into the air. Were Big-Dipper and Pinecone still with the scouts? More likely they had gone to Diablo's camp. How long before she saw her son again? She buried her face in Whipple's yellow fur, gripping him so hard that he yipped.

"Here you are." Cole was grinning like a boy who'd just been given his first rifle and brought down a bear with it.

Because she'd been worried, she said crossly, "Did Colonel Stratton ask you to take over command of the post?"

He laughed. "Not for a few days yet. You won't believe what happened. Come inside."

Once inside, he let out a whoop and picked her up, whirling her around. "Stop it!" she gasped. "Tell me what this is about."

He put her down and straightened a strand of hair that had come loose. "Dr. Lawton asked to see me and—"

"When did he ask you?" she interrupted.

"Yesterday."

"That's what was wrong this morning! And you didn't tell me," she said angrily.

"No, because there wasn't anything for you to do. I thought about this, and I didn't see how we could get away. It probably wouldn't have worked any time. And definitely not now, with all the attention on us. I had to take a chance that I could bluff my way again."

"And it worked?"

"No. Lawton had figured out I'm not Stephen Baldwin."

Martha groped dizzily for a chair. "But you're happy. Tell me!" she cried in frustration.

Only Cole's exuberance kept Martha's fear at bay as he began to recount the conversation with the doctor. At the end she still couldn't quite believe him. "You mean, we can leave—without having to run away?"

"The colonel can refuse. But I think he'll go along." Cole sat down in front of her and took her cold hands in his. "It was partly because you ran off to Diablo's camp. Then I made up that story about you. Lawton didn't want to take action against us. He admires you."

"It's more likely that he admires what you did for Fred, and especially for Peter."

"Wouldn't Peter hate it if he knew he was helping save my neck?" Cole laughed again.

"It's not saved yet," Martha said, her anxiety returning. "We'll have to go to Tucson."

"We can stay at Fort Lowell for a few days. I may find my witness and clear myself."

"You can't be Cole Wingate again as long as there are army people around who think you're Stephen."

"No, but I'm not going to worry about that now. It will work out."

Cole looked so full of confidence that she didn't express her fears. This seemed too easy. The colonel hadn't agreed yet. And she thought of Tucson with dread. Good luck didn't last forever.

Cole's confidence seemed justified when Colonel Stratton decided in favor of an immediate discharge for him. "It has to go to regimental headquarters for approval," Cole told Martha at the noon meal the next day. "The colonel is sure it will be approved. You and I are to leave for Fort Lowell in three days. I'll still be in the army until word gets there, if a wire hasn't arrived here before then."

"Then it's really true?" Aware of Lane in the house, Martha didn't say what was on her mind.

Apparently Cole guessed. "I know it will be hard for you to leave this post." His eyes added what he didn't say—she'd be farther from Pinecone.

"It will be good for you to be in Tucson for a while," he went on. "Maybe we can come back to this area again. There's good ranching land north of here." More softly he added, "The reasons for the discharge did get out. I hope that won't make you too uncomfortable."

With all the bizarre twists and turns of her life the past six months, disapproval for having had a child out of wedlock seemed inconsequential.

However, she shied away from going out where she must talk to other wives, using the excuse that she still wasn't recovered from her experiences. Harriet Fisher called, and they spent fifteen stilted minutes drinking tea. Lydia Stratton's visit was easier. Her warmth and charm convinced Martha that any post would welcome Colonel Stratton as commanding officer for the sake of his wife. As Lydia left, she hugged Martha. "I'll miss you," she said.

"I'll remember how kind you were," Martha said, "and wish I could go fishing with you again."

"Come back to visit, and we'll catch more fish."

Martha watched Lydia depart with regret.

Alice was the only other caller. She chattered on so happily about herself that Martha relaxed and enjoyed the visit. When several cups of tea had been consumed, Alice said, "We're arrangin' a good-bye party for you and Stephen. It's tomorrow night." She looked at Martha anxiously. "You will come, won't you, Elizabeth?"

"I hoped that we could just leave," Martha said.

"The garrison always has a party. One when you get here. One when you go away."

Suddenly Martha was tired of the pretense that no one had heard what Cole told the commanding officer. "I suppose since no one can admit knowing the reasons for Stephen's discharge, formalities have to be observed."

"Now, Elizabeth, don't you pay any mind to what anyone says. It's your own business why you're leavin'." Tears crept into Alice's voice. "You've been my very best friend since we met. I don't care what fool notions you have, I wish you weren't goin'."

Alice's genuine distress and her loyal defense touched Martha. She and Alice shed tears together. "Maybe we'll see each other again," Martha said when it was time for Alice to go.

"People say that but it doesn't happen," Alice said forlornly. Then her face brightened and she leaned close to whisper, "I think I might be expectin' again one of these days."

"I hope so," Martha said and gave Alice a farewell hug.

The prospect of a party reinvigorated the anxieties Martha had been ignoring. Cecil and Dorothy Hays, along with Betsy, were still at the fort. Even now, Betsy's near recognition of Cole made Martha shiver. She considered getting violently ill at the last moment, which she was genuinely beginning to feel as nine o'clock on the evening of the party arrived.

"Martha," Cole warned, "it won't do any good to hide here. I have to go to the party, even without you. So you better come along and talk to Betsy Hays. Draw attention away from me. It's supper, not a dance. After we eat, the men will go outside and drink. I'll tell them about what a damned fool I was. They'll match me with their stories. It'll be too bloody for the women. That's safe enough."

When they arrived at the Strattons' house, Colonel Stratton greeted her as if she were any wife whose husband had finished his tour of duty and was resigning. "We hate to lose your husband," he said. "My wife has enjoyed your company."

Captain Fisher looked carefully at a spot just above her left ear and said, "Your husband has been an asset to C Company."

She swallowed a nervous laugh. "Thank you, Captain Fisher."

As on the evening she'd first seen him, Doctor Lawton gave her only the attention left over from keeping track of his drink. The other men were constrained in their brief greetings, all except Major Owens. "I don't suppose you know where Dulcita is?" He asked softly.

"With her family in Diablo's camp, I believe."

"Then they're looking after her?"

Surprised at seeing the concern under his brusque manner, she said sympathetically, "I hope they are."

Most of the women treated Martha warily. She hardly noticed, though, because she was intent on locating Dorothy and Betsy Hays. Cecil Hays was there, but not his wife and daughter. At nine-thirty Lydia announced supper. Martha couldn't stand it any longer. "Aren't Mrs. Hays and her daughter coming?" she asked Lydia.

"I'm sorry that you won't get to see them again, Elizabeth. Betsy became ill this afternoon, and her mother didn't want to leave her."

Dazed, Martha walked into the dining room. She sat down at her place and took a spoonful of soup without tasting it. Maybe, she thought, she'd had ten years of bad fortune. Now she was entitled to ten lucky years.

The next morning she stopped Lane before he left for duty. "I don't know how I would have managed without you, Private Lane."

"It's been good working for you and the lieutenant, ma'am," he said. "I'm going to miss that dog. Now, ma'am, make him mind his manners. Sometimes, if you'll not be offended at my saying so, you're not strict enough with him."

"Thank you, Private Lane, for the good advice. I'll remember what you said. Whipple is to ride with me in the ambulance, so I'll see he doesn't stray."

She went out for a last look at the camp across the gorge. Pinecone wasn't there, but it resembled camps where he would grow and learn to be an Apache man. She felt tears starting and resolutely held them back. Probably her hopes for having him with her had been unrealistic all along, even though she hadn't been willing to recognize that. Still, her search had been successful in important ways. She knew where he was. She'd seen him, touched him, and earned a smile of admiration. Now she could go on mourning, or she could be happy that she'd achieved those things.

She decided to choose happiness. There would be moments of sadness, she knew. She looked back at the camp one last time, then at the surrounding mountains, and felt a kind of peace.

The Dougherty wagon was waiting at the edge of the parade ground. She was delighted to see that Sperry was the driver. Cole helped settle her inside with Whipple. "Did you see to Skinny?" she asked.

"Yes. He's in the string of extra horses," he said. "I'll be riding with Fred at the head of the line, so I'll see you at the first stop." He mounted and rode on to catch up with Fred Collins, already headed for the exit at the west end of the fort.

The six soldiers who were their escort mounted up, and Sperry called back, "You settled, Mrs. Baldwin?"

Before she could answer, a shout came from the direction of the adjutant's office. It was Corporal Wiggins. He motioned to Sperry, who got down and went back. The driver returned a few minutes later and climbed back to his perch at the front, but he didn't set the mules in motion.

"When are we leaving?" Martha called to Sperry.

"Shortly, ma'am."

She slid across the seat and looked out the window on the parade ground side. The flag whipping in the wind affected her with a feeling of loss. This army post and the people here had come to mean more to her than she would ever have expected.

The wagon lurched, and she turned toward the open door on the other side. A man was helping two women climb up to get in. Martha's heart almost stopped beating.

"Good morning, Mrs. Baldwin," Mr. Hays said. "I hope we won't be crowding you. Betsy isn't feeling well. When we heard you and your husband were leaving for Tucson today, we decided we'd best go with you. If you don't mind, Betsy will do better if she and Mrs. Hays take the forward facing seat."

Without attempting to force words past the fist in her throat, Martha nodded and moved to the seat with its back to the driver. Whipple protested, but she clutched him to her. His wife and daughter seated, Mr. Hays squeezed in beside Martha. Sperry shouted to his mules, and they started off.

29

The contingent heading for Tucson took the wagon road along the White River, then swung upward through Seven-Mile Canyon and south across the open prairie of Turkey Creek Flat. After crossing the flat, they arrived at a steep canyon that led down into the gorge of the Black River and the only place to ford. At the bottom, the march stopped to organize for the crossing.

For Cole the morning ride had gone quickly. Though uncertainty and danger lay ahead in Tucson, he rode back toward the ambulance with the high spirits of a holiday. As he approached the stopped ambulance, the side door opened and Whipple scrambled out. The dog made a dash for the river, narrowly dodging the heels of the mules and eluding Sperry, who grabbed for him.

Martha leaned out the ambulance window. "Stephen," she cried, "catch him!"

Cole hesitated, but Martha's frantic gestures spurred

him to turn his mount and start after the dog. It wasn't the first time he'd looked like an ass since he met her. Another time wouldn't hurt him, and he'd developed an attachment to the dog.

Whipple beat him to the river and was already splashing in the water when Cole caught up with him. Sliding from his horse, Cole commanded, "Whipple! Come!" The dog stopped, wagged his tail, sending up sprays of water at each wag, and ran happily back up the bank. When he reached Cole, he shook himself vigorously, depositing part of the river on Cole's boots and trousers. Cole picked up the leather leash and started walking back along the road, dog on one side, horse on the other.

Martha met him partway. "Stephen, I'm so sorry. I don't know how Whipple got away from me." In a rapid whisper she added, "Betsy Hays and her parents are in the ambulance." More loudly again she said, "I'll make sure he doesn't get out again."

Another complication. "Take care of this dog," Cole said with an appropriate degree of annoyance. "I have to see about getting everyone across the river."

Flood had swelled the Black River to a hundred feet wide, and three soldiers from Fort Apache had been temporarily stationed at the crossing to man a rope ferry. Cole made sure he stayed with them, helping with the crude arrangements of ropes and pulleys, while the ambulance was driven onto the raft and ferried across. When the last men and animals of their detail had forded and were heading up the pine-bordered canyon ahead, Cole said to Fred, "I didn't know the Hays were going back to Tucson today."

"They decided at the last minute. I forgot to tell

you." Fred grinned. "Al Parker was hoping to get escort duty when Miss Hays left next week. As we say in Georgia, he'll shit firecrackers when he finds out she's with us."

Just before the noon stop, one of the mules suddenly took off from its place in line and ran forward into the belled lead mule. The leader reacted indignantly, kicking at the interloper. Cole volunteered to stay with the animals until they were properly rounded up and back in line. "No need for both of us to hurry through dinner," he suggested to Fred. "When you go to eat with Martha and the Hays, please explain to her that I'll see her later."

By late afternoon they were still north of the San Carlos agency. "If Miss Hays is ill," Fred decided, "we'd better not push on too fast." He sent two men ahead to scout for water. When they reported a spring and grass for grazing up a side canyon, Fred gave the order to stop and make camp there.

Cole preferred to get the trip over as soon as possible, but there was no way he could object. When the tents were up, he met Martha at theirs. "How is Betsy?" he asked.

"Unfortunately she's feeling a lot better," Martha said with a troubled glance toward the tent where Betsy and her mother and father were sitting in camp chairs.

Fred stopped by to say, "Unless you object, we can share the evening meal. One of the men will cook for all of us."

"That sounds pleasant," Martha said. "Thank you, Fred."

When he walked on, she said, "I've run out of ideas about how to avoid Betsy Hays."

"I don't have any. I can't chase Whipple again. We'll

have to take our chances that she doesn't remember me."

When he and Martha joined the others, Betsy looked a little pale but animated. "How are you feeling?" Martha asked.

"I'm fine," she said, and added petulantly, "I wish Mama hadn't decided we had to leave Fort Apache."

During supper Fred, apparently enjoying his position as commanding officer and host, talked more than Cole remembered from any previous times. Following the meal, they lingered over coffee. Cole put his chair near a cedar with drooping limbs, so that his face was partly obscured. He thought Betsy gave him a couple of curious looks, but maybe he was reading too much into casual interest. By the time daylight faded completely, the tight spot between his shoulder blades was aching.

Cole hoped the evening would end, but Mr. Hays told a story about the lack of hotels in early Tucson. Tradesmen and travelers had slept regularly in the plaza in the center of town.

Before anyone began another story, Betsy said, "Do you think that two people who aren't related to each other can look almost alike?" She gave a little giggle. "Lieutenant Baldwin, you look so much like someone that I keeping thinking you must be that man. I finally remembered his name. It was Cole Wingate. I saw him when he was on trial for murder."

Cole felt the tension all the way down into his legs.

"Betsy!" Mrs. Hays objected. "You should apologize to Lieutenant Baldwin."

Betsy pouted. "I wasn't trying to insult him. But he does look a lot like that man."

"I'm not insulted by Miss Hays's comment," Cole

said. "If I made her think of the town freak, I might be."

Mr. Hays leaned forward, looking at Cole. "I don't remember Cole Wingate, but I met his father years ago. I hadn't thought about it before, but you do somewhat resemble Luther Wingate when he was younger. Where are you from, Lieutenant Baldwin?"

Cole cursed silently. "St. Louis."

"I know St. Louis pretty well. What part?"

Cole hunted through his memory for an address and couldn't find one. "Evergreen Street."

Mr. Hays gave Cole a look that mixed curiosity and an unsettling appraisal. "Hmm. I don't recall that. Which section is it?"

Cole saw that Martha's fingers were clenched in her lap. He looked directly at Fred until he had Fred's complete attention and said, "It's a pretty area. Nice houses. Fred, when you visited me before I joined the army, you said that's where you'd live if you ever settled in St. Louis."

Fred's eyes opened a fraction wider, but with only a few moments' hesitation, he said, "Yes, that's right. Have you always lived in Tucson, Mr. Hays?"

Cole didn't hear the rest of the conversation. He hoped he looked as if he had, but he was too shaken to say anything.

Eventually Mrs. Hays rose and said, "Please excuse us. Betsy may think she feels fine, but I want her to rest."

"That's a good idea," Fred agreed. "We'll have a long day tomorrow."

Cecil Hays followed his wife and daughter. Martha, her face pale, looked at Cole, nodded to Fred, and started for their tent. Cole faced his friend and said,

"Thanks, Fred, for backing me up. I'm sorry I can't tell you what this is all about. But I appreciate your help."

Fred looked at Cole soberly. Cole had the feeling Fred understood very well what had happened. "Stephen, you saved my life. Elizabeth was wonderful to Alice. You're both my friends. That's enough to know."

"Thank you." It was all Cole could say.

Fred stretched and grinned, as if they'd been doing nothing more than talking casually. "I'm going to check that the sentries are out and awake. The corporal can take care of everything without me, but I can't let him know that for sure."

After Fred picked up his lantern and started off, Cole walked on to his tent. Another close call. How many more waited for him in Tucson?

Though the Shoo Fly Restaurant in Tucson was often crowded, on this afternoon in late August it was almost empty. Napkins marked the places of the regular mealtime customers, but only Harvey Lippincott and Sidney Hubbard sat at a table in the long narrow room. The sole other person in the room was the Mexican waiter, standing, his hands tucked in the edge of his scarlet sash, looking out the front entrance.

Sidney Hubbard's face was red and his prominent jaw was clenched. "My God, Harvey, are you so damned stupid you don't know when to stop?"

Harvey, his ears heating up, gave a hasty look around.

"Dammit, Sidney, keep your voice down," he sputtered.

"Why bother, when anyone can read about it in the

Citizen? I've always known you're a greedy son of a bitch, Harvey, but I didn't think you were a fool."

"You've no call to talk to me that way. It's my brand on a few stray cattle, not yours."

"Government cattle that strayed all the way down to your ranch! And it's more like a hundred."

There was no answer to that. Harvey softened his voice. "It'll blow over. The army complains all the time, but the Indian Bureau shuts them up. That's what'll happen again."

"Maybe," Sidney Hubbard said. "It's goddamned fools like you who ruin business for everybody else. Someone in the army has been keeping track of you, and you gave them plenty to scream about." He half rose and leaned forward, both hands flat on the table. "You and I are through, Harvey. We're not doing any more business. I'm calling in your loans."

"Now, wait a minute! You owe me part of that last contract. I paid for half the wagons and mules."

"I've decided what's owed you balances the loans."

"The hell it does!"

Sidney subsided into his chair and his voice quieted to a hiss. "Don't forget the money you paid that trader to sell the Indians whiskey. It was a good idea. Keeping the Apaches stirred up brings more soldiers. And that means more business for us. But some folks might see it different. They'd call it a bribe. They'd say you caused a lot of trouble."

Harvey's chest constricted in pain. "It's not my fault he got scared and refused to sell more whiskey."

"But the Apaches killed him and his helper too. And it was your money set it all up." Sidney rose abruptly, bumping the table edge so hard that the yellow glass bottle of sauce in the center rattled in its lead castor and almost toppled over. "As of now, you're no longer in the contracting business. Tell people it's because of your health. Stay home and take care of your wife's property. You won't starve."

Furious, Harvey stood up too. "I can make trouble for you. Your hands aren't clean."

Sidney gave Harvey a look of cold contempt. "Don't try it." He retrieved his hat from the coatrack and stomped out.

Harvey picked up his hat and started for the door. Outside he started toward Leatherwood's Stables, but he had to stop. The air suddenly felt too hot to breathe, and each effort hurt. A drink. That would calm him down, help the pain in his chest. He turned into the nearest saloon, a small one-room bar with a few men inside. All of them, including the bartender, looked Mexican, and were speaking Spanish. But the bartender would know what he meant by "whiskey." All the saloon keepers knew that word.

The drink did ease his pain. He slumped down at the only table. The bartender had just brought him the fourth whiskey when a curious voice said, "Harvey, what are you doing in here?" It was Elias Wilson.

"The same as you," Harvey snapped.

"I thought you weren't drinking, because of your health."

"I do whatever I want to," Harvey said, and thought that Elias might supply some information. "Sit down, Elias." He motioned to the bartender. "Whiskey."

After Elias had sampled his drink, he gave Harvey a sly look and volunteered, "The wires are heating up between army headquarters at Fort Whipple and Washington. I hear they include your name, Harvey.

Some officer at Fort Apache must have made a special study of you."

So it was likely to appear in the *Citizen*. Harvey clamped down on his rage. "Doesn't matter. I'm getting out of the business of supplying the army."

"Oh? What are you planning to do then?"

"I have plenty to do taking care of things."

"That's right," Elias said genially, "you look after your wife's property."

Harvey's anger burst through the protection of the whiskey. "It should be my property, if Luther Wingate hadn't tied everything up. That was so it would go to his son."

"Yes, but Cole Wingate's dead. When your wife dies, it's yours. Of course," Elias added, "that probably won't help you. You'll probably die first, what with your heart and all."

"Elias," Harvey said, his rage finally diluted by the liquor, "nothing's certain in this world. Emma could die before me."

As a matter of fact, the more Harvey thought about it, the more likely that prospect seemed to him.

After leaving the San Carlos agency, the Fort Apache contingent traveled during the hours of dawn and early morning, rested in the hottest part of the day, and went on until past dark. They reached Fort Lowell the sixth morning. Cole left Cecil Hays arranging for a carriage into Tucson and found a shaded bench for Martha and Whipple under the row of cottonwood trees. Then he followed Fred to the adjutant's office.

The adjutant remembered Cole. "Sorry you're leaving the service, Mr. Baldwin," he said. "A dispatch from Fort Whipple just came in this morning. Your discharge papers were in it. Headquarters isn't usually that fast."

Cole guessed from the captain's slightly expectant pause that he was curious why there had been such prompt action. "That's good news, sir."

"My wife and I will be pleased for you and Mrs. Baldwin to stay with us for as long as you need to get settled."

"Thank you, that's generous. We'll be happy to accept for tonight." Cole didn't want to travel any farther with Betsy Hays. "We'll go on to Tucson tomorrow."

"Fourth house on the left. I'll be along there directly and introduce you to my wife."

When Cole and Fred were outside, Fred asked, "Do you know what you and Elizabeth will be doing?"

"I'm not sure. The other visitors who came to Fort Apache, the Gurnetts, asked me to visit them when they thought I'd be their escort back to Tucson. We'll pay them a call, get a recommendation for a good doctor and a place to stay." Cole didn't like keeping up the fiction with Fred, but it was easier on him if they did. "What are your orders? Return to Fort Apache right away?"

"Today everyone on the detail is off duty. Most of them will go into Tucson. We start back tomorrow, if I still have enough men for a detail. What's interesting to see in the town?"

"There's Mansfield's news depot and bookstore. The old Catholic mission south of town is beautiful." He remembered he shouldn't know details and added, "At least that's what I hear. Anyone can point you to the other entertainments."

They were approaching Martha. Before they reached her, Fred asked quietly, "Will you be all right in Tucson?"

Cole said truthfully, "I don't know."

Fred's freckled face was troubled. "Do you have to go into town?"

"Yes, I have to."

After Martha joined them, they walked on to the adjutant's house. Cole realized reluctantly that it was time to say good-bye to Fred. Of all the things he'd thought might happen in the army, making a friend he liked that much hadn't occurred to him. As they shook hands, Fred's expression showed he was moved also. They didn't speak about expecting to see each other again. Cole was sure Fred knew that was unlikely.

The next morning Martha and Cole left Fort Lowell just as the sun was probing the top of Santa Rita peak to the east. One of the Lowell mule skinners was driving the borrowed team and wagon that held their baggage and Whipple. Martha rode Skinny, and Cole was on Buttercup.

"Best way to get to the south side of town is go around it," the driver said when he learned their destination. "Roads in town are too narrow." Martha was delighted that they would avoid people who might know Cole. She also felt easier that they had kerchiefs over their faces to keep from breathing dust.

The Gurnetts' home sat a quarter of a mile back from the road. A fence of thorny ocotillo branches stretched out along the road on each side of an open gate. Cole rode through, with Martha following and the wagon last. When they reached the house, Ira Gurnett came out through double entrance doors onto the veranda.

Ira looked astonished, then in two large strides he was off the veranda and holding up his hand to Martha. "Mrs. Baldwin, I'm delighted to see you. I had no idea you were in Tucson."

Cole swung down from Buttermilk and waited until Ira had helped Martha dismount. "Our plans changed. I remembered your invitation to stop with you if we were ever in Tucson. We'd like to do that, if it's . . . convenient."

"It's fine," Ira said. "Olive and I will be happy to have you. If you don't mind sitting a moment here on the veranda, I'll see where she is and have some of the help get a room ready for you."

Martha sat on one of two cane chairs beside the door and the driver climbed down from the wagon. Whipple, tied inside, raised a fearful barking. "Please," Martha said to the driver, "would you let the dog out?"

Once freed, Whipple wriggled ecstatically and ran to Martha. After he gave her a hasty inspection, he raced off and disappeared around the side of the building. In a moment a mixture of growls, barks, and high-pitched howls resonated through the air from that direction. "Stephen!" Martha cried, half rising from the cane chair. "Please, get Whipple!"

Cole's hand on her shoulder put her firmly back in her chair. "No. He has to find out this is some other dog's territory." He leaned over and said softly, "I don't want to run into anyone who's worked here a while." In his normal voice he added, "Whipple will be back."

Cole was right. Soon a dejected Whipple came back and lay down beside her feet.

Ira returned, along with Olive. After she greeted them, the driver was directed to take the wagon around to the back. Cole tied Whipple to a post, and they all went into a large living room. No servants were in evidence, and after Ira closed the door, he said, "Now, tell us. What's going on?"

Cole sketched the events following Ira's and Olive's departure. When he finished, Ira said, "And you think the doctor won't say anything?"

"The discharge went through, just the way he thought it would. The colonel wouldn't have gone along if he'd known the truth. Dr. Lawton can't say anything now, or he'd be in trouble."

"Why do you suppose the doctor helped you?" Olive asked.

"I think," Martha said, "that he liked us and admired Cole's courage."

"We have to figure out what we're going to do now. Ira, what about the man you located who's probably blackmailing Harvey? Is he still here?"

Ira shook his head. "No. Tom Magrath is gone. I hear he's on his way to California, but I don't know for sure."

"Damn!" Cole looked apologetically at Olive. "Sorry."

She went to Cole and put her hand lovingly on the side of his face. "Never mind. But about this man—isn't it better if you let it go?"

"Olive's right," Ira said. "You need to get out of Tucson. You're welcome to stay with us, but some of our people know you. You and Elizabeth—I mean, Martha, can go somewhere else. Make a new life. People do it all the time."

The muscles of Cole's jaw tightened. "Before I leave

Tucson, I want to see my mother—and Harvey Lippincott."

The skin on Ira's bald head took on a pinker hue, but his voice kept its even tone. "That's fine about Emma, if she won't go to pieces. And if you're not seen. But as for Harvey—if you want revenge, you've got it. You dug into the suppliers' business, and now Harvey's in trouble. Big trouble with the other contractors. He's lost everything."

"That's not enough."

"What good will you do? Dammit, Cole, think! Without a witness you can't prove anything against Harvey. You'll end up back in jail. And with this army business against you along with the other charges. Don't go to Harvey."

"I have to."

Olive looked close to tears. "Cole," she pleaded, "Harvey's not well. He probably won't live long."

Cole's expression didn't change. He stood, his legs slightly apart, like a man braced for an assault. "It doesn't matter."

"Martha." Olive took Martha's hands in hers. "You tell Cole. Make him see that he's throwing his life away for nothing."

"I can't. He must decide." Martha understood Cole's need.

The argument went on into the afternoon. The driver from Fort Lowell unloaded their baggage and left. Olive found reasons for the servants who might recognize Cole to go off on errands. By the end of the day, the only concession Cole made was to agree that he should see his mother first. "I'll get Harvey away," Ira said. "Tomorrow if I can. You can see Emma and talk to her."

"Thanks, Ira," Cole said. "But if you think that will change my mind about Harvey, it won't."

Martha, who had been staying quiet, said, "I'm going too." Cole frowned and started to speak, but she hurried on. "Your mother believes that you're dead. You can't just walk in on her. I'll go in first and explain to her some of what happened."

"No," he objected. "I want you to stay out of it."

Martha faced him, as determined as he was. "We've been together in this so far. I love you, Cole. I want to do this with you."

Cole touched her face once, gently. "All right. It's settled."

30

Ira and Cole arranged that Ira would ride out to the Wingate ranch early the next day. Cole and Martha would follow half an hour later. If they saw Ira's horse, they would keep out of sight and wait. In the event that he couldn't get Harvey away, they would make the attempt the following day.

The Wingate ranch lay fifteen miles south of Tucson in the Santa Cruz River basin. Ira took the road, but Cole led Martha through the foothills of the Santa Cruz Mountains eagerly pointing out places he had gone as a boy.

"Aren't you worried about what's going to happen?" she asked.

"Yes, of course. But I can't do anything until we get there. It's a beautiful morning. I love this country." He smiled at her. "I love you. Why ruin the morning by worrying?"

That was Sharp-Knife's way too, but she knew Cole wouldn't like the comparison. "That sounds like a good idea."

In spite of his refusal to worry, his silence alerted her when they were getting close to the Wingate ranch. He turned up a small canyon and let Buttermilk pick his way around the rocks. She followed up to the crest of a hill where Cole had stopped. Through a cluster of taller cottonwoods, Martha saw the roof of a house. Corrals and outbuildings surrounded it.

She nudged Skinny over so that she could see Cole's face. Most of the night she had been mulling over what to say at this moment. "Please, Cole, listen to me. Why are you set on seeing your stepfather right now? I know we talked about it yesterday, but I still don't understand why this confrontation can't wait. Do you intend to kill him?" Cole stared down at the house without answering. His expression didn't encourage her. "Remember what you said to me—that a live child means more than a dead father."

Finally he looked at her, his eyes unhappy. "All night I thought about whether I was making the right decision." He gestured with his arm, taking in the ranch and the surrounding country. "Now, seeing all this, I know I want a place where I can raise my children. Teach them things, the way my father taught me. I don't want to be running from another murder charge. So I guess I've decided." He took a breath that sounded like a sigh. "I've let revenge against Harvey take over my life. Not any more. I won't kill him. Not if I can keep from it."

Relief made her feel shaky, but she had to say more. "Wouldn't it be better to hunt for the witness first, before Harvey knows you're alive?"

"That's exactly the point—that he should know I'm alive. I may never find the witness. But Harvey can worry every day of his miserable life whether I'm waiting to ambush him."

"If we get away."

"We'll get away." He raised his binoculars and looked in the direction of the house. "Damn! Ira's horse is still there."

"You promised you'd wait and see your mother first," Martha said quickly.

He didn't answer, but he kept the binoculars trained on the house. She strained to see. After a short while, a man came out, mounted, and started toward the valley road. Cole said, "It's Ira. Come on."

They went back down the rocky gully at a speed that made Martha fear for the horses. Cole angled across the lowest hill at a gallop, and she followed. He headed for a place where the riverbank flattened enough for willows to have grown up into trees. She had just joined him when Ira appeared on the road. At the point of the road nearest them, Cole called out. Ira rode over to them.

"Harvey's not home," Ira said.

"Thanks," Cole said, and started to ride off.

Ira moved over to block Cole's way. "Wait! Emma thinks Harvey went into Tucson, but she's not sure. He could be coming back any time."

"If he's not there now, that's all I need to know."

Ira opened his mouth to speak, then closed it and moved out of Cole's way. Martha said, "Ira, could you watch for Harvey on the road from Tucson and delay him if you can?"

"Yes, I'll do that. Good luck."

"Thank you, Ira. More than I know how to say." Cole was already ahead of her, riding fast, using the road this time. She put Skinny into a gallop.

Soon they were turning in at the ranch. Cole didn't attempt to stay out of sight, riding straight up to the hitching rail in front and dismounting. He had already tied up Buttermilk before she caught up.

"Let me go first, speak to your mother. That's what we agreed," she reminded him. "And what about servants?"

"Doesn't matter," he said, but he waited for her.

Around the edge of the veranda, ocotillo had been nailed into a lattice for shade. It also screened the entrance from view of anyone passing. Cole stood against the wall to one side of the door and pointed to a metal triangle that dangled from the roof. Martha took the spike that hung next to it and hit the triangle. The sound reverberated against the wall. After a minute she heard heavy footsteps inside. Hardly breathing, she waited.

A woman opened the door. She was middle-aged with black hair and eyes. She wore the *camisa* and full skirt of many Mexican women. "Yes, *señora*?"

Cole pushed past Martha. The woman looked at him, and her face lost all its color. She backed away and opened her mouth, but he grabbed her and put his hand over her mouth before she could scream. "Softly, Carmen. It really is me."

When he took away his hand, she whispered, "*Eres muerto!*"

"No," he said in Spanish, "I'm not dead."

She began to cry, and he put his arm around her. "It's all right, Carmen. I must see my mother. Where is she?"

Between sobs she said, "*En la cocina.*"

"I don't have much time. I'll talk to you before I go if I can. Please don't tell anyone else that I'm here."

He released Carmen and turned to Martha. "Come on. The kitchen's across the patio."

Before they stepped out of the living room, Cole looked around. The patio was empty. He walked quickly around the veranda to a door on the opposite wall and stopped. "Tell her as gently as you can," he said softly to Martha.

"Yes, I will," she whispered. His face looked pale and tight with tension.

She pushed open the door. The kitchen was large, with a raised hearth in one corner, a large black iron stove beside it, and utensils hanging on the walls. A square table took up the center of the room. At it sat a slender woman dressed in black. Streaks of gray contrasted with dark brown in her hair and the startled eyes turned Martha's way were dark brown also. She started to rise, but Martha said, "Please don't get up. I'm sorry to intrude on you, but I have some news for you."

"Something's happened to Harvey?" Emma Lippincott's voice was soft. From her tone Martha couldn't decide whether Emma feared for Harvey or not.

"No."

"Who are you?" Emma asked, as if it had just occurred to her that she didn't know.

"May I sit down?" At Emma's nod, Martha took the chair next to her. "My name is Martha . . . Wingate. I'm your son's wife."

A flash of animation lit Emma's dark eyes. "Cole's wife?"

"Yes." It wasn't true, but any other explanation would be too complicated.

The animation faded away. Emma didn't even look curious, only sad. "When Cole was here, he didn't tell me he had married. Are you looking for him? Don't you know what happened? He's dead." Tears glistened around the edge of her eyes.

"That's what I came to tell you." Martha reached out and grasped Emma's hand, lying on the table. It felt cold. "He isn't dead. He didn't die at that stage station."

Emma looked frightened and tried to pull her hand back. "They found his body. Why are you saying this?"

"Because it's true. I know because I was on the stage too. Cole and I were the only ones who weren't killed in the attack."

Emma jerked away, pushing her chair back and almost falling over it getting up. "You were on the stage with him? But you weren't at the trial. I don't believe you're his wife. I don't believe anything you're saying." She backed away and cried, "Carmen! Come quickly!"

"Please, Mrs. Lippincott. Cole is alive. He's here now." Martha ran over to the door.

Before she reached it, it opened and Cole stepped into the room. "Mother," he said, "I'm alive. I'm here."

Emma stopped as if she'd run into an invisible wall. Her eyes widened. Against the black collar of her dress her face looked like white porcelain. "Cole?" she whispered.

He started toward her. She staggered a little, but she met him partway. He held her while she sobbed and said, "I don't understand. You're really alive. I don't understand."

Feeling like an intruder, Martha made a move to go, but Cole reached a hand out to her. He soothed Emma and finally persuaded her to sit down. Patiently, he explained again that it was someone else who had been killed in the attack on the station.

"Why didn't you let me know? Why did you let me think you were dead?"

"Because otherwise I'd have ended up in the Yuma prison."

"Then where have you been? And you've shaved off your beard." She said the last accusingly, as if she'd found something she could blame her confusion on.

"Martha and I have been together. I've been waiting for a chance to get back here."

Emma drew back, her mouth trembling, her eyes fearful. "You're here because of Harvey, aren't you? Because of what you said at the trial. That he killed Luther. And the man you mur—the man who was with you."

"Mother," Cole said forcefully, "I didn't kill that man. And, yes, I believe Harvey was responsible for both murders." His voice softened. "That was part of the reason why I came. But it's more important to see you."

Martha gave silent thanks that he was putting his mother first. Maybe after this, he wouldn't insist on coming back to see Harvey.

"Can you go to the judge?" Emma asked. "You can tell him again that you're innocent."

"I have to have proof, Mother. I don't have that yet, but I will. I'll come back just as soon as I get it."

Emma seemed more in control of herself. "Then you must go, Cole. Go now! If Harvey learns you're alive, he'll do anything to find you."

Cole hesitated, and Martha waited to breathe. "Yes, you're right."

The kitchen door banged open. Martha whirled toward the sound. Standing just inside the room was a silver-haired man Martha had never seen before. She knew instantly it was Harvey Lippincott.

He said, "Whose horses are . . ." His voice trailed off as he stared at Cole. Like a seedpod that looks whole but disintegrates at a touch, he sagged against the door. It slammed shut behind him. "My God," he gasped. "Cole! You're alive."

"Yes. And here for a reckoning." Cole faced his stepfather, and Martha could see months of waiting poised in his rigid stance.

Harvey's eyes narrowed and he straightened, regaining some of his bulk. "By God, that was you! In Tucson, the officer leaving the jail. You've been hiding out, pretending to be in the army."

Suddenly he didn't look shriveled and weak any longer. Martha pressed her hand against the side of her skirt. The derringer she'd put in the pocket that morning was there.

Cole said, "Don't worry about where I've been." His voice was hoarse with hatred. "Worry about where I'm going to be. Behind any bush or rock on the way to town. Outside your window. Maybe waiting for you on the patio. Not on the way to the mine, where you murdered my father. You'll be too frightened to go there."

Harvey looked shaken, but he blustered, "You won't get a chance. I'll have the whole army after you. They'll catch you, and then you'll hang."

Emma cried out, "No, Harvey," and started to push past Cole. In the moment that she was between the two men, Harvey flipped back his coat and pulled out a revolver. Cole had his Colt out at almost the same time. But by then Harvey had his gun cocked and trained on Emma. His eyes were on Cole. "Put it down," he barked.

After an instant's thundering silence, Cole eased his

gun down onto the table next to him. Martha's hand froze next to her side. She didn't dare make a motion toward her pocket.

"Push the gun away," Harvey ordered.

Cole gave the gun a push. It spun slightly and slid partway across the table.

Harvey's mouth twisted in a cruel smile. "I won't need the army after all," he gloated. "You broke in here. Tried to attack me the way you did at the trial. I defended myself. My wife and that other woman got in the line of fire. It will turn out that you shot one of them before I managed to kill you."

Emma shrieked, "No, you can't." For an instant Harvey's gaze flicked to her. In one sweeping motion Cole pushed her aside and dived at Harvey.

Harvey swung his revolver from Emma to Cole and fired. The bullet crashed into a pan on the opposite wall with a sound like a small explosion.

Cole lunged at Harvey's legs. Harvey staggered back and fell against the door. Cole grabbed for Harvey's right arm and pinned it down, but Harvey heaved and threw Cole to one side. Harvey clutched the revolver as Cole strained to reach it. They rolled together, struggling and hitting at each other. A chair toppled over onto the tiled floor with a crash.

Martha pulled out her derringer and cocked the hammer. Trying to steady her hands, she held it in position. But with the two men grappling and turning, she couldn't fire. Cole jammed his shoulder against Harvey's head and grabbed for the revolver again.

Suddenly Harvey screamed. He screamed again and stopped flailing. His head slumped to one side.

Cole took Harvey's revolver and rose slowly, his chest heaving. Harvey groaned once, a low exhausted sound that trailed off, and then was still. His face looked as white as his hair.

"It's his heart," Emma cried. Her voice rose higher. "He's dead!"

Cole said roughly, "Mother. Stop." He turned and put his arms around her.

Martha looked back at Harvey. His eyes were open, and he was raising a small pistol up toward Cole. The derringer was in her hand, still aimed at Harvey. She fired.

Everything seemed to happen at once. Smoke puffed from the end of her derringer. Harvey jerked from the force of her bullet, but he still held his pistol. Cole spun around, the revolver he'd taken from Harvey in his hand. Martha cocked the hammer of her derringer again.

Before she could shoot, Harvey and Cole both fired. The two shots rang out simultaneously.

Cole put his hand against the side of his neck. A black mark appeared on Harvey's forehead. His arm fell back, and the pistol slipped from his hand. He sprawled against the door, staring sightlessly across the room. An irregular dark red stain spread out on the door where his head rested.

For a moment no one moved. The acrid smoke hung in the air, and the sounds of gunfire still seemed to reverberate deafeningly in the room.

Cole held the revolver a moment longer, then put it on the table and knelt next to Harvey. Rising, he nodded, "He's dead."

The sound of running footsteps came from the patio, at first faint, then loud. "*Señora!*" It was a man's voice. "Are you all right?"

Emma looked at Cole and then Martha. The voice

called again, "*Señora*! What has happened? Are you hurt?"

As if she were waking from sleep, Emma came alive. "Something terrible has happened, Pablo." She stepped quickly over to the table and picked up Harvey's revolver. Holding it in her hand, she said to Cole, "Open the door."

He took a step toward her, but she repeated, "Move Harvey's body and open the door."

Martha couldn't watch Cole moving the body. She didn't turn around until she heard the creak of hinges and saw light from the patio. Then she looked. A man was standing in the doorway, staring at Harvey's body. A white-faced Carmen was behind him.

Emma said, "He tried to kill me. I shot him. He's dead."

Cole said, "But—"

"He's been threatening me." Emma was close to screaming now. "He asked me why didn't I die so he could have everything for himself. You heard him, Pablo—the other night. And now *he's* dead." She looked at the revolver in her hand and threw it violently away. It hit the wall and fell into the pool of blood beside the body. She put both hands over her face and burst into hysterical sobs. Martha put her arms around Emma, who clung to her.

Only then did the man Emma had called Pablo notice Cole. He stepped back, an expression of horror on his face. "I'm not a ghost," Cole said quickly.

"It's really you?" Pablo whispered.

"Yes. But no one else must know I'm here."

"I will tell no one," Pablo promised. He still looked stunned, but he said to Martha, "Is the *señora* all right?"

"I think so," Martha said, and hoped that he and Carmen were loyal enough to Emma that they wouldn't say anything she didn't want them to.

Cole said to Pablo, "Mr. Gurnett is on the road to Tucson. Send someone to catch him. Right away!"

"Yes. Yes, I will. Right away." Pablo glanced once more at the body, then at Cole, and went at a run across the patio.

They waited for Ira in the living room. Emma lay on the sofa. Carmen found clean cloths, and Martha washed and bandaged the wound where Harvey's bullet had grazed Cole's neck. After that he sat in a large chair, holding Martha. While they waited, he told his mother about Martha's and his life together.

When Ira arrived an hour later, Cole described what had happened. Martha shuddered when he got to the part about how Harvey died. He held her even more closely and said, "If Martha hadn't gotten off that first shot, he'd have killed at least one of us, maybe all."

She leaned against him and felt his warmth enveloping her, warding off the terrible image of Harvey lying against the door. Once she'd thought she could never kill a man. But with Cole's life in the balance, she tried to kill two—the Apache and Harvey.

She straightened and stood up. "I'm all right," she told Cole. It wasn't true, but there were things to be done.

He stood up too and said to Ira, "Mother insists she's going to tell the sheriff she killed Harvey."

"Yes, I am." Emma sat up, looking pale and exhausted but determined. "I'll say I don't remember everything. That I shot him with a derringer first. Then I used his revolver."

Cole's mouth set in a line that resembled his mother's. "No. I'll go to the sheriff and take my chances."

"I won't let you. When Luther died, I was frightened. Harvey offered to take care of everything for me, and I let him. It was a terrible mistake. And you've paid for it, Cole. I can't let that happen again." Her voice wavered and dropped to a whisper. "I've wished that Harvey would have a heart attack. I wanted him to die. So I'm going to do what's best this time."

"She's right," Ira put in. "People knew that Harvey was furious about losing out on his business. Emma, forgive me if I'm upsetting you, but it's also generally known that Harvey had a mean temper and that lately he took it out on you. He even let out a hint to a reporter that it would be good for him if you died."

"That doesn't mean she should do this," Cole argued.

"Cole," Ira said, "there's not a jury that would convict Emma. She wouldn't even go to trial. But you—that's another matter."

Martha thought of how she would feel if Pinecone were in Cole's situation. "Cole, your mother and Ira are right."

Cole looked at his mother unhappily. Finally he sighed. "Yes, I suppose that's what we have to do. But Ira, I'll be in touch with you. If anything goes wrong, you let me know. I'll come back."

"Where are you and Martha going?" Emma asked, so wistfully that Martha could hardly stand it.

"I'm not sure. Somewhere north of here. We'll have to be Elizabeth and Stephen Baldwin for a while. At least until the army units who'd recognize us leave Arizona. Then, if I can find Tom Magrath and get him to clear my name, we can come back to Tucson."

"Emma, you can come to see us," Martha suggested. "You can say you met us at the Gurnetts' house. We'll correspond. When we're settled someplace, you can visit us."

It wasn't much, but Emma's and Cole's faces brightened. "Yes, that will work," Cole said.

Emma got up. "You need money. I have some that Harvey didn't know about. You're going to take it." When Cole started to protest, she cut him off. "This should all belong to you some day," she said sadly. "But if you can't come back, I don't suppose it will. You can't refuse what money I can give you now."

Cole and Emma looked at each other, making up for lost years. "Thank you, Mother. I'm grateful."

Ira said uneasily, "You and Martha should leave here right away, Cole. How's your neck?"

"A little sore. It'll be all right."

"I'll go into town," Ira said, "and see the sheriff and the coroner. Take care of Harvey's body. And if you're heading north, you'd better be starting."

"Yes," Cole agreed, though he sounded reluctant. "We can't take the stage from here. We'll have to buy a rig and make the trip ourselves."

"There's a good wagon at my place that you can have." When Cole started to protest, Ira said impatiently, "You can pay me for it, and for the team of mules."

Emma went to get the money. While she was out of the room, Cole said to Ira, "Will you and Olive look out for my mother?"

Ira responded gruffly, "You know we will."

When Emma returned, Martha went outside to let

mother and son have a private good-bye. In a short time, Cole came out, looking shaken. After they had mounted and were out on the road, he turned for a last look at his home. "That's a big thing Mother's doing for me. She has more courage than I've given her credit for."

Martha didn't know Cole's mother at all, but she understood why Emma would gamble her safety for her son's.

Moonlight was flooding the land as Cole and Martha started out from the Gurnetts' house that night, turning the desert plants platinum. He drove the small mountain wagon and Whipple rode behind her in the wagon bed. Buttermilk and Skinny followed on leading reins at the back.

Cole followed a route that would skirt the west side of Tucson. Their plan was to follow the stage route north and west to Florence, and then head up to the White Mountain country. North of the Fort Apache reservation, they would find a place to settle.

"You and Ira were talking about Tom Magrath," Martha said. "What did you decide?"

"I left money with Ira. After we're settled and the baby is born, I may try looking for Magrath. If I find him, I'll bribe him to go back to Tucson and clear me. When he does that, he'll get more from Ira. Or if he turns up in Tucson, Ira will make a deal with him."

"And then if the army units have changed and the Hays family isn't here, we can come back."

"Yes, if I have a plausible story for staying away all that time."

"Tell the truth. That you couldn't return until your name was cleared."

He looked at her and grinned. "Tell the truth? Do you think we'll know how after all this time?"

They topped a rise and saw the flat buildings of Tucson spread out below them. A coyote yipped from the hills to the left, and Whipple rose up to answer with a defiant bark.

Martha wondered what Pinecone was doing. Though she was resigned to leaving him with Diablo's band, the pain of the separation was still deep. Would it lessen over the years? Perhaps with other children, the hurt might ease, but she knew she would always feel the loss of her first child. However, life went on, with other problems to solve.

"What if you never find Tom Magrath?" she asked Cole.

"Then we won't come back here."

"But it's your birthright."

Cole didn't answer for a long time, leaning his elbows on his knees, holding the reins as if the mules absorbed his attention. "I don't think of it as my right any longer. The Apaches thought they had a right to hunt on lands that white people think they have a right to mine and farm. Rights don't mean the same things to me now. You're what I want. And this child, and any more we have. Pinecone too, if that's the way it works out. I'll earn those things for myself."

She moved closer and slipped her arm through his, loving him for his generous nature, and loving the feel of him next to her. "So we'll go on being Elizabeth and Stephen for now. We must do something about their families."

They rode for several minutes in silence while she

thought. "I'll write one more letter as Elizabeth," she decided, "saying you've left the army and we're not sure where we'll be. Later I'll write as a neighbor to tell them Elizabeth has died in an accident. I'll describe how happy she and Stephen were and that the tragedy affected him so much he's gone. No one knows where."

"Yes, that's a good plan."

After another period of silence, he said, a teasing tone in his voice, "One problem with being Elizabeth and Stephen—how are we going to get married if we're already married? We'll need a third identity."

"No." She shook her head for emphasis, even though he was watching the road and not her. "I feel as if I've given Elizabeth a little more life. I like that feeling. We can go to a minister and confess that we never really married. I think someone will marry us quietly, especially if I look very pregnant."

"No new masquerades?"

"No new ones."

He stopped the team and wound the reins around the brake handle, then pulled her into his arms. After a kiss that left her dizzy he said, "All right. But I damn well wouldn't have missed this one."

AVAILABLE NOW

HEIRLOOM by Candace Camp

A surefire hit from the bestselling author of ROSE-WOOD, HEIRLOOM is a heartwarming story of love between a beautiful actress and a lonely Nebraska farmer.

HEARTBREAK TRAIL by Barbara Keller

A passionate and touching tale of two people, each desperately searching for two very different things when they are thrown together in the harsh frontier wilderness of Fort Apache. A stunning western romance that is sure to entice readers.

TRUST ME by Jeane Renick

Former model Allison Shreve goes to Belize on vacation to try to get her life back to normal after the shattering experience she had three years before. There, she meets the kind of man she distrusts—Zachary Cross, a Miami cop.

CRYSTAL HEART by Candace Camp

A Candace Camp classic to capture your heart. This is a story of Lady Lettice Kenton, a titled temptress with a heart of ice, and Charles Murdock, an American rebel out of place in elegant, fashionable London. They come from two different worlds, only to discover one burning passion.

COMING NEXT MONTH

INDIGO BLUE by Catherine Anderson

The long-awaited final installment of the Comanche trilogy. Indigo Blue Wolf, a quarter-breed Comanche, has vowed never to marry and become the property of any white man. When tall, dark, and handsome Jake Rand comes to Wolf's Landing, Indigo senses he will somehow take over her life.

THE LEGACY by Patricia Simpson

A mesmerizing love story in the tradition of the movie *Ghost*. Jessica Ward returns to her childhood home near Seattle to help her ailing father. There, she meets again an old friend, the man she's secretly loved since she was a teenager.

EMERALD QUEEN by Karen Jones Delk

An exciting historical romance that sweeps from the French Quarter of Antebellum New Orleans to the magnificent steamboat *The Emerald Queen*.

THE STARS BURN ON by Denise Robertson

A moving chronicle of the life and loves of eight friends, who come of age in the decadent and turbulent '80s.

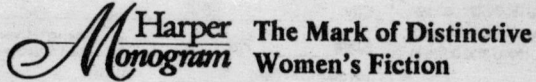

Harper Monogram The Mark of Distinctive Women's Fiction

HarperPaperbacks *By Mail*

BLAZING PASSIONS IN FIVE HISTORICAL ROMANCES

QUIET FIRES by Ginna Gray ISBN: 0-06-104037-1 $4.50

In the black dirt and red rage of war-torn Texas, Elizabeth Stanton and Conn Cavanaugh discover the passion so long denied them. But would the turmoil of Texas' fight for independence sweep them apart?

EAGLE KNIGHT by Suzanne Ellison ISBN: 0-06-104035-5 $4.50

Forced to flee her dangerous Spanish homeland, Elena de la Rosa prepares for her new life in primitive Mexico. But she is not prepared to meet Tizoc Santiago, the Aztec prince whose smoldering gaze ignites a hunger in her impossible to deny.

FOOL'S GOLD by Janet Quin-Harkin ISBN: 0-06-104040-1 $4.50

From Boston's decorous drawing rooms, well-bred Libby Grenville travels west to California. En route, she meets riverboat gambler Gabe Foster who laughs off her frosty rebukes until their duel of wits ripens into a heart-hammering passion.

COMANCHE MOON by Catherine Anderson ISBN: 0-06-104010-X $3.95

Hunter, the fierce Comanche warrior, is chosen by his people to cross the western wilderness in search of the elusive maiden who would fulfill their sacred prophecy. He finds and captures Loretta, a proud golden-haired beauty, who swears to defy her captor. What she doesn't realize is that she and Hunter are bound by destiny.

YESTERDAY'S SHADOWS by Marianne Willman ISBN: 0-06-104044-4 $4.50

Destiny decrees that blond, silver-eyed Bettany Howard will meet the Cheyenne brave called Wolf Star. An abandoned white child, Wolf Star was raised as a Cheyenne Indian, but dreams of a pale and lovely Silver Woman. Yet, before the passion promised Bettany and Wolf Star can be seized, many lives much touch and tangle, bleed and blaze in triumph.

MAIL TO: **Harper Collins Publishers**
P. O. Box 588 Dunmore, PA 18512-0588
OR CALL: (800) 331-3761 (Visa/MasterCard)

Yes, please send me the books I have checked:

☐ QUIET FIRES (0-06-104037-1) $4.50
☐ EAGLE KNIGHT (0-06-104035-5) $4.50
☐ FOOL'S GOLD (0-06-104040-1) $4.50
☐ COMANCHE MOON (0-06-104010-X) $3.95
☐ YESTERDAY'S SHADOWS (0-06-104044-4) $4.50

SUBTOTAL .... $_____
POSTAGE AND HANDLING .... $ 2.00*
SALES TAX (Add applicable sales tax) .... $_____
TOTAL: $_____

*ORDER 4 OR MORE TITLES AND POSTAGE & HANDLING IS FREE!
Remit in US funds, do not send cash.

Name _____
Address _____
City _____
State _____ Zip _____

Allow up to 6 weeks delivery.
Prices subject to change.

(Valid only in US & Canada)

H0031

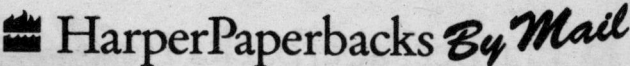
HarperPaperbacks By Mail

If you like exciting adventure and tempestuous love you're sure to like these...

FIERY HISTORICAL ROMANCES

Our bestselling authors weave stories of love, adventure and fiery passion in historical settings.

LA BELLE AMERICAINE by Barbara Keller
Sarah Taylor arrives in Paris in the Fall of 1888 to pursue her dream. But her burning desire for success leads Sarah into a world of passion and intrigue. Only the man she secretly loves can save her and help her find her true destiny. 0-06-100094-9

STOLEN LOVE by Carolyn Jewel
Elizabeth came to England in 1840 to be presented to London society with her cousin Amelia. Both girls were expected to find husbands, a task easier for beautiful Amelia than for quiet, serious Elizabeth. 0-06-104011-8

PRINCESS ROYALE by Roslynn Patrick
In 1909, a beautiful young woman from Chicago gets caught between European tradition and her own dreams and desires. 0-06-104024-X

CANDLE IN THE WINDOW by Christina Dodd
Bound by their need; they came together in a blaze of passion—Saura, the proud Norman beauty and William, the golden warrior who laid siege to her heart. These two lovers ignite a world of darkness with their breathless passion. 0-06-104026-6

TREASURE OF THE SUN by Christina Dodd
Damian de la Sola, the aristocratic Spaniard, was like no man Katherine Maxwell had ever known. Together they followed their destinies as they searched for a golden treasure in the California wilderness and discovered a love beyond price. 0-06-104062-2

YESTERDAY'S SHADOWS
by Marianne Willman

Bettany Howard was a young orphan traveling west searching for the father who left her years ago. Wolf Star was a Cheyenne brave who longed to know who abandoned him—a white child with a jeweled talisman. Fate decreed they'd meet and try to seize the passion promised. 0-06-104044-4

MIDNIGHT ROSE by Patricia Hagan

From the rolling plantations of Richmond to the underground slave movement of Philadelphia, Erin Sterling and Ryan Youngblood would pursue their wild, breathless passion and finally surrender to the promise of a bold and unexpected love. 0-06-104023-1

WINTER TAPESTRY
by Kathy Lynn Emerson

Cordell vows to revenge the murder of her father. Roger Allington is honor bound to protect his friend's daughter but has no liking for her reckless ways. Yet his heart tells him he must pursue this beauty through a maze of plots to win her love and ignite their smoldering passion.
0-06-100220-8

**For Fastest Service—
Visa and MasterCard Holders Call
1-800-331-3761**
refer to offer HO321

MAIL TO: **Harper Collins Publishers**
P. O. Box 588 Dunmore, PA 18512-0588
OR CALL: **(800) 331-3761 (Visa/MasterCard)**

Yes, please send me the books I have checked:

- ☐ LA BELLE AMERICAINE (0-06-100094-9) $4.50
- ☐ STOLEN LOVE (0-06-104011-8) $3.95
- ☐ PRINCESS ROYALE (0-06-104024-X) $4.95
- ☐ CANDLE IN THE WINDOW (0-06-104026-6) $3.95
- ☐ TREASURE OF THE SUN (0-06-104062-2) $4.99
- ☐ YESTERDAY'S SHADOWS (0-06-104044-4) $4.50
- ☐ MIDNIGHT ROSE (0-06-104023-1) $4.95
- ☐ WINTER TAPESTRY (0-06-100220-8) $4.50

SUBTOTAL .... $ _____
POSTAGE AND HANDLING .... $ 2.50*
SALES TAX (Add applicable sales tax) .... $ _____
TOTAL: $ _____

*ORDER 4 OR MORE TITLES AND POSTAGE & HANDLING IS FREE!
Orders of less than 4 books, please include $2.50 p/h. Remit in US funds, do not send cash.

Name _____

Address _____

City _____

State _____ Zip _____

Allow up to 6 weeks delivery.
Prices subject to change.

(Valid only in US & Canada)

HO321

SEVEN IRRESISTIBLE HISTORICAL ROMANCES BY BESTSELLING AUTHOR
CANDACE CAMP

HEIRLOOM
Juliet Drake, a golden-haired beauty who yearned for a true home, went to the Morgan farm to help Amos Morgan care for his ailing sister. There she found the home she sought, but still she wanted more—the ruggedly handsome Amos.

BITTERLEAF
Purchased on the auction block, betrayed British nobleman, Jeremy Devlin, vowed to seduce his new owner, Meredith Whitney, the beautiful mistress of the Bitterleaf plantation. But his scheme of revenge ignited a passion that threatened to consume them both.

ANALISE
Analise Caldwell was the reigning belle of New Orleans. Disguised as a Confederate soldier, Union major Mark Schaeffer captured the Rebel beauty's heart as part of his mission. Stunned by his deception, Analise swore never to yield to the caresses of this Yankee spy...until he delivered an ultimatum.

ROSEWOOD
Millicent Hayes had lived all her life amid the lush woodland of Emmetsville, Texas. Bound by her duty to her crippled brother, the dark-haired innocent had never known desire...until a handsome stranger moved in next door.

BONDS OF LOVE
Katherine Devereaux was a willful, defiant beauty who had yet to meet her match in any man—until the winds of war swept the Union innocent into the arms of Confederate Captain Matthew Hampton.

LIGHT AND SHADOW
The day nobleman Jason Somerville broke into her rooms and swept her away to his ancestral estate, Carolyn Mabry began living a dangerous charade. Posing as her twin sister, Jason's wife, Carolyn thought she was helping her gentle twin. Instead she found herself drawn to the man she had so seductively deceived.

CRYSTAL HEART
A seductive beauty, Lady Lettice Kenton swore never to give her heart to any man—until she met the rugged American rebel Charles Murdock. Together on a ship bound for America, they shared a perfect passion, but danger awaited them on the shores of Boston Harbor.

MAIL TO: Harper Collins Publishers
P. O. Box 588 Dunmore, PA 18512-0588
OR CALL FOR FASTEST SERVICE: (800) 331-3761

Yes, please send me the books I have checked:

☐ HEIRLOOM (0-06-108005-5) $5.50
☐ BITTERLEAF (0-06-104145-9) $4.50
☐ ANALISE (0-06-104045-2) $4.50
☐ ROSEWOOD (0-06-104053-3) $4.95
☐ BONDS OF LOVE (0-06-104063-0) $4.50
☐ LIGHT AND SHADOW (0-06-104076-2) $4.50
☐ CRYSTAL HEART (0-06-108007-1) $4.50

SUBTOTAL	$ _____
POSTAGE AND HANDLING	$ 2.00*
SALES TAX (Add state sales tax)	$ _____
TOTAL:	$ _____

(DO NOT SEND CASH. Remit in US funds.)

Name _____
Address _____
City _____
State _____ Zip _____

Allow up to 6 weeks for delivery. Prices subject to change.

*Order 4 or more titles and postage & handling is FREE! Orders of less than 4 books, please include $2.00 P/H. Valid only in the US & Canada.

ATTENTION: ORGANIZATIONS AND CORPORATIONS

Most HarperPaperbacks are available at special quantity discounts for bulk purchases for sales promotions, premiums, or fund-raising. For information, please call or write:
**Special Markets Department, HarperCollins Publishers,
10 East 53rd Street, New York, N.Y. 10022.
Telephone: (212) 207-7528. Fax: (212) 207-7222.**